AN OCCULT CRIMES UNIT INVESTIGATION

"A cool mix of cop show and creature feature. Gustainis had me at 'meth-addicted goblins'."

Marcus Pelegrimas, author of the *Skinners* series

"The cops act like real cops, the vampires act like real vampires, and the monsters aren't messing about. The plot twists and turns like a twisty turny thing, and moves like a weasel on speed. The real things feel real, and the supernatural things feel like they might be. The prose is a joy to read, and the whole thing was more fun than is probably legal."

Simon R Green, author of *A Walk on the Nightside*

"Punchy dialogue, a fun alternate history, explosive action, and a hero whose monsters haunt him even beyond the job... Gustainis has given us a fantastic supernatural cop story that just dares you to put it down."

Chris Marie Green, author of the *Vampire Babylon* and *Bloodlands* books

"I enjoyed every page of *Hard Spell*. If Sam Spade and Jack Fleming were somehow melted together, you'd get Stan Markowski. I can't wait to see what Gustainis does next."

Lilith Saintcrow, author of *Night Shift* and *Working for the Devil*

JUSTIN GUSTAINIS

Evil Dark

AN OCCULT CRIMES UNIT INVESTIGATION

ANGRY ROBOT

ANGRY ROBOT
A member of the Osprey Group

Lace Market House,
54-56 High Pavement,
Nottingham,
NG1 1HW, UK

www.angryrobotbooks.com
I'm Batman...

An Angry Robot paperback original 2012.

Copyright © 2012 by Justin Gustainis
Cover Artist: Timothy Lantz
—

Distributed in the United States by Random House, Inc., New York.

ISBN 978-0-85766-136-4
Ebook ISBN 978-0-85766-137-1

Printed in the United States of America

9 8 7 6 5 4 3 2 1

In memory of A.R. Montanaro, Jr.
The Rhino lives on, in our hearts

"There's a conflict in every human heart –
between the rational and the irrational,
between good and evil.
And good does not always triumph."
General Corman, in APOCALYPSE NOW

"Your enemy the devil, prowls around like a
roaring lion, seeking someone to devour."
1 Peter 5:8

"There's nothing in the dark that isn't there
when the lights are on."
Rod Serling

The city is Scranton. The name is Markowski. I carry a badge. The monsters from your nightmares are real, all of them. If you live in my town, protecting you from them – and vice versa – is my job.

That's pretty much all you need to know about who I am and what I do.

There are a few things in this life that I really hate, and two of them are fairies and heights.

Fairies piss me off because they act so goddamn superior. Just because they can fly, and they're all so fucking beautiful – males and females, both – and they can shift at will from Earth to Fairyland and back again, it makes them all think they're hot shit. The default setting on the average fairy's face is a smirk, and in more than one case I've been tempted to wipe it off – with my fist.

As for heights – I need to explain something about that. It's not altitude all by itself that scares me – it's only something that I might fall from and get killed that gives me the willies.

A few years back, I was in New York for a supe cop conference, and I used my free time to do some touristy stuff. So after the boat tour around the Statue of Liberty, I went to the Empire State Building and took the elevator up to the observation deck on the 102nd floor. You get a great view of the city, and I thought it was spectacular. Of course, the deck has a waist-high wall around it, and that's topped by a large gauge metal fence, and there's barbed wire on top of that – if you want to fall off that thing, you're gonna have to *work* at it. I wasn't nervous at all.

On the other hand, if you put me in one of those flimsy platforms the window washers use when they clean the building, I'd probably shit myself. I don't care if those guys think it's safe and do it every fucking day – I want something more between me and oblivion than a big plank of wood, some scaffolding, and a couple of cables. I haven't got agrophobia, or whatever they call it – I'm just not interested in doing any experiments with the force of gravity from half a mile in the air.

So, with all that, how is it I found myself on a two-foot-wide ledge that fronts the Bank Tower Building, twelve stories up from street level, trying to talk a fairy out of taking the Big Dive?

The answer to that is kinda complicated.

What happened was all my fault, too – well, most of it. Sooner or later, the lesson is going to sink into my thick Polack skull: *never leave early for work*. Every time I do, something happens – and it's never the kind of stuff that makes me smile when I think about it later.

When I said I left early, I don't mean that I was going over to the station house to start my shift ahead of schedule. I work long enough hours as it is. It's just that I was tired of my own cooking and thought it would make a nice change to have a decent meal before going off to do battle with the Forces of Darkness for another night. So I left a note for my daughter Christine, who doesn't get up until sundown, and headed off for Luigi's, my favorite Italian restaurant. I would have invited Christine to come along, but she's kind of on a restricted diet.

They say that Luigi – known as "Large Luigi" to his pals, and with reason – used to be a button man for the Gambino family in New York, twenty years or so back. But he's a law-abiding citizen now, and I don't care how many guidos he popped back in the old days. All I know is, he makes one hell of a veal scallopini. You might say it's to die for.

I don't really like eating out alone. There was a time when I'd arrange to meet my partner for a pre-shift meal once in a while. Paul DiNapoli and I used to eat together at least once a week. After Big Paul died, my new partner, Karl Renfer, would sometimes have dinner with me. But in recent months, Karl's food preferences have changed, and he's not much interested in eating anything that doesn't have a letter in it – like O, A, or AB positive.

The most direct route to Luigi's from my place is through downtown. I figured the rush hour traffic would have slacked off by then, so it was probably fastest to take the direct route. Other times of the day, I'm better off sticking to the side streets – it's longer that way, but faster.

So, driving through downtown, I noticed a bunch of red and blue lights flashing on South Wyoming Avenue. At first, I thought it might be a fire, but then I saw the half-dozen black-and-white units parked in front of the Bank Towers, the tallest building in town – it's only fourteen stories, but this is Scranton, for Chrissake, not midtown Manhattan.

I hadn't heard the call that brought these cars here, because my police radio was turned off. I was off duty – it's allowed. And since I'd turned the radio off, it stands to reason that I should've just driven past the site of whatever shit was happening, and stay on course for Luigi's and the veal scallopini.

But curiosity, which has been known to be bad for felines, is often the downfall of cops, too. Little did I know that my own downfall was literally only a few minutes away.

I parked as close as I could get to the action, put my ID folder in my jacket pocket so that the badge was visible, and walked toward the yellow tape that was designed to separate the official personnel from the gawkers.

There was a uniformed officer standing just inside the crime scene tape, but his back was to me and his head craned upward, as if he was looking at the sky. I said, "Excuse me, Officer."

He turned around, already saying, "Listen, mister, you might as well – oh, hi, Sarge. Sorry." His name was Dietrich, but he looked about as Aryan as Michael Jordan. Short – just made the height limit, I bet – greasy black hair and pockmarked skin. But he wasn't a bad cop – if he was, I'd have known.

"What's going on?" I asked him.

"Aw, we got a jumper," he said. "Twelfth floor, on the ledge. See him?"

Now that I knew where to look, it wasn't hard to spot the solitary figure, his arms pressed flat against the concrete wall as if he was crucified there. He was at least two hundred feet away, and my eyes aren't what they used to be, but there was something…

A few dozen civilians were milling around, waiting for something exciting to happen. If the guy jumped, they'd probably be overjoyed – give them something different to talk about at dinner tonight. One of the gawkers had a set of opera glasses, of all things. He was looking at the solitary figure twelve stories up as if it was the second act of the fucking *Barber of Seville*. I stepped over to him and said, "Mind if I take a quick peek through those?"

Without looking away from the subject of his interest, he said, "Yeah, I mind. Fuck off."

I said, a little louder than before, "Would you prefer to rephrase that, or just spend a night in jail getting assfucked by a couple of guys named Bubba and Leroy?"

That brought the glasses down, all right. He turned to me, and I saw his eyes go from my face to the badge and back again. "Sorry, Officer. I didn't know… here." He handed me the glasses.

"Thank you."

I looked through the lenses and tried to orient myself. After a moment, I was able to locate the figure on the ledge and get my first good look at him. I looked for maybe fifteen seconds, muttered, "Aw, shit," then handed the opera glasses back to the douche bag they belonged to. I probably couldn't have got him a night in jail just for being a douche bag – fortunately, he didn't know that.

I went back to Dietrich. "Who's ranking officer on Scene?"

"That'd be Sergeant Noonan."

"You know where he is now?"

"Yeah, Sarge." Dietrich pointed. "He's just the other side of that squad car over there, I think."

"You mind letting me through? I wanna have a word with him."

"Sure, no prob."

Dietrich lifted up the crime scene tape and I ducked under it and headed in the direction he'd pointed to.

He was right. A few feet beyond the parked squad car, Sergeant Ron Noonan was on his police radio, not sounding too happy.

"No, sir, we can't get near him. None of my men is real anxious to go out on that ledge, and I can't order them to. Once the fire department gets here, it might be different, but now… Yes, sir. I will, sir. As soon as possible, sir. Noonan out."

He was replacing the radio on his belt when he noticed me. "Markowski," he said, with a careful nod. "What are you doing here? Nobody called for Occult Crimes that I know of."

"They didn't," I said. "I was driving by, and couldn't mind my own damn business. I'm not trying to get in your hair, Noonan, but there's something you ought to know, if you don't already.

"What?"

"Your jumper – he's a fairy."

He stared at me. "A *fairy*? But those faggoty things got wings, don't they? They can fly like a bird, supposedly. What's he doin' up there – fucking with us for laughs?"

"No – it looks like his wings have been amputated."

"How the hell do you know that?"

"I borrowed some glasses from one of the rubberneckers. Got a good look at him. He won't be doing any flying until the wings grow back – assuming he lives that long."

"A fairy." Noonan shook his head. "Well, fuck me."

"Listen, Noonan – is the fire department coming?"

"Yeah, I had Chief Mertz on the horn a few minutes ago. They're sending a truck."

"With the usual equipment for this kind of thing?"

"Yeah, far as I know. What's it to you?"

I took in a deliberate breath and let it out, cursing myself for getting involved in other people's problems, especially when the one with the real problem didn't even qualify as *people*.

"Once the SFD gets here, I'll have a word with them," I said. "Then I'd like to go up there and see if I can talk to *him*."

"You know the guy – or the fey, or whatever the fuck you call them?"

"I don't think so, but it doesn't matter. I've had some experience with fairies. Look, if you want me to butt out, I will. But I think I can get him down from there alive."

Noonan looked over my shoulder. "Fire truck's here." He returned his gaze to my face. "What the fuck, Markowski. You know these damn fairies better than I do – which in my case, is not at all. You think you can get the flitty bastard down, then go for it."

I nodded. "Let me talk to whoever's commanding the truck, then I'll go on up."

About ten minutes later, I was leaning half out the twelfth-floor window that was closest to the suicidal fairy. The people in the law firm that owned the window weren't too happy about it, but I waved my badge at them and they'd let me though. I wondered if the jumper was one of their clients, who'd just got a look at his bill for legal services.

Speaking loudly enough to be heard on the ledge, I said to the fairy, "Hey, how ya doing?"

He didn't start when I spoke to him, fortunately – he'd probably heard me opening the window. He turned his head slightly in my direction and I could see that his eyes were shut tight – good.

"If you have to ask that question of me in the

present circumstances, then you are too stupid to comprehend any answer that I might give."

I'd just been told to "fuck off" in Fairy. Yeah, they talk like that – most of them. I learned a new word from *Reader's Digest* a couple of months ago that I'd immediately thought applied perfectly to fairies – *supercilious*. This specimen of the fair folk was no exception.

"Just a figure of speech," I said. "I am well aware of your predicament."

"Oh, are you?" Yup – supercilious is the word, all right.

"Well, the part that is visible to the eye," I said. "I'm sure there must be other matters I don't know about that have driven you to this… extreme situation."

Now he had me talking that way – jeez.

"Other matters, indeed. And I warn you – do not try to force me, or persuade me, off my current perch. I am *not* going back inside. For me, the only way out is down, and I shall take it as soon as I can gather my courage sufficiently."

"Of course – I respect that. My name's Stan, by the way."

He sighed dramatically, then said something in Fairy, followed by, "The closest name to mine in your language is… Butch."

Butch. I felt the smile forming on my lips, but beat it back with an effort of will. He might open his eyes and see me.

"Uh, Butch, I couldn't help but notice that your wings have been, um…"

"Amputated. Removed. Hacked off. Is that what you are trying to say?"

"Something like that. If you don't mind me asking, does that have something to do with your present… predicament?"

"It has everything to do with it," he moaned.

"I see," I said. "Or rather, I don't…"

"The matter is none of your concern, human. Go away and leave me in peace. I will seek true, lasting peace soon enough."

"Don't you want the other fey to know why you did it? Wouldn't you rather give your last act some meaning, so that others will understand what drove you to this?"

He was quiet for several seconds before answering me.

"I loved – *love* – a female of my kind who is a member of Queen Mab's court. Though I am but a common fey, she returned my love. She gave me the gift of her body – not once, but many times. We thought no one would ever find out." The way he said that last part was bitter enough to curdle milk.

"I take it someone *did* find out."

"Oh, yes – one of noble blood who also desired her but had been spurned – spurned for *me*. He wasted no time in bringing my *crime* to the attention of the Queen."

"Messing around with a member of the Court is illegal, huh?"

"It is considered an insult to the Queen herself –

which makes it the most heinous of all crimes. My punishment – well, that you see before you."

"Forgive a dumb question, but your wings will grow back, won't they?"

"Yes, in a year – perhaps two. But the shame is eternal – that, and the loss forever of the one I love."

Sounded like fairies were as fucked up as humans – just with fancier vocabulary.

Now comes the hard part.

My back to the window, I went ahead and put my butt on the sill and slowly pivoted my legs, until my feet were on the ledge. Then I carefully eased my head and shoulders through. That done, I gripped the window frame tight with one hand and slowly raised up to a standing position, my knees screaming the whole time. But finally I'd done it – I was standing on the ledge, maybe ten feet from the fucking fairy drama queen who had caused all this.

As happens every time I'm in the process of doing something stupid, I started hearing from my gut.

Uh-uh, Stan. Bad idea. You know how far up we are? Get us the fuck out of here before it's too late!

Then my brain decided to join the conversation.

Shaddup.

Now for the *real* hard part.

Two feet wide, that ledge was – give or take an inch. People say "Everything's relative," and that sure is true. Two feet would be pretty impressive if it was, say, the length of my dick. But right now that ledge I was on seemed about as slim as my chances for sainthood.

The fey opened his eyes for a second, saw what I was doing, then clenched them shut again.

Good. Keep the baby blues closed tight, pal. Don't look at me, and especially don't look down. In fact, I think I'll take that advice myself.

"What do you think you're *doing*, you fool?" he snapped. "If you try to manhandle me back inside, I will simply jump, and take you with me."

Oh, would you? If only…

"I wouldn't dream of it," I lied. "But I really want to understand your pain, your desperation, and I feel that I can only do that if I share this with you."

God, I'm so full of shit, I'm surprised it isn't coming out my ears.

Arms spread wide, palms flat against the concrete wall, I started edging toward him.

"But why should *you* care?" he said.

"Maybe I once fell in love with the wrong woman," I said. "And maybe, just maybe, I lost her forever. We may be more alike than you think, Butch."

"You have rare understanding, for a human," he said.

Another foot. Another. Almost there.

"I understand more than you know," I told him.

Mistake. He realizes my voice sounds too close. He opens those big blue eyes that they all have, stares at me in disbelief.

"You *idiot*! What are you–"

No point in stealth now. I shuffled toward him a couple more feet, then grabbed his wrist where it was pressed against the wall behind us. Butch gave something like a gasp.

Then, after a quick mental prayer, I stepped forward into nothing – taking the screaming, flailing fairy right along with me, all the way down.

I never did get to Luigi's, but, on the plus side, I arrived for work ten minutes early. Who says clouds don't have silver linings?

My partner was even earlier than me, for a change. Karl was absorbed in something on his computer monitor, but when I came in he glanced up, then did a double-take.

"Jesus, Stan, what the fuck happened to *you*?"

"Went flying with a fairy," I said. "Trouble is, neither one of us had wings."

He looked at me for a couple of seconds. "OK, you don't get to dangle something like that in front of me without providing the details. So, spill."

"Yeah, all right. I'll tell you as much of it as I can until McGuire sends us out on a call."

"Oh, that's right," Karl said. "You haven't heard yet."

"Heard what?"

"Start of our regular shift is gonna be delayed for an hour or so. A couple of Feebies are in town, and they're putting on some kind of dog and pony show for us. McGuire says the detectives on every shift have to sit through it."

"Oh, great. That means the FBI wants something from us."

"It always does," Karl said. "One of them's kinda hot, though – in a hard-ass sort of way."

"I hope you're talking about a woman here," I said. "Not that there's anything wrong, you know, if you're thinking about changing teams."

"Hey, you're the one who was goin' on about flying with the fairies. Now, let's hear it."

"All right," I said. "I left the house early tonight, with the idea of having a leisurely dinner at Luigi's…"

We weren't interrupted by Lieutenant McGuire or anybody else, for a change, so I was able to tell him the whole thing.

"Holy shit," Karl said, about eight minutes later. "You just grabbed him and *jumped*?"

"Sure. I knew the fire department was going to set up some of those big, semi-inflated air bags they use at fires, in case somebody falls from a ladder. I saw them do it once for a jumper, too – about three years ago. I made sure they did it this time, too."

"So, how'd you get all banged up?"

"Aw, I hit the fucking bag face first. I don't do this kinda thing every day, you know. The impact got my nose bleeding, although it's not broken, they tell me. And they make those air bags out of pretty rough fabric – that's where the facial abrasions came from. It'll all heal in a few days."

Karl shook his head. "What I don't get is why you even bothered, man. I mean, if the dude, uh, fairy's choices are either jump into an air bag or go back inside, he'll make up his mind by himself sooner or later. Either way, no harm."

"I'm not so sure," I said. "If he was determined to off himself, he could've found a section of asphalt the air bags didn't protect. They don't have enough to cover the whole front of the building, you know. That's why I was glad he kept his eyes closed – he didn't see the air bags deployed down below until we were on our way down. And, besides..." I shrugged.

"Besides what?"

"I hate to see city resources tied up for hours over bullshit like that. That fire truck and those black-and-whites had more important things to do than wait for *Butch* to make up his fucking mind. It offended my sense of... I dunno, efficiency, I guess."

"My partner thinks he's Batman," Karl said in mock despair. "And I thought I was the vampire on this team."

"You are, and besides–"

That was when McGuire came out of his office and yelled, "All right, everybody head to the media room. Let's go, people."

There was a general shuffling of chairs and feet as detectives got up, most of them grumbling a little.

"Time for the dog and pony show," Karl said.

I walked with him to the door. "Didn't you tell me that you saw one of those once, in Tijuana – a dog and pony show?"

"Nah, that was a donkey and a midget. A couple of chicks were involved, too, although it turned out one of them was a dude."

"Hope this exhibition's gonna be better than that," I said.

"It could hardly be worse."

How wrong we were. How fucking wrong we were.

We sat in darkness for maybe half a minute. If we were watching old-tech VHS, I would have figured it was just leader tape we were looking at. But this was a DVD, which doesn't need blank space at the beginning. I guessed the darkness was part of the program – a way to build suspense, maybe. If so, it was working.

Some people like total darkness – they say they find it restful. Me, I slept with a nightlight on when I was a kid, and I still do. Complete darkness freaks me out. I read once where Freud is supposed to have said that fear of the dark is subconscious fear of death, which the dark symbolizes. Of course, a lot of people think Freud was full of shit.

Personally, I think it goes back to prehistoric times, before man figured out how to make fire. The blackness between sundown and sunrise must've been an uneasy time for Joe Caveman, especially when there was no moon. Most predators see better at night than people do. In the dark, a man can't tell what's creeping up on him with dinner on its mind – until it's too late.

Some things never change, I guess.

Suddenly, a light illuminated the video screen – bright and sudden, like you find on a film set. You know how it goes – some guy yells "Lights!" and, *boom*, the sun comes out. What I was looking at on the screen didn't exactly fill me with eager anticipation, however.

The red circle, which was maybe ten feet across, looked like it had been carefully painted on the concrete floor. The five-pointed star inside it had also been done with care, probably by someone who understood the consequences of getting it wrong. It was easy to see the detail under those bright lights.

Inside the circle squatted two heavy wooden chairs. One of them was stained and splattered along its legs and side with a brown substance. When it was fresh, the brown stuff might have been red – blood red.

A man sat in each chair. There was nothing remarkable about them – apart from the fact that they were both naked and bound firmly to the chairs with manacles at hands and feet.

Not far from the chairs stood a cheap-looking table, its wood scarred and pitted. Someone had laid out a number of instruments there, including a small hammer, a corkscrew, a pair of needle-nose pliers, a blowtorch, and several different sizes of knives.

A man's voice could be heard chanting, in a language that had been old when Christianity was young. This had been going on for several minutes. The men in the chairs sometimes looked outside the circle in the direction of the chanting, other times at each other. The one with dark hair looked confused. The other man was blond and clearly the more intelligent of the two, because he looked terrified.

Then came the moment when the air in the middle of the pentagram seemed to shiver and ripple. The ripple grew, but never crossed the boundary of the circle. After a while, some thin white smoke began to issue from that shimmering column. Over the next minute, the color of the smoke went from white to gray, then from gray to black. The chanting continued throughout all of this.

The column of smoke gradually took the form of a Class Two demon. I blinked. Class Twos are hard to summon, being near the top of the demon hierarchy. The wizard these people were using must've been pretty good.

I'd encountered a Class Four the previous year that Karl had saved me from, and those things are so dumb they don't even have language – they're all appetite. Class Twos are different. They manifest an appearance that's almost human-looking, and they speak every language known to humankind, as well as their own tongue, developed over the millennia spent together in Hell.

The demon looked in the direction the chanting had come from and spoke angrily in Demon, demanding to know who had dared to summon him.

The voice from off-screen came back, firm and fearless. I listened for a bit, then whispered to Karl, "The wizard's threatening to lay a whole bunch of hurt on the demon if he doesn't obey the wizard's commands."

Karl looked at me. "How the fuck do you know that?" he said softly.

"I speak Demon. Sort of."

I'd studied their bastard language off and on for over ten years, and was still a long way from fluent. But I figured understanding it might save my life one day – or, more important, my soul.

The demon gave a piercing scream and doubled over. The wizard must have zapped him pretty good.

When the hellspawn spoke again, it was more onciliatory – for a demon, that is. Then it bowed its head in acquiescence. The wizard had better hope the demon never got out of that circle, or he was going to be a long time dying – and death would only be the beginning.

"The demon agreed to cooperate, and the wizard just told him to possess one of those guys in the chairs," I muttered so only Karl could hear.

The dark-haired man went suddenly rigid. He threw his head back as if in great pain, the muscles and tendons in his skin standing out all over his body. This lasted for several seconds. Then, all at once, the man seemed to relax. He looked around the room, and the circle, as if seeing them for the first time. His facial expression was one he hadn't displayed before. It combined cunning and hatred in roughly equal proportions.

Then the wizard's voice said a couple more words in Demon. He spoke sharply, as if giving a command, and that's exactly what he was doing. I swallowed. Things were about to get very ugly, I figured.

The shackles holding the dark-haired man to the chair sprang open, as if by their own accord, and fell clattering to the floor.

The dark-haired man walked slowly to the table and surveyed the instruments that had been lined up like a macabre smorgasbord. He turned and looked at the blond man, a terrible smile growing on his thin face. Then the dark-haired man picked up from the table the pair of pliers and the blowtorch. After taking a moment to make sure that the blowtorch was working, he walked over to the chair where the blond man sat chained, naked, and speechless with terror.

What happened next went from zero to unspeakable in a very few seconds. Soon afterward, it went beyond unspeakable, to a level of horror that there are no words to describe.

Twelve very long minutes later, the blond man gave one last, agonized scream and escaped into death. We sat there and watched him die.

Then somebody must've pressed Stop, because the screen went mercifully dark. A few seconds later, the lights came on.

The nine people in the room sat in stunned silence, blinking in the sudden brightness. Then everybody started talking at once.

There had been eleven people in the room when the lights were turned off. But there'd been enough residual glow from the big monitor for me to see two tough, experienced police officers quietly leave over the last few minutes, one with a hand clasped tightly over his mouth.

I was glad nobody would know how close I came to being number three out the door.

My partner Karl leaned toward me and said softly, "Sweet Jesus Christ on a pogo stick. And people say *vampires* are inhuman."

"Well, strictly speaking, you *are*," I told him, just to be saying something.

"You know what I mean, Stan."

"Yeah, I do. And I'm not arguing with you, either."

The two FBI agents walked to the front of the room and stood waiting for us to quiet down. They'd been introduced to us earlier, before the horror show started. Linda Thorwald was the senior agent, and she'd done most of the talking so far. She was average height and slim build, with the ice-blue eyes I always associate with Scandinavia. Her hair was jet black, and I wondered if she was a blonde who'd had it dyed to increase her chances of being taken seriously in the macho culture of the FBI. People have done stranger things, and for worse reasons.

Her partner was a guy named Greer, who had big shoulders, brown hair, and a wide mustache that probably had J. Edgar Hoover spinning in his grave. He moved like an athlete, and I thought he might be one of the many former college jocks who find their way into law enforcement once it sinks in that they're not quite good enough for the pros.

When the room was quiet, Thorwald said, "I regret that I had to subject all of you to that revolting exhibition of sadism and murder. If it's any consolation, I've seen more than one veteran FBI agent lose his lunch either during or immediately after a showing of this… supernatural snuff film."

Snuff films are an urban legend, probably started by the same kind of tight-ass public moralists who used to rant about comic books destroying the nation's moral fiber. But the myth made its way into popular culture, and stayed there. There's been plenty of counterfeit ones made over the years, with sleazeballs using special makeup effects to rip off the pervs who think torture and murder are fun. These days, you can see stuff like that at your local multiplex. It's all fake, but I still wouldn't want to know anybody who was a fan. If I'm going to hang out with ghouls, I prefer the real kind – they can't help what they are.

There have been some serial killers who took video of their victims to jerk off over between kills, but that was for their own private use. If by "snuff film" you mean a commercially available product depicting actual murder, then there's no such thing.

Or rather, there wasn't. Until now.

"I wanted you all to see that video," Thorwald said, "because it's important that you understand what we're up against, and what the stakes are. Copies of that DVD have surfaced within the last month in New York, Philadelphia, Pittsburgh and, uh–" She turned to her partner.

"Baltimore," he said.

"—and Baltimore," she went on. "But the Bureau

has been interested in this case for longer than a month. Quite a bit longer."

Thorwald took a step forward. "You know that expression, 'I've got good news and bad news'? Well, I'm afraid I don't have any good news to offer you today. Instead, I bring bad news, and worse news. Brian?"

I could almost see the two of them rehearsing this act in their hotel room last night. The whole thing had a stagy quality that was getting on my nerves. Of course, after what I'd just witnessed, my nerves were pretty damn edgy already.

"The bad news," Greer said, "Is that what you just saw isn't the first video depicting this kind of torture-murder. I mean, one apparently carried out by a demon that's been conjured and then allowed to 'possess' an innocent party."

That must've been the dark-haired man we'd just seen. He hadn't done all those awful things to the blond guy – the demon who'd taken him over had done them, using his body as an instrument.

"In fact, it's the fourth one," Greer said. "Same M.O. every time, with the same… gruesome result. All that varies is the technique, and the victim."

The technique varied. I guess that's why whoever was running the show had put out a selection of torture devices for the hellspawn to use. Nothing like variety.

Thorwald took over again. "The going price for one of these videos in the illicit-smut underground is one thousand dollars. To give you some perspective, you can buy one of a four year-old girl being raped for about three hundred." A look of disgust passed over her face, the first genuine expression I'd seen there. "Presumably, each one of the DVDs has sold well enough to keep those producing them in business. The economies of scale are pretty good, from their perspective. Once you've recorded the master, you can burn copies for less than a buck apiece. There's no way to know how many have been put into circulation. And no reason to think these people are going to stop doing it. That, as I said, is the bad news. But, as far as you officers are concerned, there is worse news." She paused for effect, and I wondered if she'd learned that at the FBI Academy, or in some college speech class. Maybe she'd been on the debate team – she was the type.

"We have been unable to establish the location where these atrocities were made," Thorwald said. "As with the one you just saw, what's visible on-screen doesn't give us much to go on. However, based on new information, we now have reason to believe that at least one of these DVDs was shot right here in Scranton."

Then she stood there, looking at us. I don't know what kind of a reaction she expected. If she was looking for gasps of surprise, she was talking to the wrong crowd. Most of us hadn't gasped since we found out the awful truth about Santa Claus.

Finally, Carmela Aquilina – one of the two female detectives on the Supe Squad – said, "If you're waiting for someone to feed you the next line, then I'll do it. What's this 'new information'?"

"One of the victims has been identified," Thorwald said. "A Bureau agent, who viewed the videos, recognized his cousin, who lives – *lived* – in Scranton. The cousin's name was Edward Hudzinski."

I noticed that a couple of the detectives threw quick glances my way, as if expecting a reaction. There's lots of Polacks living in the Scranton area, and we don't all know each other. We don't all hang out together, either, and some of us can't even dance the fucking polka – at least, *I* sure as hell can't. Hudzinski's name meant nothing to me. But I pitied the poor bastard, whoever he was, if he had died like the guy we'd just watched on video.

I guess Greer figured it was his turn again. "Needless to say, we didn't take the ID on faith. Instead, we queried our Scranton field office about Mister Hudzinski. They checked with Scranton PD and found that he'd been reported missing last April. There had been no suspicious circumstances about his disappearance, so it was treated as a routine missing persons case."

"Are you saying that the Department should have handled it differently?" That was my boss, Lieutenant McGuire. His voice, while polite, had some snap to it. Although he'll kick the ass of any cop under his command who fucks up, he doesn't like criticism from outsiders – even outsiders with Federal badges.

"Not at all," Greer said. "Based on the information available to you, I'd say the response was entirely appropriate. But now there's this new information, so a different response seems indicated. And this unit seems the most suitable one to carry it out."

"What is it you expect us to do?" a detective sitting down front asked.

"The answer to that should come from Lieutenant McGuire," Thorwald said. "Agent Greer and I would not presume to tell you officers how to handle a case like this. Our work at Quantico's Behavioral Science Unit involves tracking down serial killers – of the human variety. We're not experienced in matters involving the... supernatural." She managed to keep most of the distaste she felt out of her voice.

"We've requested temporary assignment to the Bureau's Scranton field office," Greer said. "We'll be available for consultation, and we want to monitor the investigation closely – without getting in the way, of course."

Of course. Until the time came to make an arrest. Then the Feebies would be right there, claiming jurisdiction as well as the newspaper headlines. Well, they could have their fucking headlines. I wanted the sick bastards who were behind this video operation. As long as they went down, I didn't give a shit who put them there.

After Thorwald and Greer left to go clean their weapons, or whatever it is that Feebies do in their free time, McGuire gave us our assignments.

"Work your snitches, all of you," he said. "If one

of these murders was committed here, the odds are good that they all were. The perps have no reason that I can see to travel all over the place, just to grab victims who're anonymous on the videos, anyway."

"Why here, I wonder," Karl said, loud enough for McGuire to hear.

"We'll know that when we nail the bastards," he said. "Maybe the wizard who's doing the summoning is based here. God knows there's no shortage of them in the Wyoming Valley."

"They all do white magic only – supposedly." That was Sefchik, Aquilina's partner.

"And we're all old enough to know what 'supposedly' is worth," McGuire said. "Besides, even those that stay on the right-hand path might have heard something about one of their brethren who's been walking on the wild side."

"And it's not just the wizard," I said.

McGuire looked at me. "What do you mean?"

"There's other people involved, too. Somebody is operating the camera while the wizard is conjuring – we saw it move while he was still chanting."

Aquilina brushed hair out of her eyes and said, "He could've done it himself, using a remote to move and focus."

"In theory, yeah," I said. "But in practice, no way. Any wizard with experience – and it looks like this guy's got plenty – knows better then to split his attention during a conjuration. The cost of fucking up is just too damned high."

"So to speak," Karl said. He's always finding puns in my speech that I didn't intend to put there.

"So there's two of the fuckers, at least," Pearce said. His nose has been broken so many times, he looks like a dumb pug. He's neither one.

"Two, and probably more," I said. "They're snatching people without being seen, then disposing of the bodies afterward. Could be that the wizard doesn't stoop to do that kind of work himself, so that means more guys are involved."

"Good point," McGuire said. "And let's not forget the people on the retail end. Somebody's got to make copies of each video, and somebody's gotta sell them. You don't buy this kind of shit at Vlad-Mart."

"Not yet, anyway," I muttered, just loud enough for Karl to hear me.

"All right, everybody, hit the street," McGuire said, just as our PA, Louise the Tease, approached him with a sheet of paper. He read it, and his face got even tighter than usual.

"Renfer, Markowski," he said, "Stick around a minute."

Karl and I traded looks. It's like when the principal tells you to stay after school – it's never for anything good.

Once the other detectives were gone, McGuire said, "There's been another witch burning."

I felt my stomach drop like a runaway elevator. "Do they have an ID?"

"No, but if you're worried about Rachel, she's still

in San Diego at that Wiccan conference. Not due back for a few more days."

I felt better, but only a little. Rachel Proctor, the department's consulting witch, wasn't the only magic practitioner I knew, although she was the one I knew best.

"If they don't know who she was, how do they know she was a witch?" Karl asked.

"Looks like the same M.O. as last time," McGuire said.

Four nights earlier, a woman had been found tied to a telephone pole in Sturgis Park – or what was left of her had been found. She'd been burned beyond recognition. But the next day, a guy named Martin Allerdyce filed a missing persons report on his wife, Brenda, who was a practicing witch. She did white magic, of course – the black kind's illegal.

Nobody thought it would serve any useful purpose to have Allerdyce attempt an identification of the charred thing found in the park. But he did provide two items, upon request: a brush containing a good quantity of his wife's hair, and the name of her dentist.

Both dental records and DNA analysis confirmed Brenda Allerdyce as the victim. I wasn't exactly surprised to hear that the funeral had been conducted with a closed coffin.

One of the fire marshals said that gasoline had been used as an accelerant, and Homer Jordan at the ME's office told me that the level of free histamines in the tissues meant that Brenda Allerdyce had been alive when the fire was lit. She must've died screaming, an ugly fact that her husband was probably all too well aware of.

And now the sick fuck responsible had done it again.

"Where's this one?" I asked McGuire.

He looked at me for a second before answering. "Lake Scranton," he said, and his voice contained no inflection at all.

Next to me I heard Karl mutter, "Well, damn."

Lake Scranton is a man-made reservoir just southeast of the city. A few months back, Karl and I, and some others, had spent a very long night in its pump house. Several people had died there, and the survivors would never be the same again. That was especially true of Karl, who'd started the night as a human and finished it well on his way to becoming a vampire.

"Tell me it's not the pump house again," I said.

"Not even close," McGuire said. "The vic was found tied to one of the trees along the shoreline. Somebody whose house overlooks the lake saw the flames and called the fire department."

"Are you sure you want us on this?" I asked. "The Feebies seem to expect us all to be out beating the bushes for whoever's been making those snuff films." I can take as much horror as anybody on the job. But after watching that video tonight, I wasn't eager to look at a charred corpse, and to inhale that distinctive odor that smells so much like roast pork that I haven't eaten any in fourteen years.

A couple of months ago, I'd spent one of my rare nights off having a few beers with Homer Jordan. He'd told me, as if I wanted to know, about some scientific paper he'd read that compared the pain involved in the various ways people die. The paper had concluded, Homer said, that burning to death was the hardest way there is to check out.

Me, I would have said that being tortured to death by somebody who enjoyed his work would have been a contender for the number one spot, but that's kind of like debating which is the hottest corner of Hell, and those kind of arguments don't interest me.

I suppose that the study Homer was talking about had made some kind of valuable contribution to medical research. But I wouldn't want to be married to the guy, or woman, who wrote it.

"I don't think the FBI expects us to abandon our regular case load just to help them with this thing," McGuire said. "And if they do, then fuck 'em. Now get moving."

We got moving.

As I drove out of the parking lot, Karl said, "Think it's those fucking witchfinders again?"

"Well, it's not Crane and Ferris, that's for sure." The last two witch-smellers to visit Scranton had died right here in this parking lot, their necks broken by a vampire named Vollman, and good riddance.

"I figure there's more where those two clowns came from," Karl said.

"I'm sure," I said. "But they're supposed to check in with the local police, whenever they come into a town – just like private eyes do."

"*Supposed to*, huh?"

"Yeah, all right," I said. "But what those bastards do is legal, unfortunately. If they'd burned a witch, they wouldn't disappear – they'd call a fucking press conference."

"Good point. So what do you figure – some lone psycho?"

"Let's wait 'til we get there," I said. "It's a mistake to theorize in the absence of data."

From the corner of my eye, I could see Karl turn to look at me. "You've been reading Sherlock Holmes again, Stan?"

"Why not?" I said. "If you can memorize all the James Bond books, I can at least read some Conan Doyle once in a while."

"I don't have 'em memorized," he said. "I'm not some geek fanboy."

"Sorry, my mistake," I said – then asked him, "What's the last line of *From Transylvania with Love*?"

Without hesitating, he quoted, "*Bond pivoted, drove the wooden stake through Rosa Klebb's heart, then slowly collapsed on the blood-red floor.*" After a second's pause, he said, "Hey – no fair. *Everybody* knows that one."

"Everybody," I said, nodding. "Yeah, you're right. My bad."

A few minutes later we reached the turnoff for Lake Scranton. It got quiet in the car as the flashing

red and blue lights up ahead reminded us why we
were here.

There's a jogging trail that goes all the way around
the lake, but it's not wide enough for cars. Neither
are any of the gates leading to it. That's why the two
black-and-white units and the ambulance were
parked outside the north gate. All three had their
red and blue lights going, creating an effect like a
madman's vision of Hell. Considering what I figured
was on the other side of that fence, the madman
would have been right on the money.

Karl and I parked and walked to the gate, which
had a uniform standing next to the strip of yellow
crime scene tape that blocked it. The cop was a pa-
trolman named Dougherty. We knew each other.

"Where is it?" I asked him.

He pointed. "Down the path and to the right.
You'll see the lights."

"Is the ME here?"

"Yeah. It's what's-his-name, Jordan."

"How about Forensics?" I asked him.

"Showed up about five minutes ago."

"Amazing."

Dougherty was right – the crime scene was easy
to find. There was no sense in tripping over something on the way, though, so Karl went first as we
followed the jogging path. He can see pretty well in
the dark these days.

There were no electrical outlets down here, but
somebody – probably the forensics guys – had

brought along three battery-powered lamps on tripods. A couple of other cops held big flashlights, their beams moving around restlessly but always returning to the charred thing that had once been a human being. Lights flashed erratically as somebody took photos of the scene.

A couple of EMTs stood patiently nearby, the stretcher they'd brought leaning against a tree. I didn't envy them the job of carrying the body all the way back to the ambulance. EMTs are tough, and they see a lot of bad shit almost every day. But what they had to transport this time would probably have given Caligula nightmares.

A guy in plain clothes stood among the uniforms, and as we got closer I recognized Scanlon from Homicide. He made lieutenant not long ago, which means he doesn't have to go to crime scenes anymore. But he still does. I wondered if he was regretting that he went to this one.

The smell of burned flesh was strong now, and if I let myself focus on it, I'd probably puke. So I focused on Scanlon, instead.

"Well, look who's here," he said. "The Spook Squad."

"Two guys doesn't make a squad, Scanlon – even a guy from Homicide should know that." I looked toward the tree and what was tied to it. "They called us because this one is supposed to be similar to the witch burning we had Wednesday night."

"Yeah, same M.O.," Scanlon said. "Such as it is. Human female, although I'm guessing on the sex, based on the remaining hair and body size. Placement of the rope is the same as last time. The knots look similar, although I'm no expert. Same accelerant, too – there's a definite gasoline smell, when you get up close."

"I'll take your word for it," I said. "You sure she's human?"

He shrugged. "Not too many species of supe fit the profile," Scanlon said. "A werewolf would have transformed and broken the ropes with no sweat. A fairy would have just vanished. She's too small for an ogre and too big for a troll or goblin." It sounded like he had been reading the manual.

"How do you know it's not a vampire?" There was something in Karl's voice that I caught, even if Scanlon didn't.

"No fangs," Scanlon said. His face, what I could see of it, was expressionless. "I had the forensics guys check, even though it's not their job." I was betting that none of them had given him an argument about it, either, although putting your face close enough to that corpse to see its teeth could be nobody's idea of a good time.

"No reason she couldn't be a witch, though," I said. "Like the last one."

Technically, witches and wizards are considered supernatural beings, or supes, but they're also human – most of them, anyway.

"No, I guess not," Scanlon said. "But why somebody who can work magic would let herself be abducted, then burned alive, is more than I can figure."

Maybe he hadn't read the manual, after all.

"Witches don't wear magic like body armor," I said, "and they can't use it instantly, like karate. Working magic takes preparation."

"Remember that guy, Kulick, a few months ago?" Karl asked. "He was a wizard, and a good one. But he was taken by surprise – and you saw what happened to *him*."

George Kulick had died hard, although it had taken a while for his spirit to move on to the Great Beyond, whatever that was. Personally, I hoped the bastard was roasting in Hell.

"But they can do defensive spells, can't they?" Scanlon said.

"Sure, if they have a reason to." I glanced toward the charred figure tied to the tree. "And if it turns out that this vic is a witch, too, I bet every practitioner in town is going to have a defensive spell in place within a few hours of getting the news."

"Which means this one should be the last," Scanlon said. "They'll be ready for him, next time."

"They fucking well better be," I said.

Homer Jordan lumbered over. He nodded to Karl and me but spoke to Scanlon. "Well, I pronounced her, Lieutenant, which shouldn't come as a surprise. Cause of death's pretty obvious, too – but I'll check the internal organs to see if she was poisoned or drugged, first."

"What about T.O.D.?" Scanlon asked.

Homer shrugged his big shoulders. "Time of death's a bitch with burn victims, Lieutenant. I'll do the best I can."

"The guy who called it in said he could see flames," I said. "The time of the call is probably a good indication of when she died, give or take a few minutes."

"That's good to know, thanks," Homer said. "I'll check the police report." He looked around at the dark trees. "Good thing we've had a lot of rain lately. Otherwise, the motherfucker could've started a forest fire, on top of everything else."

As Homer walked away, one of the uniforms came over and said, "Since the doc's done with the crispy critter, can we cut her loose, now, Lieutenant? The ambulance guys wanna get out of here."

Scanlon was in the cop's face faster than a Marine Corps drill sergeant. He didn't raise his voice, but I could hear every word he said, from fifteen feet away.

"You're talking about a woman who died in a horror and agony that your dim little brain can't begin to comprehend, and that you should pray to God you never have to learn about first-hand. But if I ever hear you refer to any burn victim as a 'crispy critter' again, I will personally tear that badge off your chest and make you eat it. Do you understand me?"

Even in the uncertain light, I thought I could see the cop's face start to perspire. "Jeez, Lieutenant, I was only—"

Scanlon's voice could have frozen Lake Scranton. "I *asked* you if you understood me."

"Yes, sir. I understand, sir."

"Then cut the victim down, and help the EMTs get her on the stretcher."

"Yes, *sir*."

Scanlon walked back to Karl and me, shaking his head. I didn't say anything – I figured he'd said it all.

"I guess your squad and mine will both be investigating this, from different angles," Scanlon said. "It would be a good thing to keep each other current on any progress – informally, of course."

"I agree, Lieutenant." *Informally* meant we'd avoid official paperwork and the interdepartmental rivalries that sometimes went along with it. It's like the CIA and FBI – they're supposed to share information, but they don't, always. And when that happens, sometimes people die.

I glanced over toward the tree, and saw the EMTs gently lowering the burned body onto the stretcher. "We probably oughta get going," I said to Karl.

I wanted to get on the path before the EMTs did. Otherwise, we'd have to follow them, and their macabre burden, all the way to the parking lot. It would slow us down, and would mean another ten minutes or so of inhaling that sickly-sweet odor from the burned corpse. I'd smelled enough of that for one night – or a lifetime, for that matter.

As I followed Karl and his vamp-vision through the dark, he said, over his shoulder, "Wonder if she has a family?"

"Probably," I said. "Most people do." Whoever the victim's survivors were, I was glad it wasn't my job to inform them of her death, and how it had happened. "We'll probably have an ID in a day or two."

"Even with the way she was burned?"

"Somebody'll report her missing, most likely – just like the other one, Mrs, uh–"

"Allerdyce," Karl said. "Brenda Allerdyce."

"Once Homer has a name to work with, he won't have much problem confirming her identity. Then we can go to work. Just like real detectives."

"Looking for stuff they had in common, all that."

"Yeah, but we'll start with finding out whether they knew each *other*. The ultimate common factor."

"Maybe Rachel can help out with that," he said. "Once she gets back."

"Assuming she's not still mad at us," I said.

"What do you mean *us*, kimosabe? I'm not the one who asked her to do the fucking necromancy."

We were kidding around, a little – we both knew that Rachel Proctor didn't hold a grudge against either of us. Although I wouldn't blame her if she did, in my case.

Last summer, I'd prevailed upon Rachel to conduct a necromancy so I could talk to the spirit of a murder victim. She'd agreed, against her better judgment. Turned out her judgment was right on the money, because things had gone very wrong. But she said she didn't blame me for any of it, and even gave me some of the credit for later getting her out of the mess that I'd gotten her into in the first place. Nice lady, that Rachel.

As we reached the gate I saw that the media had arrived in force, although the uniforms were keeping them behind a barrier of crime scene tape that split the parking lot in two. It looked like the four local networks had each sent a camera crew, and a couple of print reporters for the Scranton and Wilkes-Barre papers had shown up, too.

As soon as they saw us, a couple of mini-spotlights came on, along with the red lights atop the video cameras. The reporters were all yelling questions at us, but Karl and I just squinted against the glare and kept walking. If I made any statements without prior authorization, McGuire would disembowel me with a spoon. Anyway, I don't like journalists, much. I know they're just doing their jobs – but then, you could probably say the same thing for the guards at Bergen-Belsen.

As I started the car, Karl said, "About two hours to sunrise," which meant two hours before he had to be back inside his apartment's bedroom, in a sleeping bag with a blanket over it.

"Still time to accomplish a couple of things which might actually prove helpful. I'm gonna call Doc Watson and leave a message on his machine. See if he can spare us some time tomorrow night."

Terence K. Watson, MD, had been born in the Mississippi delta, the heart of blues country. That's where the nickname came from, although Doc says he can't even carry a tune in the shower. But he's a good psychiatrist, and he's been helpful to us in the past.

"You mentioned a couple of things," Karl said. "What's the other one?"

"I want to talk to those two Feebies."

Thorwald and Greer were set up in the squad's break room. It isn't much – a Mister Coffee that nobody every cleans, a small urn with hot water for the tea drinkers, a beat-up table, and some chairs. There's a small refrigerator that nobody ever uses, although Karl's been talking about keeping a bottle of O-positive in there, just for laughs.

The two Feds were looking through a pile of our old case files, although I couldn't figure what they thought they'd find. As we walked in, I said, "Got a minute?"

Greer glanced at his partner, then said, "Sure," with a little gesture toward the vacant chairs. We sat down, and I noticed that Karl was staring at Thorwald. Maybe he was considering her as a possible volunteer blood donor. She might've read his mind because she returned the stare and said to him, "You're undead, aren't you?"

I guess Greer wasn't as sharp as his partner, because he looked at Thorwald in surprise, then transferred the look to Karl. The surprised expression quickly turned into something wary. Maybe he thought Karl was going to jump across the table and go for his jugular. I figured Greer didn't have much experience with vampires – maybe neither of them did.

Karl just nodded at Thorwald's question. There was a time when he would've tried to charm her with a smile, but nowadays his fangs tend to spoil the effect. He usually keeps them covered around strangers.

"I didn't know that the Scranton PD was recruiting vampires," Thorwald said. She didn't have Greer's leery expression, but didn't look like she was about to ask Karl to the Sadie Hawkins Day dance, either.

"They're not, far as I know," Karl said. "I was a cop before I was a vamp." He said it as if he was discussing tomorrow's weather.

"He was… changed… in the line of duty," I said.

Karl nodded and added, "It's a long story," meaning one he wasn't interested in telling now, if ever.

"I wanted to ask you about these videos," I said.

"What about 'em?" Greer asked.

"You said there were four, so far," I said.

Greer shrugged. "Yeah. So?"

"So how do you know there's only been four?"

There was a battery-powered clock on the wall near us, and I heard it tick seven times before Thorwald said, "You've got a point, Sergeant. There could be more of these atrocities than the four we have copies of. But our agents nationwide have been pushing their contacts and informants pretty hard, especially now that they know what to look for."

She took a sip of what looked like cold coffee, and I gave her credit for not grimacing, even though it probably tasted like battery acid.

"My best estimate is that there are only four, so far," she said. "But I won't discount the possibility that there are others out there."

"And there'll probably be more soon," Greer said. "Unless we find these fuckers first."

"You've seen all four of them," I said.

Thorwald made a face that would have gone well with the cold coffee. "Several times each," she said. "It doesn't get any easier with repetition." Maybe she wasn't quite the hard-bitten Feebie that she acted like.

"Were all of them filmed in the same place?" I asked.

"We think so," she said. "Although the lights are focused on the protective circle, there are some shots, pans mostly, that give a quick glimpse of one of the walls."

"Red brick," Greer said. "We took screen caps from each video and compared them for the same basic shot in each one – a head-on view of the victim in his chair before the fun begins. The configurations of the bricks in the background are identical. That means–"

Karl interrupted him. "It means that the camera angle is exactly the same each time. It has to be. And if the camera hasn't been moved from one murder to the next, that's another point in favor of the location being the same each time."

I let my gaze drift toward the coffee maker and thought about pouring myself a cup, but fortunately sanity prevailed. Instead, I looked back at Thorwald. "That doesn't necessarily mean the killing ground is in Scranton."

"That's true, technically," Thorwald said.

"Yeah, *but*…" Karl said, and let his voice trail off.

"*But*," she said, "the only vic that we have an ID for is from here. This Hudzinski guy. We've got screen caps of all the victims' faces, enlarged and enhanced. We've sent them to all the field offices. None of the agents there recognized anybody, and we can hardly expect them to go door to door in their local areas, asking 'Do you recognize any of these people?' Not exactly an optimum use of Bureau resources."

She actually said that – "optimum use of Bureau resources" – and with a straight face, too.

Karl leaned forward in his chair. "You're talking about eight vics minimum – two per video, right?

"So what?" Greer asked.

"So they can't all be local," Karl said. "This is Scranton, not New York. Eight guys go missing over the course of–" He looked at Thorwald. "–what, a year?"

"We figure it's been going on about ten months," she said.

"Eight guys in ten months," Karl said. "Uh-uh. Not in Scranton. That many missing person reports is gonna get somebody's attention downstairs, eventually. And we'd have heard about it by now, too."

"Unless the guys were homeless," Greer said. "It's getting so that serial killers like homeless people almost as much as they target hookers."

I thought about that for a moment, then said, "No, can't be – not all eight of 'em, anyway. Scranton's not that big a town. The homeless population isn't large. I'm talking about people living in packing crates and under bridges, shit like that."

"Anyway," Karl said, "nobody around here, no matter how bad off they are, is gonna start living under a bridge."

"How come?" Greer asked him.

"Trolls," Karl said.

"Let's get back to the matter at hand," Thorwald said. "The victims represent one of the points of contact between the killers and the... public, for lack of a better term. Once we identify a victim, we can work backwards, like with any other kidnapping case. Search the vic's home for any intel about where he was supposed to be the day he disappeared, try to find out who he'd been seen with before he went missing – the usual routine."

"Scranton's not the only legal jurisdiction around here," I said. "There's lots of small towns and townships – not to mention Wilkes-Barre, which is only twenty minutes away. Some guy gets grabbed in one of those places, and the missing persons report won't pass through Scranton PD."

"You FBI guys keep track of all that info, don't you?" Karl said.

"Yeah, all police and sheriff's departments nationwide send their crime stats to Washington," Thorwald said. "The Bureau publishes the compilation every year in the Uniform Crime Report."

"That's what I thought," I said. "So, maybe ET should phone home."

She shook her head. "There's a time lag between when the raw data reaches the Bureau and when it's collated."

"How big a time lag?"

"Put it this way," she said. "The Uniform Crime Report for two years ago was just published last month."

"Shit," I said.

"Yeah, but wait a second," Karl said. He looked at me. "Don't the Staties get copied on all missing persons reports from local departments?"

"That's a damn good question." I turned to the Feebies. "Think you can get an answer for us, like maybe tomorrow?"

"Hey," Greer said, "we're not here to do your–"

Thorwald stopped him by putting her hand on his knee. I wondered if it gave him a thrill. It would've given me one. "Sergeant Markowski probably means that the people in Harrisburg will respond more readily to a request from the Bureau than one emanating from the Scranton PD." She raised an eyebrow at me. "Yes?"

"Couldn't have put it better myself," I said. I glanced at my watch. "Sorry to cut this short, but our shift's over, and we need to get out of here at least a half-hour before six."

As Karl and I stood up, Greer said, "Didn't take you for a clock watcher, Markowski. I heard you were a real nose-to-the-grindstone kind of guy."

I didn't say anything, since arguing with assholes is a waste of time, but I saw that Thorwald was looking at me thoughtfully. "What happens at six?" she asked.

"Sunrise."

• • • •

As we walked toward the parking lot, Karl asked me, "Do you suppose there's a special course at the FBI Academy called 'How to Be a Federal Douche Bag'?"

"Wouldn't surprise me," I said. "And if there is, I'm betting that Greer aced it. Probably the only 'A' he ever earned." I reached into a pocket for my keys. "His partner's not too bad, though. For a Feebie."

Karl looked at me. "You think she's hot?"

"I didn't say that. I just meant that she doesn't seem to be a revolving asshole like her buddy."

"Revolving?"

"From whatever angle the object is viewed," I said.

"She likes you, though," Karl said.

"Yeah, right," I said. "And where did that revelation come from, O wise man?"

"Her heartbeat. It speeded up a little every time she talked to you."

I didn't bother to ask him how he knew that. He'd just say, "It's a vamp thing – you wouldn't understand."

"I probably just remind her of her ex-husband," I said. "And not in a good way, either."

He shrugged. "Believe what you want."

"Think you could use some vampire Influence on Greer, maybe get him to stop being such a prick?"

"I'm a vampire," Karl said. "Not a miracle worker."

I watched him unlock his ride. It's the same Ford Exorcist he's been driving the last couple of years, except now it's got tinted windows – in case he's late getting home from work some morning.

It was Wednesday morning, and tonight would be our night off. I wouldn't have minded working, anyway, but McGuire will only authorize overtime if we're chasing a hot lead. And right now we had no leads – hot, cold, or room temperature.

"See you Thursday," Karl said.

"Dark and early." Karl slipped behind the wheel and I headed for my own car. The Toyota Lycan's got a new windshield – Karl shot out the old one while saving my life, a while back – but otherwise it's as old and dented as its owner. But it hasn't got any rust on it, and neither do I – so far.

Ten minutes later I walked into the kitchen, where a vampire sat at the table reading the morning paper. Vamps don't usually hang around my kitchen much, but this one lived here.

"Hey," I said.

"Hey, Daddy," Christine said. "I was beginning to wonder if I'd see you before I went downstairs."

"Downstairs" means the basement, where she spends the day wrapped up in a sleeping bag. I've fixed it up a little down there since she came to stay with me. No need for the place to look like a tomb, even if it sort of is one.

"Yeah, I'm running late," I said. "I was talking to some FBI assholes. It was so much fun, I didn't notice what time it was getting to be."

"What's up with the Feds?" she asked. "Some werewolf knock over a bank, or something?"

"No, it's a lot worse than that," I said. "I'll tell you

about it tonight, but there's something I wanted to ask you about before you crash – who's replaced Vollman as the local Supefather?"

She gave me a brief smile. "'Supefather' – that's cute. Well, I haven't met him yet, but I hear the new guy is a wizard named Victor Castle."

I gave her half a smile of my own. "*Castle*? Seriously?"

"That's what he calls himself. I hear his birth name was Castellino, or something, but I guess that isn't dramatic enough. He's supposed to be pretty smart, even if he does seem to lack a sense of irony."

"He and I need to have a conversation, I think. Where's he hang out – do you know?"

She folded the *Times-Tribune* and stood up. I saw she was wearing her usual bedtime outfit – gray sweatpants and a white T-shirt that mocked a certain milk ad by asking, in red letters, "Got blood?"

"I have no idea," she said. "But I'll ask around tonight, if you want. Maybe make a few calls."

"I'd appreciate it. Thanks."

She gave me a quick hug and a kiss on the cheek. "See you at sundown."

We'd agreed that saying "Good morning" as she went to sleep sounded stupid, so I said, "Goodnight, baby."

I made some breakfast, ate it, and went to bed. That night, I hung out with Christine for a few hours until she left for her job as a 911 dispatcher. Then I did some laundry, put the trash out at the curb, and cleaned Quincey's cage. Quincey's my hamster, and a good listener. I told him about the Feebies and the nasty case they'd brought us, and he seemed interested. But maybe he just likes the sound of my voice. I'm glad somebody does.

I killed a few more hours reading a book about a group of scientists who accidentally opened a portal to Hell. Some thoroughly bad shit ensued, as you might expect. The author claimed it was fiction, and I hoped he was right. We had too many people around with access to Hell as it was.

On Thursday night I got to the squad room around 7.30pm. I was going through my emails when Karl came in and sat at his desk, which is pushed up against mine so they face each other. I looked up, and said, "Hi," and went back to my computer screen. Part of my mind must have noticed that Karl hadn't booted up his own computer because I raised my eyes again and found him looking at me, a strange expression on his face.

"What?" I said.

"I was talking to a CI of mine last night." Confidential informant is the official name for a snitch – somebody who'll pass on information in return for a favor, a few bucks, or just a chance to bank some good will with the cops.

"You were working last night?" I said. "McGuire didn't OK any overtime, that I know of."

"I wasn't working," Karl said. "I just ran into him over at Scavino's."

Scavino's is a bar that attracts what you might call

a mixed clientele. Humans, mostly, but some supes go there because nobody hassles them. Ed Scavino sees to that. He's married to a werewolf, which makes him tolerant by necessity, if not disposition.

"Yeah, OK," I said. "So, you were talking to this guy, and…?"

"And he told me about a whisper that's been making the rounds lately." Karl hesitated a second, which isn't like him. Then I found out why. "Word is, Sharkey's back."

I give myself a little credit for my reaction – or lack of one. I didn't move a muscle for a good two or three seconds, except for my eyelids, which I couldn't stop from blinking rapidly. That happens when I'm scared.

"Sharkey's dead," I said.

"Yeah, I know," Karl said. "At least, I thought I did. But there was never a positive ID on his body, you know that. After the explosion, then the fire, what could you expect? The forensics guys didn't have a lot to work with."

"He was seen going into that building, just before it blew. Nobody ever saw him come out." I don't know who I was trying to convince, Karl or myself.

"Yeah – but, shit, getting in and out of places without being seen was Sharkey's specialty. He was like a fucking ninja, or something. That's why he got paid so much."

"Being a dhampir probably helps with that," I said.

"Yeah, probably."

Sharkey killed for money, but calling him a hit

man was like saying that Rembrandt was a painter. Sharkey was death on two feet. Half human, half vampire, and all lethal. To nobody's surprise, he was known as "the Shark," but I think they'd have called him that even if his name was Smith or Jones.

About eighteen months ago, a gang of vamp punks had kidnapped the daughter of Joe Guaneri, a mob boss in nearby Pittston. He'd paid the ransom, but the vamps killed the girl, anyway. Her body was found drained dry.

Even though the vamps didn't turn her, the family had buried the girl with a wooden stake through her chest, and stuffed the mouth of her decapitated head with garlic. I figured the funeral was one of those closed casket ceremonies.

Guaneri had plenty of his own soldiers to call on for payback, but none of them had any experience against vamps. So he'd hired Sharkey, instead. Guess he wanted to get more than even.

The vamp gang had taken over an abandoned public school building in Carbondale and made it their HQ. Even had a squad of armed humans to guard the place during the day. Being a dhampir, Sharkey could have gone in there at any time, day or night, but he'd waited until after sundown to make his move. Maybe he'd been told to be sure the vamps could see what was coming.

Nobody knows if that bomb belonged to the vamps, or if Sharkey brought it in himself. I wouldn't have bet either way. On the one hand, a bomb wasn't really Sharkey's style – too impersonal, not enough time for the victims to scream. On the other hand, the explosion had not only leveled the building – it had taken out two civilians walking by outside. That sounded like the Shark – he was never real careful about collateral damage.

Karl was right. Nobody had ever made a positive ID on Sharkey's body, or on any of the others. The forensics people estimated that twenty to twenty-five pounds of C-4 explosive had gone off inside that building. From what I hear, the biggest body part they found would still have fit easily inside a shoebox.

That would've killed Sharkey, all right. Dhampirs have the strengths of a vampire, like speed, strength, and the power of Influence. But they have the weaknesses of a human. A bullet in the chest will kill a dhampir just like it would you or me. So will an explosion, like the one that leveled the old Roosevelt school. It had sure taken care of the vampires.

When Sharkey wasn't seen or heard from after the blast, everybody figured he'd died inside the demolished school. Maybe we liked the idea because it was comforting. The peasants in Transylvania must've felt the same way when they heard Dracula was dead.

But Dracula keeps rising from the grave – in the movie versions, anyway.

"Have you given any thought to the possibility that your CI might be full of shit?" I asked Karl.

"Sure," he said. "But he's been pretty reliable in the past."

"He didn't say he'd seen Sharkey himself, though, did he?"

"No, he was just telling me what was in the rumor mill."

"Well, we've both been in this business long enough to know what rumors are worth. Remember the one that said a bunch of cannibals were eating people up around Lake Wallenpaupack?"

The "cannibals" had turned out to be a homeless family, living in a tent and getting by on whatever they could catch. They had eaten squirrels, fish, rabbits, and a couple of feral cats, but no people, as far as we could tell.

"Yeah, I know," Karl said, and shrugged. "You're right – the guy was probably full of shit."

"Exactly," I said. We were like two kids whistling as we walked past the old haunted house. As long as you sounded happy, nothing bad could get you.

It works pretty well, since there's usually nothing inside the "haunted house" to hurt you, anyway.

But sometimes the ghosts are real, and whistling does no damn good at all.

Pretend that there's a file folder somewhere, a big, thick one, labeled Real Bad Ideas. There's at least three things I can think of that belong in there – inviting a werewolf for a moonlight stroll, telling a witch she's got a fat ass, and pissing off an ogre.

Especially that last one.

Despite what you read in the fairy tales, most ogres are fairly mellow creatures. They're not green and cute, like that guy in the movies – Dreck, or whatever his name is, but they're not usually criminal types, either. Mostly they're just big, strong, and dumb, like the one Steinbeck wrote about in *Of Elves and Men*. But all the same, it doesn't pay to get one mad.

I figured somebody had done just that, since the inside of Leary's Bar looked like something you'd find in Berlin at the end of World War II – just after the Russians had passed through. Six tables were smashed, along with ten or twelve chairs. The big mirror was just a memory. One of the ceiling lights had been hit so hard by something – or someone – that the big fluorescent bulb hung down at the end of some thick black wire, blinking and sputtering. I had no idea how many liquor bottles had been smashed, but the odor of alcohol was so strong in there that a couple of deep breaths would probably cause you to flunk a Breathalyzer test.

If you needed additional proof of ogre outrage, there were always the three guys strewn across on the floor, who looked like they'd tried to wrestle a locomotive and come off second best. They were either unconscious, comatose, or dead.

Then there was the girl – a barmaid, judging by her outfit. She looked to be scared about half out of her mind, and I didn't blame her, since the pissed-off ogre, back against the wall, was holding her with one massive paw wrapped around her waist, like a kid playing with a Barbie doll – and not playing real gently, either.

A couple of uniforms were standing just inside the door, what they thought was a safe distance away. I looked over my shoulder and called to them, "Get Leary in here, will you? And find out what's keeping those damn ambulances."

It was quiet inside what was left of the barroom. The only sounds came from the ogre, whose breathing sounded like midnight in a TB ward, and the waitress, who was crying softly.

Keeping my voice low, I asked my partner, "Can you use Influence on him, get him calmed down?"

"I doubt it," Karl said. "I'm not real good at that stuff yet. Anyway, there's not much of a mind there to work with, haina?"

Karl's been my partner for just over a year and a half now, and a vampire for about three months. He's a good kid, even with the fangs.

I nodded. My luck never runs that good, but it'd been worth a try. "You're a lot stronger than you used to be," I said. "If it comes to a rumble, can you take him?"

Karl looked the ogre up and down. It took a while, since the guy was over seven foot from head to toe. You can find some NBA players that tall, but the ogre wasn't lean and quick, the way those guys are. He was built more along the lines of the Great Wall of China.

"I dunno," Karl said. "Let's see if we can avoid finding out."

Neither of us had drawn our weapons yet – we wanted to talk to the ogre, not kill him. We could take him out if we had to – probably. My Beretta's load included silver bullets, and I knew Karl's Glock held sixteen slugs tipped with cold iron – he doesn't handle silver anymore. Either round will take down an ogre, but you have to get him in a vital spot. It's kind of what hunting rhinos must be like – you know your gun can kill the beast, but you'd better make the first shot count, or you're in for a world of hurt.

But with a supernatural creature, just as with humans, lethal force is supposed to be the last option, not the first. The badge isn't a license to kill, and that's something I keep in mind. Besides, the paperwork is horrendous.

I heard a sound from behind me, and saw that the uniforms had brought Leary back inside. They took him over to where I was standing with Karl, about twenty-five feet from the ogre and his new girlfriend. Then they beat it back out the door. "We'll go keep an eye out for the ambulances," one of them said to me. Yeah, yeah.

"What the hell is *he* still doing here?" Leary said from behind me. "I thought you guys were supposed to be the big supe experts."

"We are," I told him, "but even experts need information. Come over here, next to me."

Leary's on the short side, with flaming red hair that's about half gone, bushy eyebrows, and more attitude than the Irish Republican Army. Some say he's got some leprechaun in him, and they'll get no argument from me.

I wanted to be able to talk to Leary and keep my eye on the ogre at the same time. Never turn your back on a supe – unless he's your partner, who you'd trust with your life. Or maybe a member of your family.

Leary was standing a few feet to my left now, so I asked him, "You get many ogres in here?"

As soon as I said it, I realized my question sounded like the set-up to a supe joke – the dumb kind, like Lacey Brennan is always telling me. Lacey works the Supe Squad over in Wilkes-Barre. She's a good cop, and not bad-looking, either, but it's not like I have a thing for her.

"Naw, this one's the first. I don't like havin' 'em around, but when something that size comes in and orders a drink, what was I gonna do?"

"Serve him, I hope," I said.

"'Course I did. Double shot of tequila. He put away that one, and eight more, in about an hour."

"Then what?" Karl asked him. "He run out of money?"

"Naw, I cut him off. He didn't take that too well."

"You wouldn't sell him any more booze because he was drunk?" I asked.

"Shit, he *had* to be. Nine double shots of Jose Cuervo – what would you expect?"

"Yeah, but was he *acting* drunk, Leary?" I was starting to get fed up with this little jerk.

"He was acting big and stupid, just like when he came in. I wanted to get him the fuck outta here before he started cuttin' up and caused some damage."

I let my gaze wander around what was left of his bar. "Looks like you did a hell of a job," I said. "Leary, did you ever consider how much booze it takes to affect something that size?" It takes a lot more than nine shots of tequila to get an ogre drunk, unless he already had some on board when he came in.

"I don't give a shit," Leary said. "I just hope the big dummy's been savin' his pennies, because I'm gonna sue him for every single one – once you guys do your job and get him the fuck out of here, that is."

I shared a disgusted look with Karl, who asked Leary, "The waitress – what's her name?"

"Why? You plannin' on puttin' a move on her or something? You're gonna have to get lover boy over there to turn her loose, first."

Karl let a little bit of vamp show in his eyes as he said, "I just wanna know what to call her. *Now tell me her name.*" Guess he was getting impatient, too.

Leary actually took a step back. "Heather, her name's Heather. Heather Collins."

"All right, Leary," I said. "That's all we needed. Wait outside while we finish up in here."

He was at the door before I finished speaking.

I lowered my voice again before I said to Karl, "Nice job. You're a scary motherfucker, I ever tell you that?"

"Yeah, too often," Karl murmured. "You know, I might be able to do the same thing to Dumbo over there, if you want me to give it a try."

"Better not," I said. "We don't want to spook him

while he's got Heather in his fist, do we? He might forget what he's holding and squeeze real hard."

"Yeah, you're right. Shit."

The paramedics showed up a few minutes later and wasted no time loading the three casualties onto the gurneys they'd wheeled in. If the ogre made a move on the ambulance crew, I'd have to shoot him and hope for the best. But he just watched them as they got the three limp forms ready for departure.

Without turning my head, I asked them, "Those guys still alive?"

"Yeah, for the time being," one of them said. "Looks like one's got a fractured skull. The other two don't seem too bad, though."

Then they wheeled the gurneys out of the bar. I hoped that a doctor or nurse with some magical ability was working at the ER tonight. Hospitals try to keep a medical magician on hand 24/7, but people with that particular skill set are hard to find – even in Scranton, which has an awful lot of supes for its size.

"Whadaya think, Stan?" Karl asked me. "Time to call SWAT?"

The Sacred Weapons and Tactics unit is trained to deal with supe hostage situations. It was tempting to let them take over, but I wasn't looking forward to sarcastic comments from their team leader, Dooley. He's something of a prick.

"Not yet," I told Karl. "Let me see what I can do, first."

It wasn't just my pride involved in the decision – there was a tactical consideration, too. Since ogre was backed into a corner, there was no way to take him by surprise. And once he saw the SWAT guys, in their distinctive black uniforms, the big guy might panic. And panic could be pretty hard on Heather the waitress.

I made eye contact with the ogre and spoke to him for the first time. "Hey, how ya doin?" I said. "I'm Stan, this here's Karl." I paused to give him a chance to process the information. Ogres aren't real quick, even when they *haven't* put away half a bottle of tequila. After a few seconds, I went on. "What's your name, pal?"

Another couple of seconds went by. "Igor," he rumbled.

I didn't let any of the humor I felt appear on my face — you learn quick, on the street, not to show what you're feeling. But *Igor*, jeez. Ogre parents aren't usually known for having a sense of humor – or maybe they just didn't see the irony.

"Igor, listen," I said slowly. "Why don't you let the girl go? She doesn't look like she's having a real good time, you know?"

Igor looked at Heather. Then he lifted her up, like she was a Barbie doll – a shrieking, terrified Barbie doll – until her hair was a couple inches from his nose and sniffed a couple of times before putting her back down, his big hand still around her waist. "She smells good," he said to me, as if that explained everything. Maybe to an ogre, it did.

Some supes have senses of smell that will put a bloodhound to shame, but not ogres. Otherwise he'd have been able to smell the fear on her, too. To the right kind of nose it was probably a stronger scent than whatever perfume she was wearing. Maybe then he'd have let her go.

"We can't all just stand here until tomorrow, Igor," I said in a reasonable tone. "We're all gonna get pretty hungry, for one thing."

I hoped the suggestion would encourage Igor to ask for food. We'd get it for him, too. That's standard procedure in hostage situations. I'd order him the biggest pizza in town, including every topping known to man – along with a liberal dose of horse tranquilizer. That's standard procedure, too. Once Igor was in dreamland, maybe we could get a block and tackle set up in here to lift him out of the room.

But instead of asking for something to eat, Igor said, "You gonna take me to jail?"

No sense lying to him about that. Even ogres aren't *that* dumb. "Yeah, for a while," I said. "Until you make bail, anyway."

Igor shook his immense head. "No! No jail. I *hate* jail." I guess he'd been inside before. "People there are *mean*."

The idea of anybody, guard or prisoner, being mean to something Igor's size was hard to imagine, but maybe he meant they taunted him through the bars of his cell. There's guys who get off on that, taunting the powerful when they're helpless. They forget that the helplessness is usually temporary, and even ogres have memories.

There's all kinds of cells in the supe wing of the county jail. Some of them have bars with bits of silver imbedded; others have got doors made of cold iron. They've got some ogre-proof cells, too. Those rooms have some kind of magical spell on them that prevents–

Magic. Ogres are afraid of magic. There's some kinds of magic that it's smart to be afraid of, but ogres are notoriously skittish about any kind of spells, and those who can use them. Meaning witches.

I brought out my phone, opened it, and acted like I was looking in the directory. "I guess you're leaving us no choice, Igor," I said. "We'll have to call in Rachel Proctor."

The immense eyebrows came together as Igor tried to parse what I'd just said. After a couple of seconds he asked, "Who's that?"

"She's the police department's consulting witch." That much was true, but nothing else I was about to say would be. "She doesn't care for guys who frighten girls like Heather," I said. "The last time I called her out to a scene like this, we had a werewolf who'd gone a little nuts and taken some hostages. Rachel turned the poor guy into a toad."

Igor looked at me for a couple of seconds. "She can do that, this Rachel?"

"Saw her do it with my own two eyes," I said. "And here's the funny thing – once we got the guy to jail and she was supposed to turn him back – it didn't work."

The ogre's eyes opened wide. "You shittin' me?"

"Nope, it's God's truth," I said. "Karl was there, too – he saw it."

On cue, Karl nodded several times. "Very sad," he said. "Guy had a family, too."

"Things didn't end up too bad," I said, lying the truth right out of town. "At least they found a home for him – in the Nay Aug Park Zoo. You go to the zoo much, Igor? You've probably seen him there. Excuse me."

For obvious reasons, I had Rachel Proctor on speed-dial. I pressed the tiny icon next to her name and brought the phone to my ear. After a couple of seconds, I said into it, "Rachel? Hi, it's Stan Markowski. How you doing?"

I paused to listen for a moment, then said, "Listen, Rachel, I've got a problem that might be right up your alley – or in your cauldron, as the case may be. See, there's this ogre–"

That's as far as I got before Igor the ogre bellowed, "Wait, wait! I give up! No witches – I surround!"

I was pretty sure he meant "surrender," although Igor was big enough to surround you all by himself, if he wanted to. Fortunately, I was right. He let Heather go, then put his hands up.

I said into the phone, "Never mind, Rachel. The problem seems to be solved," and heard Rachel's voice say "…be back until next Monday. So wait for the beep, then leave a message."

Fifteen minutes later, Igor was in the back of a police department prisoner van, his wrists bound by chains of cold iron, on his way to County. Heather the waitress was sitting in the back of an open ambulance, a blanket around her, drinking coffee from a thermos. I asked one of the uniforms to take her statement, once she was feeling more composed.

As Karl and I left the scene, a couple of uniforms were cordoning off the area with the yellow tape that reads *Police Line. Do Not Cross*.

Leary stomped over, not looking any happier for Igor's arrest and departure. "What are they *doing*?" he yelled, pointing at the two cops.

"Securing a crime scene until Forensics gets in there and does their work," I said. "If nothing else, they'll need to take a lot of photos. You might want to take some yourself, for the insurance people."

"But what about my fuckin' *bar*?"

I took a look through the open door of the tavern and the wreckage it contained.

"Don't sweat it, Leary," I said. "I don't think you were gonna do much more business tonight, anyway."

As we walked back to the car, Karl said, "Well, that ended with nobody gettin' hurt – apart from those dummies who tried to fight Igor."

"Yeah," I said. "Maybe our luck is changing."

After all these years on the job, I should know better than to tempt fate that way.

• • • •

Doc Watson had left a message that he'd see us at 4am, and it was twelve after the hour when Karl and I arrived at his reception room. The woman behind the desk looked to be in her mid-fifties. A lot of vamps have night jobs, but I was pretty sure this one was human, more or less.

"He's expecting us," I told her.

The look she gave me would've done credit to Sister Yolanda, who'd made my life hell in eighth grade. Despite all the weres, zombies, and vamps I've had to deal with since then, Sister Yolanda was the one I still had nightmares about.

"The doctor was expecting you *at 4 o'clock*," she said. I wondered if she had a big wooden ruler somewhere in her desk.

I was in no mood for this shit, and I guess Karl wasn't either. He put his hands on her desk and leaned forward. The smile he gave her displayed his fangs nicely. "I'll make you a deal," he said pleasantly. "You'll tell the doc that we're here, and I'll try to forget that I haven't fed tonight and I'm *real* thirsty. Sound like a plan?"

I heard the castors protest as she quickly pushed her chair back, her eyes huge.

"Y-yes, of course. I didn't mean to – excuse me, please."

Then she was heading for the oak door behind her at a pace that was not quite a run. She knocked twice and didn't wait for a reply from inside before entering Doc Watson's inner sanctum.

"Where were you when I was in eighth grade?"

I murmured to Karl. He looked at me, but before I could explain, the receptionist was back.

To me she said, "Doctor Watson will see you now." She didn't look at Karl at all.

Terence K Watson was a thin guy who wore his thick black hair brushed straight back. Combine that with the goatee and his fondness for black clothing and you've got a look that Rachel Proctor once described to me as Faustian. What she meant was the doc would have looked good as Mephistopheles in a staging of Marlowe's play. Faust himself was no fashion plate, by most accounts.

Rachel is one of the smartest people I know, but she's wrong on that one. I've seen the real Mephistopheles, and he looks like nothing human – unless he wants to. Besides, Doc Watson isn't into stealing souls. He's in the business of saving them, or trying to.

The doc and I go way back, and he's met Karl before, so no introductions were called for. But as we sat down, he looked at Karl and said, "I heard you'd been turned a while back, Karl, and now I see that the stories are true. If you don't mind my asking, how are you doing? It's quite an adjustment you've had to make."

Karl thought for a few seconds before answering. Maybe he was deciding how much to say. "It's an adjustment, like you said, Doc. But it's not too bad most days – most nights, I mean. And when it is, I just remind myself that being undead beats the alternative."

"Does it? You're sure?"

"Yeah, pretty sure."

Doc nodded. "Good."

"You must treat a few vampires yourself, Doc," I said. "Since you've started offering night appointments, and all."

He looked at me and his expression grew, if possible, more serious. "The confidentiality of my relationship with patients is absolute, Stan. It has to be – even to the point of declining to answer that question."

"I didn't mean anything by it, Doc. Just making conversation."

He let his long face relax in a sort of smile. "I know, Stan. But it's not the kind of small talk that I can join in."

"We're here to ask you about somebody who isn't one of your patients," Karl said. "At least, I hope he's not."

"Even if he is, Karl, you'll never know it." He spread his hands for a second and sat back. "Ask away. I'll tell you what I can."

Karl and I took turns telling him about the witch burnings. When we were finished, Doc was silent for several seconds.

"I suppose telling you that the person responsible for these crimes seems to hate witches would be an exercise in the obvious," he said.

"Yeah, kind of," I told him.

"Of course, that assumes the victims are chosen randomly, within the witch community," Doc said.

"There's always the possibility that his grudge was against these two women in particular."

"We've got people working that angle," Karl said. "They're looking for a common factor – clients, boyfriends, relatives, all that."

"If they find something, it'll make my life a lot easier," I said. "But since God seems to be part of an ongoing conspiracy to make my life difficult, let's assume for now that it's a serial killer who's obsessed with witches."

"All right, then." Doc was sitting in an expensive-looking leather swivel chair. He tilted it back as far as it would go and closed his eyes. He sat like that without speaking for fifteen seconds or so. "He's choosing witches because they symbolize some-thing for him – something that he wants to kill, or wishes he had, but can't. It's possible that an actual witch did him dirty sometime in the past, of course. However, when the victims are female, we tend to believe that they are serving as stand-ins for a woman in the killer's past, often the mother, or a mother-figure." Doc opened his eyes and shrugged. "Trite, but true."

"So, you figure the guy's mother was a witch?" Karl asked.

"Maybe," Doc said, "but it's rarely that simple. By the way, I've been using 'he' because it's easier, but I don't mean to prejudice your investigation by im-plying that the killer is necessarily male. However, the odds favor it, since the vast majority of serial killers who have been identified were male." Doc thought for a moment. "That doesn't apply to supernaturals, of course."

"How come?" Karl asked.

"Because the distinctions aren't as clear. For instance, do you consider a vampire who kills people a serial killer, or just hungry?"

"I know what I'd consider him," I said.

"No doubt," Doc said. "But then, you've got some issues of your own with vampires, don't–" He stopped himself, then looked at Karl. "Sorry," he said. "I meant no offense."

"None taken, Doc," Karl said. "When you're right, you're right – Stan *does* have issues with vampires. Although he hasn't put garlic in my locker for a couple of months now."

Doc stared at Karl for a couple of seconds, as if he wasn't sure whether he was being kidded. Karl was telling the truth – I do have problems with vamps, but maybe not as many as I used to.

Doc turned to me. "There's one other possibility that might apply to your killer's motivation," he said. "It could be political."

It took me a moment to realize what he was talking about. "You mean human supremacists," I said.

Doc nodded slowly. "Exactly. I know we have some locally. Every once in a while, the *Times-Tribune* publishes one of their hate letters. And I think I remember reading something about a demonstration once."

Karl looked at me. "Pettigrew's bunch," he said.

"Could be a conversation with the HSR is in order," I told him.

Doc Watson tilted his head a little. "HSR?"

"The Homo Sapiens Resistance," I said. "That's the name of the national organization – although from the members I've met, calling themselves *Homo sapiens* may be a bit of a stretch. Cro-Magnons, maybe."

"Was there any kind of signature left at the crime scenes?" Doc asked me. "Anything that might make a statement about who was responsible, or why?"

"Nothing," I said. "And we went over those crime scenes pretty damn thoroughly. So did Forensics."

"And I haven't seen any statements released to the media, either," Doc said.

"What's your point, Doc?" Karl asked.

"Terrorism – and that's what we're talking about here – is only effective if the people doing it let the world know *why* they did it. Lenin said, 'The purpose of terror is to terrify', and it's hard to terrify people if they don't know who you are."

"Could be that the local haters haven't read Lenin – or much of anything else," I said. "We'll have a word with them, anyway. Shake their tree a little, and see if anything falls off."

"Besides," Karl said, "it's fun."

We'd learned what we came for, and it was time for us to go. As I stood up, I said to Doc, "I guess you've come into some money recently."

He looked at me with narrowed eyes. "It's true – my dad died a couple of months ago and left me a good-sized share of his estate. How did you know, Stan?"

One of the guys at the station house had told me about Doc's good fortune, but I decided to play Sherlock Holmes.

"That painting on your wall over there is new, and it looks like an original oil, not a copy," I said. "I haven't seen that sports coat on you before, but it's made of pricey fabric and looks tailored. Instead of getting your hair cut, like usual, you've had it styled. I can only see the edge of the watch under the sleeve, but it looks like an Omega, and the cheapest one they make goes for about fifteen hundred bucks." I gave him a casual-looking shrug. "You're too smart to live beyond your means, so I figured you'd had a windfall of some kind."

"I thought cops only did stuff like that in the movies," Doc said. "That's fucking amazing, Stan."

Since I knew that Doc had inherited some big bucks, it wasn't hard to work backwards and look for signs of affluence. But I had no intention of telling him that.

I followed Karl to the door, then turned back. Looking at Doc with what I hoped was a straight face, I said, "It was quite elementary, my dear Watson."

Doc's building isn't in a high crime area, and I wasn't worried about the police-issue Buick we drove getting stolen or stripped. As we came outside and turned the corner, I saw that I'd been right – the car was still there, and wasn't missing anything. But something had been added, in the form of the ghoul who was leaning against the driver's door.

I can recognize a ghoul on sight. I don't even need to smell his breath, although you can usually do that from several feet away, and it isn't pleasant. Their diet has what you might call a distinctive odor. They're all short, too. Not dwarf short, but I've never seen a ghoul who topped five foot six, and this one was no exception. He had a goatee like Doc Watson's, but where Doc looked suave and a little sinister, this flesh-muncher came across like a beatnik that had wandered through a 1950s time warp. I half expected to hear him call me "Daddy-o."

Karl and I braced him from about six feet away, where his breath wasn't too bad. "You leaning on our ride because you got no place else to be?" I asked him. "Or do you want something?"

He took his time straightening up, as if it was his own idea and not a strong suggestion from a representative of law and order. He stared at Karl for a couple of seconds, then turned to me.

"You'd be Sergeant Markowski," he said.

"Tell me something I don't know," I said. "Like who you are, and what's on your mind."

"You may call me Nikolai, if you wish," the ghoul said. "As to my purpose, it is to tell you that an important man would like to see you."

"If the president sent you, tell him I'm busy," I said. "I didn't vote for him, anyway."

He gave me a tight little smile. "Not someone quite that important, perhaps. But he is – or rather he represents – a man of substance, who has an interest in your current case."

"We usually have several cases going at once," Karl told him. "Which one does your 'man of substance' have in mind?"

The ghoul looked at Karl again, his eyes narrowed. After a moment he said, "Interesting. I was not told that the police employed *nosferatu*."

"My name's not *nosferatu*, it's Renfer. Detective Renfer. And I asked you a *question*, punk."

Karl's a James Bond nut, but now it sounded like he'd been watching one of Clint Eastwood's old "Dirty Harry, Monster Slayer" movies.

He didn't seem to scare Nikolai. The ghoul looked Karl up and down before turning his gaze back to me. "I refer to the case of those... unsettling... DVDs, and the persons who are making them."

Calling those DVDs "unsettling" was like telling a Jew that the Holocaust had been an "inconvenience". I guess Nikolai hadn't been affected by those horror shows the way Karl and I had. Maybe he'd even enjoyed them.

"What do you know about those?" I asked him.

"I?" The ghoul touched fingertips to his chest in an exaggerated show of innocence. "I know very little. But the man who sent me knows rather more. That is why he wishes to speak to you... officers."

"And what's *his* name?" Karl asked. From the tone of his voice, he was getting ready to go all Dirty Harry on this little prick – for real. I was tempted to let him.

"I'm sure he would rather tell you that himself, in person," the ghoul said. "I have a car parked down the block. If you would accompany me...?" He reached one hand into his pants pocket, but before he could withdraw it, the barrel of my Beretta was pressing against his forehead. "Don't," I said.

The ghoul became as still as if he'd just been exposed to a Gorgon statue. My weapon was loaded with a mix of silver and cold iron, either of which would decorate the roof of the car with Nikolai's brains. Ghouls live a long time, but they're not immortal – and they sure as shit aren't invulnerable.

"Two things," I said. "One: we're not going anywhere with you. Tell us where your mysterious employer is, and we'll consider paying a call on him sometime. Two: unless you're just real glad to see us, I'm pretty sure that pocket you're reaching into contains a good-sized knife, probably a switchblade, which is illegal in this state. If your hand comes out holding anything but car keys, I'll give you a third eye – right between the two you have now. Understand me?"

The little bastard's eyes were wide now, and instead of another smart-ass remark, he just said, "Uh-huh."

"Not to worry, though," Karl said, and I could hear the nasty smile in his voice. "If things don't work out for you, there's a real nice funeral home here in town, run by a guy named Barney Ghougle. That's not his real name, but it's what we all call him. Maybe he's a relative of yours? I bet he'd find you real tasty."

Although ghouls eat human flesh, they are terrified by the idea that someone might do the same to them after death. That's why every ghoul I've ever known has standing instructions for cremation when they die. Go figure.

Even in the feeble light from a nearby street lamp, I could see that the ghoul was sweating now. He said, "I – I meant no offense, I assure you."

"Of course you didn't," I said, without moving the gun a millimeter. "Now – where does your boss hang out?"

"Radisson hotel, room 431." It was like he couldn't get the words out fast enough.

"And his name?" I pressed the muzzle against his skull a little harder.

"Milo. His name is Milo."

"Milo *what*?"

"We just c-call him Mister Milo. Dunno his first name."

I took the gun away from his forehead and stepped back. "Tell Mister Milo that we'll be around to see him sometime, and if he gives us any shit I'll make him regret it. Follow me?"

A slight nod, as if he was still afraid to move his head. "Yessir."

"Now blow."

He blew.

I made no move to get into the car. Instead, I stood

watching the ghoul as he rapidly walked down the street.

After a couple of seconds, Karl looked at me. "What?"

"I want to see what he's driving," I said. "Here's hoping he didn't park around the corner."

I needn't have worried. About half a block away now, Nikolai was unlocking a car parked at the curb. As he pulled away, I got a better look at his ride: a big sedan that looked like an Oldsmobile, probably rented.

"Can you get his license number?" I asked Karl. Not only do vampires see in the dark, but their distance vision is a lot better than a human's.

Karl got up on his toes for a better look. "Pennsylvania plates PLV 198," he said.

"Good, thanks." I reached for my car keys. "Get in."

Inside the car, Karl looked at me again. "You've got something cookin', don't you?"

"Despite what I told Nikolai, you *know* there's no way we're waiting a couple of days to follow up on a possible lead. Not for this case."

"Yeah, that's what I figured."

"And I wanna brace this Mister Milo when he's not expecting us, try to catch him off balance. I want every edge we can get."

"But he'll know we're coming sometime," Karl said. "You already told his pet ghoul."

"Yeah, but he doesn't know it *yet*."

I reached for the police radio.

"Dispatch, this is Markowski."

"Read you loud and clear, Sergeant," the female voice said crisply.

"Is there a patrol unit anywhere near the 700 block of Taylor Avenue?"

"Wait one."

She was back within ten seconds. "Roger that, Sergeant. A black-and-white is three blocks away, on Prescott. Do you want them directed to your location?"

"Negative, but patch me through to their unit, will you?"

"Roger. Wait one."

It wasn't long before I was listening to a male voice saying, "This is Four Baker Nine. Over."

"Is that you, Bradshaw? It's Markowski."

"Yeah, it's me, Stan. What do you got?"

"A dark green Olds heading north on Taylor from downtown, Pennsylvania license PLV 198. You have reason to believe that the driver is wanted for questioning."

"Is he? Wanted for questioning, I mean."

"Better you should be able to say you never knew the answer to that," I said. "But if you frisk the driver, who's a ghoul calls himself Nikolai, you'll probably find an illegal weapon, which will allow you to bring him in."

"What kind of weapon? Is he packing?"

"Just a switchblade, far as I know."

"OK, Stan. But you owe Meyer and me a cold beer."

"I'll buy you two apiece," I said. "Thanks."

As I put the radio back in its bracket, Karl said,

"So, Nikolai isn't going to be reporting to his boss anytime soon."

"That's the idea." I started the engine.

"He might've done it already, by phone."

"Could be." I was watching the traffic, waiting for a gap to pull into. "But if this Mister Milo is a big enough player to have a ghoul as an errand boy, he might be too paranoid to talk business on the phone. A lot of them are, you know."

Karl fastened his seat belt. "So, I guess I don't need to ask where we're heading now."

"Not unless you've started eating Stupid Flakes for breakfast."

"I don't eat breakfast anymore, Stan. Strictly speaking."

"Just an expression." I pulled away from the curb, made an illegal U-turn, and headed for the Radisson hotel.

The Radisson is in what used to be the old Lackawanna train station. They've kept the basic architecture of the building, but spent a lot of money on the interior to make it the best hotel in town. All modern conveniences at the Radisson.

The fifth floor is known as "Floor V" – which means it's specially designed to accommodate guests of the undead persuasion. Each of the rooms has two layers of blackout curtains, and when you click on Do Not Disturb from inside, it triple-locks the door. Room service has a special "Midnight Menu" that's heavy on Type A and Type O, either whole blood or plasma. If you prefer your nourishment directly from the source, the hotel has certain employees who will pay a discreet visit to your room, and depart a pint or two lighter – in return for a *very* good tip. It's interesting that selling your body's still illegal, but taking money for your blood isn't.

Mister Milo was on Four, which meant that whatever else he was, he wasn't a vamp.

I gave the door to 431 the three hard raps that most cops use, although I don't know why. I guess it's supposed to send a message to those inside that somebody in the hall wants your attention, and wants it *now*.

The door opened a little. It was on its chain and through the six-inch gap I could see what I was pretty sure was another ghoul looking out at me. I had my ID folder ready, and I made sure the guy inside got a good look at my badge. "We're here to see Mister Milo," I said. "Open up."

"Well, I'll have to see–" the ghoul began.

"No," I said. "What you have to *do* is close that door just long enough to drop the chain, then open it again. Because if that door isn't open three seconds from now, I'll kick it down on top of you. *Do it.*"

The door was new-looking and solid, and I probably couldn't have kicked it down on the best day I've ever had. But I bet Karl could've, even if he wouldn't be able to go inside afterward, without an invitation.

The ghoul looked at me for a second, his eyes widening. I heard a voice from somewhere behind him say, calmly, "Do as the man says."

The door closed hastily. A moment later, I heard the sound of the security chain being disengaged, then the ghoul opened up, all the way this time. I walked right at him, figuring he wouldn't want to play linebacker with me. He scrambled aside and I said over my shoulder to Karl, "Come on in."

We were in the living room of what was obviously a suite. It contained a coffee table, big-screen TV, a desk, some overstuffed chairs and a sofa where a man had just been seated. As he stood up, I saw that Mister Milo was human, or appeared to be.

He was below average height, which still made him taller than his ghoul gofer. He had slicked-down brown hair, a thin mustache, and a suit that probably didn't cost much more than my car when it was new.

He walked toward us, a pleasant expression on his face, and extended a hand. I'm not usually inclined to shake with lowlifes, but this time I thought I might learn a couple of things so I went along.

As he grasped my hand I said, "Sergeant Markowski, Scranton PD." When he let go and turned to Karl I said, "And this is Detective Karl Renfer."

The handshake backed up my conclusion that Mister Milo was human. His skin was too warm to be a vampire, and he lacked the small patch of hair on his palm that is characteristic of weres. Of course, that didn't rule out the possibility that he was a practitioner of some kind.

He let go of Karl's hand, stepped back, and said,

"The fact that you're here means that you already know who I am."

"I was told the name was Milo," I said. "But I don't know if that's first or last."

He gave me a tight smile. "It's both, actually."

"Your name's Milo Milo?" I didn't let the humor I was feeling touch my face or voice, I hope.

"That's correct. My parents had an unfortunate affection for the novel *Catch-22* by Joseph Heller. They thought it would be… amusing to name me as they did."

"No offense," Karl said, "but I'd want to have a long talk with my parents about that when I grew up."

"Oh, I agree with the impulse, Detective, but I never got the chance," Milo said. "When I was fifteen, our house caught fire in the middle of the night. Both Mommy and Daddy were burned to death. It was very sad." He might have been discussing something that happened to people he'd read about in a book on ancient history.

He made a gesture toward the armchairs. "Shall we sit down, gentlemen?"

When we were all seated, I looked toward the ghoul, who was still standing near the door. He was pissed off and trying not to show it.

"Do you want to talk private business with him here?"

"I trust all of my associates implicitly," Milo said; then, with barely a pause, told the ghoul, "You can go for a walk, Winthrop – but don't go too far. I'll call you when I need you."

The ghoul left without a word, but he still didn't look happy. "You ever wonder why all ghouls have such fancy-ass names?" I asked Milo.

"No, I haven't actually," he said. "But, tell me – what would your reaction be if you met one who called himself Rex, or maybe Spike?"

"I'd probably laugh out loud," I said.

"That may be the reason, then." Milo, who was back on the sofa, leaned forward. "Let me get to the reason I wished to have a conversation with you officers, which is the same reason that brought me to your... charming little town."

Snotty little prick. "Brought you here from where?" I asked him.

"I live in Los Angeles," he said, as if it meant something. Maybe to him it did.

"What was it you wanted to talk about?" Karl asked him.

"These DVDs that have been circulating that show a demonically possessed man torturing and murdering another man."

"What's that got to do with you?" I asked. "I don't suppose you're here to confess that you're responsible."

Mister Milo gave me a tight little smile. "No, not hardly." The smile disappeared as if it had never been there at all. "I represent certain interests in the Los Angeles area who are very concerned about these videos. It is feared that eventually knowledge of them will become public, causing an outcry against an industry that is utterly innocent of any wrongdoing."

It took me a moment to figure out what he was saying. "You represent the porn business."

"We prefer to call it the adult entertainment industry," he said.

"You can call it the fucking Girl Scouts, for all I care," I said. "I still don't think the term 'utterly innocent' is a good description of your business."

"I meant innocent of involvement in these so-called 'snuff films'," Milo said. "Feel free to moralize to your heart's content, Sergeant. But the same laws that guarantee your right to wax indignant about adult entertainment also give your fellow citizens the right to choose it as their own private form of amusement – and they do, in very large numbers."

Getting this scumbag to admit that he was a scumbag was a waste of time, and we had bigger fish to fry.

"So, if your 'industry' has nothing to do with these snuff videos, what are you doing in Scranton – protesting your innocence? You could've just sent an email. Quicker and cheaper."

The smile made another brief appearance. "But then I would have been denied the pleasure of making your acquaintance, Sergeant," he said, and I wondered if I could just shoot him and get away with it. Maybe if I called it "pest extermination".

"I'm here to act as a go-between, Milo said. "A liaison, if you will, between the local authorities and my employers."

Karl snorted. "And what fucking good do you figure that's gonna do?"

Milo spread his hands and shrugged at the same time. I wondered if he practiced it in front of a mirror. "I hope to serve as a conduit for information, Detective. I could pass on to you anything relevant that might be discovered back on the West Coast, and I hope you officers would reciprocate by sharing with me developments in the case as they arise."

I was about to get all hard-ass and tell this creep that the police didn't share confidential information with scumbag civilians, when my brain finally got out of first gear. So I asked him, just to see what he'd say, "And suppose we did share information about the case with you, what purpose would it serve? What would you use it for?"

Another elegant shrug. "Well, that's impossible to say at this point, of course. But I find that all information proves useful, sooner or later – don't you?"

He was good, I'll give him that. I figured that Milo had been lying from the cradle and only got better at it with each passing year. The fact that some porno king had sent him out here was probably a testament to his skill as a bullshit artist. He was lying like the pro he was, and I knew it.

He was looking at Karl when he finished speaking, but for what I was about to do, I wanted him looking at me. "Milo," I said quietly.

When he turned his innocent-looking gaze my way, I leaned forward in my chair, to bring my face as close as possible to his. Looking closely at his eyes, I said, "You hired Sharkey, didn't you?"

He didn't blink or turn a hair. But the pupils of

those brown eyes instantly dilated, and that was all I needed to see.

I once spent some time reading a book called *Deception Detection*. About ninety percent of it was stuff any experienced cop knows, but the chapter on pupil dilation movement caught my interest. Pupil dilation movement (or PDM) was what the author, some PhD from Berkeley, called an "autonomic response". That means it operates outside the conscious control of the will. It's like blushing when you're embarrassed, or breaking out in a sweat when you're nervous about something.

Not everybody blushes from shame, or sweats due to tension, but every human's pupils dilate or contract in response to sudden, strong emotion. Every damn one. That's what the guy said in his book, anyway – and he's a PhD, so I figure he knows his shit.

As soon as I said "Sharkey", Milo's pupils had gone from the size of a dried pea to something more like a dime.

From the corner of my eye I could see that Karl had turned his head to stare at me, but I kept looking at Mister Milo. His raised eyebrows were a study in mild surprise, and the smile made a guest appearance on his lips before he spoke.

"Sharkey?" he said. "Don't believe I recognize the name. It sounds like the title of yet another rip-off of *Jaws*."

I shook my head. "Nice try, Milo. You're a credit to whatever law school taught you how to lie, cheat, and steal. You *are* a lawyer, aren't you?"

He sounded irritated for the first time since we'd arrived. "Yes, I'm a member of the bar. So what?"

"So nothing," I said. "Just confirming a suspicion. But what I said about Sharkey – that wasn't a suspicion. That's a fact, you stupid son of a bitch."

No smiles this time. His lips were a pencil-thin line. "I repeat, I have no idea what – or whom – you're talking about. But, just for the sake of discussion, if I had hired this Sharkey, why would doing so make me, in your words, 'a stupid son of a bitch'?"

"Because Sharkey's what the Grim Reaper would look like if he had a better tailor and traded in the scythe for an Uzi. He's fucking Death incarnate."

"I would hardly have expected such poetic language from… a representative of law and order, Sergeant."

Milo walked over to the desk, where some bottles, ice, and glasses had been laid out. As he poured Scotch into a glass, I said, "If you think that was poetic, then you need to start reading a better class of poet."

"Um, perhaps." Milo took a sip of his drink, then said, "Pardon my manners. May I offer you gentlemen a drink?"

I shook my head again. "We're on duty."

Then Karl chimed in. "Stan's right," he said. "Besides, I never drink… Scotch."

I bet he'd been waiting to use that Bela Lugosi line ever since he was turned.

"You pay Sharkey for a body, you get a body," I

said. "Trouble is, you sometimes get a bunch of other bodies that you *didn't* pay for."

"I heard a story about him not long after I started on the force," Karl said. "Sharkey was sent after some mid-level mobster named Wiley, and Wiley heard about it before Sharkey could find him. So he decided to hole up in his condo until Sharkey gave up and went away."

"What he didn't understand," I said, "is that Sharkey *never* gives up."

"Fuckin' A," Karl said. "So Wiley stocks up on food, keeps the drapes closed, and never answers the door for *anybody*. He stayed in there over a month, I hear."

When neither of us said anything for a few seconds, Milo gave a loud sigh. "I suppose I'll have to feed you the next line, if only to move things along. So – then what happened?"

"Sharkey blew the building up," Karl said. "He likes explosives – the guy he was after should have known that."

"Didn't even have to buy any TNT," I said. "He got into the basement and dug up the gas line that ran underneath the building. Then he figured out a way to make it blow. The whole thing looked like an accident, if you didn't know better."

"Sharkey got his man," Karl said. "Along with a bunch of other men, not to mention over a dozen women and children who were in the building when it blew. Now, this next part I'm not sure about, some say it's made up. But supposedly the mob boss who'd hired Sharkey got all kinds of upset over all the innocent people who'd been killed in the explosion. When he said something about it, Sharkey's response supposedly was, 'What's the problem? I didn't charge you for any of them'."

Milo finished his drink and put the glass down. "This is all fascinating – or, rather, it would be if I had actually hired this Sharkey person, which I didn't."

He sounded so convincing. If I hadn't seen his eyeballs do the hokey-pokey earlier, I might even have believed him.

"The adult entertainment industry isn't run by mobsters, gentlemen," he said. "That might not have been the case more than thirty years ago, but in *Miller v. California* the Supreme Court essentially decided that our product is legal. Disreputable in the eyes of some, perhaps, but entirely legal."

"What about all the human trafficking that goes on?" Karl said.

"It's regrettable, to be sure," Milo said, although he didn't seem especially sad about it. "But it has nothing to do with the people I represent."

He turned to me. "Do you actually believe, Sergeant, that the adult video studios in California have to kidnap young women off the streets of Budapest or Juarez, to force them to appear in, say, *Debbie Does Dallas 19*? Hundreds of girls seek work at the adult modeling agencies every month, and many are turned away for being insufficiently attractive. There is no need to kidnap anyone, even if we were so inclined."

"But human trafficking does go on," I said.

"Of course it does," Milo said. "And its victims either end up in forced prostitution or, if they are young enough, in child pornography. Neither of which has anything to do with my principals. Adult entertainment is a legal business, run by legitimate businessmen."

"And those legitimate businessmen are getting worried," I said.

"With good reason," Milo said. "There's no shortage of right-wing politicians eager to exploit something like this 'snuff film' phenomenon for their own benefit, to tar the whole industry with the same brush, as it were. And if these videos continue to be made, it's only a matter of time before they become public knowledge."

"And so they sent you," I said.

"They sent me to act in a legal capacity and protect their interests. My principals certainly would not countenance my hiring some... dhampir assassin to murder those responsible, tempting though the idea is."

I stood up, and Karl did the same. "Well, thanks for seeing us, Mister Milo. Since you're planning to stay in Scranton awhile, I'm sure we'll talk again."

"I look forward to it," Milo said, sounding almost as if he meant it.

We had the elevator to ourselves for the ride down. "What do you think?" Karl asked softly.

"I think a couple of things," I said. "One is, his eyeballs jumped when I said Sharkey's name."

"That PDM stuff you were telling me about."

"Uh-huh. Sudden changes in emotion produce immediate pupil dilation. And here's the other thing I think."

We reached the lobby and the doors slid open. Before leaving the elevator, I said, "I never said anything to Milo about Sharkey being a dhampir."

When we reached the street, I saw a young guy in a scraggly beard was standing on the corner trying to hand out leaflets. Even in Supe City (which some people call Scranton) there isn't a lot of pedestrian traffic at almost five in the morning, so the guy was either an optimist or a lamebrain – or whoever sent him was.

As we got closer, he held a leaflet out toward us. It was in color, printed on slick paper. Better than the usual stuff these street guys hand out, which tends to look more like crayon on a paper bag than an IPO for a software company. "Learn the truth about the Catholic Church, fellas. The time is nigh." He didn't seem very enthusiastic about it all. How can you respect a weirdo who doesn't even believe his own rhetoric?

I took one, more out of pity than anything else. We still had half a block to go, so I handed it to Karl. "You can see better in this light than I can," I said. "What *truth* about the Catholic Church are they peddling now?"

He gave it a quick flip through as we walked. "Looks like the Church of the True Cross is at it again."

"Figured it was them – or somebody like them."

"Let's see," Karl said. "The Mass in English is a sacrilege, supes are the devil's children, all nuns are lesbians, and…" He glanced at the back cover. "… the pope is the Antichrist."

"In other words, business as usual."

"Seems like." He dropped the leaflet in the next trash can we passed. I was glad he did that – I hate littering.

"I dunno about that lesbian thing," Karl said. "I mean, aren't nuns supposed to be the brides of Christ, or something?"

"That's what they say." I shrugged. "Maybe He likes to watch."

On the way home, I stopped at Sup'r-Natural Foods to pick up some plasma for Christine. You can buy whole blood lots of places, but plasma is considered a specialty item. It's expensive, and only a few stores carry it. For vamps, plasma is to whole blood what prime rib is to hamburger. Christine won't buy the stuff for herself because of the price, but every once in a while I'll bring some home for her as a treat – even if it means going into Sup'r-Natural Foods to get it.

Anyway, I figure if she has plenty of commercial product available in the refrigerator, she won't feel the need to tap the source, if you know what I mean. She wouldn't go around attacking people, like some vamps do – I ought to know, since I've busted a lot of them over the years. But the idea of

Christine picking up some guy, or letting him pick her up, just so she can get her fangs into his neck – that makes make my skin crawl. I can't explain it; maybe it's a parent thing.

So I stop at Sup'r-Natural Foods (Open 24 Hrs!) every once in a while, but that doesn't mean I enjoy the experience. You can imagine the kinds of customers the place attracts, especially during the hours of darkness. Vamps, of course. Sup'r-Natural has the best selection of the red stuff in town – both whole blood and plasma.

You'll find some weres in there, too. Usually they're looking to pick up a double rack of goat, which is hard to find elsewhere. I don't know what it is with weres and goat meat – must be an old-country thing. I've seen trolls in the place a few times, too, buying monkey steaks. I once heard a troll tell another one, "It tastes just like children!" And you don't want to know what's for sale in the Ghoul Specialty Section.

I picked up a one-pound bag of Type A frozen plasma and turned to head for the checkout. A second later I wondered if I'd managed to walk into a wall, because something big was in my way that hadn't been there a minute before. I took a step back and saw it was an ogre, like the one Karl and I had busted earlier in the evening. In fact, I thought I saw a family resemblance. He looked down at me and rumbled, "You're Markowski, right?"

I took a couple more of steps back – not out of fear, but to give myself room to maneuver. I switched the plasma package to my left hand, and let my right hand hang down by my side. To get at my weapon, all I'd have to do is sweep the sports coat back and draw. Like I said before, ogres aren't generally violent – but that doesn't mean that some don't believe in payback.

I tilted my head back so I could see his face clearly. "Yeah, I'm Markowski. Who're you?"

"I'm Ivan." If he was known among his friends as Ivan the Terrible, it wouldn't have surprised me any. I lowered my gaze a little, so I could take in more of him.

Watch his body, they'd taught us in training. The other guy can fake with his head or his hands, but not with his trunk. Watch the body.

I waited for the ogre to say something more, but he just stood looking at me, his expression unreadable. After a couple of seconds I said, "Something on your mind, Ivan? I'm kind of in a hurry."

"I'm the brother of Igor."

Fuck. Looks like I was right about payback. I let my right hand drift under my jacket and push the material back a little.

"You arrested Igor tonight, yeah?" the ogre went on.

"That's right, I did. He'd busted up a bar, hurt a couple of humans, and grabbed a woman as hostage. I didn't have much choice."

"I know," the ogre said quietly – for an ogre. "I wanna thank you."

OK, that *wasn't* what I'd been expecting.

"Thank me? For what – doing my job?"

"Yeah, kinda. Igor drinks too much – we knew he would get in bad trouble, sooner or later. Maybe jail will teach him something, yeah?"

"Could be," I said. "It works that way, sometimes."

"And you coulda killed him, is what I hear. He gave you the excuse. But you didn't."

"There was no need to," I said. "So I didn't."

"That's why I say thank you," Ivan said. "And I owe you. If you ever need something that an ogre can do, you let me know, yeah?" He gave me a piece of paper with a phone number scrawled on it.

"I'll keep it in mind, thanks," I said. I held up the package I was holding. "I gotta get going, before this stuff thaws."

"OK, see ya around, Markowski."

When I entered the kitchen, Christine was staring intently at the screen of her laptop, which was facing away from me. Vamps have pretty acute hearing, so she must have been really focused on what she was looking at for me to surprise her when I walked in.

The movement at the edge of her vision must have caught her attention, because she looked up with a start. "Oh, hi, Daddy."

"Hi, baby. What're you doing?"

She was logging off even as I spoke to her. "Oh, just the Help Wanted section of last Sunday's paper."

"How come? You're not having trouble at work, are you?"

"No, work is cool. But I don't want to be an emergency services dispatcher the rest of my life – which is likely to be rather lengthy."

I've been a cop long enough to keep what I'm thinking off my face, if I want to. I maintained the pleasant expression I'd worn coming in, but it wasn't easy. Vampire or not, I know when my daughter is lying to me.

I held up the bag from Sup'r-Natural Foods. "Got you something." I brought out the frozen package of plasma and said, "Type A – your favorite."

She clapped her hands together a couple of times. "Oh, Daddy, how sweet. Thank you!" She rose, came around the table, and gave me a hug. As she stepped back, I said, "Do you want some now?" Warming it up in the microwave wouldn't take long.

"I better not," she said. "Gotta go beddy-bye in less than fifteen minutes. I'll save it for breakfast."

"Sure," I said, and put the package in the freezer.

"Oh, I found out about Victor Castle for you."

"Who? Oh, the Supefather, right."

"You probably ought not to call him that when you meet him, which you can do at 'Magic Carpets, Mystic Rugs', on Susquehanna Avenue."

I smiled at that, a little. "The *capo di tutti supe* is a rug merchant?"

"He has a bunch of business interests, or so I hear, but that's the one he uses as headquarters."

"OK, I'll be paying him a visit. Thanks."

"No prob." She grew a smile of her own. "*Capo di tutti supe*," she said, and shook her head. "You've been watching *The Sopranos* again, haven't you?"

"I sneak one every once in a while." I didn't mention that one of the reasons I liked the HBO series was that all the bad guys were human, and whenever somebody shot one of them, they stayed dead. No wonder it was considered fiction.

Not long afterward, Christine was on her way downstairs for her day's rest. She left the laptop on the kitchen table.

I waited a couple of minutes to be sure she wasn't going to come back for something. When I saw the first rays of sunlight creep in through the kitchen window, I went over and sat down where Christine had been when I'd come home. I opened the laptop and the screen came alive immediately, asking me for a user name and password.

Her email account was christinevamp@aol.com, and I was pretty sure the first part of that was her user ID. She'd never told me her password, but I understand my daughter better than she realizes. I typed in *ritaelainemarkowski*, clicked, and watched the screen welcome me back to the world of cyberspace.

The password was her mother's name. Like I said, I know my daughter.

She'd logged off from whatever page she'd been viewing, but I went to the bar that ran across the top of the screen and clicked on the drop-down menu. The most recent site visited was something called "Drac's List." It was a name I'd heard before. I double-clicked on it.

A second later, I was looking at

DRAC'S LIST
For Vampires & those who love them

It's my job to know what's going on in the supe community, and I was aware of a couple of websites, like Witch.com, that are devoted to bring together supernatural creatures for whatever it is that they want to do together. But this place, I knew, was different.

"Looking for a bite?" it said. "Drac's List is the place to go for vampires looking for a willing... partner, as well as humans who just can't wait to know what the undead's 'touch' feels like."

This was a business that brought together vampires and those who wanted to be bitten by one. And Christine had been looking at it, then tried to conceal that fact from me. I didn't go any deeper into the site. If she had a profile in there, I didn't think I could stand to read it.

I shut the computer down and lowered the lid. The "click" as it closed seemed unnaturally loud in the quiet kitchen. I sat looking at the vampire rights sticker that Christine had put on the lid. It had a drawing of a wooden stake, and superimposed on it was a red circle with a diagonal line through it – the kind of thing they use in airports over a picture of a cigarette to mean No Smoking. Inside the circle were the words: "Van Helsing bites it."

I don't know how long I sat there, but eventually I got up and went to bed. There have been days when I've slept better. Quite a few of them, in fact.

I left for work without waiting for sundown. It didn't matter if McGuire wasn't paying overtime – I wouldn't put the extra couple of hours on my time sheet. I didn't know yet what I was going to say to Christine about Drac's List, and I didn't want to sit around the house with her and pretend nothing was wrong. She knows her old man pretty well, too.

I decided to pay a call on Harmon Pettigrew, head of the local chapter of the Homo Sapiens Resistance. It started out as an anti-vamp organization back in the Fifties, when it was known as the Johannes Birth Society. The name was a reference to a guy who was supposedly the first human vamp victim in the USA, but that story's a myth. In the late Sixties, the Birthers changed the name and broadened their focus to include all supernatural creatures. These fuckers hate everybody – except humans, that is. And they don't always respect the law.

I thought a conversation with Pettigrew might go easier if Karl wasn't with me. Those HSR jerks don't like cops much – they regard us as human race traitors, or something. You can imagine what their attitude is toward a vampire cop.

Having Karl with me when I talked to Pettigrew would be fun, in some ways. Pettigrew would hate having Karl there, but the badge meant he'd have to be civil – just like in that old movie *In the Bright of the Day*, about a vampire cop from Philly stranded in the Bible belt. Rod Steiger was great in that, but Jonathan Frid should've won the Oscar.

But that conversation with Pettigrew, fun though it might be for me and Karl, probably wouldn't produce any worthwhile information. Talking to the guy alone increased the odds that I might actually learn something useful.

Pettigrew runs a motorcycle repair shop called Born to Be Wilding at the edge of town. A lot of HSR types hang out there, which isn't too surprising. Don't get me wrong – not all bikers are human racist assholes. But a lot of the local racist assholes do seem to be bikers.

As I walked into the main repair bay I saw Pettigrew kneeling on the cracked cement floor with the engine from a beat-up Harley spread out on the floor all around him. He was alone, which was my good luck. I don't think any of these HSR clowns would ever make a move on me, but Pettigrew's an even bigger asshole when his posse's around – it's like he has to show the others what a tough guy he is.

He heard my footsteps and pivoted his head toward me at once, like an animal does when it hears a twig snap in the forest. Seeing who I was, he got slowly to his feet, the tool he'd been holding still in his right hand. I walked a few yards closer, then stopped, my eyes pointedly on what he was holding, which looked like a Number Seven flare nut wrench. After a second, Pettigrew got the idea and tossed the wrench on the floor, as if that was what he'd intended to do all along.

"Sergeant Markowski – to what do I owe the pleasure, if that's what it is?"

Unlike the rest of him, Pettigrew's voice was restrained and fairly cultured – at least when his homies weren't around. Not many people knew that he has a degree in economics from Penn State – or he would have, if they hadn't kicked him out three weeks before graduation for starting a species riot.

Physically, he was what you'd expect: weightlifter's build, shaved head, the grease-stained sleeveless sweatshirt displaying the tats that ran the length of both muscular arms.

"You mean, apart from the delight I always experience in your company?" I can talk fancy, too, if I want.

Pettigrew's mean-looking mouth turned up briefly at the corners. "Yeah, besides that."

"I wanted to ask you about a couple of things. You hear about stuff that I wouldn't, since there's people who'll talk to you that won't talk to me."

"Hard to imagine, isn't it?" Then the playful note left his voice. "Why should I do anything for the porkers? All you bastards do is help the supie-loving government oppress real warm Americans."

"I don't suppose saying 'the goodness of your heart' is enough of a reason," I said.

"Not fuckin' hardly."

I gave him a shrug. "So, what do you want?"

Pettigrew walked slowly over to a nearby workbench, picked up a rag, and started carefully wiping his hands. From the looks of the rag, I didn't think he was gaining much ground in the cleanliness department.

Without looking up from what he was doing he said, "Jackie Marcus."

It took me a moment to place the name. Then I remembered that John Robert Marcus had been busted a month ago on six charges of child molestation involving a couple of kids who lived in the same trailer park he did. The girl was seven, I think. The boy was five. I knew Marcus's name because he had been a longtime member of HSR, even editing their so-called newspaper for a couple of years.

"You want him sprung?" I asked Pettigrew. "You can't seriously expect me to say yes to that."

"I don't." He finally looked up, his expression grimmer than usual. "He's in County, awaiting trial. They've got him in the protection wing, along with the snitches, welchers, and faggots. I want you to get him released into population."

"You want him in the yard, with the rest of the inmates? What the hell for?"

"So a couple of our guys who are already inside can get to him. Fucker betrayed the movement, made us all look bad with his little *hobby*."

The last word had some snap to it, and I remembered that Pettigrew had kids of his own. Going against type, he was said to be a pretty good husband and father.

"You want your people to shank him," I said.

"Shank?" He gave me a crooked grin. "Don't believe I'm familiar with that word, Officer."

Now that I had Marcus's name rattling around in my memory bank, something else popped up.

"The DA's trying to make him a deal, isn't she? A lighter sentence in return for everything he knows about the HSR and all of *your* little hobbies. He hasn't made up his mind yet, has he?"

The grin was gone now. "All the reasons don't matter. What's important is that the son of a bitch has got to go down before his case goes to trial."

"And if I promise to talk to the warden over at County and see if I can get Marcus sent out in the yard to play, you'll answer some questions for me?"

"Yeah, something like that."

I shook my head slowly. "No can do, *hombre* – even if I was so inclined, and I might just be. The warden at County's new, only been on the job about four months. I've never met him, and he sure as hell doesn't owe me any favors."

"Maybe he owes a favor to one of your buddies. One hand washes the other, or so I hear."

"It's not real likely. Like I said, the guy's only been in place four months – not long enough to run up too many IOUs." I paused to let that sink in. "That mean we can't do business?"

Pettigrew looked at me. "You could've just said, 'Sure, I'll take care of it', knowing all the while that you couldn't."

"Yeah, I guess. But I don't work that way."

"So I hear," Pettigrew said. "So I hear."

He dropped the rag in a trash can and leaned his butt against the workbench, his still-dirty hands gripping the edge for support. "Ask your questions," he said. "I'll either answer, or I won't. But I won't lie to you – I don't do that."

"So I hear," I said. "All right, then. There's some

people with a Scranton connection making and selling snuff films."

"I thought all that stuff was some bullshit urban legend," Pettigrew said.

"This stuff isn't," I told him. "I've seen one, and it's the real deal. There's four different ones that we know about, and they all follow the same pattern. Two guys are chained up inside a pentagram. A demon is summoned, and it possesses one of the guys. Then he's set free, and the demon makes him torture and kill the other guy. It's the nastiest shit I've ever seen – and I've seen a lot."

"Jesus," Pettigrew said. "That is *beyond* sick."

"No argument from me," I said.

"Demons, huh? Well, that's supies for you – fuckin' perverts, every damn one."

"Let's not generalize," I said. "So I take it all of this is news to you?"

"Yeah, it's the first I've heard of it," he said, and I believed him.

"If you come across anything that smells like this, I'd appreciate a call."

He shrugged those big shoulders, not committing himself. "What else you got?"

"Somebody's been burning witches," I said. "Two, so far. We don't know why, and we sure as hell don't know who."

"Yeah, I saw something on the news about one of them," he said.

"Is that all you know about it – what was on TV?"

Pettigrew was silent, looking at the floor in front

of him, as if he'd found a crack that made an interesting pattern in the concrete. "I hear things, all kinds of shit," he said finally. "It's hard to know how much of it's true, and what's connected to what, you know?"

"Yeah," I said. "So?"

"I get a feeling it's not going to stop with the witches," he said. "Pretty soon, other supies are going to turn up as members of the true dead, and you know what I call that?"

"What?"

"A good start." He frowned at the floor. "But this is some crazy shit, if the whisper stream has it right. These motherfuckers are looking to start the Big Party." He looked up at me then, and I saw something in his face that was a mix of eagerness and fear. "*Helter Skelter*, man. *Helter* fucking *Skelter*."

Helter Skelter. Years ago, a crew of Charlie Manson's bloodthirsty wackos had written that in blood on the interior walls of a house, out in the Hollywood Hills. The blood came from the bodies of four women who'd been having a social evening when the killers broke in. One of the women was the wife of the famous were actor, Larry Talbot.

The next night, a different bunch of crazies, also sent by Manson, had invaded an elegant house in LA, not far from the La Brea tar pits. Armed with holy water, wooden stakes, and an Uzi that sprayed silver bullets, they'd left behind three dead vamps and "Helter Skelter" written all over the place in vampire blood.

The Talbot-La Brea murders had scared the shit out of undead Southern California, but it wasn't long before the police, acting on a tip, busted Charlie and his bunch of misfits at some ranch they had out there in the desert. It was at their trial that the prosecution explained to the jury in detail what Manson's conception of Helter Skelter really was.

The name came from an innocent little song on the Beatles' *White Magic* album, but there was nothing innocent about what Crazy Charlie had in mind for America: race war.

Out of Manson's deranged mind had come the notion that the Bible predicted a final showdown between humans and supes, or what Charlie called the "Children of Light" and the "Children of Darkness." When it became clear to the supes that humans were targeting them, courtesy of Charlie and his troops, they would strike back indiscriminately. This would bring a swift response from humans, prompting a struggle that would eventually result in the annihilation of every supe on the planet.

Or something like that.

Charlie was currently serving ninety-nine years to forever, and the rest of his tribe also went down for long stretches. A few of them were released eventually, and one of the women actually tried to assassinate President Ford. But somebody in the crowd grabbed the gun away before Betty could take a bullet.

In any case, the visions of Helter Skelter were locked up with the madman who had dreamed them, and that particular brand of craziness wasn't going to trouble the world again.

Or so everybody thought.

I looked at Pettigrew. "If you really believe that, you oughta be happy as a pig eating garbage," I said.

His mouth tightened at my insulting metaphor, but what he said was, "I don't know, man. I just don't know. It's a cool idea to rap about over a few beers or some weed, but making it really happen…" He let his voice trail off.

"You afraid you might get killed, is that it?"

He shook his head. "No, within the context of the struggle, my life is nothing."

I just looked at him. After ten seconds or so, his somber expression broke and he snorted with laughter.

"Guess you still know bullshit when you hear it, huh?"

"I encounter so much, you might say it's pretty familiar," I said.

"Yeah, well, sure, I'm afraid I might die, if the capital 'S' shit hits the capital 'F' fan. I've got a wife and kids that I love the hell out of, most days. And I'm pretty damn fond of myself, too. But that's not the real reason why this Helter Skelter stuff scares me."

"What, then?"

"I'm afraid we just might lose."

It was time for me to go to work for real. When I got to the squad room, I saw that Karl had already arrived. He was alone in the place, apart from Lieutenant McGuire, who was in his glass-enclosed office at the far end.

Karl looked up, said, "Hey," and went back to work on his computer. I wanted to let him know about my conversation with Pettigrew, even though he might be pissed that I went there without him. I walked around to his side, grabbed an empty chair from somebody's desk, and wheeled it over to where Karl was sitting. As I plopped down he turned and looked at me curiously. "What's up, Stan?"

"I got out of the house earlier than usual tonight. Christine and I have some shit going on, and I didn't feel like dealing with it right now, so I left before she got up."

"Is she OK?" I sometimes wonder if Karl has some kind of a thing for Christine. I hope he doesn't, although I couldn't have said why, exactly.

"It's complicated, but, yeah, she's OK. I'll tell you about it sometime. Maybe you can even give me some advice, since you're uniquely qualified. But now you need to hear about the conversation I just–"

That was far as I got when McGuire came out of his office and yelled, "Markowski, Renfer – you got one." He didn't need to yell, since we were the only ones here, but I think it's just habit with him now.

I swiveled the chair around and stood up. "We've already got two cases going, boss," I said carefully. "If you count the snuff film thing, that is."

"And now you'll have three. You see anybody else around here to catch it?"

Karl was on his feet by now. "What and where, boss?"

"Looks like a dead werewolf in Nay Aug Park. Your buddy Scanlon is on the scene and asked for somebody from what he likes to call the spook squad."

"The park's a pretty big place," Karl said. "Got any info about where the scene is?"

"Yeah," McGuire said. "The tree house."

There's this company that goes around the country building enormous tree houses in parks and other public green spaces. They charge a lot, but the city was able to get a matching grant from some Federal agency a few years back, and I have to admit the final product was impressive.

It's basically just a big, open platform with a roof on it, but the thing is built in the middle of an immense oak tree. The trunk shoots up right through the middle of the thing, and the designers put holes in the roof where the branches go. The tree house overlooks Nay Aug Gorge and the Roaring Brook, which runs through the middle of it. If you were crazy enough to jump over the railing, you'd have a 150-foot drop straight down before you hit the water, and that creek isn't nearly deep enough to dive into with any hope for survival. The tree house is as steady as the Sphinx, but it might not be the best place to visit if you're nervous about heights.

There's been a couple of suicides over the years – lovelorn teenagers looking to make a romantic final exit. I'd seen the aftermath of one of those idiotic gestures when I worked Homicide, and the result didn't look romantic at all.

That hasn't been a problem in a long time, though, ever since they closed the park after sunset. If you're some emo determined to make a dramatic exit, I suppose you could sneak in there some night. But the odds are you'd run into a werewolf, and the results of that encounter might make the remains of a jumper look positively dainty by comparison.

The city lets the weres have the use of the park at night as a public service – both to the weres and the rest of the city's population. Wolves need to run, it's in their nature.

Back when the city council was composed of sentient beings, they realized that it would be better for everybody concerned if the weres had a big, open space to do their collective thing, instead of doing it in their backyards. Less risk to the neighbors that way – and to the weres as well. Every human knows about silver bullets, and although the cartridges tend to be pricey, they're not exactly hard to find. I'm pretty sure that I saw some for sale in Vlad-Mart last week.

To get to the park tree house, you walk up a gently sloping ramp that makes a sharp right turn about halfway up. I'm sure there's some principle of engineering that explains that, although nobody has ever bothered to enlighten me.

It was the usual homicide scene: flashing red and blue lights, yellow crime scene tape, obnoxious yelling reporters – and Scanlon. He was waiting for us at the base of the ramp, along with a couple of uniforms that I knew.

"I would've been inclined to call you guys anyway," Scanlon said, "considering that this place is Were Central after dark. But once I laid eyes on the vic, I was pretty damn sure it was something you'd be interested in."

"Where's the body – up there?" I nodded toward the tree house.

"Uh-huh."

"Then let's go have a look," I said.

Scanlon took the lead up the narrow ramp, with me behind him, followed by Karl.

"Who called it in?" I said to Scanlon's back.

Without stopping, he said over his shoulder, "Anonymous call to 911. They've traced it to within the park, but the number isn't getting us anywhere. Probably a disposable phone."

I wondered if Christine had been the operator to take the call, and if she'd known it would bring her old man to the scene. Then I decided that I'd better stop thinking about Christine.

There was more crime scene tape across the entrance to the tree house. Scanlon produced a pocket knife and cut it loose. Must have been a sharp blade – it went through the plastic tape without a snag.

The naked man lay on his side, what was left of his mouth frozen into a snarl. Weres have to undress before transforming, or they'd just have to fight their way out of the clothes with teeth and claws once the change is complete. And as every-body knows by now, a werewolf returns to human form post-mortem. So if you kill a were, you end up with a dead, naked human – like the one we were looking at now.

I heard Karl draw in his breath sharply – a good trick when you no longer need to breathe. He was reacting to the pool of blood under the corpse's head. There wasn't much of it, though, compared to some other crime scenes I've been at. Bullet wounds to the head often bring instantaneous death, and corpses don't bleed much. But there was another, larger pool of blood a few feet beyond the corpse.

"What do you make of the other blood pool?" I asked Scanlon.

"Don't know yet," he said. "It's not consistent with the head wound. Maybe the vic managed to hurt the killer before dying."

"With a bullet in his brain?"

"I mean before the perp got a shot off. Maybe some human idiot got into the park, the were at-tacked him, and the guy was defending himself. Could happen."

"Not unless the shooter was a goat," Karl said.

Scanlon and I looked at him. Karl was kneeling next to the second blood pool, and I saw that his index finger was dark from where he'd dipped it in the blood for a sniff, and maybe a taste.

"This is goat blood," he said, looking up at us. "Not human, not were. Just your basic old-McDon-ald-had-a-farm goat."

"There's an expert opinion for you," I said to Scanlon.

"I don't doubt it," he said. "But that raises an interesting question, the same one that I often find myself asking at murder scenes."

"You mean 'What the fuck?'" I said.

"That's the one."

Karl was looking closely at the section of railing that overlooked the gorge. He wasn't using a flashlight, but then I guess he didn't need one.

"There's a couple of blood drops here," he said, "and the smell of goat is pretty strong." He turned to look at Scanlon. "I'm betting that if you send some guys down into the gorge tomorrow, you'll find a dead goat, probably with its throat cut. Even if it went into the creek, it won't have traveled far downstream. Water's pretty shallow, this time of year."

"You're on a roll, man," I said. "Care to tell us what you think it all means?" I was beginning to get an idea myself, but Karl deserved a chance to shine, especially in front of Scanlon, who'd voiced his doubts about vampire cops to me once, over a beer.

"I think it was a set-up," Karl said. "The perp led the goat up here, killed it – and waited. He knew that weres were gonna be in the park, and they have a powerful sense of smell, better even than… some other kinds of supes." I think he'd been about to say "vampires," but thought better of it.

"He knew the blood smell would bring a were-wolf up here, sooner or later," Scanlon said. "And it would probably be strong enough to mask the shooter's scent, as well."

"Sure," Karl said. "And there's only one way for the wolf to get here – right up that ramp. Talk about shooting fish in a barrel."

"So the wolf comes bounding up the ramp," I said, "and the killer's waiting, maybe sitting or lying down. Just him and his piece, loaded with silver."

"That's what I'm thinking," Karl said. "So the guy shoots the wolf, who dies and transforms back to human. Then the killer heaves the goat over the railing, steps over both blood pools real careful like, then walks down – and out."

"Why not do the same with the vic?" Scanlon said. "That way, he might not be found for days, even weeks. Which would give the perp lots of time to set up an alibi, or even leave town."

We stood there in silence until I broke it by saying, "He didn't throw the body over, because he wanted it to be found. He wanted us to know that somebody killed a werewolf here tonight."

"Why the fuck would anybody do that?" Scanlon asked.

"As a step in bringing on Helter Skelter." They both looked at me as if I'd grown a second head. I took a deep breath and let it out. "I had a conversation earlier today with a guy. I haven't had time to tell you about it, but it's time I did."

It was Karl's turn to drive, but he didn't start the

car when I slipped into the seat next to him. Instead, he turned and looked at me.

"If somebody hadn't offed a werewolf tonight, were you ever gonna tell me about the little talk you had with Pettigrew?"

"I started to tell you about it as soon as I got to the squad room tonight, remember? Then McGuire gave us this thing to deal with. I could've mentioned it in the car on the way over, but it's a short trip and I knew I wouldn't have the chance to finish before we got to the park. And I wanted to make sure you got the whole story at once, not just a piece of it."

After a couple of moments he nodded. "OK, I remember you sitting down next to me when you came in. And then McGuire comes out of his office, and it's *Who else am I gonna give it to*?"

His impression of McGuire was really terrible, but I thought this wasn't a good time to mention it.

"OK, that answers one question, Stan, but here's another one. How come you went to see that fuck-face Pettigrew without me?"

"It's like I started to tell you back at the squad," I said. "I've got a problem with Christine and I don't know how I want to deal with it yet. So I got out of the house before she was up."

"Yeah, all right, you wanted to leave early and avoid Christine. But that doesn't explain Pettigrew, Stan. You could've taken in a movie, or maybe stopped off for coffee someplace. Nothing says you had to go see Mister Master Race by yourself."

"You just showed why I did it."

Karl blinked a few times. "What the fuck does *that* mean?"

"The 'master race' thing. Going to see Pettigrew was a spur of the moment decision, OK? But it did occur to me that having a conversation with him would probably go smoother without the two of you growling at each other like a couple of pit bulls."

"I'm your partner, dammit, you should've–"

I held up a hand that stopped him mid-sentence. "Karl, let me ask you something. Say we needed some info on a case from a real hard-ass vampire, the kind who thinks the only thing humans are good for is lunch, OK? In a situation like that, would you consider – would you at least *think about* – asking me to wait in the car while you went and talked to the dude?"

Karl looked at me for what I guessed was a slow count of three. Then he nodded, faced front, and turned the ignition key.

"So, where we goin'?" he asked.

"Time to go see a wizard about a rug."

The establishment calling itself Magic Carpets, Mystic Rugs was located on the western edge of downtown, on the last commercially zoned street before the residential section began. The place was located a few doors down from 3 Witches' Bakery, which is where we found a parking space. I'd never been inside the place, but remembered hearing their commercial jingle on the radio – "Nothin' says lovin' like something from the coven." I was glad they were closed. It's hard to resist a bakery, and I eat enough junk food as it is.

There were a couple of those newspaper vending boxes in front of 3 Witches – the kind where you put in your fifty cents and pull out a paper. The vendors said it worked on the honor system, but I think it was more a recognition that nobody would want more than a single copy of one of those rags.

The *Times-Tribune*'s headline was about our latest political scandal:

JUDGE INDICTED IN REFORM-SCHOOL SCAM

In the adjoining machine, that new tabloid, the *People's Voice*, was using three-inch tall letters to announce:

VATICAN TO AMERICA: GO TO HELL!

I thought I knew what that was about. Some bigwig cardinal over in Rome had said, where a reporter could hear him, that he'd be just as happy if North America sank into the sea, taking the population with it.

I don't take a lot of interest in religious politics – and if you think that term's an oxymoron, welcome to the twenty-first century. But even I knew that the big guys in Rome have a love-hate relationship with North America, especially the USA. On the one hand, we're a big, affluent country with lots of Catholics – and a percentage of the money being dropped into all those collection plates every Sunday finds its way into the Vatican's coffers. Without America, they'd probably go broke.

But American Catholics don't always toe the party line real well. The Church says contraception's a sin, except for the rhythm method. You can always tell couples who use that approach, by the way – they usually have twelve kids. But the stats show that in the USA, Catholics use artificial birth control about as often as the rest of the population, which I'm sure pisses off the pope no end. And there are some Catholic priests who care more about social justice than the law, like the Brannigan brothers, who were always getting arrested a few years back for protesting the war in Transylvania.

So I wasn't exactly amazed to hear that there's some frustration in Rome about us, and only a little surprised that some cardinal would be indiscreet about it. But it wasn't what I'd call a big news story. The *Times-Tribune* had carried it last week, on page 12, I think. If the *People's Voice* thought they were going to make money attacking the Vatican in heavily Catholic Scranton, they were in for a hard lesson in both faith and economics.

In the rug store's big windows, I could see displayed – behind what looked like triple-thick safety glass – seven or eight gorgeous Oriental rugs. Their total price tag would probably beat what I'd paid for my house.

Karl was looking, too. "Wonder if any of 'em actually fly?" he said.

"Probably costs extra."

We had barely taken three steps into the brightly lit showroom when a trim, well-dressed guy in his thirties hurried over to meet us.

"Welcome, gentlemen, to our humble establishment," he said, probably for the twentieth time that day. "What kind of beautiful carpet may I show you this evening?" He had an accent that sounded Lebanese.

"We'd like to see Victor Castle," I said.

He nodded a couple of times, as if I'd said something profound. "Certainly, good sirs. I shall immediately determine if he is on the premises at the present time. May I say who is enquiring?"

I showed him my badge. "This is enquiring."

His head bobbed a few more times. "Of course, officers. Please excuse me – I shall return momentarily."

He vanished through a curtained door behind an antique-looking counter and a second later I heard his voice, with no accent whatsoever, yell, "Hey Chico – tell the boss that a couple of cops are lookin' for him!"

I glanced at Karl. "What d'you think – Lebanon?"

"By way of Swoyersville, haina?"

Abdul-from-Swoyersville never reappeared from the back of the store. Instead, the curtains parted and a man I assumed was Victor Castle – born Castellino – strode into the showroom area.

He was a little below average height and was wearing the vest and pants of a three-piece suit. I assumed the jacket was still in the back. The outfit was clearly expensive, but it didn't stop the beginnings of a gut from protruding under the vest's lowest button. He had thick black hair, although some of it had been replaced by a pink bald spot that reflected the glare from the ceiling lights. If he was supposed to be such a big-deal wizard, I wondered why he hadn't worked a little magic on his own appearance.

Karl and I showed him our badges while I gave him our names. He stared at Karl for a few seconds, and I realized he could tell that my partner was undead. Then he shifted his gaze to me and said, "The reason why I haven't used my magical skills to make myself tall, lean, and hirsute, Sergeant, is that while I have a number of vices, physical vanity is not among them."

I blinked at that. "I didn't think there was a spell, in white magic anyway, that allowed mind-reading."

The smile he gave me didn't reach his green eyes. "You are correct, Sergeant. In fact, I'm not even sure that black magic can confer that ability, although I am much less knowledgeable of that variety. But I did follow your gaze as I entered. Your eyes traveled the length of my form, doubtless estimating my height. Then your gaze lingered for a moment at my lower stomach and traveled upward again – not looking into my eyes but at the top of my head, which I expect appears quite shiny in this harsh light. Then you wondered why, with my much-touted magical powers, I had not employed them to correct my... physical imperfections. Correct?"

I nodded slowly. "If you really did all that without magic, then it's pretty damn amazing."

Karl murmured in my ear, "I thought it was quite elementary."

Castle gestured to my right. "As you can see, we have some comfortable armchairs, from which our customers sometimes view our wares. Perhaps we might sit down?"

He walked us over to where three upholstered chairs sat in a rough semicircle. When Karl and I were seated, Castle took the third chair and turned it toward us before sitting down. Each of these chairs probably weighed close to two hundred pounds, yet Castle had handled his the way I might move a metal folding chair. Magic or muscle? No way to know.

Castle spread his hands for a moment and said, "So, then?"

"I understand you're Ernst Vollman's successor," I said, "as... leader... of the local supernatural community."

"Ah, yes, Vollman," Castle said. "A very interesting man. He will be missed. I understand you were both present when he died?"

"Yes," I said. I had no intention of discussing with this guy the night that Ernst Vollman and his son Richard had both come to the end of their long lives. Vollman had died fighting, and the son, who was also known as Sligo, had died one of the ugliest deaths I'd ever seen.

When I didn't say anything more, Castle shrugged and said, "In answer to your question, it's fair to say that I enjoy a certain amount of respect from what you call the local supernatural community. Leader?" Another shrug. "I'm more of an ombudsman, really, called upon sometimes to settle disputes between factions, or individuals. Now, how may I be of assistance to the police this evening?"

"There are a couple of matters I'd like to discuss," I said. "One involves the fact that somebody is going around burning witches."

Castle's pleasant expression, which I assume was the one he wore out of habit, became grim. "Yes, I am aware of these atrocities. Two women, who had done harm to no one, subjected to such an agonizing death. It's like something out of the Middle Ages."

I wondered if Castle's knowledge of the Middle Ages came entirely from books, or if he'd been there personally. Sometimes these wizards are older than they look.

"Two – so far," Karl said. "And we don't want the number of victims to get any larger."

"A goal we share, Detective," Castle said. "Believe me."

"If we knew why those particular women were chosen, it might help us figure out who's been doing the choosing," I said. "Are you aware of any common factor, other than both being practitioners?"

"It's likely they knew each other," Castle said. "The community here in Scranton is not a large one. But they did not socialize together, nor were they related, either by blood or marriage."

"Sounds like you've been doing some investigating of your own," Karl said.

"As I told you, Detective, stopping these attacks is of great importance to us. I have no intention of sitting idly by as they continue. Not, of course," he made a pacifying gesture, "that I lack faith in the forces of law and order."

"Of course not," I said, keeping most of the sarcasm out of my voice.

Castle went on as if I hadn't spoken. "However, there are certain... sources of information available to me which you might not find readily accessible."

"Other than the fact that the witches didn't know each other, what have these sources had to say?" I asked him.

Castle studied his hands for a moment. I couldn't see the pentagram tattoo on his palm from where I sat, but I knew it was there.

"So far, nothing of value. I find it most frustrating, especially since another of these terrible attacks could occur at any time."

"Is it possible somebody's holding out on you?" Karl asked.

"Oh, no, Detective. I doubt that very much. The word has gone out that any useful information about this matter will be amply rewarded. And the corollary, also."

I frowned at him. "Corollary?"

"Simply that if any member of the community keeps such valuable knowledge to himself, the consequences will be... severe."

Something in Castle's face made me not want to ask what "severe" might entail.

"You said there were two items you wished to discuss with me, Sergeant," Castle said. "May I know the other one?"

"All right," I said. "Somebody's out there making, and selling, snuff films."

Castle's eyebrows climbed toward what was left of his hairline, like caterpillars scaling a wall. "I thought such things were myths, invented by the religious right to justify censorship of all mass media."

"That may have been true once," I said, "but not any longer. These are the real deal. Detective Renfer and I had to sit through one, and the FBI says there are at least three more in circulation."

Castle looked from me to Karl and back again. He took his time about it. "I assume you are telling me about this because there's some connection to the supernatural world?"

"You assume right," I said, and told him about the videos – as well as their Scranton connection.

He listened with what I can only call morbid fascination, elbows on knees and fingers tented under his nose. When he'd finished he dropped his hands and sat back. "Ye gods," he said softly. "Just when I thought I understood the depths of savagery that humanity was capable of…" He shook his head, as if to drive out the images that I'd planted there.

"The real savagery isn't being committed by humans," I said. Maybe I was feeling a little defensive. "The demon is the one who does the butcher's work."

"Yes, I understand that," Castle said. "And I'm no fan of demons, believe me. Nasty things. But permit me a hypothetical example, Sergeant. Let's say that someone were cruel enough to toss a live infant into the tiger's cage at the zoo. Who would you hold responsible for the ensuing tragedy? Not the tiger who, after all, was merely acting like a tiger. You would, quite properly, blame the individual who put the two of them in proximity – right?"

"OK, you've made your point," I said. "But the demon isn't being conjured and controlled by Sam the barber, or somebody. The one doing *that* is a wizard."

"Quite right," Castle said. "In this matter, it would seem, there is plenty of blame to go around."

"I'm less interested in moral discussions," I said, "than I am in nailing the fuckers who are doing this. At least one of the victims was a local boy."

"Mister Hudzinski," Castle said.

"That's him," Karl said.

"We live in a highly mobile culture, as you know," Castle said. "It's entirely possible that Mister Hudzinski, although a citizen of our fair city, fell into his misfortune a long way from home."

"If he did, we'll know it soon enough," I told him. "There are detectives digging into every detail of the guy's life, even as we speak. But for now, I'm going on the assumption that he was killed locally. And there's something else for you to think about."

Castle raised his eyebrows politely, but said nothing.

"If one of these videos was made locally, then they all were." I explained how the physical layout of the killing ground was the same in all four of the snuff films. "The camera angles are identical, too," I said. "The cameras are on tripods, and it doesn't look as if they're moved from one of these atrocities to the next."

Castle thought about that. "Even if Hudzinski disappeared locally, that doesn't mean he was killed here. Most car trunks contain ample room for a body, either living or dead."

And I bet you'd know, I thought.

"That's stupid," Karl said, which earned him a glare from Castle. I don't know if the Supefather was pissed at being talked to that way by a cop, or by a cop who was also a fellow supe.

"It makes no sense," Karl went on, "for them to transport a prisoner from Scranton to, say New York. There are lots of risks, haina? You could get pulled over for a busted tail light, or the guy could escape somehow. Hell, he might even die on you along the way. It's too complicated."

"He's right," I said. "If they wanted to film their fucking torture sessions in New York, or even Altoona, it'd be a lot simpler just to grab a couple of guys in those local areas."

Castle made a small gesture acknowledging

defeat, which I thought was gracious of him. "All right," he said, "for the sake of discussion, let's posit that all of this 'torture porn' is being made locally. What do you want from me?"

"Names," I said. "That's what I want. If this stuff is being filmed around here, there's two possibilities. One is that the wizard doing the conjuring is from outside the area and came to town fairly recently. You know of anybody like that?"

Castle shook his big head slowly. "No one comes to mind. He wouldn't be required to check in with me upon arrival, but any practitioner who expected to remain in this community would probably have the good manners – and the good sense – to pay a courtesy call."

"The first of these videos was made while Vollman was still alive," Karl said. "Maybe the wizard checked in with him."

"That could be," Castle said. "But there's no way to know for certain. Vollman and I weren't close, and he didn't leave any written records that I've come across."

"The other possibility," I said, "is that the wizard is a local boy gone bad. How about it, Castle? Anybody in your community dabbling in black magic these days?"

"From what you've described, this individual is doing more than just dabbling," Castle said. "But in any case the answer is no. If I were aware of any such activity, I would of course have reported it to the police." He said that with a straight face, and any irony in his voice might have been my imagination. Or maybe not.

"Or you might've just handled it yourself," Karl said. "To avoid troubling the authorities, and all that."

The look that Castle gave Karl said, *Just be glad you have that badge to hide behind, pal, or I would have your balls for breakfast.* I hoped Karl would never have to deal with Castle without his status as a cop to back him up.

What Castle said was, "I suppose there is that possibility. But if I had, we would not be having this discussion, would we?"

We left the rug shop with Castle's promise that he would shake the supe community's tree a bit to see if any black magicians fell out, and would let us know if they did.

As we walked to the car, I said to Karl, "You gave the Supefather a fair amount of attitude back there."

"The guy's an asshole. Just rubs me the wrong way."

"You weren't like that with Vollman."

"Yeah, well," Karl said, "that was fucking then and this is fucking now."

Yeah, back then you weren't undead, and didn't have to prove your independence to anybody – including yourself.

I decided not to share that observation with my partner.

"I notice you didn't say anything about the werewolf in Nay Aug Park," Karl said.

"I'm keeping that as my ace in the hole," I said. "Although what game we're playing here, I have no clue. Besides, if Castle really is the Man, like Vollman was, he'll know about it from his own sources soon enough."

When we returned to the car, the red light on the police radio was blinking, which meant that we'd had a call while we were in the rug shop. I got in on the passenger side and picked the radio out of its holder.

"Dispatch, this is Markowski. A call came in for us sometime in the last half hour."

"Wait one, Markowski."

A couple of seconds later, a female voice in my ear said, "This is Agent Thorwald."

I'm pretty sure I blinked at that. "This is Markowski. How is it you're on the police radio net?"

"Lieutenant McGuire let me borrow one of the units. I've been trying to raise you for the last twenty minutes," she said, not sounding happy about it.

"Sorry, we were engaged in a gunfight with a gang of desperate criminals."

"Really?"

"No, not really. What can I do for you, Agent Thorwald?"

When she spoke again, her voice was matter-of-fact. She had controlled her temper, rather than ream my ass out for joking around with her. That earned her a point in my book. A small one.

"You and your partner had best return to the squad area," she said. "ASAP."

"Can I ask why?"

"An agent from the Scranton field office brought over something that arrived there today, special delivery. It's another snuff film."

I felt my guts contract. Some other poor bastard had died in unimaginable pain, for the amusement of a bunch of fucking sickos.

"I agree that we should take a look at the video," I said. "But can't it wait until near the end of our shift? We've got a couple of other stops to make." I was in no hurry to sit through another episode of Grand Guignol with real blood, although I knew that I was just postponing the inevitable.

"Up to you," she said, "but I'd recommend you come in now. This one's different from the others."

"How so?"

"There's a woman in it."

The set-up was the same, except that it wasn't. They had the pentagram, all right, and the red protective circle surrounding it. What looked like the same blood-spattered wooden chairs sat within the circle, and nearby you could catch glimpses of the table with its instruments of agony all ready to go.

One of the chairs contained another naked man, manacled and clearly terrified. He looked to be about thirty, with close-cropped black hair, a heavy five o'clock shadow of beard, and a tat on one shoulder that looked like a coiled cobra.

The other chair, just like Thorwald had said, held a woman. Her face was turned away from the camera, but the sex was pretty clear from the styled blonde hair, the smooth-shaven leg visible in its shackle, and a side view of one of her breasts.

I guess whoever was behind this operation had decided to give the pervs a real treat this time.

The same voice off-camera was chanting the same words in Demon as before, with an identical result.

The air within the circle shimmered, then produced smoke that went from white, to gray, to black. The demon appeared, and was driven into submission by pain. Then the male prisoner jerked as the demon invaded, and I gave a small nod as my expectations were confirmed. I'd assumed that the woman had been brought in to play the role of victim. That's a common feature of torture porn, or so I hear, and I was assuming this exercise in sadism was aimed at the same general audience – or at least the portion of it that had a thousand bucks to spare.

It was at that moment that the woman first turned her face toward the camera, and an instant later I felt like I'd just been stabbed in the chest with an icicle. I couldn't breathe, I couldn't speak, but worst of all, I couldn't take my eyes off the video screen.

Karl must have realized that something was seriously wrong, because he grabbed the remote, pointed it at the DVD player, and pushed Pause. Part of my brain wished he'd hit Stop instead, and that the show would never start again. Ever.

"Stan? What is it, man? Your heart's going like a million beats a minute. You want the paramedics? Stan!"

I closed my eyes, and when I opened them a few seconds later, I found out that I was capable of speech, after all. "Karl, oh dear Jesus God, Karl! This can't be real, I must be fucking dreaming and I wish I would wake up. It's impossible!"

"What, Stan? What's wrong? Is it the woman? We already knew there was gonna be one this time – Thorwald said so. What's going on, man?"

"Jesus, Karl, don't you fucking *see*?"

"See what, Stan? Come on, work with me. What is it?"

"You've met her, I know you have, that time in Pittston. Don't you fucking *recognize* her?"

"The woman in the video? I've never seen her before, Stan. Who is she?"

"What're you, fucking *blind*, you with your fucking vampire sight, you can see in the dark and you can't even fucking see *that*?" I said.

"Stan–"

"Karl, *it's Lacey Brennan*."

Karl grabbed my arm. Even through my shirt and sports coat I could feel how cold – and strong – his grip was.

"Stan, take a deep breath. Stan, listen to me – *it's not Lacey*. It isn't her, Stan. I'm sure of it."

"What makes you the fucking expert? You only met her once, you said so yourself."

"No, Stan, that's what *you* said. I know she was

at that crime scene in Pittston last summer, but I saw her twice before then, and I remember what she looks like. There's a resemblance, yeah. I can see how you'd get faked out by it. But it's *not* her, Stan."

"How can you be so–"

"And I think I can prove it."

I stared at him. "And how the fuck are you gonna do that?"

"Stan, does Lacey have a long scar that runs down her right calf?"

"I don't — how am I supposed to know *that*? How the fuck do *you* know that?"

"That crime scene in Pittston was in the top floor of a duplex, remember? I was behind Lacey going up the stairs, and we had to go slow because the stairs were shaky. There was nothing better in my field of vision at the moment, so I looked at her legs. She had a skirt on, remember? A little short for official business, but on her it looked good."

"Karl," I said, "are you telling me you're hot for Lacey?"

"Nah, she's too sarcastic for my taste. But following her up those stairs I noticed her legs, and they were first-class. Shapely, and without a mark or blemish. Perfect skin – I remember thinking that at the time."

"Perfect, huh?"

"Yup. Apart from that, I'm sure it's not Lacey's face, but that's not proof. The scar is."

"Christ, she could have picked it up since the summer," I said. "It could've happened anytime."

"Not this one – the scar I'm talking about is old. See for yourself."

He pressed Play and the DVD started again. But instead of letting it run, he used the Reverse button to bring the action back to a point before the real action started. Then he paused it again.

"Look, Stan – it's a long scar, pretty hard to miss, especially close up. And it's *old*, man. Look at it."

"Yeah, OK, all right, it's an old scar. Years old, probably."

"Absolutely. Now, take a look at this."

He advanced the recording slowly, a few frames at a time. When he hit Stop, the screen showed a good, clear shot of the woman's face.

"See that? Really look at it. Her face is fuller than Lacey's. In fact, her whole body is at least twenty pounds heavier than I remember Lacey to be, haina?"

I looked at the image for several seconds, and something inside me that had been clenched hard started to loosen up. "Yeah, I think you're right, Karl."

"And this chick is older than Lacey, too, wouldn't you say? By at least ten years."

I looked some more. "I guess you're right about that, too. Thanks, buddy."

I reached inside my jacket pocket for my phone.

"What're you doing?" Karl asked.

"Something I should have done five minutes ago."

I opened the phone, selected a number in the

directory, and touched Call. After two rings, it was answered.

"Occult Crimes Unit – this is Sandra. How may I help you?"

"Hi, Sandy. It's Stan Markowski, in Scranton."

"Well, hi, Sergeant. How you been keeping?"

I decided to lie. "Not too bad, thanks. I'm surprised you're on the night shift – I thought you worked days."

"I do, but the night girl is out with the flu, so I'm putting in some OT. Can always use the money."

"Is Detective Brennan available?"

"No, she's out on a call, Sergeant. If it's urgent, I can patch you through."

"That's OK, Sandy, don't bother. But she *did* come in to work tonight?"

"Sure, I saw her less than half an hour ago. Care to leave a message?"

"No, that's all right. I'll give her a call tomorrow."

"OK, Sergeant. You take care now."

I put the phone away and said to Karl, "I can't handle watching the rest of this right now. Why don't we go get a cup of coffee – or, in your case–"

"Yeah, I know. Sounds good to me. We'll watch this shit later. Come on."

As we waited for the elevator – which, like usual, took forever – I looked at Karl. "Listen, some of the stuff I said to you back there in the room – I got no right to talk to you that way. I was just crazy for a couple of minutes, that's all."

"Forget it. If it was me, I'd have been worse.

A lot worse. But then, everybody says I'm a gutter-
mouth."

The elevator finally pinged, signaling the car was
about to arrive.

"Do they really?" I said.

"Fuckin' A."

After a cup of java – and a lightly warmed glass of
Type O for Karl – at the place around the corner, we
went back to the squad and made ourselves sit
through the rest of the torture video. Apart from the
gender of the victim, this one wasn't very different
from the one that the Feebies had shown us a couple of nights earlier. Thorwald had been right about
one thing, though – looking at that stuff doesn't get
any easier with repetition.

Afterward, we went looking for the two FBI
agents, to see if they had any insights they'd like
to inflict on us. However, Louise the Tease – whose
real name is Louise Brummel, if anybody cares –
said the two Feds had left a couple of hours earlier.
Probably went off to spit-shine their holsters, or
something.

I checked my watch. We could either find some
busywork until our workday ended in twenty minutes, or just leave now. After the shift we'd had, I
knew what I favored.

I turned to Karl. "What do you say – wanna call
it a night?"

"Works for me."

As we walked through the parking lot, I said,

"Hey, you got a minute? I'd like your opinion on something."

"That business with Christine you were talking about before?"

"Uh-huh."

Karl checked his watch. "We're not exactly pushing sunrise, so – sure."

As it happened, we were parked next to each other, so Karl leaned against the side of his car and said, "What's on your mind, Stan?"

I had my butt braced against the Lycan. "You ever hear of something called Drac's List?"

He nodded slowly. "Yeah, I think so. What about it?"

"You know that it's a kind of, I dunno, dating service that puts vampires together with humans who want to get bit by one."

"Yeah, that's what it is – more or less. So?"

"When I got home yesterday, Christine was on her laptop, looking at something. But she closed the computer when I walked in, and gave me some bullshit story about scanning the employment ads in the Sunday paper. Then she went downstairs."

"And you snooped."

"I'm a parent, remember? Not to mention a detective. Bet your ass I snooped."

"And you found she'd been scoping out Drac's List, instead of the *Times-Tribune*," Karl said.

"Yeah, exactly. I was pretty upset."

"Because she lied to you? Or are we talking about something else?"

"The lying didn't help," I said, "but what got to me was that she was cruising those ads. You know, looking for a… vamp freak."

"Stan." Karl's voice didn't sound happy.

"Look, nothing personal, OK? You know my feelings about vamps, uh, vampires have gone through some changes. I don't look at it the same way I used to."

"Gee, that's good to know," he said with a touch of sarcasm. "But…?"

"But she doesn't have to *do* that. She makes a good salary – she can afford all the bottled blood she needs. Even if she couldn't, I'd buy it for her. I even bring her plasma sometimes. She won't buy it for herself, it's too expensive."

Karl just looked at me.

"Dammit, she can drink it out of a fucking glass, just like you do. She doesn't have to act like a goddam…"

"*Parasite? Bloodsucker? Undead leech?* Which expression were you looking for, Stan?"

"That's not fair, dammit! I never think of her like that – or you, either."

We were quiet for a bit. Then Karl said, "You like fruit, don't you, Stan?"

"'Course I do. So what?"

"Apples, oranges, bananas, strawberries…?"

"Yeah, all of them, and some more besides. Is there a point you're trying to make here?"

"What if, starting tomorrow, you were told that you could never have fresh fruit again, Stan? No more frozen, either. Only the canned stuff. For the rest of your life. How would that make you feel?"

"That's not the same thing, and you know it," I said.

"You're right, it's not. Canned fruit tastes pretty good, if I remember right. But the difference between bottled blood, or even plasma, and the real thing, from a living person, it's like a choice between that powdered orange drink the astronauts used to drink, and fresh, sweet, juicy oranges."

More silence.

"I didn't realize it was that different," I said, finally.

"It is. Just ask any vamp."

"Karl–"

"And here's something else for you to keep in mind, buddy. Both Christine and me, we're vamps because of *you*. Because of choices *you* made, not us. We weren't even consulted, remember?"

"*Consulted?* You were both almost *dead*. If I *could've* consulted either one of you, I wouldn't have *needed* to."

Karl reached in a pocket for his keys. "Time for me to head home. I wouldn't want to get you all upset by burning to death in front of you." He opened his car door and got in.

"Jesus fucking Christ, Karl – are you saying you'd rather be *dead*?"

"I dunno, Stan. I never got to find out what it's like."

He closed the door, started up, and backed out of the parking space. Then he drove away, without looking back.

I got in the Lycan and cruised around town for a while before heading home. I had some things to think about. Just as well that a puppy didn't try to cross the street in front of me, though. I'd probably have run it over, then backed up to nail it again.

When I finally arrived home, Christine was at the kitchen table, reading a magazine. She put it down as I came in and said, "Hey, Daddy." She looked a little wary – maybe my face still showed something of what I'd been feeling after talking to Karl.

"Hey, yourself," I said.

"I'm glad it's not fifteen minutes later, or I'd have missed you again. You weren't here when I got up tonight." The way she said it wasn't an accusation, just a statement of fact.

"Yeah, there's a guy I wanted to talk to without Karl along. Karl and this guy, they don't get along too well. So I started my shift a little early."

"Oh, OK. How's Karl doing, anyway?"

"He's all right," I lied. I cleared my throat, which didn't seem to do a lot of good. "Listen, uh, I wanna say something, and I'd rather not have a discussion about it right now. But if you need to talk about it when you get up, we can."

She gave me a careful nod. "OK, sure. What's up?"

I'd composed this whole damn speech in my head while driving, and now I couldn't remember any of it.

"Christine, listen, I don't know what it's like to be a… vampire. I realize that. There's probably lots I don't understand about it, and maybe I never will.

But I want you to be happy, babe – or as happy as you can manage to be."

"Yes, I believe you."

"So, look – whatever you do when you're out, whatever you need to do, is none of my damn business, as long as you're safe, and you don't hurt anybody else. That's what matters to me."

Another one of those careful nods. "All right. Thank you."

"What I'm trying to say is, what happens in the night stays in the night. As far as I'm concerned, it's don't ask, don't tell."

She gave a little laugh. "You mean like that policy they used to have for supes in the military?"

"Yeah, I guess. Something like that. I hope it works better for us than it did for Uncle Sam."

She got up then, came over, and put her arms around me. "I think it will. Those people in the service didn't love each other. And we do."

"You got that right, kiddo."

She let go and stepped away. "Well, time for me to hit the hay. Will you still be home when I get up?"

"I should be, yeah."

She gave me a smile that didn't show her fangs. She's gotten pretty good at that, but if the fangs appear now and then, I'm going to try not minding. "I was just wondering. I don't have any discussions planned."

"OK, fine. Goodnight, baby."

"'Night, Daddy."

After she left, I realized I was famished, the first time I could remember feeling hunger all day. I checked the fridge – good, we had eggs I could scramble.

As the pan was heating, I idly picked up the magazine Christine had been looking at, which turned out to be the "Super-Special Undead Issue" of *Cosmo*. I started to smile as I looked at the cover stories: "7 Clues He's Batty Over You," "Is Your Coffin Clunky?" "A-Positive Or O-Negative: How To Know If He's Your Type," and "Sharpest. Fangs. Ever." Then I saw the one on the top left: "That Secret Place He *Really* Wants You To Bite Him."

I haven't laughed so hard in quite a while. Too long, really. Too damn long.

The next night, I came in to work a little early. I was hoping to have a quiet word with Karl, but he didn't show up until our shift was due to start. When he plopped down at the desk opposite mine, I opened my mouth to speak but he beat me to it.

"You seen the paper today, Stan?"

"Just glanced through it. The comics, mainly. Why?"

"There was an article about some company that's found a way to sell blood in powdered form. Just add water, and you've got yourself a nice snack, if you're a vampire."

I didn't know where he was going with this, but I suspected I wouldn't like it when he got there.

"That right?" I said, just to say something.

"Yup. They've even got a name picked out for it."

He was waiting, so I said, "What's that?"

"*Fang*," he said and grinned at me, vampire teeth and all. "Gotcha!"

He made a fist and slowly extended his arm across the desk toward me. After a second, I reached out and bumped it with my own fist. "We cool?" I asked.

"We cool."

"If you two soul brothers are done signifying," McGuire said from his office door, "I've got work for you."

After last time, I knew better than to protest being assigned another case. Besides, a glance at the assignment board showed that every detective team, on all shifts, was carrying four or five open cases. Things were busy for the Supe Squad these days, and it wasn't even Halloween.

We went back to the office, and McGuire handed me a slip of paper with an address on it. "Looks like a vamp, er, vampire attack. There was one last week, in case you didn't hear – Aquilina and Sefchik caught it. Compare notes with them, when you get a chance. Maybe we've got a serial fanger on our hands."

As we walk out of the squad room, I said to Karl, "Think the boss should get some of that sensitivity training?"

"Nah," he said. "I bet you could teach him all he needs to know."

In the elevator Karl said, "You check your email yet tonight?"

"Haven't had time. Why?"

"I was just wondering if you heard from the same guy that I did – Mitchell Hansen."

"That name rings a bell," I said, "but I can't remember why."

"Dude's a reporter for the *T-T*, does a lot of their crime stuff."

"That's right – he was bugging me about something a couple of months ago. And what does the *Times-Tribune* want to know this time?"

"He was asking if I knew anything about snuff films," Karl said, deadpan.

"Uh-oh. The Feebies are gonna shit when they hear about that. What'd you tell him?"

"That, far as I knew, it's an urban legend. I said he should stop wasting his time – and mine."

I nodded. "I'll tell him something like that if he writes to me. Good answer, by the way. You ever think about a career in PR?"

"As a liar, I'm strictly amateur, man. Not ready to turn pro just yet."

The elevator door opened, and we headed down the corridor that led to the parking lot.

"But talking about public relations," Karl said, "always reminds me of this dumb-ass I knew in high school."

"Did the dumb-ass go into PR?"

"Nah, he had this idea that he was gonna move out to Nevada and run one of those legal brothels they have there."

"Interesting career path," I said. "Don't know about the pay, but I bet the benefit package is outstanding. So, what'd the guy do – head out west after graduation?"

"Uh-uh. He wanted to go to college first, so he applied to the U. He said they had a degree program that would be good preparation."

"He really *was* a dumb-ass, then. The University of Scranton is a Catholic college, and I'm pretty sure the Church still discourages prostitution."

"Yeah, I know. Turned out he'd read their catalog wrong."

"What do you mean, he misunderstood the catalog? It's written so high school seniors can understand it, for Chrissake."

"Like I said, he wasn't too smart. He thought they offered a degree in Pubic Administration."

There are several nice apartment complexes just outside of Scranton that spread over several acres, allowing quite a lot of people to live there while creating the illusion of open space. But in town, real estate is too expensive for stuff like that. There are plenty of apartments, but they're mostly in buildings like Franklin Towers on McEvoy Avenue. Like a lot of these places, it doesn't live up to its pretentious name. There may have been somebody named Franklin involved in the design, but there wasn't a tower to be seen – just the usual big concrete rectangle on its side with a bunch of windows.

Lester Howard had lived, and died, in apartment 518. The uniform stationed at the door peeled back the crime scene tape to let us in.

The uniform's name was Meroni. I knew him well enough to nod "Hi" in the halls, but that was all.

"Forensics been here yet?"

"Not yet, Sarge. Busy night for them. There was a murder over in Dunmore – looks like a domestic, I hear." Dunmore's a suburb of Scranton. They've got their own police department, but it's too small to afford its own Forensics and SWAT, so they share with us.

"Another crew's over on Mulberry," Meroni went on. "I hear a couple of vamps were found staked in their house. Good riddance, you ask me. Somebody should stake 'em all."

I glanced at Karl, but apart from a mildly disgusted expression, he didn't react. I didn't say anything about it, either – but there was a time when I might've agreed with Meroni.

"Just let us in, will you?" I said.

The apartment looked like it had seen the services of an interior decorator. Not only was it not done in Early Man Cave – which is the style most young single guys adopt – I'm pretty sure most men living alone don't have curtains that coordinate with the walls. Hell, most guys don't even have curtains.

That impression of quiet good taste continued in the bedroom – apart from the corpse on the bed, which probably wasn't part of the decorator's original plan for the room. I figured it sure wasn't part of Lester Howard's plan.

In life he had been a thirty-something white male, in decent physical shape, who wore his hair long and his beard short. His penis was large and uncircumcised. In death he was just an extremely pale naked corpse on the bed with two small holes in his neck, his brown eyes staring at something only the dead can see.

I've been to a few vampire murder scenes. Not many. Vampires don't have to kill to get nourishment, especially in this age, with everything out in the open. But just as there are sicko humans who'd rather rape a woman than have consensual sex, there are some vampires who think that blood tastes best when you take it by force.

Other times, it's just loss of control. A vampire, especially a baby vamp who's new to the undead state, might be having such a good time at somebody's neck that he can't make himself stop. And the victim, if that's the word, won't always call a halt to it, even when vision starts to fade. I understand that being fanged feels *really* good, which is why there seem to be so many humans willing to part with a pint or two of their life's essence in return for the pleasure involved in giving it up.

But something about this murder scene was *off*, and it took me a minute to figure out what it was. "Look at his facial expression," I said to Karl.

"Doesn't have much of one, does he?"

"The guy looks… placid, like somebody laid out in a funeral home – what Mom used to call a 'corpse house'."

"Your mom sounds like somebody I could've learned to like," Karl said. "But you're right – he doesn't look like any vampire victim I've ever seen."

"If he gave it up willingly, he oughta look... blissful, not neutral. Like somebody who'd died from an overdose of marijuana."

"Um, I don't think that's possible, Stan."

"I'm just sayin'."

"Yeah, I know. And if he was attacked, there should be bruising and contusions. And his face would look frightened, or angry. Just like anybody else who's being murdered."

"Which means we have a serious case here of *whiskey tango foxtrot*."

He looked at me. "Say what?"

"Phonetic alphabet for WTF, or–"

"What the fuck. Yeah, OK. That's pretty good."

"Christine says they use it at work all the time."

"Not to the people calling in, I hope." Karl went to the bed, leaned over the corpse, and inhaled loudly. Then he moved a couple of feet down and did it again.

"You're gonna let me in on what you're doing eventually, right?" I said.

He straightened up and turned to me. "Vampire senses are more acute than human. All of them, not just sight. You knew that, right?"

"Yeah, I guess I did."

"Not all vampires are alike, and I hope you know that, too. But they all give off that characteristic vampire scent. I don't know how to describe it, but it smells like nothing else. And I'm not getting it from this guy, Stan. Not even a whiff."

"So we're back to…"

"*Whiskey tango foxtrot,*" Karl said. "Exactly." He walked slowly around the bed, staring at the corpse of Lester Howard the whole time. "I think we better give Homer, or whoever does the post, some specific instructions, Stan."

"Such as?"

"Have him look at the wound track, if he can work with one that small. See if it gradually narrows, the way it would if fangs made the puncture – or if it's uniform the whole way down, as if somebody used…"

"A couple of needles. Yeah, I gotcha. And I agree. Anything else you wanna tell Homer?" I said.

Karl was looking closely at the bite marks – or whatever they were.

"Yeah, let's have him test the wound for vampire saliva," he said. "He might not do that unless we ask him. Could be he sees what looks like fang marks, figures 'vampire', and never gives the wound a close look. But it *needs* a close look."

"Goddamn right it does. And I was thinking we oughta ask him for a tox screen, too. If somebody drained this guy using some kind of needle, they'd need a way to make him lay still the whole time. And no bruises means they didn't just hold him down while they did it."

"I like the way you think," Karl said.

"All this stuff is leading us to a bigger question," I said.

"You mean *whiskey tango foxtrot* again?"

"Kind of. Assuming it wasn't one of the undead who chilled this guy – why the fuck would somebody kill him and want to make it look like a vampire did it?"

"Could be misdirection," Karl said. "Point suspicion away from the human killer. A jealous husband, maybe. Judging from the size of this guy's schlong, it isn't out of the question."

"Maybe," I said. "Or it could be something a lot worse than that."

"Such as?"

"Helter Skelter, buddy. Helter fucking Skelter."

Karl blew breath out between pursed lips. "You figure they're working both sides at once? Killing supes to make the supe community pissed off, and killing humans in a way that looks like a supe did it?"

"I hope I'm wrong," I said. "Because if I'm not, this isn't the work of one lone nutcase, or even a couple of them. This could be bigger than we thought."

Karl gave me the grin again. "Bigger than both of us?"

"Nothing's *that* big."

A Dell desktop computer sat on a small desk in one corner of the room. I made a mental note to have Forensics copy the hard drive for me to look at later. The computer was still on, but had gone into sleep mode. Using the tip of my pen, I moved the mouse a couple of inches – just enough to wake the machine up, and see the last thing that Lester Howard had been doing with it.

The screen came to life, and I was looking at

DRAC'S LIST
For Vampires & those who love them

No matter who the murder victim is – or the killer, for that matter – the detective routine is the same. A forensics crew arrived as we were leaving Howard's apartment, and went in to do their CSI thing. Scanlon and his boys from Homicide never did show up. I guess the word had already gone out that this was a vampire kill, which made it a problem for the Supe Squad alone. I'd send Scanlon a copy of our report anyway.

Karl and I checked for witnesses by interviewing every tenant on Howard's floor. Nobody we talked to said they had seen or heard anything unusual. Nobody *ever* sees or hears anything, but you still have to go through the routine. We made note of the apartments where nobody answered the door, so they could be canvassed later. All told, we spent about three hours inside Franklin Towers.

Back at the car, we'd barely got the doors closed when my cell phone started playing "Tubular Bells". The caller ID simply read "Unknown Caller."

"This is Markowski."

"Sergeant, it's Victor Castle. We spoke recently at my place of business."

"Yeah, how you doing?"

"Less than optimal, I'm afraid. That's what I wanted to talk to you about."

"So talk."

"I much prefer to discuss this kind of thing in person, Sergeant."

"Listen, Castle," I said, "we haven't got time to swing by the rug store right now. Maybe we–"

"That won't be necessary. I'm only a hundred feet or so away from you. With your permission, I could appear in your back seat almost immediately."

"If you're so close, why don't you just walk over and get in?" I said.

"I'd rather be unobtrusive. Your car is not under observation – I determined that while waiting for you to complete your business in that apartment building," he said. "Still, I would prefer not to take the chance that we be seen speaking together at this stage."

"All right. If that's the way you want it, come on in."

"Very well. I will see you very shortly."

I closed the phone and said to Karl, "Don't jump – Castle is about to magic himself into our back seat."

"Huh? Why the hell would he do that?"

"Because I think it wise not to be seen talking with you officers," Castle's voice said from behind us. Despite my warning, Karl jumped a little. We turned, and there was the Supefather. He was wearing the jacket that went with his three-piece this time.

"If you can do this," I said, "and it seems pretty clear that you can, why wait until we got back? You could've been waiting back there when we got in."

"That would show rather bad manners on my part, Sergeant. In any case, I did not want to startle you officers, and run the risk of a violent response on your part."

Karl turned to me. "Isn't there a spell on all police vehicles designed to repel magic?"

"Yes, there was," Castle said, as if he'd been the one Karl asked. "Very competent journeyman work. I dismantled it while waiting for you to return."

"Who the fuck said you could do that?" Karl said. "Now we're helpless against magic!"

Castle gave him a tight smile. "If you'll pardon a little professional hubris, Detective, as long as you are with me, you will never be helpless against magic." He shrugged those well-tailored shoulders. "In any case, I will replace the protective spell when I leave. In fact, I worked out a variation that will make the spell even stronger than before. It helped pass the time while I waited."

As long as Castle was feeling generous with his magic, I toyed with the idea of asking him to give the car a bigger engine, plush carpeting, and a kick-ass stereo system. But then Karl would want an ejection seat and machine guns under the headlights, just like James Bond. Fuck it – McGuire would probably consider the whole thing a bribe and report us to Internal Affairs.

"OK, fine, whatever," I said. "You're here now –
so what's on your mind?"

"Recent events," he said, "have taken a turn that
disturbs me greatly."

"What events are we talking about here?" I asked.

"In addition to the recent witch burnings, you
mean? Well, there was that tragic business in Nay
Aug Park the other night."

"You know about that, huh?" I said.

"Such a bizarre event could hardly remain a secret for very long, to one with my resources.
Besides," he said, and gave a brief laugh, "the story
was in today's *Times-Tribune*."

That's what I get for not reading the paper
every day.

"Yeah, that was some fucked-up shit, all right,"
Karl said, earning him another thoughtful look
from Castle that made me glad Karl carried a badge.

"What was not in the paper just yet," Castle said,
"was the news that two vampires, a husband and
wife, were staked in their home sometime today."

That must have been the case Meroni had referred to, the one keeping the forensics techs busy.

"You probably know more about that than we do,"
I said. "It's not our case, and I just caught a mention
of it in passing from another officer."

"And now," Castle said, "I find you officers at the
scene of an alleged vampiric murder of a human."

"That's private police business!" Karl snapped.
"You've got no right to that until it's released by the
department."

Castle turned his head slightly so that he was looking at Karl directly. He studied Karl in silence for a second or two, then said quietly, "*Benimm dich, du Grünschnabel. Solche Unverschämtheit passt einfach nicht für Neuankömmlinge.*"

Castle and Karl had locked eyes, but Karl looked away first. I didn't know what Castle had said – I recognize German, but don't speak it – but it sure got Karl to chill out.

"Regardless of whether you *should* know about this case, you obviously do," I said. "So I might as well break a few regulations of my own and fill you in on what we know. Your use of 'alleged' to describe this vampire attack is a good choice of words, as it turns out."

I told Castle what we had observed in Howard's bedroom, as well as what we suspected. I laid out for him what we were going to tell the doc who would perform Howard's autopsy.

When I finished, Castle was quiet, staring out the side window as if the solutions to all his problems were out there in the night somewhere. When he spoke his voice was pensive.

"We have witches being killed by humans..." He looked at me. "I gather that's the working assumption?"

When I nodded, he went on. "Then a werewolf murdered by persons, or beings, unknown. Two vampires, staked in broad daylight."

"Which is the best time, if you're going to do that kind of thing," I said.

"Yes, to be sure," he said absently. "And now we have what on the surface appears to be a human murdered by a vampire, although that conclusion may not stand up to close examination."

He glanced at Karl, who seemed fascinated by the knobs on the radio, then looked at me. "What in the name of all the gods is going on here, Sergeant?"

"We have a theory about that," I said, being sure to give some of the credit to Karl.

"Would you care to share it?" Castle asked.

"It boils down to two words, I told him. *Helter Skelter.*"

Castle blinked a couple of times. "*Helter Skelter.* Wasn't that an old movie about that murderous lunatic, Charles Manson?"

"Yeah, and before that it was a song by the Beatles," I said, "but now it's a crackpot idea, and somebody around these parts seems to think its time has come."

I told him what I'd learned from Pettigrew. When I was done Castle just sat there, looking stunned.

"Race war?" he said. "Between supernaturals and humans? That has got to be the most ridiculously absurd notion I've ever heard of."

"It's up there on my list, too," I said. "But *somebody* seems to believe in it. And he's trying to make it a reality. Or they are."

Castle looked at me. "They?"

"I can't believe that one guy is doing all of this," I said. "It's either a bunch of loonies who all believe the same thing, or one guy with enough money to hire a lot of help."

"If you had to bet it was one or the other," Castle said, "where would your money go?"

"At this stage, I'd keep my money in my pocket," I told him. "We don't have enough information yet."

Castle pondered this for a few seconds, then said, "If we lack data, perhaps logic will get us somewhere. Isn't there an expression you detectives use – *cui bono*?"

"Who benefits? Yeah, we use that one sometimes."

"So who stands to benefit if this so-called race war were to take place?"

"Nobody," I said, "unless some dude's been stockpiling wooden stakes and silver bullets."

"Detective Renfer," Castle said, "as one who might be said to have a dual perspective on such matters, who do *you* think would emerge victorious, in a worldwide race war?"

Karl started when Castle spoke to him, but he answered quickly enough. "Humans," he said. "It would take time, and the cost in human blood would be high, but I'm pretty sure the humans would win in the end."

"I'm not disagreeing with your conclusion," Castle said, "but I'd be interested to know what led you to it."

Karl shrugged. "Numbers, for one thing. Although the census data is bullshit, it's still clear that humans outnumber supernaturals – ten to

one, twenty to one, who knows? But it's a big difference."

"I would agree with that," Castle said, "even
though I don't know the exact proportion myself.
Anything else?"

"Supernaturals have weaknesses – some of them
do, anyway."

Karl had said "some of them", not "some of *us*".

"Vampires are stronger and faster than humans,"
Karl went on, "and they have other advantages,
like using Influence. But during daylight hours, a
vampire is as helpless as a corpse – because that's
what he is."

"And werewolves are just like humans, most of
the time," I said. "They can only transform in moonlight, and then if they run into a silver bullet, they're
toast."

Castle nodded, as if we were the two brightest
pupils in class. "And what about magic practitioners?"

I looked at Karl, who said, "Some witches and
wizards are real powerful – but nobody's all-power-
ful. Magic is limited by time and space and a bunch
of other stuff I don't really understand."

"And practitioners aren't invulnerable, either," I
said. "Especially if they're taken by surprise. What's
happened to those poor witches is proof of that."

"Right on both counts, unfortunately," Castle said.

"I'm pretty sure we'd win, but the supes, uh, supernaturals would do a *lot* of damage first," I said.
"Humans would survive, but I'm not positive that
human society would."

Castle nodded. "A costly victory, to be sure."

"So the bottom line," I said, "is that in a war between humans and supernaturals, there'd be no real winner."

"Yes, Sergeant," Castle said. "That conclusion is both true, and irrelevant."

I stared at him. "Where do you get 'irrelevant'?"

"I mean, it doesn't matter whether a race war would be a good idea. The important thing is whether someone *thinks* it's a good idea."

"OK, now I'm confused," Karl said.

I waited for Castle to explain, although I was pretty sure that I'd grasped his meaning.

"It's like invading Russia," Castle said, "which military experts have said for centuries is a truly bad idea. The country is simply too vast for an invading army to subdue quickly, and the Russian winter makes an extended campaign impossible."

"Makes sense to me," Karl said with a shrug, and I just nodded.

"And yet that obvious fact didn't stop Napoleon from trying it in 1812, or Hitler in 1940. And each time, it cost the lives of a great many people – on both sides."

Karl nodded slowly. "It really doesn't matter if a race war is a bad idea, as long as some dumb-ass somewhere thinks it's a *good* idea."

"Exactly," Castle said. "Which brings me back to the original question: *Cui bono*? Or maybe I should rephrase it as: *Cui cogitat bono*?"

"Who thinks to benefit?" I said. I'd had four years

of Latin in high school, and when the nuns teach you something, it tends to stay with you a long time. Terror and pain will do that.

Karl just shook his head. "So what you two professors are getting at is – what nut, or group of nuts, is crazy enough to try starting Helter Skelter here in Scranton?"

"Admirably put, Detective," Castle said.

There was silence in the car until I said, "I don't know how much weight I want to put on this, but the Catholic Church comes to mind. After all, they've declared all supernaturals to be 'anathema'."

"I know," Castle said. "Such nonsense."

"*Nonsense?*" Karl said. "Then why can't I go to church anymore, huh? How come the sight of a cross makes me want to puke my guts out?"

"I have given much thought to that question over the years," Castle said, "and have concluded that vampires' aversion to religious symbols is psychological, more than anything else. Popular culture has told you, over and over, that vampires fear the cross. Therefore, once you became a vampire, you felt fear and revulsion when in the presence of a cross, or other religious symbol. You believed you were supposed to, therefore you did."

"That's what you think?" Karl said angrily. "Well, *I* think you ought to–"

"Nine Alpha Six, this is Dispatch. Come in, please."

I don't usually consider radio calls a blessing, but this one sure was. I grabbed the radio.

"Dispatch, this is Markowski. Go ahead."

"We have a report of a 666-Bravo at the Radisson hotel. Lieutenant McGuire says it's all yours. Over."

666-Bravo was a homicide involving a supernatural. Was this stuff *never* going to stop? And I know McGuire's a fair boss – if he was giving this call to us, it meant the other teams on shift were busy elsewhere.

Helter Skelter, baby. Helter Skelter.

"Roger that, Dispatch. You got a room number for us, or should we knock on all the doors until somebody dead answers?"

Come to think of it, having a corpse answering the door at that place might not be such a big deal.

Ignoring my feeble attempt at sarcasm, the dispatcher said, "Affirmative, Markowski. Room number is four three one. I repeat, four three one. Do you copy?"

"Roger that, Dispatch. We're on our way. Markowski out."

I wished I'd let Karl take the radio call – he likes saying stuff like that. It might've cheered him up a little, too.

Karl turned to me. "Four thirty-one at the Radisson? Isn't that–"

"Mister Milo and his pet ghouls," I said. "It sure is."

I turned to look at Castle. "I guess you heard. We'll have to continue this conversation later."

Castle nodded. "Of course, Sergeant. I look forward to it." And then he was just – gone. A fucking show-off, in more ways than one.

"Siren and lights?" Karl asked me.

At this hour of night traffic wasn't heavy, but I know Karl loves using our "get out of the way" equipment.

"Sure," I said. "What the hell."

Karl pulled the portable revolving light from the glove compartment, turned it on, and stuck it on the dash between us. I started the siren screaming, checked the mirror for traffic, and got us moving.

Five police cars – three black-and-whites and two unmarked, like ours – were parked haphazardly in front of the Radisson, the light from their red and blue flashers bouncing off the elegant façade like special effects at a Plasma-matics concert. I hoped nobody on that side of the building was trying to get some sleep.

I figured that at least one of the unmarked cars belonged to Homicide, so there was a good chance that Scanlon was already upstairs. Maybe he'd have it solved by the time we got there.

As Karl and I strode toward the elevators, I noticed a lot of people milling around the lobby – too many for this time of night. Maybe they were waiting to see something exciting. As for me, I hoped the excitement was already over.

Upstairs, the usual crime scene tape blocked off the hallway on both sides of room 431, but one of the uniforms who was standing around lifted it to let Karl and me through and into a suite that was already pretty crowded. Scanlon was there, all right, along with a couple of homicide dicks, Homer Jordan, and some guy in a suit who was taking pictures. He had a lot to photograph.

Milo Milo was sprawled across the couch. He wore gray slacks and a white dress shirt covered in blood that I assumed had come from the gaping wound under his jaw. The only way to kill somebody that way is to force the blade through the lower jaw, into the facial cavity and up into the brain. Doing that took skill, strength, and one hell of a big knife.

But the killer had saved most of his ingenuity for the two ghouls who'd served Milo as drivers, gofers, and, I suppose, bodyguards. Some bodyguards.

"You remember their names – the ghouls?" I said quietly to Karl.

"Nikolai and Winthrop." Under some circumstances, saying those two fancy-ass names out loud might have brought a smile to Karl's face. But not this time.

The ghouls were posed – I can't think of a better word to describe it – in the living room's two armchairs. Each one was showing the same wound under his jaw that Mister Milo had suffered, but that's where the similarity in mayhem ended. Both ghouls were disemboweled, the slick intestines gleaming wetly in the light from the room's lamps, which were all turned on. I wondered if Milo had liked a bright room, or the killer had just wanted to light up his little exhibition.

I thought I could see something on one of the ghouls' mouths that was too big to be a tongue. I went over to the body and bent down for a closer look. Just as I thought – it was his penis.

I didn't bother to check the other ghoul. I knew it would be the same. He was thorough, our killer was.

On the carpet near one of the chairs lay an open switchblade. The handle was smeared with blood, and nearby lay two pale severed fingers. I figured one of the ghouls had tried to knife-fight the killer, and come out second best.

"Forensics been in yet?" I asked Scanlon.

"Nah. One unit is tied up over near the university. Some werewolf mauled one of the students, from what I hear."

"He still alive?" I asked.

"*He's* a *she*," Scanlon said, "and, no, she's dead. Hard to keep breathing with your throat's been torn out."

"They got anybody in custody?" Karl asked.

"Not as far as I know."

Helter Skelter.

"Isn't it kind of weird," Karl said, "for the boss, here, to die quick, but the thugs get to suffer? I mean, you take out a hit on somebody, it's usually the boss you're pissed off at. If anybody's gonna get butchered, it'd be him."

"You think it was a hit?" Scanlon said.

"Wasn't no bunch of Girl Scouts that did this," Karl said.

"You got a point there," Scanlon said, then turned to me. "You must know who the guy on the couch is, if you know the names of his hired help."

"Yeah, we do. His name, and I shit you not, was Milo Milo."

Scanlon's expression didn't change. "Is that right?" One of the homicide detectives that had come with Scanlon gave a little chuckle. Scanlon turned his head toward the guy slowly, like a tank turret taking aim.

"Something on your mind, Smalley?"

The detective's face reddened. "No, boss. Not a thing."

Scanlon looked at him for a moment longer. "That's not surprising." To me he said, "OK, that's who the guy was. Now *what* was he?"

"He said he was a lawyer representing the porn industry – or what he insisted on calling 'adult entertainment'."

"What the fuck was he doing in Scranton?" Scanlon said. "I don't work Vice, but if there's a porn operation in the Wyoming Valley, nobody's ever said anything to me about it. I thought all that crap was based in Southern California."

"Most of it is," I said. "But there's a branch that's stayed below the radar until recently, and it seems to have a Scranton connection. That's what Milo Milo over there was concerned about."

"I'm not gonna stand here and pretend that makes sense, Stan," Scanlon said.

"I know it doesn't – yet," I said. "Any part of this happen in the bedroom, far as you can tell?"

"No, it looks clean."

I made a small gesture that took in the other

people in the room. "Why don't we talk in there, and stay out of everybody's hair."

"I dunno," Scanlon said. "I mean, I like you, Stan – just not that way."

Fucking homicide guys aren't exactly known for their sensitivity. They'd probably make jokes during a guided tour of Auschwitz.

"Come on," I said, and headed toward the suite's bedroom. Scanlon and Karl followed me inside, and Karl closed the door.

"This is supposed to be a big secret, and the FBI wants it kept that way. I think I oughta tell you, but I'd rather those other guys in there not hear about it. OK?"

"Oh, damn," Scanlon said, deadpan. "And here I was planning to post it on my blog."

"Yeah, all right," I said. "Here's what's going on."

Karl and I took turns telling him all about the snuff films, but I didn't share my theory about Helter Skelter – not just yet.

"So, Mister Milo out there was in town trying to find the sick bastards who're making these snuff films," Scanlon said, "before they hurt the reputation of the porn industry. If you ask me, that's kind of like a Mafia family worrying about its public image, but OK."

"Even the Mafia does PR these days," Karl said.

"Whatever," Scanlon said. "So, who hit him?"

"The logical answer is – whoever's making the snuff films," I said. "Only problem with that is, Milo didn't know anything worth killing him over. Or if he did, the oily bastard didn't share it with me."

"Hard to imagine, isn't it?" Scanlon said.

"Maybe he shared it with Sharkey, instead," Karl said.

Scanlon looked at him quickly. "Sharkey's dead."

"Be nice to think so," I said. "But there's a rumor going around that he's back in town, and the pupils of Milo's eyes gave him away when I mentioned Sharkey's name."

"Sharkey," Scanlon said. "Jesus."

"The fact that Milo got hit *must* mean that he stumbled onto something useful, even if he didn't tell us about it," I said.

"Not necessarily," Karl said. "Maybe whoever's making these fucking snuff films is just real thorough, that's all. The Columbian drug lords operate the same way, I hear. The slightest threat to their operation appears, they don't worry about how important it is – they just wipe it out."

"That still doesn't explain why the killer, or killers, went to work on the ghouls and not Milo," Scanlon said.

"No, it doesn't," I said. "Maybe we don't have enough information to answer that yet."

"We don't have enough information to blow our fucking noses," Scanlon said.

"Fuckin' A," Karl said.

"Speaking of information, you'll send us a copy of the case file?"

"Yeah, sure. It'll help me fool myself that I'm actually accomplishing something on this case."

"I'll be sending you a file, too," I said. "We've got

a murder that looked at first like a supernatural case, but now I'm not so sure."

"I can hardly wait," Scanlon said.

In the car, Karl said, "There's something about the way Milo was knifed that's been nagging at me."

"It's pretty unusual, all right," I said.

"That's not what I mean – it reminds me of something I heard about once, but I can't remember the details."

"Stop thinking about it, you'll drive yourself nuts," I said. "Your subconscious will come up with the answer when it's good and ready."

"Hope it's ready before Helter Skelter gets here."

"Well, with any luck – *what did you say*?"

Karl was looking at me strangely. "I said, 'I hope I remember before–'"

"Helter Skelter. Damn!"

"You can start making sense any time now, Stan."

"That's why the killer back there mutilated the two ghouls, but not Milo. He was going for a twofer."

"Stan–"

"He cut up the ghouls because, once word got out, it would piss off the supe community. And somebody's been working pretty damn hard lately to rile up the supe community – and the humans, too, if that fake vampire kill we saw tonight is any indication."

"Wait – I thought Milo was killed by the snuff film people," Karl said.

"He was – *because they're the same people*."

• • • •

Back at the squad, I asked Louise where the two Feebies were.

"No idea, Stan. They haven't been in all night."

"Did they leave you contact info?"

"No, nothing. I asked, but…" She made a "What can you do?" gesture.

"Yeah, I know," I said. "The pricks think they're too good for us – as usual. Where's McGuire? He's not in his office."

"Went home an hour ago. Says he's maybe got that twenty-four-hour bug that's going around."

"Great, just great. I guess I'll have to tell everybody about my brilliant deduction tomorrow night."

"If you really need to tell somebody, you can tell me," she said with a smile. "I don't mind listening."

Louise is pretty sweet, most of the time. It's hard to believe that she's Civil Service.

"That's all right, Louise," I said. "It would take me an hour to give you the background, and I'm not sure if the payoff would be worth it for you. But thanks."

She gave a toss of her head that sent the blonde curls bouncing. "That's OK."

"When you see the Feebies again, ask them to do something for me, will you?"

She pulled a pad over and grabbed a pencil. "Sure – go ahead."

"Tell them I think it would be a good idea to find out who owns the *People's Voice* – I mean who *really* owns it, not what it says in small print on page 2."

She wrote busily for a few seconds. "Got it, Stan – I'll tell them the next time they come in."

"Thanks. Hey – how'd the tournament go last weekend? Did you take First again?"

Louise is an absolute genius at Scrabble, and she's got the trophies to prove it.

She made a face. "Nah. Second."

"You'll get 'em next time."

"Damn straight I will."

Karl and I spent about an hour catching up on paperwork – or whatever we should call it these days, since no paper's involved. Then we signed out for the night. Fifteen minutes later, I was home.

As I closed the front door behind me, I noticed there was no light on in the kitchen. Christine can see fine in the dark, but she usually leaves the light on for my sake. I flipped the switch – no Christine. Tonight had been her night off, so I knew she hadn't gone to work.

Living room – nothing. I looked in the basement, although Christine never goes down there until she has to. Nothing. Then I checked the bathroom and upstairs. *Nada*.

A cold hand had gripped my chest as soon as I saw the darkened kitchen, and with every room I looked in, it grabbed a little tighter. I checked my watch – sunrise in seven minutes.

If she was stuck somewhere and couldn't get home before dawn, she'd have called – either to have me come get her, or at least to let me know that she was OK. But my cell phone hadn't rung all night. It occurred to me to check the house phone – we still have a landline, call me old-fashioned – and felt a surge of relief when I saw the red light blinking on the answering machine. I started toward it – and then heard the sound of a key in the front door.

A moment later, Christine walked in. I resisted the temptation to go all fatherly and give her, "Where have you been, young lady?" She was an adult now, and besides, she's a *vampire* – people are probably afraid of *her*.

She closed the door and said, "Hi, Daddy." To my ears she sounded a little like a teenager coming home way past curfew, but I might have been projecting my own feelings onto her.

I took a deep breath, let it out and said, "You're cutting it pretty close tonight, baby. Sun's up in–"

"Six minutes. I know. I hope you weren't worried."

"What – me worry? I'm a regular Paul Newman."

She laughed a little. "I think you mean Alfred E." She came over and gave me a hug, and when she stepped back I saw, at the corner of her mouth, a tiny smear of red.

As she went over to put her purse on the kitchen counter I said, because I had to, "Mind if I ask where you were tonight?"

She turned back at once. The look she gave me wasn't angry, exactly, but I didn't think she was about to nominate me for Father of the Year, either.

She raised one eyebrow – something I've never

been able to do, but her mother always could – and said, "I thought the new policy was 'Don't ask – don't tell.' Was it only good for twenty-four hours?"

We stood looking at each other for a little bit, then I blinked a couple of times and nodded slowly. "Yeah, you're right. I withdraw the question, and I'll try not to ask it again." I gave her half a grin. "Guess maybe I was a little worried, after all."

Her face relaxed. "I know, and I'm sorry I put you through it. I tried to take a shortcut home. Like most shortcuts, it ended up taking longer than the regular way."

"You could've transformed and flown home," I said.

"Yeah, I know. If I was really pushing the dawn, I would have. But I'd hate to just leave the car, with my purse in it, parked on some street all day. So I'm saving going batty as a last resort."

"You're the best judge," I said. "Just call me Paranoid Papa."

She gave me a smile that looked genuine. "I don't think it's called paranoia if you're scared for someone else." Glancing toward the window she said, "Well, time for nighty-night. See you at sundown."

She was opening the basement door when I said, "Don't get pissed off, but I need to ask you a very specific question, baby. Either answer it, or don't."

Her expression became wary. "All right, but be quick, huh?"

"Do you know a guy named Lester Howard?"

"Is he warm?"

He wasn't when *I* saw him, but to avoid confusing her I just said, "Yeah."

Her brows furrowed, then she shook her head slowly. "Nope, the name doesn't ring any bells. Why?"

"I'll tell you about it tonight. Sleep well, honey."

"OK, then. Goodnight, Daddy." She closed the door behind her, and I could hear her footsteps on the stairs.

I'm not going to say it's impossible for Christine to deceive me. Any parent who thinks that is a fool. But I've known her a long time – her whole life, and then some – and I believed her.

Then I remembered that answering machine message. If it wasn't Christine, then who…?

"Stan, hey, it's Karl. I've gotta hit the hay in a couple minutes, but on the way home it hit me why that weird knife wound in Milo rang a bell. I was at the Supernatural Law Enforcement Conference in LA last year – you got me that grant, remember? So I met this chick from Chicago, she's a detective on their Spook Squad. Spent all my free time buying her drinks and trying to get into her pants. I never did, but I remember she told me about a bunch of homicides where each one of the vics had a long blade shoved through the soft tissue under his jaw and up into the brain. Familiar, haina? She said the Chicago cops had a pretty good idea who the hitter was, they just couldn't prove it. And catch this: she said the guy would kill anybody for money, but the dude specialized in supes.

I'll call her tonight and try to get a name and some more info. Catch you later, man."

When Christine got up, I told her about Lester Howard, and then about the whole Helter Skelter thing. Since these bastards were going around killing supes as well as humans, I figured she ought to know.

When I finished, she took a last swallow from the cup of warm plasma she'd been drinking, pushed the cup to the side and said, "Race war? Seriously? These people have *got* to be insane."

"I wouldn't doubt it," I said.

"I mean, they're crazy enough for wanting it, but if they think they can actually make it happen..." She shook her head.

"Yeah, I know. But the fact that it's a pipe dream doesn't mean they won't kill people trying to achieve it, just like Charlie Manson and his followers did, back in the day. Or Hitler, before him."

"Hitler wanted Helter Skelter too? I never knew that."

"No, what I mean is he had a crazy racial dream – a completely Aryan world. Ridiculous idea, but Adolf and his buddies wiped out millions trying to achieve it."

"Yeah, OK, I get you."

"Which is why I'd like you to be extra careful when you're out, wherever you go. These lunatics have killed at least six supes so far, two of them vampires. And they're not going to quit until somebody stops them."

"I assume that's where you come in," she said.

"Goddamn right I do – but it's gonna take a while, which is why I want you to be alert and cautious at all times."

"Yes, Daddy." Usually, there's a teasing lilt to her voice when she says that. But not this time.

"I've got a locksmith coming over tomorrow," I told her. "He's going to put better locks on the doors and install a deadbolt on the door to the basement. It'll ease my mind a little about leaving you here alone all day."

"Fine with me," she said. "I want to rest, in peace, during the day, not rest in peace forever."

"Do you really?"

She frowned at me. "Huh?"

"I mean, would you rather be undead than true dead? Karl and I had a conversation about that the other night."

"Doesn't sound like an easy talk to have."

"It wasn't. Karl reminded me that he's a vampire because of me, just like you are. I asked if he'd prefer that I let him die, back there at the pump house."

"And what did he say?"

"He said he didn't know, since he's never been dead."

"'Course he has," she said. "So have I – twelve hours every day, or however long the sun's up. It's boring, frankly. When Chandler called it 'the big sleep', he wasn't kidding."

"What about the afterlife? For the truly dead, I mean. Heaven, and all that."

"Far as I'm concerned, that's still an open question. Nobody's offered an answer that makes sense to me, so I'm not willing to take my chances just yet, if I don't have to." She pushed her chair back. "I need to jump into the shower and get dressed."

She took a few steps toward the doorway, then stopped and turned back to me. "I know this would sound *really* weird out of context, but – thanks for making me a vampire, Daddy." She gave me a big grin, fangs and all. "And remember to get two sets of keys for those new locks."

"Already ordered," I said. Then she was gone.

Christine usually leaves for work about an hour before I do. After we said goodbye, I toasted an oversize English muffin and ate it with peanut butter, shaved, took a shower, and cleaned Quincey's cage. I swear, that hamster seems to shit more than he eats.

As I pulled the front door shut behind me and felt the lock click into place, I was thinking about Karl and his onetime lust object, the detective in Chicago who might be able to give us a lead on Mr Milo's killer. Fortunately, I wasn't giving it all of my attention, or I'd be dead now.

Standing in the driveway, I pushed the button on my keychain that opens the garage door. Then my brain got around to processing a sound I'd heard a second or two earlier – something that sounded like a quickly stifled screech, and it had come from *inside the garage*. And there was an odor, as if somebody had left the lid off a garbage can – but trash pickup had been yesterday.

I backed up fast, drawing the Beretta as I moved.

Once the door had risen five or six feet, the goblins came pouring out, screeching like a platoon of scalded cats. Light from a nearby street lamp glittered on the blades of the long knives they held.

The only thing that'll kill goblins for certain is cold iron, and that fact put me in a good news/bad news situation.

Good news: I had cold-iron tipped slugs in the Beretta.

Bad news: I only had four of them. The clip holds eight rounds, but I usually carry half cold iron and half silver, alternating them when I load the clip. I never know what I'm going to have to deal with, and cold iron's no good against vamps or weres. I carry a round under the hammer, but that's silver, too – I have more confrontations with the undead and shifters than with goblins and other fey, so my ammo load reflects that.

Worse news: I had more goblins than bullets. As I backed down the driveway, the fucking gobs kept coming out of the garage, like clowns from a circus car. I counted six of them. They were all making that screeching noise they do in battle, which sounds like claws on a blackboard. It would have really annoyed me if I wasn't busy being scared shitless.

Thank God, or whoever's in charge, that Christine usually parks in the driveway. I don't know how well a vampire would have done against six goblins, but I'm glad Christine didn't have to find out. Whatever happened to me, she was out of danger – I hoped.

Despite my hasty retreat, the goblins were getting close now. I double-tapped the nearest, putting two rounds into his furry green chest. One was silver, which had no effect, but the cold iron slug did the job just fine. The goblin clutched at himself, screeching even louder for a second before he fell on the asphalt and was immediately trampled by his buddies, who just kept coming.

I dropped the second goblin the same way. That left me with two rounds of cold iron, and four goblins who wanted to kill me.

I pointed the Beretta at them two-handed and yelled, "Police officer! Freeze!" in my most authoritative-sounding voice. If I could get them to hesitate, I'd have the chance to make a break for the street. The gobs might not want to follow and kill me in front of witnesses. I was sure the neighbors had heard the shots. They might've called for help by now, but whether they dialed 911 or 666, nobody was going to get here in time to do me any good.

My Dirty Harry act was a flop. The goblins didn't even break stride. The light was better here and now I could see that their eyes, usually hooded and barely visible, were wide open and crazed. *Meth? Again?* A meth-addicted goblin had killed my partner eighteen months ago, but things had been quiet on that scene since, and I'd figured that the problem had burned itself out. Looks like I was wrong – maybe dead wrong.

Another goblin was closing, eager to stick that long blade in my guts. I fired twice and put him down. Another one was right behind him, so I fired my last three rounds, knowing one of them would be the cold iron that would ruin this greenie's night. It did. But now the Beretta's slide had locked open, meaning that I was out of ammo, and almost out of hope. I had a spare clip in my pocket, but I'd never be able to reload before the little green bastards were on top of me.

Two goblins left. Two knives. And me with no cold iron at all – except...

I snaked my left hand back near my hip and grabbed the handcuffs off my belt. I wasn't hoping to restrain the two goblins, but the cuffs are made of an alloy that contains silver – and cold iron.

I wrapped three fingers around one of the cuffs and swung the other one like a flail. I caught one of the goblins full in the face and he yelped and jumped back. It wasn't pure cold iron, but the blow had both hurt and surprised him.

The other one hesitated, and I thought for a second they might back off and give me room to run, but then the first goblin gave his misshapen head a quick shake and came in again. After a moment, his buddy joined him. I swung the cuffs again, but this time he ducked and the other one came in under my raised arm. I stiff-armed him back, but that was only going to work once – even goblins aren't *that* dumb. They separated a little now, muttering in their incomprehensible language, and I tried to console myself with the thought that Karl would track down these little bastards, and whoever had sent them, and then God help the whole fucking bunch. I figured that thought was going to be one of my last when a deep voice behind me said calmly, "Drop flat."

I didn't hesitate. A half second later I was on the ground, trying to turn my head around and see what was happening. I heard a loud *thump* and looked up in time to see the nearest goblin's face explode in a bloody mass of fur and bone. The last one stopped, looked at the remains of his pal, then screeched and threw himself at whoever was behind me. He got maybe half a step before another shotgun blast practically cut him in half.

I rolled over on my back to get a look at whoever had just saved my ass. He'd only said two words, but that was enough for me to know that the voice wasn't Karl's.

The first thing I saw was the weapon – a cut-down shotgun with smoke drifting from the end of a foot-long tube attached to the barrel. I'd heard they made silencers for shotguns, but never saw one in use until now. Very handy, if you were looking to kill somebody with certainty and not make a lot of noise about it.

I tried to focus on the man who was now lowering the weapon. He wore a long black leather coat that hung open to reveal the bandolier of shells across his chest, a wide-brimmed hat keeping his face in shadow, and Oakley sunglasses, even after dark. On a lot of people that getup would look silly, but on this man it seemed exactly right. Of course, I'd seen him once before – even though, until recently, I'd thought he was dead.

"*Sharkey*." It wasn't a question – I knew who he was.

He looked down at me and a smile split his thin face for an instant. He touched the brim of his hat, said, "Evening, Sergeant," in that Darth Vader voice, then stepped back into the gloom at the end of the driveway.

I scrambled to my feet and went after him. I couldn't tell you what I wanted – to say "Thank you," or ask him why he'd saved me, or even arrest him. That last choice was the least likely. Even if I'd had a loaded gun, I'd have hesitated before trying to arrest Sharkey all by myself.

It didn't matter, anyway. By the time I got to the street it was empty. A couple of my neighbors were out on their porches, but I didn't yell over to ask if they'd seen the man in the hat and leather coat. Most people only saw Sharkey when it was too late.

Sirens off in the distance now, wailing like the souls of the damned.

I spent the next hour at my house, answering questions from fellow detectives and giving statements. Then they let me go to work, where I spent three straight hours with Internal Affairs. But it didn't go too bad, for Internal Affairs. They had a couple of new guys, Boothe and Durkin, doing the Q-and-A, and I guess they hadn't yet been through the "Advanced Asshole" course that seems mandatory for everybody on the Rat Squad, because it wasn't nearly as unpleasant as such sessions have been in the past.

It also helped that all the ones I shot were goblins. If I'd iced four humans – with two more courtesy of Sharkey – I'd have been with IA all night and into the next day. But nobody cares too much about a bunch of dead goblins. Maybe they should.

After that it was McGuire's office, where at least I was offered a decent cup of coffee. The lieutenant considers himself a coffee gourmet. He's got a Braun coffee maker in his office, and a can of Maxwell House has never been anywhere near it. He orders these Jamaican Blue Mountain beans from someplace, grinds them at home as needed, and brings the result into work in sealed sandwich bags. He doesn't share it very often, and I don't blame him – that stuff is too good for the common people.

Karl and I sat there with McGuire and the three of us tried to answer the latest Whiskey Tango Foxtrot question – why would a bunch of goblins want to kill me, and why did Sharkey, of all people, stop them?

We were getting exactly nowhere when McGuire's desk phone buzzed. I knew he'd told Louise no calls, but she let this one through. A minute later, I knew why.

McGuire mostly listened, saying "Uh-huh" a couple of times. Then he said, "Thanks, Homer, I appreciate it," and hung up.

He looked at me. "I called in a favor Homer owed me and got him to rush a tox screen on one of the goblins – I told him any one of them would do. Looks like you were on the money, Stan. That little green bastard was wired up to his furry eyebrows. I'd be surprised if the others weren't exactly the same."

"Meth," Karl said. "Jesus H. Christ on a pogo stick."

"I thought after Big Paul got killed" – that was mostly my fault, but I decided not to bring it up – "the State Police raided the goblins' little encampment out there by the city dump."

McGuire nodded. "They did."

"They were supposed to confiscate all that dumped cold medicine the gobs were using to cook with."

"They did that, too," McGuire said. "And the DA told the Loquasto brothers – the city subcontracts dump operations to them – that they'd face criminal prosecution if cold medicine in any quantity was ever found there again. Dom and Louie believed him – they've got people checking every truck that goes in there now."

"So, if there's no more cold medicine at the dump," I said, "how come a bunch of meth-head goblins were after my scalp tonight?"

"Other people are still making meth," Karl said. "Here in the Valley and elsewhere. They must be – the profit on that stuff is *huge*."

I looked at Karl, then turned to McGuire. "So, if the gobs didn't make it themselves, where'd they buy it?"

It was quiet in the little office until McGuire said, "I figure they got it from whoever sent them to kill you."

"*Sent* them?" I said, frowning. "I was assuming they just wanted payback for the goblin I killed in the liquor store."

"That was a year and a half ago, Stan," McGuire said.

"The boss is right, Stan," Karl said. "For gobs to hold a grudge that long would be like a squirrel remembering that you gave him some peanuts last fall. They're not real smart, haina?"

"And here's something else to ponder," McGuire said. "How did those goblins get to your house from where they live, out near the dump? That's what – three miles?"

I shrugged. "Some of them drive, even if they don't have licenses."

"Yeah," McGuire said, "but what were they driving? I got the deputy chief to assign me some manpower, and they used a goblin-sniffing dog to check every parked vehicle for a radius of three blocks from your place. Not a whiff."

I sat and thought about that. "So somebody got these little green fuckers wired on meth, drove them to my place, let them in through the side door of the garage, and told them to wait until I raised the door. Then he just drove away?"

"Could be," McGuire said. "He might've just abandoned them, figuring that no survivors would be able to tell us anything useful, what with the meth and their natural stupidity."

"Or maybe he was parked someplace where he could see your driveway," Karl said. "When you and Sharkey smoked all six of the gobs, he figured there was no reason to hang around any longer, and split."

"Speaking of Sharkey," McGuire said, "that's something else that puzzles me – why did he intervene? I'm glad he did, mind you, but I can't figure his motivation."

"Yeah, me neither," Karl said.

"You two aren't exactly best buddies," McGuire said to me, "and Sharkey isn't known for his compassion. He doesn't just help people for giggles."

"I've been thinking about that," I said. "You're right about the Shark – he doesn't do anything on impulse. The only explanation that makes any sense to me is – Mister Milo."

"You mean the vic from the Radisson?" McGuire said. "I don't get it."

"Milo was sent out here to take care of whoever's been making those snuff films, right?" I said. "When he and his ghouls didn't turn up anything, maybe he figured Karl and me were his best bet for finding the bad guys. So he hired Sharkey to follow us around until we identified the source, then the Shark could step in and do what he does best. Milo must have told him to make sure nothing happened to us in the meantime."

"Yeah, but Milo's dead," McGuire said.

"Doesn't matter," I told him. "Sharkey always gets paid up front, and he's got a strange sense of...

professional ethics – strange, considering what he is, I mean. If he takes your money, he does the job. Period. He doesn't stop until the contract is fulfilled."

"Sounds like you know this dude pretty well, Stan," Karl said.

"Better than I ever wanted to."

Karl looked like he was waiting for me to say more, but when I kept quiet, he didn't push.

"All right, so maybe we know why Sharkey's acting like your guardian angel," McGuire said. "But what we still don't know is who he's guarding you *from*."

"I'd say it's gotta be related to one of the cases we're working, but so far we haven't got shit on any of them. Suspicions and theories – that's it."

"If somebody's trying to take you out, maybe that's a validation of your suspicions and theories," McGuire said.

"Could be," I said. "And that reminds me – in all the excitement I didn't get around to telling you my latest theory – and it's a doozie."

McGuire sat back. "I'm all ears."

I told him my idea that the snuff films and murders of supes – and maybe a human, too – were all being carried out by the same people.

When I'd finished, McGuire didn't say anything. He checked his coffee mug, dumped a mouthful of cold coffee into the wastebasket and poured himself a fresh cup.

"It's a reach, Stan," he said at last. "Especially the part about the snuff films being part of this big Helter Skelter conspiracy. I don't see how they can get the public all upset if the torture murders are all underground – and that's exactly where they are."

"They *have* to be sold on the sly," I said. "It's like kiddie porn – just *possessing* that stuff means you're going to jail, let alone selling it."

"My point exactly," McGuire said.

"Yeah, maybe you're right," I said. "Could be that whoever killed Milo just hates ghouls for some reason, and that's why he gave them special attention. Although I figure all the mutilation was post-mortem, which means it wasn't torture."

"Post-mortem?" McGuire said. "How do you know that? The ME's report hasn't come out yet."

"They weren't restrained," I said. "Nobody who's still alive is going to just lie still while you disembowel him, let alone cut his dick off."

McGuire thought about that for a second. "Could be that your perp is extremely strong. Or maybe he had help, to hold the vics down while he cut on them."

"There's something else to consider, too," I said. "Blood splatter."

McGuire frowned at me. "What about it?"

"There wasn't any," I said. "Or none to speak of, anyway. You cut somebody like that while his heart's still beating, blood's gonna spray all over the place. It'd be on everything. Plus, the vic is sure to struggle, which would increase the mess." I spread my hands. "I saw the room, boss. No mess."

"Sounds like you've proved your new theory," McGuire said. "But that doesn't make the big conspiracy true. You can't horrify people with this stuff if they don't *know* about it."

"They'd know about it if they read it in the fuckin' papers," Karl said. We both stared at him.

"Papers?" I said. "What fucking papers?"

"Remember, Stan? I told you the other night. I got a call from this dude at the *Times-Tribune*, asking if I knew anything about snuff films."

"You didn't say anything to me about this," McGuire said.

"I didn't figure there was anything to say, boss. I told him snuff films were a myth, and not to bother me with that bullshit again." Karl shrugged. "End of story. Or that's what I thought at the time."

"What was his name again?" I asked. "The reporter."

"Mitchell Hansen," Karl said.

"That's right, I remember now," I said. "He left a message with Louise last week for me to call him – I just tossed it. Haven't heard from him since."

"Well, now." McGuire took a sip of coffee and put the cup down carefully. "I got a call the other night from a so-called journalist, asking me to comment about snuff films. I told him my comment was to stop wasting my time with fairy tales." He looked at Karl, then at me. "He said his name was Tod Solin, and that he worked for the *People's Voice*."

We left McGuire's office more puzzled than when we had gone in – and that was saying something. If the local media had the snuff film story, how much did they have? Who had leaked it to them? And even if they figured out what was going on, how could they turn it into a news story without grossing out all their readers? Maybe that was the whole point of this – to make people sick to their stomachs and eager for payback against somebody, anybody.

As we reached our desks, I asked Karl, "Did you talk to that detective in Chicago about those knife wounds?"

"I haven't had the chance to track her down yet, but I'll do it now – as long as McGuire doesn't send us on another call."

"Didn't get the chance? Our shift's half over – what've you been doing all this time?"

"Well, uh…" If vampires could blush, I'm pretty sure Karl would have been.

"Karl – come on, this is me, remember? I don't give a shit if you were buggering a goat on the front steps of City Hall."

Karl shook his head. "That's not fair, Stan – it wasn't a goat, and, besides, we're just good friends. Anyway, those weren't the front steps. There's two side entrances, you know."

"You crack me up, Karl. Now cut the crap. What have you been up to?"

He wouldn't look at me. "Watching your house."

"Watching my – what the fuck for?"

"To make sure nobody came back and set any more traps for you while you weren't home. I figured one attempt on your life is enough for one night, even for a tough bastard like you."

"But how did you–"

"I was here when the OIT call came in. And once I found out the officer in trouble was you, I figured I'd better get over to your place, pronto."

"McGuire OKed that?"

"I didn't bother to ask."

"Jesus, Karl, you took–"

"Just let me finish, all right? When I got there, a couple of black-and-whites had already arrived. I could see that you were OK, and that a bunch of goblins weren't. I didn't figure you noticed me."

"No, I didn't."

"So, after a while," Karl said, "they take you away in a black-and-white, and Forensics does their thing, than a couple of ambulances cart off the dead goblins, then – nothing."

"What do you mean, 'nothing'?"

"I mean no cops stayed around to secure your house. Whoever sent those gobs could've come back and planted a fucking cobra under your welcome mat, and the first thing the department would know about it would be when somebody found your body. So I stayed in the yard and watched. Nothing happened, by the way."

"Shit, man, I–"

"I'm not done," Karl said. "McGuire finally got hold of the patrol commander, who agreed to send a couple of guys over to your place. When they got there, McGuire called me on my cell and said to get my ass back here. So here I am – with my ass intact, in case you didn't notice. Doesn't look like McGuire's too pissed at me, either. Maybe because he'd have done the same thing, if he'd thought of it."

"Can I talk now?" I asked.

"OK, as long as you don't make any fucking speeches."

"No speeches. Just – thank you."

He looked at me for a few seconds. "You're welcome."

"So, are you gonna try to find that Chicago chick now?"

"I'm on the case, Ace."

"Somebody told me that Rachel Proctor is back from her conference. I'm gonna pay her a visit."

"Maybe by the time you get back, I'll have some news from Chi-town."

"Here's hoping."

The office assigned to the department's Consulting Witch was on the floor below us. I took the stairs instead of the elevator. I'd been doing a lot of sitting tonight, with one thing and another. Of course, after those goblins had tried to kill me, sitting down had seemed like a real good idea.

Rachel tends to work nights, for the same reason I do. Her door was open, but I knocked on the glass before walking in.

Rachel's not a very big woman – five foot even and probably 105 soaking wet. Not that I've ever seen her soaking wet – I think she likes me, but not that way. She was wearing her thick auburn hair swept back in a ponytail, and she wore reading glasses that made her look like a schoolteacher –

but the kind of schoolteacher who could turn you into a toad instead of giving you detention, if provoked.

At my knock, she looked up from the thick old book she was reading and smiled. The smile seemed genuine – proof of her good nature, considering the kind of trouble I'd got her in some time back.

"Hello, Stan," she said, pushing back her chair and standing.

"Hey, Rachel. Welcome back from, uh…"

"San Diego. The weather was beautiful." She looked at me more closely. "What's the matter, Stan? What happened?"

"What makes you think anything special happened? I'm a cop – stuff happens around me all the time."

"No, this is personal to you. Your aura's usually a strong turquoise, but there's some gray in it tonight. It's pulsing, which means a reaction to something recent."

She sat down again. "I'm not trying to pry. If it's something you'd rather not talk about, that's up to you. But you can't hide your emotional state from me."

Auras. Jeez. I sat down in one of her visitor's chairs. "I had a little trouble earlier tonight, is all. Some goblins tried to kill me."

"My goddess, Stan! Are you all right? Physically, I mean."

"They never laid a glove on me – or a knife, which is what they had in mind."

Her brow furrowed. "Goblins aren't usually aggressive, unless attacked. I assume you weren't the one doing the attacking."

"Not six of them, I wasn't. But you'd be surprised how aggressive goblins can get when they're pumped full of meth."

"*Meth*." She tilted her chair back and studied me. "There was a problem with some meth-addicted goblins a couple of years ago, wasn't there? You asked me for a potion that would make them compliant."

"Yup. Worked like a charm, too, if you'll pardon the expression."

She looked at me some more. "That was the night Paul DiNapoli died."

"Uh-huh."

"You're still blaming yourself for that, aren't you?"

"Who says I'm blaming myself?" I said that maybe a little louder than I'd intended.

"You did. Just now. But it was already apparent."

"Rachel, no offense, OK? But I didn't come here for psychotherapy, or whatever witches call it."

She nodded calmly. "All right, Stan."

"I'm actually here to warn you."

"*Warn* me? About what?"

"Somebody in the area has been abducting and burning witches," I said.

"Yes, I know. The first one happened before I left. I read about the other one while I was away."

"You checked out the *Time-Tribune*'s online edition?"

"No, the news was posted to a discussion board that I follow," she said.

"Witches have discussion boards?"

"Why not? Everyone else seems to. Sometimes technology is better than magic. But only sometimes."

"Did you... know either of the victims?"

A deep sigh escaped her. "Not personally, although I'm friends with the sister of one." She moved a small paperweight from one part of her desk to another. "And here we thought the burning times were over."

"This isn't the state doing it this, time, Rachel. Or the Catholic Church. It's some lunatic, or a group of them."

"I doubt that made the flames any less painful for the victims, but I take your point. If you don't mind me asking about police business – are you close to catching whoever's responsible?"

"It's not that I mind telling you," I said. "But the answer is kind of complicated, and I've got to get back upstairs. The short answer is, we don't know who's been doing the actual murders, but we may be getting a handle on why it was done. And knowing *why* brings us one step closer to *who*."

"I understand – I think. And I appreciate your candor."

"So, if you already heard about the burnings, you know enough to take precautions until we nail these bastards."

"Yes, I've got a spell prepared to defend myself. I

can invoke it instantly by using a single word of power."

"If you have to use it," I said, "try not to kill the perp. I need him alive and talking."

"I can't kill anyone, Stan. White magic, remember?"

"Just checking." I stood up. "Well, thanks for your time. Good to see you again."

"Stan, before you go…"

"What?"

"Come here a second, will you?"

"Mrs Robinson, are you trying to seduce me?"

"You should live so long." When I stood in front of her desk she said, "Let me see your right hand."

I held it out to her, saying, "You haven't added palmistry to your talents, have you?"

"That stuff's bunk. Turn your hand over."

She gently held my hand with her left, and with her right index finger she began to trace some kind of pattern on my palm.

"That kinda tickles," I said.

"Sssh." She bent over my palm and said a few words in a language I didn't recognize. Then she looked up at me. "Stan, do you remember that night in the liquor store? The night Paul died?"

"Damn right I do." My throat felt tight as I spoke.

"Good." She said a few more words in that unfamiliar language. "Now close your hand and squeeze it. *Tightly*! Tight as you can!"

I did what she asked, feeling foolish.

And then something loosened deep in my chest, like untying a knot I never knew I had in there. I felt like I could take a full breath for the first time in – well, in a year and a half.

Rachel let go of my hand and sat back. "Thanks for indulging me, Stan."

I stared at her. "What did you just do?"

She gave me an enigmatic smile. "Nothing of consequence. Just helped you relax a little, that's all."

I looked at her a little longer. The smile remained in place. "There's something I've been meaning to ask you, Rachel."

"What's that?"

"Why do you wear glasses for reading? Can't you magic up some twenty-twenty vision for yourself?"

"Don't I wish," she said. "No – unlike the black variety, white magic cannot be used for the benefit of the practitioner – at least, not directly. It only allows us to serve others."

"Oh. I was wondering. Well, I've gotta get going."

She nodded. "Of course. Say hi to Karl for me."

"Yeah, I will." I walked to the door, then stopped and turned around.

"Rachel?"

She gave me raised eyebrows. "Yes?"

I wanted to say something about what she'd just done, but no words came out. After a moment I just said, "Goodnight, now."

"Goodnight, Stan."

When I got back upstairs, Karl was talking to his computer – or that's what it looked like. I sat down at my desk and looked over at him.

"So now they're all standing there," he said to his monitor. "Mom, Dad, the three kids, Grandma, the family dog, and a parakeet. They're all naked, dripping sweat and God knows what else. So the talent agent, who's looking a little stunned, says, 'That's quite an act you've got there. What do you folks call yourselves?' And Dad steps forward and says–"

I figured it was time to clear my throat, so I did. Karl looked up, and I said, "What's going on?"

"Oh, Stan, you're back – good. Hey, we're in luck. That lady I was telling you about? Not only does she still work for Chicago PD's Spook Squad, I caught her at her desk. Come on around – bring your chair."

I rolled my desk chair around to where Karl was sitting. As I'd figured, he was using the Sky-Cape media spell that allows people to talk to each other face-to-face online.

Looking at Karl's monitor, I could see a woman sitting at her own computer. The room behind her looked not very different from the one we were in.

"Stan, meet Roz Pavlico," Karl said. "Roz, this is my partner, Stan Markowski."

"Pleased to meet you, Stan," she said. Detective Pavlico looked to be about forty, with brown hair worn short and a round face. She had a hard look about her, but then I've yet to meet a female cop who doesn't. Funny how I never notice that on male cops – maybe because I take it for granted.

"Likewise, Roz – or do you prefer Detective Pavlico?" Even though Karl had introduced us by first names, I thought I'd ask. Women in this job can be touchy about respect, maybe because of all the shit they have to take from male cops.

"Roz is fine," she said. "Karl tells me that you're interested in a guy who we like for a series of killings."

"Have there been more since you talked to Karl about the guy at that conference?" I asked.

"Three or four. We're pretty sure he travels around a lot, although Chicago seems to be his home base."

"So you know who's doing it, but you have no evidence to nail him?"

"Yeah, you know how it is with guys like this. People talk to us but refuse to get on the stand, or witnesses disappear before a grand jury can be convened. And every witness who goes missing, or who's found dead, makes the next witness that much more reluctant."

"You were telling me that this dude seems to specialize in supes?" Karl said. Interesting how he continues to use that word, although some supernaturals consider it a slur.

"That's right," Roz said. "Vampires, mostly, although we've found his trademark on a couple of trolls and an ogre. A few humans as well."

"This guy took down an *ogre*? With a *knife*?" Karl sounded impressed, and I didn't blame him.

Roz nodded. "Looks that way. Around here, he's pretty much regarded as a bamf."

"As a *what*?" I'd never heard the word before.

"Bamf," Roz said. "B-A-M-F. Stands for Bad Ass Motherfucker."

Karl gave a snort of laughter. "Sounds appropri-ate," I said. "So, what is this bamf's name, anyway?"

"Neil Charles Duffy," she said. "He's known lo-cally as 'Duffy the Vampire Slayer'."

"Cute," Karl muttered. Clearly, he didn't think it was.

"Any chance you could send us a copy of this vampire slayer's file?" I asked her.

"I'll have to check with my boss," Roz said, "but he'll probably be cool with it. Anything that gives somebody a shot at nailing Duffy is fine with us. If you guys manage to take him down, we'd prob-ably chip in and send you a bottle of Scotch, or something."

"Thanks, we appreciate it," I said. I gave her my email address and we said our goodbyes. Karl touched a button to deactivate the spell, and the monitor went dark. I stood up and wheeled my chair back where it belonged.

"Think she might be persuaded to send a bag of AB plasma along with the Scotch?" Karl asked.

"If she doesn't, I'll buy you one myself," I told him. I glanced at the wall clock and said, "We've got about an hour before we knock off. You got anything to do – paperwork or something?"

He gave me half a smile. "When *don't* I have pa-perwork?"

"Why don't you work on that for a while? I want to give Lacey Brennan a call."

"Oh, you mean about the–"

"The woman in the snuff film, yeah. The

resemblance looks too close to be coincidental, although I hope I'm wrong."

"I hope you are, too," Karl said. "I like Lacey – but even if I didn't…"

"Yeah, I know."

"Sure, Stan, go ahead. If I run out of forms to fill out, I can always play Angry Bats for a while."

"I think I'll call her from outside. Get some air at the same time."

Karl looked at me for a second, then nodded. "Sounds like a good idea."

I went down to the parking lot. Since we were between shifts, I had the place to myself. I got in my car and called the number for the Wilkes-Barre Supe Squad. On the second ring I heard, "Occult Crimes Unit – how may I help you?"

"Hi, Sandy. It's Markowski again."

"Good evening, Sergeant – or morning, as the case may be. You still lookin' to talk to Detective Brennan?"

"That's right. Is she available?"

"Yep, she's sittin' right at her desk. Hold on just a sec."

There was a click, and a few seconds later Lacey's voice was in my ear. "Hey, Stan."

"Hi, Lacey."

"So, two vamps are in some bar, having a blood together. And in walks this human chick – and she is *hot*. Know what I mean?"

"Sure," I said. I knew better than to interrupt – I'd just have to endure.

"She goes over to the bar and orders a drink. One of the vamps is married, and scared of his old lady besides, so he's out of the running. But the other one's single and something of a stud, as vamps go. So the married one says, 'Get a look at that, will ya? Go on over and buy her a drink, man.' And the other vamp gives this chick the once-over and says, 'Nah, I'll pass.' The married one says, 'How come? She's *gorgeous*.' The other vamp shrugs and says, 'She's just not my type'."

"I don't get it," I said, although I did. "Ohhh, you mean 'type' as in *blood* type. Hey, that's pretty funny, Lacey." It's an unspoken rule between us that I never laugh at Lacey's supe jokes.

"Yeah, whatever," she said. "What's up, Stan? You're not in the hospital again, are you?"

I'd picked up a bad concussion a few months back while saving the world from a race of super-vampires, and Lacey had come over to visit me a couple of times. She'd also sent a few smutty get-well cards, but she doesn't have some kind of a thing for me. Probably.

"No, I'm fine, Lacey. But I want to ask you something kind of unusual."

"It's shaved bare, except for a little landing strip of hair just above. That what you wanted to know?"

For Lacey, the concept of *too much information* doesn't really exist.

"Uh, no," I said, "but thanks for the image. This is something serious – potentially, anyway."

"Now you've got me intrigued," she said. "What is it, Stan?"

"Do you have a sister?"

After a brief silence she said, "Yeah, I have two. One older, one younger. I'm in the middle. Why?"

"Do either or both of them live in the area?"

"Sarah's been in Oregon for years, but Mary Beth lives in Exeter someplace."

"She's the older one, right?"

"Yeah, but how do you know that? What's going on, Stan?" I could hear a thread of unease running through her voice now.

"Maybe nothing. It's hard to say yet. Listen, Lacey, um, your sister, Mary Beth. Have you seen or heard from her lately?"

"We're not close. I get a card at Christmas, that's about it. And I'm not answering any more questions until you stop fucking around and *tell me what this is all about, Stan.*"

"All right," I said. "It's like this: we've come into possession of a video recording which shows a woman being... murdered. And I'm pretty sure it's real, not some fake shit for the pervs to drool over."

"Sweet Christ," Lacey said softly.

"The woman in the video... she bears a resemblance to you. A pretty strong resemblance, actually. In fact, when I first saw it, for a couple of seconds I thought..." I had to stop and clear my throat. "But then Karl pointed out to me – you remember Karl."

"Yeah, sure. Go on."

"Anyway, Karl pointed out that the woman in

the video appeared to be older than you, and a bit heavier – maybe twenty pounds or so. She also had a scar on one leg."

"Oh, dear God. Dear Jesus God." It was almost a whisper.

"We don't have any way to ID the victim, apart from the video. There's no, uh, body that's been found, so far. So, since I thought it was possible that there was some kind of family connection–"

"How did she die?"

"Excuse me?"

"You fucking heard me." Her voice was like flint. "*How did she die*?"

"Lacey, there's no need for this. We don't even know if the woman is–"

"Stan, I want you to listen to me very carefully. I'm going to speak slowly, and I want you to get every word. Understand?"

"Sure." What else was I gonna say?

"If-you-ever-want-even-the-slightest-chance-of-getting-in-my-pants-from-now-until-the-day-you-retire-you-will *tell me how she died*."

For me, getting into Lacey's pants wasn't quite the Holy Grail she seemed to think it was. Or maybe she assumed that was all any man would want from her. I wasn't moved as much by a desire to do her someday as I was swayed by the passion behind her words. That, and the knowledge that if I didn't give her what she wanted, she would probably never talk to me again – and that would hurt a lot more than being denied her charms.

All this went through my mind in a second or so.

"All right, Lacey. But I promise it'll only add to your pain. It's gonna put images in your head that you'll wish had never got there."

"That's my problem. Tell me."

"She died hard, Lacey."

"Somehow, I figured that. Tell me. All of it."

So I did.

I tried to pretend that I was giving a deposition to a grand jury or coroner's inquest. I tried to describe what had been done to the victim in proper sequence, to the best of my recollection. I tried to be cold and clinical, neither adding unnecessary details nor leaving anything out. I tried not to pay attention to Lacey's breathing and the other small sounds she was making. I tried to do all those things, and the only one I failed at was the last one.

At some point, Karl came out of the building and headed for his car. He saw me on the phone and waved, to let me know he was going home. I nodded, but didn't stop talking to Lacey.

"And then she became unresponsive," I said finally, my voice flat as a corpse's EKG, "even to flame from the blowtorch. From this I concluded that the woman had expired. The video ended shortly thereafter."

It was a cool evening, but I hadn't turned the heat on in the car. Still, I was sweating buckets.

Now that my "deposition" was finished, I didn't know what else to say, so I sat there and listened to the sound of Lacey quietly crying. Finally she spoke, in a voice that sounded like she was being choked. Maybe, in a sense, she was.

"Thank you, Stan. That must have been very... difficult for you."

"It was a lot more difficult for you – I know that. I only did it because you wanted me to, Lacey – and it had nothing to do with getting into your pants someday. Nothing."

"I-I believe you, Stan. Thank you."

What was I supposed to say now? *You're welcome*? *I told you so*? I decided to keep my mouth shut, a decision I should make more often.

Eventually, Lacey managed to say, "I have to go now, Stan. I will always remember that you did this for me."

"Lacey – you're not about to do something stupid, are you?"

"No... nothing like that. I am going to sign out early, and tell them I'll be taking a vacation day tomorrow. Then I'll go home, where I will proceed to get very, very drunk. I'll talk to you in a few days, Stan."

"Lacey, if there's anything..." I let my voice trail off.

"I know, Stan. I know. Gotta go. Bye now."

"Bye, Lacey."

Sometimes I hate my job, my life, and the world I live in. I wondered if Rachel had a potion for *that*.

After I finished ruining Lacey's life, I didn't waste any time signing out and heading home. Even so, there were only about five minutes left until sunrise as I pulled into the garage – which was, fortunately, goblin-free this time. I was relieved to see Christine's blue Ford Carpathia parked in the driveway. Worrying about her was about the last thing I needed right now.

Christine was at the kitchen table with the paper, but she stood up as soon as I walked in the door.

"Daddy! Oh my God, are you all right?"

She threw her arms around me and hugged me more vigorously than usual. If it was anybody else applying that much pressure, I'd have made them stop – vampires are pretty damn strong, and I was starting to worry about my rib cage when she finally let go.

She stepped back, and must have seen something in my face because she said, "Oh, my gosh – that must've hurt! I'm sorry, I wasn't thinking. I've just been so worried."

I opened the refrigerator and was glad to see that we still had some pineapple juice. It's pricier than OJ, but nothing tastes better after a long night than a tall glass of cold pineapple juice. Actually, a couple of beers would have been even better, but I had to stay awake for the locksmith, who was coming at 9am. After the shift I'd had, two beers would probably put me in dreamland.

As I poured my juice I asked, "What's got you so upset, babe? Is there something in the paper about my little goblin infestation last night?"

"Oh, is *that* what the smell is? No, there's nothing in the *T-T*, but the driveway's half covered with this sticky green stuff and it smells just *awful*. And I found some of these, too."

She picked up several small round objects from the table and showed them to me. I knew at once they weren't silver, or she couldn't have handled them.

"Let me see," I said, and took them from her.

Each little sphere was the size of a dried pea and the color of an old nickel. "Shotgun pellets," I said. "Double-ought buckshot, looks like. These appear to be cold iron. And the green stuff in the driveway is definitely goblin blood."

"Why were you shooting goblins with a shotgun in our driveway?"

"I wasn't," I said. "Not with a shotgun, anyway. That was my guardian angel."

She ran a hand over her face. "Now I am *really* confused."

"I'll explain everything later," I said, and looked out the window. Dawn was just reaching the horizon. "You better get downstairs, babe, and quick. I'm OK. Stressed beyond belief, but physically undamaged. Now go – I'll fill you in at sundown."

"OK. She gave me a quick kiss on the cheek. "I'm glad you're all right." And then she was through the cellar door and gone. Vampires can move fast when they want to. And at thirty seconds to sunrise, they usually want to.

Hank, the locksmith, showed up at 9.05am and installed state-of-the-art locks on the front and back doors. I've known him for years, and can trust that he won't be giving out duplicate keys to anybody but me. He noted the window alarms and said, "Never saw much point in those. They don't do much good, some guy breaks in while nobody's home."

Or while Christine is – literally – dead to the world. I kept that thought to myself.

"These don't make noise," I said. "Anybody breaks the circuit, they send a signal to the security company, Semper Fi."

"Oh, I see." Hank nodded, keeping his face blank.

"I know – you're thinking that rent-a-cops are pretty much worthless, and you're right, for the most part. But Semper Fi only hires ex-Marines with combat experience. And they're all licensed to carry."

"That's not too bad, then."

Next, I had him install a heavy-duty deadbolt on the basement door. I told him that I wanted the kind that could be opened by a key, from either side.

"Why would somebody wanna lock themselves *inside* the basement?" Hank asked me. Guess he didn't have any vampires in the family.

"Sometimes I throw an orgy down there," I said, my voice as matter-of-fact as my expression. "My guests like their privacy – you know how it is."

He looked at me for a couple of seconds, as if unsure whether he was being kidded. Then he snorted and set to work.

After Hank left, I was finally able to stagger off to bed. As my head hit the pillow, I prayed that I wouldn't dream. But, like most of my prayers, that one went unanswered, too.

● ● ● ●

It was full dark when Christine and I shared break-fast – well, we shared the table, but our menus were different – and I told her about my eventful night. I left out the part about the end of my visit with Rachel, since I wasn't sure yet what exactly she had done, or how I felt about it. But Christine heard everything else.

"Just listening to it makes me feel like my head's going to explode," she said. "I can only imagine what it must have been like to go through it. Pretty tough dude, my old man. Takes a real lickin' and keeps on tickin'." I knew she was referencing an old Timex commercial.

"We'll see how well I keep time tonight," I said. "I feel like the crystal's cracked and the mainspring is about to break from being wound too tight."

"You'll be fine," she said. "But poor Lacey – what an absolutely horrid thing to listen to."

"I only told her because–"

She held up a pacifying hand. "I know, I know. I'd have done the same thing in your place – and in her place too, for that matter. Sometimes there's no easy way out."

"Yeah, I think I heard that somewhere," I said.

"And speaking of easy ways out," she said, "who the fuck is sending goblins after you?"

"Oh, that would be Mister X," I said.

She cocked an eyebrow at me. "Really? Is that his first or last name?"

"For now, it stands for both."

"OK. So who is Mister X, and why does he have it in for my daddy?"

"He's probably the guy – or the gang – behind the snuff films. Karl's theory is that he's like the Columbians. Apparently down there, if somebody so much as whispers something about going after those guys, they take him out. Don't even wait for him to become a nuisance. Just bang-bang."

"And Karl feels Mister X has the same bloody mindset?"

"It explains why somebody took out Milo – who, as far as I know, hadn't turned up anything new about the snuff film operation," I said. "Although he did have Sharkey waiting in the wings, just in case."

"And now Sharkey's your guardian angel."

"I figure Milo paid him to follow me – well, Karl and me – around until we found Mister X. Then Sharkey would step out of the shadows and hit him. And since I can't lead him to Mister X if some goblin sticks a knife in my gizzard, he's keeping me alive until then. And the way this case is going, Sharkey's gonna have to watch my back for a long time to come."

"Even though Milo's dead," she said.

"Sharkey's the most ethical man in the business, they say. As well as the deadliest."

"Well, it would seem better to have him on your side, rather than on your case."

"Amen to that," I said.

"I don't know who Mister X is, obviously," she

said. From deep in her eyes, I saw a glint of red. "But if I ever meet him, he'd better guard his throat."

"That's my girl."

"And in the meantime, somebody's killing supernaturals, in the hope of starting this Helter Skelter race war?"

"They're killing humans, too, and framing supernaturals for it."

"This Howard guy you were telling me about," she said.

"Lester Howard, yeah. If he was really the victim of a vampire, then I'm Mary, Queen of Scots."

"Let's hope you're not," Christine said with a grin. "You wouldn't like the wardrobe, and she came to a bad end, as I recall."

"I'm probably safe," I said.

She took a sip from her cup of heated plasma. "And who's behind this Helter Skelter bullshit?"

"I'm still working on that. For now, let's call him Mister Y, although 'he' is probably a 'they'."

"Except you think X and Y are one and the same."

"I think they might be," I said. "At first, we all figured that the motive behind the snuff films was purely financial – same as the pervs who make kiddie porn."

"Let's not talk about kiddie porn – please. I may be a vampire, but those fuckers are the real monsters."

"No argument from me. But their motive is to make money, and we figured the same was true of the guys behind the snuff films. But now…"

"The press has got hold of the story."

"Looks that way," I said. "Maybe some nosy reporter just stumbled over it. But if info about these videos was deliberately leaked – well, a lot of people are gonna get real upset when they hear about these supernatural torture sessions."

"More ammunition for Helter Skelter."

"Could be, honey. Could just be."

I could see that McGuire had visitors. Thorwald and Greer were in the office with him, looking serious. I think there's a course they offer down there at Quantico called "Federal Gravitas 101." Or maybe it's just that their job doesn't present too many occasions for giggles. Come to think of it, neither does mine.

I looked at Karl, who was sitting at his desk. "How long have J. Edgar's finest been in there with the boss?"

"Beats me," he said. "I just rolled in a couple of minutes ago myself, and they were already here."

"I want to talk to the Feebies, but I don't think we oughta just sit here with our thumbs up our asses waiting for the privilege."

"Amen to that," he said.

"Let's get out of here," I said. "I had a long, painful talk with Lacey last night. I wanna tell you what she–"

McGuire must have noticed that I'd come in, because he went to his office door and waved me over.

"Great," I said to Karl. "Well, let's go."

"Not sure I was included in the invitation."

"You are now," I said. "Come on – maybe you can intimidate Thorwald with your fangs."

"I've got something else I could intimidate her with," he said, getting to his feet. "But the boss probably wouldn't appreciate my whipping it out in his office."

"You mean your pistol."

"'Course I do," he said. "What else?"

McGuire's office wasn't built to accommodate five people comfortably, but then sometimes comfort's overrated.

I guess Thorwald didn't think so. "It's kind of cramped in here, so perhaps Detective Renfer could excuse us?"

"No, he couldn't," I said. "We work as a team, just like you and your partner."

"If it gets bad, I could always turn into mist and float above everybody," Karl said.

"You can really do that – create mist?" Greer asked him.

"Sure," Karl said. "Every time I fart."

"Let's cut the crap," McGuire said. "Agents Thorwald and Greer have been working on identifying the victims in the snuff videos," he said. I guessed the issue of Karl's presence was settled.

I looked at Thorwald. "Any luck?"

"At the Bureau, we don't believe in *luck*," she said. "But intelligence and hard work did pay some dividends, yes."

Looks like Greer wasn't the only one to complete the "How to Be a Federal Asshole" course.

I kept my mouth shut. Next to me, Karl muttered a word in my ear that sounded like "hunt", but probably wasn't.

Seeing that I wasn't going to rise to the bait, Thorwald said, "We have been able to identify three of the victims. None of them are from Scranton, which is why they didn't appear on your department's missing persons list. But only one of the three even had an MP report filed – by his mother, who lives in Arizona and became alarmed when her son never answered his phone or returned her calls. These are solitary men, which probably explains why they were marked for abduction by the snuff film makers."

She reached into her big leather bag and pulled out three manila folders. She put them, one at a time, on McGuire's desk.

"Albert Becht, 41, of Old Forge. Daniel Cossick, 29, of West Pittston. And Gregory Ryfa, 38, of Wilkes-Barre."

I noticed that the files didn't look very thick. But at least they were files, and they did have victims' names on them.

Thorwald pulled a notebook from the bag, opened it, and flipped some pages. "Becht was in video number 2 as the torture victim. Cossick and Ryfa both appeared in video number 3 – Cossick the possessed torturer, Ryfa the victim."

"Did they know each other?" Karl asked.

"We're working to determine that," she said. "Thus far, I'm inclined to say no. As I said, they tended to keep to themselves."

"Didn't they have jobs?" I asked her.

"No, they didn't. Cossick and Ryfa were both on public assistance, while Becht was living off a trust fund."

"Welfare and a trust fund," I said. "Can't get much more different than that."

"Naturally, we obtained warrants to search their residences," Thorwald said. "They each owned a personal computer, which isn't surprising. The hard drives have been removed and sent to Washington for analysis."

"So now you're looking for common factors," I said.

She nodded approvingly, as if the special needs kid had actually answered a question correctly in class. "Exactly. A cursory study of their homes doesn't tell us much. They shared the usual male interests – sports, beer, and pornography, but the last reflected nothing as extreme as the snuff films. Just the usual tits, ass, and gash."

I wondered if she'd used that last word to prove that she was really one of the guys, or to show her contempt for us.

"Oh, and they all seemed to have an interest in vampires," she added.

If I didn't know better, I'd have said it was chance that she happened to be looking at Karl when she said that last part.

"Lots of people do, from what I hear," Karl said evenly. He wasn't letting himself be provoked, either. "How'd you establish that as a common factor?"

"Different things that we found," Greer said. I guess he felt he was supposed to contribute something. "Books, DVDs, magazines, posters – stuff like that."

Karl nodded. "Makes sense to me. I assume you also checked the contents of their furniture – bureaus, and like that."

"Of course." Thorwald sounded mildly offended.

"Did all three of these guys, by any chance, have… a sock drawer?"

Thorwald gave McGuire a "See? Told you we should've kicked him out" look and said, "Is there some point that you're attempting to make, Detective?"

Karl shrugged. "Since they all have socks in common, I was just wondering if maybe we were dealing with a bunch of foot fetishists."

I tried to keep the smile from growing on my face, I really did. Greer appeared puzzled, and McGuire apparently felt the need to cough.

It's a pity that nobody took a photo of Thorwald's face right then. It would have been a perfect illustration in some dictionary, next to the definition of "Rage (barely suppressed)".

Before Thorwald could grab a pencil from the nearby desk and try to drive it through Karl's heart, McGuire said, a little louder than necessary, "Is there anything else we have to talk about here?"

"Well, there's one thing," I said. McGuire shot me a look that said, "This better not be something smart-ass." I went on, "I think I have an ID on the female victim in the latest snuff video."

Thorwald had her notebook out again before I'd even finished speaking. Fast hands. I hoped I'd never have to outdraw her – or try to.

"I think her first name's Mary Beth. If it is, then her maiden name was Brennan, although she might've gotten married along the way and changed it. She lives – lived – somewhere in Exeter, which is a little town–"

"I *know* where Exeter is, Sergeant," Thorwald said. "What I'm uncertain about is exactly what *you* know. I'm hearing 'think', 'might've', and 'somewhere'. None of that exactly inspires confidence in your information. Do you have an ID on the victim, or don't you?"

Karl had her pegged, all right. *Hunt* – or something like that.

I took a deep breath and let it out, in an effort to calm myself down a bit. Then I said, "I used all those qualifiers because I wanted to be precise about what I know at this point, and what I don't. I think it's highly probable that the female vic started life – and maybe ended it – as Mary Beth Brennan. I'll probably have more solid information in a day or so, including an ID based on a screen cap of the woman's face, if you'll loan me that DVD again, or let me burn a copy."

"Why 'a day or so', Markowski?" Greer said. "You holding out on us?"

Control. Keep calm. Shooting FBI agents is a felony, even if they deserve it.

"I'm not holding out anything," I said. "It's just that the situation's complicated. Here's why."

I told them about my initial mistaken ID of the victim, then about my phone conversation with Lacey the next day. I left out the part where she threatened to deny me access to her beautiful ass forever if I didn't spill the beans – it would've given them the wrong impression, both about Lacey and about me.

When I was done, both Thorwald and Greer were looking at me with the kind of expression you see on a Statie when he pulls you over for doing fifty in a school zone.

"I cannot believe," Thorwald said, "that you would be so unprofessional as to reveal the very existence of these videos, let alone the contents of one, without clearing it with us first."

"I would have," I said, "but you two haven't been around the last two nights. And I understand that you refused to give your contact information to our PA."

McGuire looked at me, then at Thorwald. "You haven't given us any way to contact you?"

"That information is released on a 'need to know' basis," Thorwald said.

"And you don't think that these officers," McGuire said, "who are working on the case that *you* brought to us, might have a need to know how to get in *touch* with you?"

"Messages left at the local FBI field office will be forwarded to us," Thorwald said primly. "And right now I don't wish to be distracted from the issue of Sergeant Markowski's carelessness in revealing what is essentially confidential information."

"I didn't give it to the *New York Times*," I said, "or even to the *Times-Tribune*. I told a veteran detective who knows how to keep her mouth shut."

"A veteran detective who's now got an emotional involvement in the case," Greer said.

"Some people are funny that way," I said. "When you tell them that one of their close relatives has been tortured to death, they get all upset."

"I still say you shouldn't have told her," Thorwald said. "She could have been shown one of those screen caps you were talking about earlier, and asked to make an identification of the woman in the photo."

"Yeah, that would work," I said. "You show Lacey Brennan a photo of a woman's face and ask, 'Is this your sister?' And when she wants to know why you're asking, you say 'Sorry, that's classified information.' I'm ninety-nine percent certain she'd tell you to–" I turned to Karl. "What's that expression she uses?"

"You mean 'Go fuck yourself'?"

"That's the one." I turned back to the Feebies. "She'd tell you to go fuck yourself. And you know what – she'd be right."

The two FBI agents looked at each other for a couple of seconds, then Thorwald gave a long-suffering sigh. "Well, since the cat's out of the bag, we may as well make use of it. I'll need contact information for this Detective Brennan."

I gave her a tight smile. "Sorry. That's classified."

She glared at me, then turned to McGuire. "Lieutenant, would you *please* tell your officer to–"

"All right," I said. "All right. What I meant was, it would be a bad idea to try to talk to Lacey about this today."

Instead of asking the question, Thorwald just gave me raised eyebrows.

"Because she's still in the initial hours of grieving," I said, "and because right now she is either *a*) drunk, or *b*) viciously hung over. You shouldn't try to talk to her in either condition."

"Unless you enjoy being told to go fuck yourself," Karl said. "And if that's your kink, we can save you the ride to Wilkes-Barre and do it for you right here."

"Let me talk to her," I told Thorwald. I tried for a reasonable tone of voice. "Tomorrow. If you'll give me a screen cap of the victim's face, I'll show it to her. If she IDs it as her sister, then I'll get all the information I can from Lacey about her."

"I thought you said the two women weren't close," Thorwald said, but she sounded like she was trying for reasonable, too.

"I did, but Lacey also told me that they exchange Christmas cards, so she'll have the address, at least. I'll get that, along with the sister's current last name and anything else that Lacey knows. Just give me twenty-four hours, forty-eight at the most. What do you say?"

"*I* say you ought to–" Greer began, but Thorwald made a sharp gesture and cut him off like a guillotine. "Very well, Sergeant," she said calmly. "If you'll give me your email address, I'll have some screen caps made, showing only the victim's face, and send them to you. When you have some information about said victim, I'd like to know about it. Fair enough?"

I gave her a nod. "Fair enough."

Her voice was mild, but the message in her eyes was the same one you'd get from a high school bully whose torments have been interrupted by a teacher: "We'll finish this later."

As I got behind the wheel I said to Karl, "Still think Thorwald likes me?"

Karl fastened his seatbelt and pretended to ponder it. "Well, maybe the same way that Cain liked Abel, something like that."

"Yeah, I was thinking along those lines myself."

"Where we going?" he asked.

"Let's pay another call on the rug merchant," I said. "I wanna ask Castle how it is that a few hours after we're talking to him about Helter Skelter, I've got a bunch of goblins in my garage, wanting a close-up look at my liver."

"You think Castle's on the same side as people who are killing supes and making snuff films? Those guys oughta be Castle's worst enemy, man."

"Yeah, you'd think so, wouldn't you? But if we're working off the assumption that the gobs were sent after me because we're on the trail of those Charlie Manson wannabes, how many people know that? Castle sure did."

"That's true," Karl said. "Plus whoever Castle told about it. Maybe he put the word out to the local supe community – 'Anybody heard anything about Helter Skelter? A couple of cops think someone's trying to make it happen here in Scranton'."

"If he did that, wouldn't *you* have heard something?"

"Not necessarily," Karl said. I caught his grin out of the corner of my eye. "I haven't been going to the meetings."

"We'll see if we can get Castle to tell us who he's been talking to."

"You know who else could've put out the word that we're looking into Helter Skelter?" Karl asked.

"Who?"

"Pettigrew. Our favorite human supremacist."

"Why would he do that?" I said. "He doesn't want Helter Skelter to start – he isn't sure his side would win."

"Maybe he didn't do it deliberately," Karl said. "Could be he told somebody he trusted, who told somebody else, who told the bad guys – whoever they are."

"Yeah, that's not exactly impossible, is it? Guess we better add Pettigrew to our list of people to see."

"*We*? You mean I get to go along this time?" To his credit, there wasn't a lot of sarcasm in Karl's voice. A little, maybe – but not a lot.

"Sure," I said. "Maybe your fangs'll scare him."

"They didn't work real well with Thorwald."

"Shit, Pettigrew's not *nearly* as tough as Thorwald."

Karl snorted laughter. "You know, it occurs to me, Pettigrew's little Nazi playpen is closer than the rug shop from here. Save us from doubling back if we go there first."

"Sounds like a plan, man," I said, and turned right at the next corner.

About five minutes later, we pulled into the parking area of Born to Be Wilding. The only other vehicle there was a customized Harley that I was pretty sure belonged to Pettigrew. Good – he was still here. I would've figured that anyway, since all the lights in the place were on.

As I turned the engine off, I said to Karl, "Look, I don't expect you to put up with any shit from Pettigrew, but try not to start something, OK?"

Karl unlatched his seatbelt. "I seek peace, and pursue it," he said, the way you do when quoting somebody.

I looked at him. "Where's that from?"

"Psalm 34."

"You've been reading something besides James Bond," I said.

"No Bibles for me anymore. I just remember it from school."

We were walking toward the open service bay when Karl suddenly stopped. "Uh-oh."

"What?"

"Blood, close by," he said. "Fresh, and lots of it."

"Human?"

"I think so."

As we started forward again, I drew my weapon and saw Karl do the same. That turned out to be unnecessary – the only one in there was Pettigrew, and he wasn't going to be dangerous to anybody ever again.

The human supremacist lay on his back near one of the big workbenches, splayed out like an abandoned rag doll – except you never find Raggedy Andy in a pool of his own blood. Pettigrew's lips were drawn back in a snarl, as if he were defying what had recently killed him. Most of his throat seemed to be missing.

After a quick look around to be sure that nobody was lurking, we walked toward Pettigrew, stopping at the edge of the blood pool.

"Pardon the stupid question," I said to Karl, "but is he dead?" If by some fluke Pettigrew was still alive, I'd be legally and morally obligated to try CPR and call an ambulance. Otherwise, I planned to stay out of the blood and not mess up the crime scene.

"No heartbeat at all," Karl said. "He's gone."

"Can you tell how long?"

"Uh-uh. But it's a fresh kill."

Karl's voice sounded a little shaky. It couldn't be because he was grieving for Pettigrew – if anything, he'd probably have a drink of plasma to celebrate. That's when it hit me. My vampire partner was in the presence of an awful lot of the stuff that constituted his diet. His training as a detective was probably warring with a strong impulse to start drinking the evidence.

"Listen, Karl, you wanna wait in the car? It's cool."

"No, I'm all right." His voice didn't completely support his words.

"Are you sure? Because I–"

"*I said I'm all right.*"

"OK, then. OK."

I knelt down and touched a finger to the blood on the floor. It was only slightly tacky, which supported Karl's conclusion that the attack had been fairly recent – probably within the last couple of hours.

We were supposed to call this in, but I figured there was no hurry. And I wanted to have a look around before every cop and forensics tech in town started traipsing through the place.

As I stood up, I said to Karl, "You're the one with the super-acute vision. See anything that I'm missing?"

He didn't answer for a couple of seconds, and I wondered if he had zoned out on me. But then he said, "There are some hairs in the blood. See there?" He pointed, and I could just make out three or four hairs, a couple of inches long. "There's more over there," Karl said, and pointed again. "And some more, over near the body."

"Nice of the killer to leave us with so much evidence," I said.

"Yeah, I was just thinking that myself," Karl said. "And get this – I'm pretty sure it's not human."

"What, then? Dog?" I was pretty sure that Pettigrew didn't keep a dog here. And if he had, it would probably be howling over his body – that, or lapping up the blood.

"Close," Karl said. "I'd say wolf."

"Well, fuck me," I said. "You saying our perp's a werewolf?"

"I'm saying that's what somebody *wants* us to think."

I turned and looked at him. "And where did *that* come from?"

"Main reason is, there's no wolf smell," Karl said. "I got a good whiff of it the other night at Nay Aug, so the scent's fresh in my memory. And I'm getting – *nothing*. There's probably some on the hairs, or fur, but the blood is masking it."

"Anything else you've noticed?"

"Yeah, no blood spatter or trail of blood drops."

I glanced around the garage, "Yeah, it is pretty clean, isn't it – apart from the pool he's lying in."

"And it makes no fucking sense," Karl said. "Think about it, Stan. We're supposed to believe that a great big wolf attacked Pettigrew and tore his throat out. But there's no defensive wounds, no claw marks, nothing like that. Guy like Pettigrew, he'd fight."

"Yeah, I'm with you."

"And, shit, you've seen animal attacks before – we both have," Karl said. "Tearing somebody's throat out, even if you've strong jaws and a good set of sharp teeth, is gonna be messy. Blood flying all over, arterial spray, the whole nine yards."

"In contrast, what we got here is almost… surgical."

"Fuckin' A. And if our hypothetical werewolf did kill the guy, he couldn't help but get blood on him – all over himself, probably. And yet he ran off without getting a drop of it on the floor, all the way to the door and beyond."

"So somebody set up a fake werewolf attack for us to find." I nodded slowly. "You wanna say it this time?"

"What – Whiskey Tango Foxtrot?"

"Uh-uh. Helter Skelter, man. Helter fucking Skelter."

We called Homicide, which was a nice change from them always calling us. Scanlon arrived with a couple of his guys shortly after a couple of black-and-whites pulled in, lights flashing and sirens wailing. They didn't have to hurry – Pettigrew wasn't going any-where.

Karl and I had just started to explain to the uni-forms how we'd come to discover Pettigrew when Scanlon walked over and said to them, "I'll take care of interviewing these officers. You two secure the scene – the media jackals have police radios, and they'll probably be here any minute. I don't want them fucking up my crime scene by walking all over it."

My crime scene. Scanlon was taking over – good. That's exactly what I wanted.

"Something I wanted to ask you, Lieutenant," I said. "How come you still show up at these things, while my boss stays back at the office instead of coming to ours?"

"It's his choice," Scanlon said. "We all have our own ways of doing things. I like to be on the street, and fortunately, I've got a sergeant who stays in the squad room and runs things pretty well when I'm not there." He gave me a quick grin. "From what I hear, McGuire doesn't have that luxury. Now – you wanna tell me about this?"

Karl and I took turns filling him in on what we knew, and what we suspected. As we were finishing up, an ambulance arrived with the guy from the ME's office. Actually, it wasn't a guy, but a painfully thin woman named Cecelia Reynolds, one of the three pathologists who work for the ME and the only one that I never joke around with. A very serious lady, is our Doctor Reynolds. But then, I hear she grew up in the South Bronx and proceeded to work and study her way out – all the way to a full scholarship at Columbia University's med school. I guess *serious* is her default setting.

I asked Scanlon to excuse us, and Karl and I drifted over to where Cecelia was pulling on a pair of latex gloves. "Good evening, Cecelia," I said.

She looked up. "Hi, Stan. Karl."

She looked at Karl a second or two longer than necessary, something I'd only noticed her doing a few months ago. Maybe she found Karl's new state intriguing. I sometimes wondered if she was a vamp vixen – a human woman who's into the undead – but any vampire who put the bite on Cecelia had better not be looking for a big meal.

"So," she said, "looks like we have us a nice, messy homicide here."

"At first glance," I said, "it looks like a werewolf killing."

"Do tell. I never worked one of those."

"Well, I hope you didn't have your heart set on it, because this probably isn't your lucky night."

"What are you talking about, Stan?"

"There's a good chance that whoever killed the dude over there tried to make it look like a werewolf is responsible."

She frowned. "Why on Earth would someone do that?"

"The answer to that's long and complicated, and I'm sure you've got better uses for your time tonight. I'll tell you all about it some night over a beer."

Cecelia looked at me, her head tilted a little to one side. "That promise is based on the assumption that I would consent to the behavior in question, Stan – an assumption that has yet to be tested."

"Could I have that in English, please?"

"You're assuming that I'd be willing to have a beer with you sometime."

"Does that mean you won't?"

"No, it merely means you should be careful about your assumptions."

"Duly noted," I said. "Now, about the deceased over there…"

"Yes?"

"When you're doing the post, you might want to check the ratio of serotonin to free histamines, to see if he was alive, or at least conscious, when he was killed. And while you're looking at his blood, it might be worthwhile to check for poison or some sort of tranquilizing agent."

The smile she gave me was as bright as it was false. "Goodness me, Sergeant, if I didn't know better, I'd have sworn that you were just telling me how to do my job."

"Not at all," I said. "And I apologize if I gave offense. But tell me something: *would* you have checked the serotonin-free histamine ratio as part of your regular procedure?"

One of the things I like about Cecelia is her utter honesty. After a couple of seconds she said, "No, Stan, I probably wouldn't have. The snarky comment is hereby withdrawn."

"Fair enough. I was–"

Karl's head lifted a couple of inches, like a hunting dog that hears the far-off sound of geese approaching. He said, "Pardon me," and started walking rapidly toward the open bay door.

"Something wrong?" I called after him.

"Think I hear the radio." Can't beat those extra-sharp vampire senses. It was nice to have them on my side, for a change.

I chatted with Cecelia for another minute or two, then Karl came back in the garage. "Stan."

"What's up?"

"Radio call. It's McGuire."

He turned and went back out, and I followed him. Over my shoulder I said to Cecelia, "Gotta run. Talk to you after the post, OK?"

I saw her nod and then I concentrated on getting out to the car without quite running. McGuire wouldn't get on the radio personally just to ask us to pick up a pizza.

As we reached the car, I asked Karl, "Did he tell you anything?"

"Better hear it from him," Karl said.

No, definitely not a pizza run.

I got in, and grabbed the radio. "This is Markowski."

"This is McGuire."

Yeah, I knew that already – get to it.

"Yes, boss."

He said, "Sefchik and Aquilina are in the house, but I thought I'd try to reach you first. Figured you might want this one, since it concerns Rachel Proctor."

Please don't tell me that she's the latest witch to be burned. Please, for the love of God, don't tell me that.

"What happened?" I didn't yell, but everything in me wanted to.

"For starters, she's OK. So cool those jets of yours."

Guess McGuire could tell that I'd wanted to yell.

"All right, boss. What's up with Rachel?"

"Looks like our witch burner may have made a try for her tonight."

"And…?" I asked.

"She had a spell of some kind ready, and she zapped the bastard," McGuire said.

"Good for her – but 'zapped' how?" I already knew she couldn't have killed him. White magic, and all that.

"Froze him in place, apparently. Maybe you ought to get over there, have her thaw out the suspect, and bring him in. There's a black-and-white on scene already, but I figured you'd want in on this."

"As my partner likes to say, *Fuckin' A*. Where's 'over there'?"

"Rachel's house," McGuire said. "I guess the guy made his move on her front porch."

"We're on the way. Markowski out."

As I started up, Karl said, "*Fuckin' A*? You stealing my lines, now?"

"I was only borrowing that one, Mister...?" I let my voice trail off, figuring that Karl would get what I was doing.

He did. He gave a laugh, then said, in his best Sean Connery imitation, "Renfer. Karl Renfer."

The black-and-white unit, red and blue lights flashing, was parked in front of 1484 Stanton Street, and I slid our car in behind it. Rachel's front porch light was on, and under its illumination I could see Rachel, two uniformed officers – and a strangely posed mannequin. At least, it *looked* like a mannequin.

As we approached the porch, I could see that one of the uniforms was talking to Rachel, his notebook and pen in hand, while the other one stood next to the thing that looked like it belonged in a display window at Boscov's, or maybe in Madame Tussauds wax museum.

We mounted the creaking steps and went over to Rachel, who looked like she'd had a shock but was holding herself together pretty well. Karl probably would have said that she appeared shaken, but not stirred.

I nodded at the uniform who'd been talking to her. His name was McHale, and I'd been seeing him around for the last five years or so. He was tall and broad, the dusting of freckles across his nose an odd contrast to his King Kong physique. He took a couple of steps back as I approached Rachel.

"How you doing, kiddo?" I said to her.

"I'm not bad, considering, and stop calling me 'kiddo'."

I tried not to smile. Same old Rachel.

"Wanna tell me what happened?"

"As I was saying to Officer McHale, I got home about half an hour ago. I was standing in front of the door, sifting through my keys to find the right one. I heard a sound off to my left. I looked, and he–" she pointed with her chin toward the still figure "–was coming at me quite fast, his arm extended the way you see now."

"You didn't notice him before that?" I asked. I glanced around her porch. "There isn't anyplace to hide up here."

"The porch light was off – I only went inside and turned it on after the excitement was over. He'd been hiding in the shadows over near the side railing."

"Gotcha. So you look over your shoulder and see him coming at you. Then what?"

"As I told you when we talked last, I had a spell ready, the kind I could invoke with a single word –

and the proper gesture. So I made the gesture, said the word, and *voila* – instant statuary."

"Nice casting," I said. "I'm glad you were prepared."

"Me, too." Her lips compressed grimly. "Especially considering the fate I would probably have suffered, if this *motherfucker* had been successful in abducting me."

Rachel rarely swears. The fact that she'd done so meant that she wasn't feeling quite as calm as she looked. Not that I blamed her.

"So then I went inside," she said, "turned on the outside light and got my phone out. I called 911 and reported the attack, then realized that I probably should have called 666 instead. So I did."

"Never hurts to cover all the bases," I said, then turned to Karl. "Keep Rachel company for a few minutes, will you? I wanna check out our perp."

"Sure," Karl said, stepping forward. "Hey, Rachel. How's the witch business?"

"Not bad, Karl. How the vampire business?"

"It kinda sucks, but that's not always a bad thing."

I left those two to trade bad puns and went over to the human statue.

If this was a museum, the exhibit could be titled "Cat Burglar – Early Twenty-first Century". Or maybe the guy had Googled "Commando", then clicked on "Illustrations" and copied the results – to the letter.

His wiry build was right for the role, anyway. He looked flexible and strong, but without a lot of bulging muscles. Rachel's attacker seemed to be around thirty, and that was all I could tell about him, apart from the outfit.

He was dressed completely in black – pullover sweater, gloves, jeans, and shoes. I'd have to check later, but I was betting he wore black socks, too. To top it off, he even had the black stocking cap pulled down low over his ears. Put some black camo paint on his face – the one part of the look he'd passed up – and this role-playing asshole would be all ready for a raid on some Nazi ammo dump. He was perfect.

His posture now looked like what you get when you hit Pause on your DVD player. His feet were well apart, one in front of the other, as if he'd been moving fast when the magic hit him. His right arm was extended, fist clenched. He was holding something white in his clenched hand, so I stepped close for a look and saw what appeared to be a folded handkerchief. Then I stepped closer, and took a whiff. Chloroform.

Old school all the way. Jesus.

He was being guarded, if that's the word, by the other uniform, whose name was Perrotta. I'd seen him around before. He had smart-looking brown eyes, and the thick mustache that covered his upper lip was within department regulations, but only by a millimeter or so. I nodded to him and said, "Have you advised the prisoner of his Miranda-Stoker rights, yet?"

Perrotta shook his head. "No way for him to show that he understood 'em, Sarge, the way he is now. Don't want some shyster lawyer gettin' him off later on a technicality."

"Good thinking," I said. "We'll Stokerize him ourselves, once he's thawed out. You frisk him?"

"Sure, Sarge. He had this on him."

Perrotta produced an evidence bag – which is just a plastic sandwich bag with "Evidence" stamped on it – and handed it to me.

It took me a second to realize what I was looking at. "Christ, it's a fucking blackjack," I said. "I haven't seen one of those in years." I handed the bag back to him. "Anything else of interest?"

"Just the usual – wallet, keys, handkerchief, pocket change. I left it all in place."

"Did you check the wallet for ID?"

"Yeah, I did – and get this: there was *nothing*."

"No ID, you mean?"

"I mean *no nothing*," Perrotta said. "Only thing in the wallet was cash. No drivers license, no registration, no credit cards, not even a fucking library card."

"How much cash was he carrying?"

"Exactly $440."

"You mentioned keys," I said.

"Just a set of car keys, left front pocket."

I reached into the guy's pocket and pulled out a key ring. No helpful bauble dangled from it – I'd been kinda hoping for a plastic tab that said *Witch Burners Club*, with an address and phone number. But my luck never runs that good. All I got were two Ford keys on a plain metal ring.

I handed the keys to Perrotta.

"Once Detective Renfer and I have secured the suspect, I want you and your partner to check every Ford vehicle parked on this block, until you find the one that the keys fit."

"OK, Sarge."

"You shouldn't have to look real hard – he's got to be parked close by. You don't go carrying a limp body any distance around this neighborhood, even at night."

"Maybe the scumbag had an accomplice," Perrotta said.

"One who drove off when Rachel zapped this guy? Yeah, could be. But we gotta look for the car, anyway."

"Yeah, I know. What do you want us to do, assuming we find it?"

"First thing, check it over, including the trunk. I wanna know if this dude was carrying a can of gasoline and maybe some rope. Stuff like that."

Perrotta nodded. "Sounds like you like this guy for the witch burnings."

"Yeah, and I'll like him even better for it if there's rope and gas in his back seat." I handed him my card. "If you turn up something, I want you to call me – ASAP."

"Sure, will do."

"Then have the vehicle towed to the impound lot. Tell whoever's on duty that the vehicle is *not* to be released to *anybody* without my specific authorization."

"Got it, Sarge."

"Be sure to get a receipt from the impound lot. Leave it, with the keys, in my mailbox at the house. If you didn't find the car, then just leave the keys. There's no big hurry about that last part," I said. "I won't get to the car until tomorrow." I looked at the frozen figure next to me. "I'm gonna spend the rest of tonight having a nice chat with Chuck Norris, here."

I went over to where Rachel and Karl were quietly talking. "Rachel, did you happen to notice if some vehicle, maybe one parked nearby, took off in a hurry once you took care of that guy?"

Rachel bit her lip for a few seconds, then shook her head. "I don't remember anything Stan – but I have to admit I was kind of distracted for a while there."

"OK, just thought I'd ask. Now, you wanna thaw this jerk out for me? We're taking him down to the station house, and it's gonna be tough getting him in the car if he can't bend."

"Sure, Stan. The sooner you take this garbage off my porch, the better."

She stood facing the still figure. "Tell me when you're ready."

Karl and I positioned ourselves on either side of the still figure. "OK," I said. "Go ahead."

She pointed her index finger at the frozen man and said what sounded like "*Keslungi pasha notro*!" – then she dropped her hand abruptly, with a slicing motion.

A second later, the guy lunged for her, but Karl and I were ready for him. We each grabbed a wrist and twisted his arms up behind his back. We had handcuffs on him before he fully knew what was happening.

"What? Hey, let go of me! Where'd you come from? Let me *go*, dammit!"

He was struggling to get free now, but it was a waste of time and energy. Karl held his arm on one side, and I had a tight grip on the other. With my free hand, I showed him my badge. "Police officers," I said. "You're under arrest for trespassing, attempted abduction, attempted assault, and a bunch of other stuff we'll think of later. You have the right to remain silent. Anything you say can and will be held against you in a court of law. You have the right to speak to an attorney. If you cannot afford an attorney, one will be appointed for you. If you are a supernatural being, you have the right–"

Our commando prisoner gave a nasty laugh. "Supernatural being?" he said. "Are you fucking *kidding* me? Do I look like one of those subhuman scum to you?"

I shook him hard enough to get his attention. "Shut up until I finish. If you are a supernatural being, you have the right to have someone of your own kind present during questioning, in addition to an attorney. Do you understand these rights as I have explained them to you?"

"Yeah, sure, I understand. I want a fucking lawyer!"

"You can call one after you're booked," I said. "Let's go."

He didn't fight us as we got him down the steps and over to our car, then put him in back. I glanced over my shoulder towards the porch and saw that one of the uniforms had resumed taking Rachel's statement while the other one bagged the chloro-form-soaked rag the suspect had dropped when he unfroze. A few seconds later, we were on our way to the station house.

The commando didn't say anything en route. There was a time when I might have tried to draw him out. Once he's been Stokerized, anything he says in the car is admissible, although we're not sup-posed to interrogate him without his lawyer. Back in the day, I might've said to my partner, a little louder than necessary, "Boy, that witch sure looked scared, didn't she?" If the suspect wanted to offer his opinion, who were we to stop him?

But not with a vampire riding up front. If the DA tried to introduce as evidence something com-mando boy said in the car, his lawyer would claim that Karl had used Influence to get him talking – and how could we prove otherwise?

Back in 1975, the Supreme Court ruled in *Barlow v. Maine* that information obtained under Influence was inadmissible in any trial, criminal or civil. The DA won't even allow Karl in the room when a sus-pect is being interrogated, even if the perp's lawyer is present.

I've been learning that there are some advan-tages to having a vampire partner, but getting information from suspects under arrest isn't one of them.

Of course, that doesn't apply when we want to know something from a guy – or creature – who *wasn't* under arrest. I hoped Karl would get better at using Influence soon. It would come in handy when talking to informants who we thought might be holding out on us.

At the station house we brought our commando prisoner upstairs, where we turned him over to the booking sergeant. Tonight that was Ron Beck, who's been booking suspects longer than anyone can remember. Some say he once fingerprinted Jesse James, but I don't believe it. Everybody knows Jesse never got this far north. Ron's got thick white hair and a potato nose whose color suggests some experience with alcoholic beverages.

We brought the suspect over to Ron's desk and took the handcuffs off. If commando boy tried anything cute, there were plenty of cops in the room to stop him.

"Have somebody bring him upstairs when he's processed, will you, Ron?"

"Absolutely, Stan," he said. He took our prisoner firmly by the arm and led him off to be fingerprinted.

In the squad room, Karl and I briefed McGuire about the attack on Rachel and the guy who had tried it. I was describing what the perp had been wearing when my phone started playing music. I glanced at it and said, "I'd better take this, boss."

McGuire nodded, so I answered the call.

"This is Markowski."

"Sarge, this is Officer Tom Perrotta from the crime scene earlier tonight."

"Right, Perrotta. What've you got?"

"You pegged it right, Sarge. Three houses down from Rachel's place, other side of the street, we hit the jackpot with an Econoline van. You want the tag number, all that?"

"No, I want to know what you found inside it."

"It was just like you said. In the back of the van he had a five-gallon can of gas, full, and a couple coils of nylon rope. Oh, and a Bible."

I asked, "Which version?" Catholics still stick with the Latin Vulgate edition, while Protestants use the King James. It might give us a clue as to which side of the Christian fence our perp called home.

"Version? Hell, beats me, Sarge. I don't know there was more than one."

"It's all right, forget it – you and your partner did good. Now get that van over to Impound, will you?"

"Already called the tow truck – they're on the way. I'll leave the keys and paperwork in your box, like you said."

"That's great, Perrotta. Thanks."

I closed the phone and said, "The uniforms found the guy's ride – Econoline van parked across the street from Rachel's. Wanna guess what was inside?"

"From the way you're smiling," McGuire said, "I

figure it was something along the lines of gasoline and some rope."

"Fuckin' A," Karl said.

"You both win the prize, gentlemen," I said, "although the real winner is the DA."

We'd all been worried that the commando would only be charged with what had actually gone down at Rachel's tonight. We had him on trespassing – which is a misdemeanor – attempted assault, and attempted abduction. And if that was the whole indictment, the bastard might well make bail.

But since rope and gasoline had been used in both witch burnings, finding it in Mister Commando's van meant the DA could charge him with two counts of abduction and murder, along with the stuff involving Rachel. And since a case could be made that he was motivated to burn the women because they were witches, a trio of civil rights violations might be involved, too – although that's a Federal rap.

Which means that at arraignment, the district attorney's office could ask the judge either for a remand into custody, or for bail so high that the fucking Rockefellers couldn't pay it. And there was a real good chance that any judge would go along.

The last thing I wanted to see was the commando released on bond. He'd disappear faster than a politician's ethics – and be just as hard to recover.

The three of us were grinning at each other when a uniformed officer came into the squad room, looked around until he spotted me, then headed toward McGuire's office.

"Excuse me, Lieutenant," he said to McGuire, then turned to me. "Sergeant, your John Doe is in interrogation room 2."

I looked at him. "My *what*? John Doe?"

"That's what he is, Sarge. Guy refused to give his name. And since he didn't have any ID on him…" The officer shrugged. "He's John Doe."

"Jeez," Karl said. "I would have at least expected name, rank, and serial number."

I stood up. "Well, guess I'll go talk to him. If I can figure out what movie he's got playing in his head, maybe I can tweak the ending a bit."

Karl said, "I'll get started on the arrest report while you're doing that. Don't want him to get sprung because of a paperwork error."

"Let me know how your conversation goes," McGuire said.

"Hell," I said. "You'll probably be able to hear the screams from here."

"His or yours?" Karl asked.

The interrogation room is about eight feet square, with acoustic tiles on the walls and ceiling. The purpose of the tiles is to block out distractions from outside, but if a suspect wants to think the point is to muffle screams, that's not usually a bad thing.

Carmela Aquilina followed me into the room, closing the door firmly behind her. Procedure says at least two cops have to be in there with a suspect. Unlike a lot of procedures, that one makes a certain amount of sense. One-on-one, it was just possible that a suspect could overpower the detective and grab his gun. Then all kinds of bad shit would follow.

Since Karl wasn't permitted in the room, I'd asked Aquilina to back me up. Part of that decision stemmed from the fact that she was available, although I knew that a couple of other detectives from the squad were also in the building someplace. But my other reason for asking her was based on her gender. We didn't yet know what scabs on his psyche our commando was trying to scratch with his witch-burning, but I thought hatred of women might come into it somewhere. If so, having an attractive female cop present might get under his skin, with interesting results.

The commando was seated at the big square table, so Aquilina and I took chairs opposite him. "You and I have already met," I said, "although I didn't get the chance to introduce myself. I'm Detective Sergeant Markowski." I made a nod to my left. "This is Detective Aquilina. And you are…?"

He just stared at me. He was trying for impassive, but the hatred burned in his eyes like twin bonfires. They'd taken the stocking cap off him downstairs, and I saw that his hair was what my mother would have called dirty blond. He had the blue eyes to go with it, too – a regular storm trooper. Pettigrew would have loved him.

"I don't know why you're playing cute about your name," I said. "If you've been in the system, your fingerprints will ID you soon enough. Same thing if you've ever been in the service." I pretended to study him. "You're ex-military, aren't you? What were you – special ops?"

I didn't believe that for a second, but sometimes a little flattery goes a long way. Not this time, though. He just kept that basilisk gaze on me.

"Maybe he's ashamed to tell us," Aquilina said.

I cocked an eyebrow at her. "You think?"

"Could be. If we knew his name, we could look into his background. I wonder what we'd find?"

"Maybe he was a war hero," I said. Aquilina and I had slipped into good cop/bad cop without even planning to. That's another reason why I'd wanted her in the room. She's smart as hell.

"No, I don't think so." She ran her eyes slowly over the prisoner. "Anybody trying that hard to look tough is probably overcompensating for *something*."

"That's not fair, Carmela," I said. "We don't know anything about him."

"We know what we can *see*. I mean, look at the size of his nose, and those short fingers. I think he dresses like a tough guy because he's got a teeny weenie, and he's afraid somebody will find out."

"Oh, come on – you've got no call to say stuff like that."

She gave the prisoner a nasty smile. "Betcha ten bucks he's hung like a hamster."

"How do you figure to win *that* bet?" I asked. "I'm sure not gonna make him undress in front of you."

"Wait until he's been in the county jail for a couple days – and nights." The nasty smile became an evil grin. "Then we can ask his cellmates."

"All right, Carmela, that's enough," I said, making myself sound irritated. "Take a walk. Go get some coffee, or something."

"All right, Stan." Aquilina stood up slowly, as if it had been her idea all along. "I'll leave you and your new boyfriend alone for a while, if that's what you want."

We were violating procedure now, leaving me alone in here with a suspect. But I thought the payoff might be worth it.

When the door closed behind Aquilina, I said, "I'm sorry you had to put up with that. She's not my regular partner. But he's undead, and not allowed to participate in interrogations. That Influence thing, you know."

I was about to offer him a cup of coffee when he spoke for the first time since I'd entered the room, his voice quiet, but filled with contempt. "Bloodsuckers, and witches, and–" He looked toward the door where Aquilina had exited. "–stupid cunts who don't know their place. With those for pals, how does a human like you look at himself in the mirror?"

I shrugged, and tried for a sheepish expression. "Sometimes it isn't so easy."

The smile he gave me matched Aquilina's for nastiness. "Well, don't worry about it, Markowski. You won't have to do it much longer."

"What's that supposed to mean?"

He just shook his head. "I want a lawyer."

"How about you explain what you meant, first?"

The headshake again. "Lawyer. Court-appointed lawyer."

"Uh-uh. You only get a court-appointed lawyer if you can't afford to hire one."

He gave me a shrug of his own. "Fine – so I can't afford one."

"Your wallet, which I'm sure had its contents inventoried downstairs, contained $440. Less than half of that will buy you an attorney to represent you at your arraignment."

"And how am I supposed to hire this cheap lawyer from in here?"

"Just a minute," I said. I got up and left the room. A few minutes later, I returned with a landline phone and a telephone book. Cell phone reception in here, I knew from experience, was terrible. I plugged the phone into a jack in the wall.

"I'll leave you alone for a while," I said. "You can find yourself a lawyer in the phone book. Here's a tip – look under 'A' for attorneys, not 'L' for lawyers. And if you need to take notes – here."

I tossed him a pad of paper and one of those four-inch pencils we give to prisoners. They're supposed to be too small to use as weapons.

He stared at the phone as if I had dropped a fresh warm turd on the table in front of him.

"You'll listen to the call," he said.

"No, I won't," I said. "One, because it's against the law, and two, anything we heard would be inadmissible in court, anyway. What passes between you and your lawyer is privileged."

He chewed on that for a couple of seconds. "You'll still have the number I called."

"So what? We'd be able to figure *that* out based on what lawyer showed up to rep you. We know 'em all, believe me."

He seemed to deflate a little. "How much time do I have?"

"Twenty minutes is customary. Should be plenty of time – all you need to do is hire the guy. You can tell him your story when he gets here. Maybe," I said, "you'll even tell him your name."

He nodded solemnly. "All right – thank you."

Thank you. That was the first thing he'd said that surprised me.

Back in the squad room, I saw Aquilina at her desk, with a cup of coffee. When I walked over, she gestured with the mug. "It seemed like good advice," she said, "so I took it, although the coffee's as bad as ever."

"Thanks for your help in there," I said. "You played the son of a bitch perfectly."

"Did it do any good?"

"Actually, no – but that's not your fault." I looked at her for a second. "Remind me never to do anything that'll get you talking to *me* like that."

Aquilina took a swig of the terrible coffee. "Pretty unlikely, Stan," she said. "You don't look a *thing* like my ex-husband."

I stopped by McGuire's office and told him what

we'd gotten out of commando boy, which was exactly zip.

"Can't say I'm surprised," McGuire said. "Maybe his prints will get a hit – FBI, DOD, something like that."

"I hope so. Although there's millions of people who've never been printed by anybody, anywhere."

"Yeah." McGuire gave me a crooked grin. "What kind of police state is this, anyway, where we can't even make people get fingerprinted?"

"Maybe we'll get his name in court," I said. "He can't be arraigned as a John Doe, can he? At least, I've never seen that happen."

McGuire raised and lowered his eyebrows. "Why not? What are they gonna do – threaten to put him in jail?"

"Guess we'll find out in the morning," I said.

I was sitting at my desk, describing for Karl how Aquilina and I had unsuccessfully tried good cop/bad cop on the suspect, when Karl's head came up suddenly.

"What's up?" I asked. Even though I'd been feeling pretty damn tired, I was suddenly very alert.

"Blood," he said. "There's fresh blood close by, and a lot of it."

It took me two heartbeats to realize what that meant, then I was out of my chair, through the door, and racing down the hall.

A second later, a blur went past me, and I knew my vampire partner would get there first. When I arrived at interrogation room 2, Karl was pushing at the door and meeting a lot of resistance, by the look of it. The door was open about four inches and didn't want to go any farther. This close, even *I* could smell the blood inside the room. Commando boy, it would seem, had done something rash.

"He's got furniture braced up against it, somehow," Karl said. "It's a pretty tight fit."

"Fuck it," I said. "Can you tear the door off its hinges?"

He studied the frame for a second. "Yeah, probably," he said. "The gap where the door's open will give me some leverage."

"Then do it."

"One thing, Stan. Once the door's down, I've gotta get the fuck out of here. That much fresh blood around... I could lose control, and that'd be pretty embarrassing."

"Fine," I said. "Yank out the door, then take off. I'll see you upstairs."

"Right."

Karl reached into the gap and got a grip on the edge of the door. His hands were wide apart, with one set to push while the other pulled. He strained against the door, and after a few seconds the top hinge tore out of the wall. That gave Karl even better leverage, and a moment later the door pulled free with a banshee screech and slammed into the opposite wall. Karl said, "See ya," and was gone before the door crashed onto the carpeted hallway.

Cops – uniformed and not – came running from all directions, drawn by the noise. They were all asking their own versions of "What the fuck happened?" but I didn't answer at first. I was staring into the interrogation room through the empty space where the door had been.

It was pretty clear that commando boy wouldn't be needing a lawyer, after all.

"They searched him down in Booking," I said to Karl. "They emptied the fucker's pockets, then checked him for weapons and contraband. He didn't have anything on him when he was brought into that interrogation room. He was *clean*, Karl."

"I believe it."

"Then I had to go and give him a pencil."

"Don't beat yourself up over it, Stan. Sure, you gave the guy a pencil – that's standard procedure. That's why they keep that box of pencils down there. And they're special pencils, too."

"Four inches long," I said. "With a sharp point."

"Hell, it's *got* to have a sharp point, or you can't fucking *write* with it."

"Yeah, I guess so," I said. "But still…"

"'But still' my ass," Karl said. "They give the prisoners those dinky little pencils for a reason – they're supposed to be too small to be used as a weapon, for either homicide or suicide."

"The motherfucker managed it, though."

"I don't figure whoever ordered those pencils had in mind a guy so determined to off himself that he would dig the thing into his neck, and keep pushing until he opened the carotid artery."

"That does seem to call for a certain amount of determination, doesn't it?" I said.

"*Determination*? It calls for a fucking psycho, that's what. It's like… cutting off your arm with a pocketknife."

"A guy did that, though, didn't he? There was a movie made about it."

"Sure," Karl said. "And the reason they made a *movie* about it is because ninety-nine point nine percent of human beings would never have the guts to do something like that – even if the alternative was dying of thirst in a fucking cave."

"I guess commando boy belonged to that one-tenth of a percent," I said. "Maybe he was special ops, after all."

"I doubt it," Karl said. "He was just nuts. How'd he manage to barricade the door, anyway?"

"He pushed the table against the wall," I said. "Then he wedged a chair against it, and then another chair behind *that* – which brought the whole fucking Tinkertoy setup within a few inches of the opposite wall."

"Shit, no wonder I couldn't force it open."

"I did find something kinda interesting down there, though – after they carted commando boy off to the morgue."

"Interesting how?"

"Well, I gave him a pad of paper along with the pencil."

"Also standard procedure," Karl said. "So?"

"So, he'd thrown the pad into a corner – a corner where the blood pool didn't reach."

"I don't suppose he wrote out a confession, did he?"

"No, but he did write something on it."

Karl sat up a little straighter. "Don't keep me in suspense, Stan."

"It looked like it wasn't intended for us. God knows why he bothered to write it down at all. Maybe he found it comforting, because it looks like he wrote it over and over."

"Hope do you know it wasn't for us?"

"Because he tore off the sheet he was writing on, and shredded it before he started digging into his neck with the pencil. The pieces of paper were so small, they look like confetti."

Karl smiled a little. "But he forgot that the pencil would leave the impression of what he wrote on the sheets underneath, huh?"

"No, he seems to've remembered that, too. He not only shredded the top page – he tore out the next three or four and did the same. Like I said – confetti."

Karl rubbed the bridge of his nose. "OK, so why're you telling me about it, then?"

I produced a little smile of my own. "Because he didn't tear off enough of them."

"Aha – the light dawns," Karl said. "Although I probably should stop using that expression, haina? So, what did you get?"

"I got another pencil and gently shaded all the places where the writing had been. It came through pretty faint, but it was there. He wrote the same thing, over and over, about twenty times. McGuire's got the original, but I copied down the words for myself. Here."

I took a sheet of paper from my jacket pocket and handed it to Karl. He looked at it and frowned. He kept looking, and the frown only got deeper. Looking up at me, he said, "Well, Whiskey Tango Foxtrot, and like that. Latin?" Karl handed the paper back to me.

"Looks like it," I said. "*Ad verum Dei gloriam.*"

"You're the one who knows the lingo – what's it say?"

"For the true glory of God."

Karl blinked a couple of times. "And what the fuck is *that* supposed to be about?"

"Beats the shit out of me," I said. "But in a few hours, I'm pretty sure I can find out."

The man I wanted to talk to wouldn't appreciate being awakened at 5am for something that wasn't an emergency, and I figured about 8 o'clock was about the earliest I could get away with calling about something that wasn't urgent. I said goodbye to Karl as he left for his day's rest at about 5.30am, but remained at my desk.

I could've gone home and called Garrett from there, but depending on what he told me, I might want to make additions to the case file, and I had to do that here. McGuire said he'd OK a couple of hours of overtime, and there was always paperwork for me to catch up on while I was waiting for 8 o'clock to roll around.

I called Christine to let her know that I wouldn't be home in time to say goodnight to her. I got her voicemail and left a message saying I hoped to see her when she got up.

I was writing my report on the suicide of John Doe, aka commando boy, when Thorwald and Greer, the Bureau's finest, came in to see McGuire. They both looked at me as they passed through the squad room en route to the boss's office, but neither one spoke. Greer glared at me, as I would've expected, but the look Thorwald gave me was... harder to read. Maybe she was letting her imagination create a Spanish Inquisition fantasy, with me as the star attraction. That would've surprised me a little, since no one expects the Spanish Inquisition. Or so I hear.

I'd reached the point in my report where I was trying to describe the way that commando boy had barricaded himself in the interrogation room when I heard footsteps approach from behind me – just one set, and by the sound, I figured them for Thorwald's. A couple of seconds later, I found that I was right.

She was wearing a navy-blue blazer over a pair of khaki pants that might've been a little tighter than regulation. Female law enforcement officers don't wear dresses or skirts on the job – not if they're street cops. Skirts make it hard to run, and even harder to fight.

Her black hair was cut in front into bangs that went about halfway down her broad forehead. Beneath them, the ice-blue eyes were looking at me without the glare I'd started to get used to.

"Long night," she said.

"For both of us, I guess."

"I thought your shift ended a half hour before sunrise," she said. If there was anything in her voice besides mild interest, I didn't catch it.

"It usually does," I said, "for the sake of my partner. But I'm putting in a little overtime."

"Did something new break in the case?"

"Nothing you don't already know about." If she thought I was holding out on her, she'd raise the roof. "There's a guy I need to call," I said, "and he won't be available until about 8am."

She nodded, as if this was actually interesting to her. Then she said, "It looks like Greer and I got off on the wrong foot with you and your partner. The two of us came into town very focused on nailing the people behind this butchery, but we may have pushed a little too hard. If we did, I apologize."

I didn't change my facial expression, but I fancied that I could hear the Hallelujah Chorus being sung by angels in the background. An apology from Thorwald, as far as I was concerned, was right up there with that old trick involving the loaves and fishes.

"It's not necessary," I said, "but thanks. Having to watch this stuff on video, over and over, would put anybody on edge."

"Yes, on edge," she said. "And with damn few ways of blowing off steam."

"Yeah, I know," I said, just to be saying something. What was I going to do – suggest she take up bowling?

She looked past me for a moment, I assume at McGuire's office, where her partner was still yakking with the boss. Then she glanced at the big clock on the wall. When she brought her gaze back to me, there was something in her face that hadn't been there before. I couldn't have said what it was, exactly, but she looked softer, somehow.

"It's almost 7.30am," she said. "After you talk to your guy at eight, are you going off duty?"

"Yeah, I was planning to," I said, "unless he gives me something I have to act on right away, and I don't think it's gonna be that kind of conversation."

She nodded again. "We're going off duty, too – as soon as Greer gets done whining to your lieutenant about interagency cooperation. We're staying at the Hilton, downtown. I'm in room six-oh-four."

I gave her a nod of my own. I kept my poker face but my mind was going *Whiskey Tango Foxtrot*?

"If you're not too tired, why don't you swing by after you get off – shift, I mean?"

"To discuss the case, you mean?"

The look she gave me said she thought I'd probably be able to tie my own shoelaces after a few more months of training.

"No, dummy – for a couple of hours of good hard fucking. It'll do us both good, and I'll spring for breakfast after. The Hilton's room service is pretty good. We can discuss the case then, if you want."

I won't claim that I was incapable of speech – it's just that I couldn't think of anything to say that wasn't going to get me in some kind of trouble with somebody.

So I decided to go pragmatic. It seemed safest, and would buy me a little time.

"What about your partner?" I managed to keep my voice level, I think.

"What about him?" She shrugged. "His room's down the hall. And if you were thinking of having him join us, don't bother. Greer's as gay as San Francisco – couldn't you tell?"

Before I could reply to that bit of news, she held up a hand, palm toward me like a traffic cop.

"Don't say anything more. You'll either show up, or you won't. If you do, fine. If you don't, it's your loss" – then her voice returned to the tone I was familiar with – "and this conversation never happened."

"What conversation?"

She nodded one last time and walked back to McGuire's office. As for me, I remained at my computer, but I can't claim that I got much more done on my paperwork.

I waited until 8.05am before I picked up the phone. I won't say the past half hour had gone by fast, exactly – but time passes quicker when your mind is occupied, and I hadn't exactly lacked for stuff to think about. And I only spent a small portion of that time imagining Thorwald naked.

I tapped in the number I'd looked up, and it was answered on the second ring.

"This is Father Garrett."

"Morning, Dave. It's Stan Markowski from Occult Crimes. Hope I'm not calling too early."

"Not at all, Stan – how've you been?"

"Can't complain, I guess. How about yourself?"

"Reasonably well, I like to think. I haven't seen you since that messy business over on Spruce Street last summer."

Garrett is a Jesuit who teaches theology at the U. He's also a volunteer member of the city's SWAT – Sacred Weapons and Tactics – unit. And not the prayer team auxiliary, either. When there's a SWAT call-up, Garrett straps on his body armor, grabs his weapon, and kicks supe ass with the best of them. The order not only says it's OK – they actually encourage him. Warriors for God, and all that.

"Yeah, it has been a while, hasn't it?" I said. "Dave, I've got what is going to sound like a dumb question for you."

"I always tell my students that there's no such thing as a dumb question, Stan. What's really dumb is not asking what you need to know. Fire away."

"OK – what's the motto of the Jesuit order?"

There was a pause. He said, "Well, that's not what I'd expected, but the motto is 'For the greater glory of God'."

"And in Latin?" I asked.

"It's *Ad majorem Dei gloriam*. What's this about, Stan? You thinking about joining up?"

"No, not yet. I'm asking because in a case I'm working, I came across a phrase in Latin that sounded familiar."

"And that's what it was? The Jesuit motto?"

"Almost, but one word's different. It's *ad verum Dei gloriam* – for the *true* glory of God."

Another pause. "Really? Well, now, that's interesting."

"Interesting how?" I asked. "Have you heard it before?"

"Oh, yes – far too often. Don't you know what that is? It's the motto taken on by that bunch of heretics who call themselves the Church of the True Cross."

This time, the pause was mine. "No, I didn't know that. It *is* pretty interesting, now that you mention it."

"They haven't been trying to recruit you, have they?"

"Not exactly, no," I said. "I met a guy recently who, I guess, was one of their members."

"Give those people a wide berth if you can, Stanley. They've got some rather… disturbing ideas. And some of them, I think, may be flat-out crazy. The way fanatics are."

"Looks like I need to find out some more about these guys," I said. "All I know about them is what I've read in a couple of their flyers. They seem to hate practically everybody."

"Not a bad description, really. Listen, Stan – the guy you want to talk to about this so-called church is Pete Duvall. He's our comparative religion expert, and I believe he's written a book – or a series of articles, I forget which – about those people."

"Sounds like a man I ought to see," I said.

"Where can I find him? Please tell me the order hasn't sent him to Peru, or someplace like that."

"No, he's a little closer than that," Garrett said. "When I said 'our expert', I meant here at the university. You can find him in St Thomas Hall, three doors down from my office."

"He teaches at the U? Well, that's good news. When's he likely to be around?"

"I can check his office hours for you on the university's webpage," Garrett said. "I know you could do that yourself, but I'm already online, so it's quicker for me. Hold on."

He wasn't away long. "Stan?"

"I'm here."

"Since you're a night owl by necessity, this should work to your advantage. Pete teaches an evening class that meets three nights a week from 7pm to 7.50pm. He's got an office hour posted for right after class, from eight to nine. You won't even have to stay up past your bedtime to see him. Feel free to use my name, although you shouldn't need to."

"That's great, Dave – thanks a million. Now I've got just one more dumb question."

"Only one? You're a lucky man. Go ahead."

"What day is it?" I said.

"Today's Wednesday, Stan. And I recommend you spend a good part of it getting some sleep. Sounds like you've been pushing too hard, as usual."

"Yeah, I know. I'm going home as soon as we

finish here. No, wait – I think I have one more stop to make, first."

The Hilton has its own parking garage, but I prefer to park someplace I can get out of in a hurry. I was able to find a space on the street, not far from the hotel's main entrance. And the main entrance was what I sat there looking at, for several minutes.

I tried to remember the last time I'd gotten laid – not the day, but the year. I revisited my fantasies about Thorwald's naked body, and she looked fine indeed. I thought about my wife, dead these last six years, and found that didn't help at all. Finally, I let go a sigh and reached for the door handle.

And then "Tubular Bells" started playing in the car.

I got my phone out and looked at the caller ID. *Lacey Brennan*.

"Markowski."

"Hi, Stan – it's Lacey." No dumb supe joke this time, I noticed. Her voice had a raspy quality I hadn't heard before. A lot of crying will do that to you.

"Hi. How're you doing?"

"I'm assuming that's a rhetorical question." Her tone was about as light as mercury.

"Yeah, sorry."

"I want to talk," she said.

"I'm listening."

"No, I mean face-to-face. Can you meet me at the Skyliner on Route 315 outside Pittston? That's about halfway for each of us."

I hesitated, but only for a second. Maybe two. "Sure, no problem. When do you want me there?"

"Five minutes ago."

Morning rush was in progress, so it was about twenty minutes before I pulled into the parking lot of the diner/truck stop/motel/local landmark that is the Skyliner. It's the only eatery – if I can call it that – around that's open twenty-four hours. I used to go there when I was a teenager sometimes, and the place was an area fixture back *then*. The food's pretty good diner chow, but you'd be a fool to stay in one of the motel rooms, and an even bigger fool to patronize one of the hookers who sometimes worked out of the place. Both were known to have bugs.

It occurred to me that I didn't know what Lacey's personal car looked like, so I just went inside. A quick look around satisfied me that she hadn't arrived yet.

The place is self-seating, so I took a booth that gave me a clear view of the door. When a waitress, who looked like Regis Philbin, asked if I wanted coffee, I said, "Absolutely." I had the feeling I was going to need a lot of coffee today. The doctors say that caffeine's no substitute for sleep, and they're right. But sometimes in my job, sleep's a luxury – and I can't afford many luxuries on my salary.

A couple of minutes later, Lacey came through the door, looking like something no self-respecting cat would drag in. Her blonde hair hadn't been washed in a while, she was pale, and I was betting that her blue eyes were bloodshot.

As she sat down opposite me, I saw that I'd been right – if her eyeballs contained any more blood, she'd have every vampire in the Valley hitting on her. How much of the redness was due to crying, and how much from vodka, I wouldn't even try to guess.

I stifled the usual "How're you doing?" I didn't need any more comebacks about rhetorical questions. Instead, I just said, "Hey," and got the same in return.

She was sitting there, elbows on the table and head in both hands, her eyes closed against the fluorescent glare, when the waitress came over and asked her about coffee.

Without moving her head an inch, Lacey said, in that flat, scratchy voice, "Do you have cyanide?"

"*What?*"

"I asked if you had cyanide on the menu."

"Why… of *course* not!"

"Then coffee will have to do."

The waitress looked like she wanted to give Lacey some shit, but the realization that she'd be taking her life in her hands must've sunk in. She just turned and stomped away.

"So, what–" I began.

"Not yet," she said, not moving anything but her lips. "Coffee first, then talk."

The waitress didn't waste any time bringing coffee. After she finished pouring, Lacey said, still without moving, "Thank you."

Looking at me, the waitress asked, "You folks want menus?"

I knew better than to ask Lacey about food, so I told the waitress, "Just coffee, for now."

Lacey took hers black, and, as usual, there was no nonsense about waiting for it to cool. She'd blow on it, take a sip. Blow on it, take a sip. Lacey Brennan could finish a cup of coffee before most people would dare start one.

When her cup was empty, I gestured the waitress over. She refilled Lacey's cup and warmed mine up without a word. She didn't bother to ask about menus again.

I figured rather than ask any more questions, I'd let Lacey talk when she was ready. After a couple of fearless sips from her new cup of java, she did.

"What do you know," she said, "about the people who made this... video?"

"On that subject, facts are few, but theories abound," I told her.

"Start with the facts," she said.

"Maybe the most important fact is that there are four others – at least."

"Four other versions of... what you described for me the other night?"

"Almost exactly the same," I said. "Only the victims differ."

She closed her eyes for several seconds, then opened them and asked, "Why did you say, 'at least'?"

"This isn't the kind of... product... that you can put on the shelf at Target," I said. "It's sold clandestinely, so the FBI – they're running the case, supposedly – had to rely on snitches and CIs for the copies they have. There's no way to know if there are others that haven't floated up out of the sewer, yet."

"Dear sweet fucking Jesus," she said softly. "This is a – a *business*? I was assuming it was just the latest wrinkle in serial killer perversity. Most of them take trophies of one kind or another, and I figured that one of the sickos had decided to sell a video version of his *fun*. But people are doing this for… *money*?"

"That was the assumption the FBI was making – still is, I guess."

She pressed her hands against her head again, as if to keep it from exploding. Then she put her hands down and said, "The way you just put that suggests an alternate assumption. Is that where those 'theories' you were talking about come in?"

"Yeah. One of them, anyway."

Lacey turned her head slowly and looked out the window. There wasn't much to see. Plenty of parked cars and trucks, a couple of guys poking around under the hood of a big Peterbilt, a young couple holding hands as they walked toward the diner's front door, a stray mutt wandering around the parking lot sniffing the trash.

Maybe Lacey needed to remind herself that there was another world out there – one where people weren't abducted and tortured for the amusement of some and the profit of others.

Then she turned back and glanced at her near-empty cup. "We need more coffee."

We each put away three more cups over the next

half hour while I told Lacey what I knew, and what I suspected. I made a mental note to leave the waitress an especially good tip – she'd done a lot of running back and forth for what was going to be a pretty small check.

"The Church of the True Cross," Lacey said musingly, when I was done. "I don't think I've heard of them before."

"I probably wouldn't, either, except that they're based in Scranton, for some reason. Their head honcho, or whatever they call him, is an excommunicated bishop named James Navarra. Maybe I'll know more about him and his church after I talk to the Jesuit expert tonight."

"So these guys are trying to start Helter Skelter by killing humans to make the supes mad, and killing supes get them pissed off at humans? It's *crazy*, Stan."

"No argument from me, Lace. But then, Charles Manson was crazy, too."

"But if the idea is this huge worldwide struggle, with supes and humans at each others' throats all over, they're sure as shit not gonna cause it from *Scranton*, for Chrissake."

"Maybe it's a pilot project," I said. "Try it on a small scale, and if it works, then go national – or bigger."

"Sort of like a weed in your garden. First there's one, and after a while there's a bunch of them – unless you stamp out the first one before it has a chance to spread." Lacey drank the last of her coffee. "I want you to keep me informed of developments in this case, Stan."

"Not a problem," I told her. "I'll copy your office with all the stuff that comes in and the reports that go out."

She shook her head. "No, don't do that – I'd like you to keep in touch with me, personally."

I must have looked at her funny, because she said, "I'm on an indefinite leave of absence, Stan. The official story is that I'm grieving over the death of my sister – and I would be, too, if there weren't more important things to attend to."

"Leave of… Jesus H. Christ." I shook my head slowly. "You should've told me that before I started running my mouth, Lacey. If you're a civilian, for however long it lasts, you've got no right to that information."

"On the contrary, Stan," she said in a voice that chilled me. "Who has more right to that information than I do? Can't you hear my sister's spirit, crying out for vengeance? *I* sure as hell can."

"Lacey…" One of her hands was lying flat on the table, and I gently covered it with my own. "You can't go running around like some kind of vigilante. This is real life, not some fucking Charles Bronson movie, for Chrissake."

"Movie? There's already a movie being filmed, Stan. You described one of the scenes for me yourself, remember? I'm just planning to add to the cast of characters – and maybe change the ending, too."

Something moved behind her eyes, then. I can't

say what it was, exactly – but it made me very glad that I wasn't one of the people who had put her sister in front of those video cameras.

"Lacey, you'll just get yourself killed – either that, or arrested. You know what happens to cops who end up in prison, even a women's prison."

"That doesn't scare me, Stan. And anyway, if I should end up in the slam, I guarantee you that within a week those other bitches will be afraid of *me*."

I believed her, too.

Lacey covered my hand with her other one, as if we were choking a bat to see who had to play left field. "Stan, you want to stop looking at my civilian status as a problem, and think of it as an opportunity."

"An opportunity? For *what*?" I asked her.

"An opportunity to get things done that the job won't let you do yourself. I don't have to worry about warrants, Stan, or about probable cause. I can go where you can't, and do the things you'd never be allowed to."

As I thought about that, she gave me a crooked grin. "And besides, your chances for getting in my pants will be much improved."

"Lacey, I'm going to risk my career by letting you know about this case as it develops – but it's not because of interest in your body. In fact, I'd rather you didn't bring that up again until this business is over, assuming we're both still alive and at liberty, and maybe not even then. Now, give me your personal contact information."

She pulled out her business card and began to write on the back. Then she stopped and looked up at me. "You're an unusual guy, Stan – and not in a bad way, either."

I got home still wired from all the coffee I'd had in the diner with Lacey, but I needed to get some sleep. Carbohydrates usually make me sleepy, and I was hungry anyway, so I had a plate of rigatoni with spaghetti sauce over it. I make great spaghetti sauce – it's all in the way I open the jar.

Then I checked on Quincey, gave him some food pellets, and went to take a long hot shower. The warm water, combined with the digesting pasta and extreme fatigue, helped make me drowsy, so I decided to try and get some rest.

A while later – which turned out to be an hour and twenty minutes – I found myself wondering why music was playing while I was in the process of undressing Agent Thorwald. Then part of my brain registered that I was listening to "Tubular Bells". Thorwald and her French bikini underwear disappeared, my eyes snapped open, and I grabbed the phone.

"Yeah. This is Markowski."

"Stan, this is Harry West, over at the squad."

It took me a couple of seconds to process this, then I remembered that Sergeant Harry West was head of the day shift at the Supe Squad. McGuire's the boss and usually works nights, but Harry supervises the detectives who work the non-peak daylight hours. I don't see him too often.

"Yeah, Harry, what is it?" I was just awake enough to start feeling worried. West wasn't calling because he wanted my recipe for clam dip.

"I got a call from Homicide about something that went down a little while ago. Even though you're off duty, I figured you'd want to be in on it."

"What happened? Where?" I said.

"There's been a shooting. One dead that I know of. It's at 1440 Monroe, apartment 4-C."

Until that moment I wasn't fully awake, but the effect that address had on me was like being dropped into the Susquehanna in January.

"Fuck, that's Karl's place!" I said. "Is he all right?"

"The shooting vic is human, but that's all I know right now. You heading over there?"

"Bet your ass I am."

There was a black-and-white unit in front of Karl's building with its lights going, next to an unmarked car with a portable flasher that I assumed belonged to Homicide.

The elevator brought me up to Four, and even if I hadn't known which apartment was Karl's, it wouldn't have been hard to find, since only one had a cop standing at the door. I realized that my badge wasn't on display and I was reaching for my ID folder when the uniform at the door said, "It's all right, Sarge. Go on in." He opened the door for me and stood aside.

When I walked into Karl's living room, Scanlon looked up from the corpse he was kneeling over and said, "Took you long enough to get here."

"Jesus, Scanlon, don't you *ever* sleep?"

"Sleep is overrated. I'd rather work – especially if it involves coming to little parties like this one."

The party in question was small, but colorful. It consisted of me, Scanlon, a couple of his homicide guys, and the forensics techs. I wasn't sure whether to include the corpse on the floor, or not. As for the color – I'll get to that.

In life the deceased had been a human, probably male. He wore fancy cowboy boots, new-looking jeans, and a light nylon jacket of dark green. I'd based my assessment of his gender on clothing, body size, and the look of the one hand I could see. I couldn't be certain because he didn't have a head anymore. Most of it was decorating one wall, looking like a painting by that Jackson Pollack guy I'd once seen a movie about.

The only thing I knew about my partner right then was that he wasn't the one lying dead on the living room floor. "Is Karl OK?" I asked Scanlon.

"Far as I know. I assume he spends the day in there."

Scanlon jerked a thumb at the door to one of the bedrooms. When Karl joined the ranks of the undead, he had some modifications made to the place. One of them involved installing a lock on the bedroom door – and not just any lock. This thing was a double-bolted monster made by Gardall and the only way to open it, short of blasting, was by touching the right sequence of numbers on a keypad. Since a lock is only as good as the door it guards,

Karl had installed a new one of those, too – iron, surrounded by a steel frame.

"Yeah, that's his bedroom," I said.

"For obvious reasons, we couldn't go in there and check on him. You got the lock combination?"

"Yeah, he gave it to me."

Scanlon nodded toward the monster of a door. "You mind?"

"Not in the least," I said. In fact, he'd have had a hard time stopping me from going in there.

I tapped in the eight-digit code, being careful to shield the keypad with my body. I trusted Scanlon, but with *this* information, Karl didn't trust anybody – except me.

I heard the lock disengage after I'd touched the final digit. I turned the knob and pushed the door slowly open.

Karl's bedroom looked the way it had the only other time I'd been here – a couple of bureaus, matching nightstands, and the bed – that was it. The human-sized lump in the bed was covered by a heavy blanket, which I carefully peeled back to reveal the sleeping bag where Karl spent the day. I pulled the zipper down a couple of feet and looked at my partner. Karl Renfer looked dead – but that time of day, he was supposed to. More important, there was no sign that anything had been done to change him from "undead" to "true dead".

I only realized I'd been holding my breath when I started breathing again.

I zipped up the sleeping bag and replaced the

blanket. I left a note where Karl would be sure to see it, briefly explaining what had happened in his living room. I didn't want him to freak when he got up at sunset and went in there. Then I left the bedroom, closing the door firmly behind me until I felt the lock catch.

"Karl's fine," I said to Scanlon. "You don't need to let anybody else in there, do you?"

Scanlon shook his head. "No reason to. It's pretty obvious this is where all the action went down."

I was glad he said that, because if he'd wanted to send the forensics people poking around Karl's bedroom, I was going to have a sudden attack of amnesia regarding that lock combination. That might lead to some unpleasantness.

"Who called it in?" I asked Scanlon.

"Lady down the hall. She works part-time as a medical transcriptionist, and today's her day off. Says she heard what sounded like a thud coming from this end of the hall. Took her a couple of minutes to make up her mind to check it out, which is just as well. If she'd run into the perp as he was leaving, he'd probably have iced her, too."

"Most likely," I said, "but I hope you didn't tell her that. She'll never come out of her apartment during the day again."

"I decided not to share my conclusion with her," Scanlon said. "So, she decides to check out this 'thud' and takes a slow walk down the hall. God knows what she expected to find, but she did notice that Karl's door was ajar a couple of inches."

"I thought that kind of thing only happened on TV," I said.

"Yeah, I know what you mean. It's not unreasonable, though. The perp is in a hurry, he closes the door behind him, but doesn't stick around to make sure the latch has caught, the door falls open a couple of inches."

"Cheap locks," I said. "No wonder Karl installed his own."

"I would, too," Scanlon said. "So, Mrs Randall sees the gap between the door and the frame, comes over, and peeks through it. Turns out the line of sight gives her a clear view of the dead guy here, along with the mess on the wall. So she runs back to her apartment and calls 911."

"A public-spirited citizen," I said. "We need more of those."

I walked over to the wall decorated with most of the contents of the victim's skull. Amid the blood, bone fragments, and brain tissue were a number of small holes, each about the size of a dried pea.

I went over next to Scanlon, and we stood there staring, side by side, like a couple of dweebs visiting an art museum for the first time.

"Shotgun," I said to Scanlon.

"Uh-huh."

"By the size and number of the holes, I'd say double-ought buck. Those pellets are so big, the cartridge only holds eight of 'em."

"That's what Forensics thinks, too."

I looked down at the corpse. "They make sup-pressors for shotguns these days, you know."

"Yeah, I've read about those," Scanlon said.

"'Course, you can only do so much with a shot-gun, when it comes to sound suppression."

"Those fuckers are pretty loud, all right."

"Best you can hope for, even with a good suppres-sor, is to reduce the noise from *blam* to something kind of like a *thud*."

"Sounds about right," Scanlon said. He turned and looked at me. "I read a report the other day about a dude who supposedly used a suppressed shotgun to take out a couple of goblins, who were attempting to eviscerate an officer of the law."

"That's what happened, all right."

"According to the report, the officer in question was able to make a tentative identification of the suspect."

"Yeah," I said. "He was."

"Which leads us to the question," Scanlon said, "of what the fuck Sharkey was doing here, blowing the head off some would-be vampire slayer."

"You're sure that's what the vic was? Not some run-of-the-mill B and E artist?"

"Oh, that's right," Scanlon said. "You haven't seen this stuff, yet. Come here."

I followed him over to Karl's sofa. On it was a long canvas bag, like the kind tennis players carry their rackets in. Scanlon sat down next to it and snapped on a pair of thin latex gloves.

"We found this next to the body," Scanlon said,

and pulled the bag's zipper open. I had my own gloves on by now.

Scanlon removed from the bag a two-foot-long wooden stake with a sharp point and handed it to me. "He's got two more of those in here," he said.

I turned the stake over in my hands. "Made on a lathe," I said. "Wonder if he learned that in high school shop class."

"No wonder they call it 'occupational training'," Scanlon said. "Then there's this."

He produced a big mallet with a black rubber head and showed it to me. "Why rubber, and not metal?" he asked.

"Rubber on wood – less chance of slipping than iron on wood," I said. "You don't want to risk whacking your fingers when you're dispatching the bloodsucking undead."

"Trust you to know something like that," he said. "And we have this, which I don't figure was his lunch."

He handed me a large plastic baggie with a zip-lock top. It contained a freshly cut flower with a four-inch stem and a bushy white head.

"Wild garlic," I said, handing it back to him. "Tra-ditionalists use it, along with the wooden stake. It's the Van Helsing method, which some people still swear by. Stake through the heart, cut off the head, and fill the mouth with garlic."

"That would explain this, then." Scanlon pulled from the bag and handed me a saw with a foot-long blade and orthopedic pistol grip. I recognized it as an amputation saw, the kind surgeons use. The blade was splattered with brown stains that I figured had once been red.

"He came well prepared," I said to Scanlon, and gave the saw back to him.

"The only thing that puzzles me is this."

He handed me a device that looked like what you'd get if you crossed an iPhone with an expensive calculator. It had two wires dangling from it with odd-looking plugs at the ends.

I looked at it, and then it occurred to me that the little keypad looked like the one on Karl's lock. That's when I realized what I was holding.

"I've never seen one of these," I told Scanlon, "but I've read about them. It's a gizmo that's supposed to crack the code on an electronic combination lock." I nodded toward Karl's bedroom. "Like that one."

Scanlon took it back from me. "I thought that was strictly James Bond stuff."

"Don't say that around Karl," I said, "unless you want a twenty-minute description of every similar gadget that ever showed up in one of those movies."

Scanlon started putting the vampire-killing gear back in the bag. "Guess yesterday's James Bond fantasy is today's reality. This dude really *was* well prepared."

"My guess is, he broke in for the first time a few days ago, and did a little reconnaissance."

"You figure he saw the lock, and realized he'd need special equipment to beat it."

I nodded. "Looks like if Sharkey, or whoever it

was, hadn't stepped in, one of those fucking sticks would now be sticking out of Karl's chest."

They scream, when you pound the stake in. They scream, and they writhe, sometimes they beg, and the blood spurts all over – just like if it were you or me.

It looked like I'd have to buy Sharkey a beer sometime – or a blood, or whatever the hell he drinks.

"I know you'll be sending this guy's prints out on the wire," I said to Scanlon. "But you might save some time and trouble if you send them to Chicago first. Ask them to check the prints against those of a guy they call Duffy the Vampire Slayer."

Scanlon's face twitched, which I suppose was his version of a smile. He's not a big smiler, Scanlon. "Duffy the Vampire Slayer? No shit?"

"No shit."

I got home – again – a little after two in the afternoon. I was still riding the adrenaline wave that Harry West's call had given me, so I figured I'd better make some coffee and face the fact that I wasn't going to sleep again until my next shift was over.

Once the coffee maker was burbling away, I went into the living room to see if anything interesting was on TV. I didn't think my brain could handle anything complicated, like reading a newspaper. I got interested in a show on AMC that I'd never seen before, about a candidate for president who's secretly possessed by a demon. The next thing I knew, Christine was gently shaking my arm and saying, "Wake up, Daddy. Time to get ready for work."

I came awake with a start. "Shit!" I said. "Must've dozed off." I rubbed my face a couple of times and yawned. "Although, come to think of it, that's the best thing that could've happened." I checked my watch. Three and a half hours of sleep was better than none.

I saw that the answering machine's red light was blinking. I'd been down so deep, I hadn't even heard the phone ring.

"Hey, Stan – it's Karl. Thanks for the note you left me, man. At least I was prepared when I walked out of the bedroom and found the two homicide dicks waiting for me. Looks like I need a better lock on the front door, too, haina? Not to mention new plaster and paint in the living room. Listen, the homicide guys say they want to talk to me, although I figure I'll just keep tellin' 'em, 'Beats me, fellas, I was dead to the world when it all went down. Literally.' But that means I'm gonna be late coming on shift – tell McGuire, will you? See you soon – I hope. Bye."

Christine had heard Karl's message, too. She looked at me and said, "What the hell was *that* about?"

"I'll tell you about it over breakfast, honey. But right now I need a shower and a change of clothes."

"Want me to make you some eggs while you're upstairs? Save you some time when you come down."

"Hey, they'd be great, thanks. Messing with human food won't gross you out?"

"No, I don't think so. Watching you eat eggs with ketchup – now *that* grosses me out."

A little later, while eating the scrambled eggs she'd made – yeah, I had 'em with ketchup; sue me – I filled Christine in on the latest series of crises.

She frowned into her cup, swirling around the small amount of Type A that remained in it. "So, do you figure this guy was after Karl because he's" – she made a face – "one of the bloodsucking undead, or because he's your partner?"

"Could be either one, I suppose. But there's lots of vampires in Scranton, so the odds are against him being randomly targeted as just another step toward Helter Skelter."

She nodded. "Good point."

"Besides," I said, "that bunch of goblins came after *me* the other night, remember? That could be more Helter Skelter too, I guess – just another human murdered by supes. But the likelihood of both Karl and me being chosen by chance for that shit is pretty damn low."

"I was thinking about that attack on you last night," she said, "when things got slow at work, and it doesn't make sense. I mean, how would a human go about assembling a goblin hit squad? You can't just stroll through Goblin Market calling, 'Hey, anybody wanna knife a cop tonight? I'll throw in all the meth you can snort'."

"Yeah, I see what you mean. Any outsider who tried that would be lucky not to get knifed himself."

"He'd have to use a middleman, wouldn't he, our Mister X? Or middle-goblin. Someone to do the recruiting for him."

I put my fork down as my brain finally started working again. "He'd have to put the word out, somehow. And whenever any kind of word goes out to the supe community, there's a guy who's sure to hear it."

"You mean Mister Castle?"

"No, he might be a little too high up for something like that to reach him. I was thinking of someone lower in the food chain."

"How low?" she asked.

"Low enough to consider human flesh a delicacy."

"Oh, ewwww."

I grinned at her. "Nice talk, for one of the bloodsucking undead."

She gave me a shrug and a grin. "Hey, everybody's gotta have standards."

"Tell Christine if she ever gets tired answering emergency calls, there might be a slot for her on the police force," McGuire said. "How did the goblins get organized – you should've thought about that before now – and so should I."

"Better late than not at all," I said. "I told you I wanted to drop by the U tonight. Father Duvall's got an office hour from eight to nine."

"Yeah, I'll be interested to hear what he has to say about these True Cross nutjobs – if that's what they are."

"Well, since Karl's gonna be tangled up with Homicide for a while, I thought before I visit Father Duvall I'd stop in at Renfield's."

"For what?" McGuire asked.

"I'm hoping to see a ghoul about a goblin."

Renfield's is Scranton's biggest bar catering to a supernatural clientele. They let humans in, of course, just as a supe can get a drink, of whatever he wants, at any other bar in town. Discrimination's illegal – the courts have been very clear on that point.

But it's not surprising that supes prefer the company of their own, even if the different species aren't always on the best of terms with each other. Vampires and werewolves, for instance, don't always get along too well – but anybody who starts trouble in Renfield's is banned for life. And for some of these folks, that can be a very, very long time.

I noticed that the volume of conversation ebbed for a few seconds when I walked in. It always does, even though I'm on pretty good terms with most of the supe community. In my job you have to be, regardless of your personal feelings. The talk had returned to its normal level by the time I reached the bar.

I ordered a ginger ale from Elvira, the bartender, then turned around to lean on the bar, facing the room. I scanned the tables and was relieved to see that Barney Ghougle was here, having a drink with his brother. Algernon keeps getting into trouble with the law – he's got a little indecent exposure problem – so Barney and I have done a certain amount of business over the years. Nobody knows the current dirt like a ghoul, and Barney is the gossip king of Wyoming Valley.

It's better that I not go walking around amongst the tables in Renfield's. Having a cop on the prowl makes some people – and a few others – nervous. So I waited until I caught Barney's eye, then made a slight nod. A few moments later he got up from his chair and made his way toward me.

Barney Ghougle looks like somebody you'd see in a painting by the great American portrait artist, Charles Addams, although Barney always reminds me of the late actor Peter Lorre – short, a little stout, with hair plastered over his head with too much gel. Barney owns a funeral home, and even in Renfield's he wears the professional outfit – black suit, dark gray tie, white shirt. I guess in that place he never knows when he'll encounter a future customer – or a former one.

As he reached me I said, "Hello, Barney – buy you a drink?"

"Certainly, Sergeant," he said, with grave formality. "A bourbon and water would be most enjoyable."

Yeah, he really talks like that. Occupational hazard, I suppose.

When his drink arrived, Barney took a sip and said, "Now, then – what pressing matter has brought you to this fine establishment tonight?"

"Goblins."

"Oh, yes?" Barney wrinkled his nose. "Unpleasant creatures." Like I said, there's not always a lot of love lost between different varieties of supes.

"You'll get no argument from me," I said. "In fact,

a bunch of them were extremely unpleasant around me the other night. With knives, no less."

"Yes, I heard of that dreadful incident." Of course he had. "I was also relieved to learn that you came through the ordeal unscathed."

"Unscathed, maybe, but distinctly pissed off. I don't want something like that happening again."

Barney permitted himself a tiny smile. "My understanding is that those six impertinent goblins will not trouble you – or anyone else – ever again. My congratulations, by the way, on your prowess in combat." He raised his glass to me, then took another sip. "I did not receive any of their custom, alas – goblins bury their own."

If Barney thought I'd taken down all six greenies by myself, then let him. My reputation as a badass can always use a little polishing.

"Whoever sent those six could always send more," I said. "That's why I'm very interested in finding out who exactly *did* send them."

Barney gave me raised eyebrows. "You believe they were hired to kill you, and not simply paying off a grudge? There is bad blood between you and the goblin community that goes back some years, I understand."

I gave him a look. "Barney, when's the last time you met a goblin who could remember what he had for breakfast yesterday, let alone something that happened eighteen months ago?"

The little ghoul nodded slowly. "That is a reasonable point you raise."

"More important, can you imagine six goblins, acting alone, who could stay organized long enough to build a campfire, let alone plan and carry out a hit?"

"When you put it like that, I cannot help but agree. Someone would appear to have used the goblins as stalking horses against you."

"Finally, the light dawns," I said. "So what I want to know is, what human's been hanging out with the goblins lately."

Barney frowned into his glass. "Oh, dear."

"Don't give me 'Oh, dear', Barney. This is me, remember? The guy who keeps getting your brother out of jail?"

"I am well aware of your efforts, Sergeant. And I hope I have not proved ungrateful in the past. I am thus most distressed that I cannot be of assistance to you on this occasion."

"Can't – or won't?"

"I most certainly would, were it within my capabilities. But I have no lines of communication into the goblin community. They are very secretive, and do not mingle much outside their own numbers. Except for their cousins, of course."

"Their *what*? Cousins?"

"I refer to the ogres, naturally."

"Ogres?" I almost spilled my drink. "The giants and the greenies – are you fucking *kidding* me?"

"I grant you there is little physical resemblance. But they are both creatures of the fey, and feel a certain kinship with each other. It is rather like the

Russians and Serbs, in human society. Different countries, different languages and cultures. Yet in 1914, the Russians came to the defense of Serbia, thus igniting the First World War."

"Goblins and ogres. Jesus, why didn't I know that?"

Barney shrugged those well-tailored shoulders. "It is not a fact that either side advertises. Ogres are, in their own way, rather secretive, too."

"Son of a bitch."

"I am thus most regretful of my inability to offer you assistance on this occasion. But perhaps if you know a friendly ogre…"

I put my glass down so suddenly that I sloshed ginger ale over my hand. "Mother *fuck*," I said. "I think I just might."

Now I needed to see an ogre about a goblin, but it was almost time for Father Duvall's office hour, and that was an opportunity I didn't want to miss.

Just inside the main entrance to St Thomas Hall was a building directory, which informed me that Peter Duvall, SJ, had his office in room 309. Turned out I didn't have to worry about room numbers as I reached the right hallway. Only one room had light streaming from an open door, and I was glad to see that Father Duvall, unlike some profs I've heard about, actually kept his office hours.

I stepped into the doorway and rapped my knuckles against the open door. When the man in black with the clerical collar looked up, I said, "Father Duvall? I'm Stan Markowski, from the Scranton Police Department's Occult Crimes Unit." I showed him my ID. "Dave Garrett said you might be able to help me with a case I'm working on."

Father Duvall had manners. He stood up and walked around his desk, hand outstretched. Once I got a good look at him, I knew what thought often ran through the minds of his female students. It was the same feeling I'd had in high school, whenever I looked at beautiful Sister Mary Alan.

What a waste.

Father Duvall reminded me of nobody so much as Jean-Paul Belmondo, who was the essence of French cool in the 1960s. He had the same disarrayed black hair, hooded eyes, and thick, sensuous lips. Duvall even had the same kind of dimple on his chin.

What a waste.

"Good to meet you, Sergeant," he said, shaking hands with a smile. "I don't know what you're working on, but if Dave thinks I might be able to help you, then I'll give it my best shot."

He invited me to sit in one of the wooden visitor's chairs that faced his desk. I told him that I was interested in the Church of the True Cross, but I didn't go into why. I just said that the Church had come up in an investigation of mine, and that I wanted to learn more about it.

"The Church of the True Cross," he said softly, sitting back in a big leather chair that looked a lot more comfortable than mine. "You know, back in the Middle Ages, when Mother Church was the toughest kid on the block, heresy was punishable by death. We live in a more enlightened age, I'm very glad to say, but while most heretics these days are merely annoying, those who constitute the Church of the True Cross are, I suspect, truly dangerous."

"Dangerous in what way?" I asked.

"In the same way that Islamic fundamentalist terrorists are dangerous. Both share a sense of utter self-righteousness combined with an often violent contempt toward those who are different, either in beliefs or in nature."

I put a hand to my forehead for a moment. "I'm just a simple cop, Father, who hasn't had much sleep in the last three days. Can you put that into words of one syllable for me?"

Duvall tilted his head and looked at me. "'Simple cop'? I'm not so sure about that, but I'll try to stop talking as if this is a theology seminar. Fair enough?"

When I nodded, he leaned forward, placing both hands on his desk. "What I meant by that last bit was that the Church of the True Cross will hate you if you either *think* differently than they do, or if you *are* different from them."

"Different, you mean, the way supes are."

"Yes, exactly."

"But hasn't the Pope declared all supes to be anathema, too?"

"Yeah," he said, and sighed again. "But that's not going to last, especially if the next pontiff isn't a Neanderthal like the current one."

"Nice way to talk about the Big Boss," I said. "Not that I'm disagreeing."

"The Big Boss is the Lord, my friend," Duvall said. "He's the CEO and Chairman of the Board. His Holiness is more like the corporation's president. Presidents come and go – only the Big Boss, as you call him, is eternal."

"So you think the Church is likely to change its position on supes?"

"Yes, inevitably. How soon depends on who the next pope is, but there's already a lot of sentiment in the College of Cardinals that Paul VI's condemnation of supernaturals was shortsighted, as so many of his views were."

"How about you, Father?" I asked him. "What's your view of supernaturals?"

"My view is that we are all God's creatures, and thus worthy of His love. If God did not want vampires, for instance, to exist, then they wouldn't."

"But that's not an opinion shared by the Church of the True Cross, I take it."

"Hell, no. Those guys would like nothing more than the return of the Inquisition – but with them in charge, of course. They'd be burning vampires and werewolves left and right."

"And witches, too?" I asked quietly.

"Yes, witches, of course." He stopped and looked at me for a second or two. "That's what this is about, isn't it? Those poor women who have been burned alive in the last few weeks."

"That's *part* of what it's about," I said. "But there may be more going on than that – a lot more."

"I wish I could say that I'm surprised," Duvall said grimly.

"How did these True Cross guys get started, anyway? I tried to look up the Wikipedia article on them, but it's been taken down."

"That's because the True Cross propagandists keep trying to rewrite it to conform to their own cracked version of history."

Duvall steepled his fingertips and looked at them for a few seconds. "OK, you know how the Puritans came over here and settled New England because the old England just wasn't holy enough for them?"

"John Winthrop and all those guys."

"Right – and the logical conclusion of the Puritans' extreme self-righteousness was the Salem witch trials of 1692, in which, uh–"

"Twenty," I said.

"Yes, twenty innocent people were executed. You know your history," Duvall said.

"That's the kind of history I'm supposed to know, just like I know that something like twelve other people were executed for witchcraft around New England, years before Salem."

"Not many people know about those," Duvall said, nodding his approval. "But it all goes to show the lengths fanatics will go in order to preserve their power."

"You're saying the Church of the True Cross is like the Puritans?"

"In some respects, yes. Their church was founded in 1994, when a group of people broke with the Society of St Pius X, which was founded by Marcel Lefebvre, himself a defrocked archbishop and heretic."

"He was the guy who thought the Second Vatican Council was a Commie plot to take over the world, right?"

"Something like that," Duvall said. "He came out of the tradition of right-wing French Catholicism, and there's nobody more reactionary than *that* crowd."

"Except for the Church of the True Cross," I said.

"You got it. They decided that Lefebvre and the Society were too accommodating, because they weren't calling for John XXIII to be lynched after the reforms that brought us out of the Middle Ages. All Lefebvre did was put on his boogie shoes and leave Mother Church. But that wasn't enough for 'Bishop' James Navarra – he wanted a more militant posture. So he split, and took a bunch of the Society's members with him."

"How big a bunch?" I asked.

"Seventy or eighty, something like that."

"I take it they've grown some since those days."

"Oh, sure," Duvall said, "although they refuse to release any membership numbers. In terms of people who regularly attend his services here in Scranton, maybe a couple of hundred. That doesn't count the curiosity-seekers who go once and are so turned off that they never go back. And there are a number of people from outside the area who send him money, although how much is between him and the IRS."

"Some folks will send money to anybody," I said.

"Sad, but true – but here's the ironic thing: Navarra and company don't even *need* it."

"Why the hell not?" I asked.

"Because he's got a sugar daddy – a rich nitwit who's been bankrolling the Church for years."

"Anybody I might have heard of?"

"Probably not," Duvall said. "But I bet you've heard of one of his kids. The guy's name is Patton Wilson. He's got six kids, one of whom is Matt Wilson."

"Mister Kiss-Kiss-Bang-Bang? The movie star?"

"The very same. Although I don't think Matt talks much about his dad in public – he's probably too embarrassed."

"Is that the source of Dad's money – his movie star kid?"

"Not at all," Duvall said. "Dad's filthy rich all on his own. Used to own a chain of newspapers in the Midwest, I understand."

"Used to?"

"Far as I know. He cashed in and sold all the papers years ago, or so they say."

"I wonder," I said. "So Dad's a true believer, is he?"

"Hard-core, all the way. Some say he's even more extreme than Bishop Navarra, although I figure that the good bishop is exactly as extreme as Patton Wilson wants him to be."

"It's like that, huh?"

"I believe so," Duvall said. "Wilson pulls the strings, and Navarra dances as required."

"You said these guys are dangerous? Why? There's no shortage of religious nuts around."

"Most religious nuts don't have millions of dollars to play with," Duvall said. "And Navarra preaches a gospel of hate, pure and simple. He's like Hitler, in the 1920s – except Navarra wears a clerical collar, to which he is not entitled. And I'm no longer sure that he's all talk and no action."

I leaned forward, which didn't make the chair any more comfortable. "Father, I think you'd better tell me exactly what you mean."

"Duvall says there's supposed to be twelve of these guys," I said. "You know, like the twelve apostles."

"Twelve enforcers," McGuire said.

Karl looked at me. "There's eleven of 'em now."

"Apparently, they've been trained by some ex-special forces types," I said.

"Commandos," Karl said with a snort.

"Duvall said he's pretty sure these guys do the Church's dirty work," I said, "although he had no specific idea of what that work might be."

"But he mentioned the witch burnings," Karl said.

"That's what he thought of when he saw them on the news – that it was the kind of shit these guys might be willing to do."

"Why the fuck didn't Duvall come in?" McGuire said.

"He has no proof," I said, "and without that, he figured we wouldn't be interested in talking to him."

"If only he knew how desperate we've been for a lead," Karl said. "Hell, speculation without evidence would've been an improvement over what we had, which was nothing."

Whatever McGuire was going to say was interrupted by the ringing phone on his desk. He never did get around to finishing the sentence.

"McGuire. Yeah." I watched the knuckles of his phone hand slowly turn white with the pressure of his grip. For some reason, he glanced at me. "Of course." He wrote something on a pad. "I'll put somebody on it right now. Thanks."

He hung up the phone and sat staring at it. "Looks like the Church's enforcers have been busy." He spoke softly, as if talking to himself. Then he looked at me.

"There's been another witch burning," he said. His voice was not quite steady.

I immediately thought of Rachel. Did they send someone to finish the job, with Rachel not expecting trouble anymore?

"They have an ID?" I asked, my chest tight.

"No. All I've got is this." He pushed the pad toward me. Written on it was "921 North Webster Ave."

"Son of a motherfucking bitch," I said. *"That's my house."*

• • • •

As Karl and I walked, very fast, out to the parking lot, I opened my phone and keyed 911.

The woman who answered was not Christine.

"Emergency services. How may I assist you?"

"I want to talk to Christine Markowski – she's one of your operators. Put her on the line."

"Sir, I'm sorry, but this number is only for–"

"This is Detective Sergeant Stanley Markowski, Scranton Police Department, badge number 4341. I don't know who you are, but if you don't put Christine on right now, I promise you'll be charged with obstruction of justice. Now *do* it!"

"Y-yes, sir."

The line went silent. God doesn't hear from me all that often these days, but I was praying in my head now, for all I was worth.

Please don't let her come back and say that Christine didn't make it to work tonight. Please don't let—

"Hello, Daddy. What's wrong?"

You can have your symphonies and concertos and angelic choirs singing. As far as I was concerned, the sweetest sound in the universe right then was my little girl's voice.

"Chris–" I tried to speak, but my throat was clogged. I cleared it noisily and managed, "Christine."

"Yes, I'm here – what's going on? You scared Roberta half to death."

We were at the car now. It was my night to drive, but I flipped the keys to Karl, who didn't need any explanation. I got in the passenger side and slammed the door.

"Christine, in case we get cut off somehow, you need to know this: do *not* go home this morning. Do. Not. Go. Home. Understand me?"

"Yeah, OK, sure. I can crash at a friend's place. But what the fuck is going on?"

"There's been another witch burning – apparently at our house."

"*What*? Our house? Why?"

"I dunno," I said. "But they haven't ID'd the victim yet, and for a second I thought the evil bastards had moved up from witches to vampires, and the charred body was you."

"Oh, my God, you must've been – no, I'm fine. I've been here the last three hours or so."

"Baby, I am *so* glad you're all right," I told her. "I've got more calls to make, so I have to go. I'll call you tomorrow night. Don't go home until I tell you it's OK – all right?"

"Sure, Daddy, that's no problem. Make your calls – I'll talk to you tomorrow."

"OK, bye."

Karl had the flashing light on the dash going, and the siren screaming. Under other circumstances, he'd have been grinning like a kid. But his face was serious as he glanced at me.

"Christine's OK, then?"

"Yeah, thank God."

"Thank God is right."

I brought up the directory in my phone and pressed a number.

"Who're you calling now?" Karl asked.

"Rachel."

Rachel's line started ringing. One. Two. Three. If she didn't answer, that didn't necessarily mean anything bad. She could be out getting a cheeseburger, or something. Four. "Come on, Rachel, answer the fucking–"

"Hello?"

"Rachel, it's Stan."

"What's wrong? It's bad, I can tell."

"There's been another witch burning. I was afraid it was you."

"*Another one*? But I thought the man doing that was dead!"

"He is. Apparently he'd got friends."

"Oh, goddess – that poor woman, whoever she is."

"That spell you used the other night," I said, "the freezing one – I'd reactivate that, or whatever the proper term is."

"Yes, of course. I'll do that at once."

"And you might want to call your sister witches and put the word out. Tell them the danger hasn't passed."

"All right, Stan, I'll take care of it."

"The other witches are probably OK for tonight," I said. "These bastards have never done more than one a night. But then, they never did one in my yard, either."

"Your *yard*! Oh, Stan, that is so awful–"

Karl made the corner onto my street on what felt like two wheels. Ahead, I could see flashing lights.

"We're almost there. Gotta go. Talk later. Bye."

I wasn't even surprised to see Scanlon anymore. He stood at the bottom of my front steps, hands in his overcoat pockets, and watched me approach. Karl went to talk to the uniformed officers who'd responded first.

I took a few seconds to look at the tree, a poplar that I'd planted on the day Christine was born. But I saved most of my sympathy for the victim. Like the others, she was reduced to a charred lump of meat, tied to the tree with rope at her chest and shins. The odor was – well, it was all too familiar by now, although I never imagined that I'd be smelling it here.

"Ten minutes ago, McGuire said you didn't have an ID on the vic. Anything change since then?" I asked.

"No, she's still a Jane Doe," Scanlon said. "We'll do the usual – send dental work out, DNA, look for a missing persons report that fits. We'll probably have an ID in a couple of days, if the earlier cases are any indication."

I made myself look at what was tied to the tree. Without taking my eyes away, I said, quietly, "I wonder what husband is asking, right about now, where his wife is, or what kid is worried because Mom is late getting home. Or what father–" I had to stop for a second. "What father is going crazy because his daughter's missing."

"You talk to Christine?" Scanlon asked.

"Yeah, she's fine."

"How about Rachel Proctor?"

"Talked to her, too. She's OK."

We stood there in silence, gazing upon the remains of one of the cruelest things one human being can do to another. Finally Scanlon said, "I thought this was supposed to be done with."

"Yeah, we all did."

"As that partner of yours would say, Whiskey Tango Foxtrot?"

"I'm pretty sure I know what happened," I said. "Problem is, I can't prove diddly-squat."

"Tell me what you think."

He listened closely as I told him what I'd learned about the Church of the True Cross.

When I was done, he was quiet for a bit, then asked, "What do you figure the point was of doing this in your front yard? Revenge? Defiance? A warning?"

"I think it was their way of saying, *This isn't over, motherfucker*. And you know something?"

"Um?"

"They're right."

I had to let homicide detectives traipse through my house, to make sure there wasn't anything in there connected to the atrocity out front. I guess Scanlon had told them not to be annoying about it, because they weren't – for the most part. But just having a couple of cops walking around inside your home is enough to annoy most people, me included.

Finally the forensics techs had all the photos and soil samples they wanted, the body of the victim was on its way to the morgue under a Jane Doe tag, and I was free to go back to work.

Once we were in the car, I pulled out my wallet and started sorting through all the junk I've stuck in there and keep meaning to get rid of.

Karl watched me for a few seconds. "What're you doing?"

"Looking for – ah, there it is." I retrieved from amidst all the crap a piece of paper with a phone number on it. I got my phone out and, before Karl could ask, said, "There's an ogre I need to call."

Karl looked at me. "An ogre."

"Yep."

As I started touching numbers, Karl nodded calmly. "Makes perfect sense to me," he said. Maybe he'd read somewhere that you're supposed to humor lunatics.

Midway through the second ring a voice answered. "Yuh?"

"I'm looking for Ivan." If he asked me for a last name, I was sunk. I didn't know if ogres share phones, or what the hell they do.

"This Ivan."

"This is Sergeant Stan Markowski, Scranton Police Department."

"Mark who?"

I tried not to sigh into my mouthpiece. "The cop who could've shot your brother Igor, but didn't."

"Oh, yeah, Markowski. OK, I remember. Hi."

"You said you owed me a favor, remember?"

"I did? Oh, right, 'cause you didn't kill Igor. Yeah, I owe you, Markowski."

"Well, tonight's the night I collect on it. I need to talk to you somewhere, face-to-face."

"You wanna talk? That's the favor?"

This time, I couldn't stop the sigh from escaping.

"No, I want to talk to you and tell you what the favor *is*."

"Oh. OK."

I waited, but the ogre didn't say anything more. "Where can I meet you?" I asked, finally.

"Meet? You mean tonight?"

"Yeah, tonight. Soon."

I listened to several seconds of heavy ogre breathing before Ivan spoke again.

"How about Leary's Bar?" he said. "Nice place."

That idea was so brilliant, I knew something must be wrong with it. In a moment, I knew what the flaw was.

"I think maybe they're closed," I said. "For re-modeling."

"Nah, I pass by there last night. Didn't go in. Bar is open. Look like all new stuff inside."

"That's a *great* idea, then. How soon can you get there?"

"I leave now, maybe... ten minutes?"

"OK, Ivan, I see you in Leary's Bar. Ten minutes."

God, now he had me doing it.

"See ya," the ogre said, and the call ended.

Karl was looking at me. Of course, he'd only heard my end of the conversation.

"Do I have this right?" he said. "We're gonna meet an ogre who owes you a favor – in *Leary's*?"

"That's about it."

Karl turned the ignition key. "Then we better get a move on. I wouldn't miss this for the world."

As we pulled into traffic he said, "Siren and lights a little too much?"

"What the fuck," I said. "Go wild."

Leary's place looked good as new. Of course, a lot of the stuff in there *was* new.

He'd replaced the tables and chairs – not just the broken ones, but all of them. I guess he wanted everything to match. The mirror behind the bar still had manufacturer's stickers on it, and if Leary hadn't completely restored the collection of bottles that usually lined the shelf in front of the mirror, a lot of them seemed to be there. I checked the ceiling lights – yep, repaired or replaced. Even the floor looked as if it had been refinished.

I took all this in during the time it took Karl and me to walk from the door to the highly polished bar and sit down. I checked out the two waitresses, but neither one was Heather, who'd had such a stressful time with Igor the other night. I wondered if she'd ever come back to work here.

Leary came through a door behind the bar, saw us, and swaggered on over. He was one of those guys who look like they could strut while sitting down.

"Well," he said with false bonhomie, "look what the bat dragged in!" When he caught the look Karl was giving him, Leary just smiled and said, "No offense, of course."

"I'm amazed how fast you got this place put back in order, Leary," I said. "Must've cost you a fortune to have it done in only a few days."

The shock of red hair bobbed up and down. "That it did," Leary said. "But if I'm closed, I can't make money. And if I stay closed very long, my regulars'll find someplace else to do their drinkin', that's for sure. Besides, I plan to stick the insurance company with the bill for most of it."

He slapped the bar with his big hands. "Now, what can I get you fellas? First round's on me."

"Really?" I said. "Pity we're on the job, or I'd ask for a nice single malt." I'm not exactly sure what "single malt" means, except that it's expensive booze. "As it is, I'll have a ginger ale, and my partner here will have...?" I looked at Karl, who said, "Club soda is fine."

Leary cocked an eyebrow at Karl. "Club soda, is it? Well, just as well you didn't ask for a Bloody Mary, since mine aren't made with real blood." He laughed, which made one of us who found him funny.

Leary drew our drinks from his dispenser and brought them over. Setting them down with exaggerated care, he said, "A ginger ale for the good Sergeant Markowski, and a mere club soda for Detective Renfer. I didn't even know you people could drink this stuff, Karl – it lackin' the hemoglobin, and such."

"It doesn't do much for me, tell you the truth," Karl said with a friendly smile that displayed his fangs, "but I can drink it without puking. Besides, if I get an uncontrollable urge for the real thing, I know what to do." He looked Leary up and down. "You'd be a Type O, wouldn't you, Leary?"

Leary forced a grin at what he probably hoped was humor, then turned to me. "What brings you gentlemen here, then, if not for spirits? If you came by just to see how old Leary is gettin' on after the great ogre invasion of a few nights ago, well, I'm touched at your concern, I am."

"No, actually, we're meeting someone to discuss police business," I said, "and this was a convenient location for everybody." I saw something large moving in my peripheral vision and turned to look. "And here he is now, right on time."

Leary was looking in the same direction I was, and his eyes were suddenly the size of drink coasters. "What in the name of all the saints is *he* doin' here? The bastard's in jail, ain't he? Don't tell me he made bail, because the judge didn't set any. I called and checked."

I acted like I had just figured out what he meant. "Oh, you mean you thought this fella is… no, no, you're quite right. That one's in the slam, and likely to remain there for some time." I paused for effect. "This is his brother."

"Good Lord between us and all harm," Leary breathed. To me he said, "What does he *want*?"

"A drink, I expect," I said. I waved to the ogre. "Come on over and sit down, Ivan."

And so he did, taking up two bar stools in the process. I noticed Ivan lowered himself down carefully even so, as if used to the fragility of human furniture.

"What'll you have to drink, Ivan?" I asked. "The

good innkeeper, Mister Leary, here is buying – isn't that so, Leary?"

Leary seemed incapable of speech. He just looked at Ivan and nodded.

"Cognac," Ivan rumbled. "I like cognac."

"My friend here will have a cognac, Leary, a double. The good stuff, if you please."

The look that Leary gave me could be bottled and used to poison pit vipers. But off he went, and soon came back with a snifter of cognac that he set in front of Ivan. No dramatic flourishes this time, I noticed.

Before turning away, Leary caught my eye and mouthed what I'm pretty sure was "You're responsible."

Ivan took a sip of his cognac – I noticed he didn't swirl it around in the snifter first, the way people do in the movies. I never understood that ritual, either. He put the glass down and said, "Good stuff. Thanks."

"You're welcome, Ivan. Now I want to ask you something. Is it true what I've heard, that your people are related to... goblins?"

The ogre sat staring into his glass, and I wasn't sure he was going to answer. But then he nodded slowly and said, "Not close relations, but yeah. Some say like 'cousins', but I'm not sure what they mean."

"Do you speak Goblin?"

Another slow nod. "Some."

"Do you know any of the local goblins?"

"A few, yeah."

"Do any of them owe you a favor? Or is there maybe one who you can scare into doing something for you?"

Ivan turned and looked at me. "Depends on what 'something' means."

I turned my stool toward him and leaned forward a little. "OK, here's what I had in mind."

By the time we finished talking with Ivan, who promised to stay in touch, it was getting near the end of our shift. But I wanted to do one more thing, before Karl and I parted company for the night.

"Since the bad guys know where I live," I said, "I told Christine to spend the day someplace else."

"Sounds like a good idea," Karl said. "You planning to follow your own advice, for a change?"

"Yeah, I am, as a matter of fact. I thought I'd get a room someplace until this mess of a case is resolved."

"Probably for the best. Got someplace in mind?"

"I want a hotel, not a motel," I said. "If I can get a room four or five stories up, or higher, I won't have to worry about anybody coming at me through the windows. And I'll set up some stuff at the door to give me a few seconds warning if anybody tries to get in that way."

"As long as you don't blow away some poor maid who just wants to change the sheets."

"I'll notify housekeeping to leave me alone," I said.

"So, there's five high-rise hotels in and around town, haina? Which one floats your boat?"

"I was thinking of the Radisson."

Karl whistled. "Stan the man is going first class."

"Fuckin' A," I said. "The city will reimburse me, since this is work-related, so I may as well make the most out of it."

I didn't tell Karl why I hadn't considered staying at the Hilton.

"Thing is," I said, "I need to go home first and pack a bag."

"And you want me to watch your back." One of the things I like about Karl is I don't have to draw him any diagrams.

"Exactly," I said. "Which is why I'd like us to go now, while there's still some night time left."

"So, let's do it."

Karl drove us back to the station house, where we signed out and got in our own cars. We'd agreed that Karl would leave first, and park a couple of streets over from my house. He'd quietly make his way through the neighbors' yards and get in position to watch my place before I drove up.

And if I encountered trouble from somebody already waiting inside, Karl's acute vampire hearing would pick it up, and he'd move in fast. He's been in my place many times, Karl has – he doesn't need to ask permission to enter.

I went in through my front door carefully, ready for trouble. But I needn't have worried. The only living soul inside was Quincey. Bringing his cage with me to the Radisson might draw attention, so I quickly changed his bedding, overfilled his food bowl, and attached an extra water bottle, so the little guy wouldn't dehydrate.

As I packed my suitcase, I kept one ear cocked for sounds of commotion outside. "If somebody does show up," I'd said to Karl, "take him – or them – alive, if at all possible."

"Fine with me, but if you're thinking of interrogating another one of these clowns – well, you saw what happened last time."

"Yeah, I know – they tend to be obstinate. That's why I have in mind something different to try, if we ever get our hands on another one."

But I guess the Church of the True Cross wasn't interested in me any more tonight. I locked the front door, waved in the general direction of where I figured Karl would be, and drove off to spend a few days in the lap of luxury. Of course, it's easier to enjoy elegant accommodations when you're not concerned about people trying to kill you.

On my way to the Radisson I called Christine. She had another half an hour to go on her shift at Emergency Services, but I wanted to be sure she knew where I was before she went to ground for the day. She's not supposed to take personal calls at work, and I'd already caused enough disruption over there for one night. So I called her personal number and waited for the voicemail to kick in.

"*Hi, baby, it's me. I just stopped over to the house, and it's fine, but I still think we should both stay away for a few days. I'm going to be at the Radisson, under the*

*name Michael Pacilio, P-A-C-I-L-I-O. But if you want to
call, you're probably better off just using my cell number.
Love ya."*

Michael Pacilio was the hero of that novel I'd
been reading about scientists who'd opened the
door to hell. I didn't think anybody would recognize the name – the book hadn't exactly been a
bestseller.

I knew that using a phone while driving is
against the law, and it's a law I usually agree with
and obey. But shit happens, sometimes. I was
tempted to arrest myself for the violation, but I decided to let me off with a warning, instead.

At the Radisson I talked to the assistant manager,
Tim Walsh. I've known Tim a long time, and he
agreed to let me check in under the false name I'd
selected.

He also promised to override the computer's request for a credit card number to go with Michael
Pacilio's name. Anybody with the resources of the
Church of the True Cross might be able to access my
credit card statements online. If they saw a current
charge for the Radisson, they might send some people after me. Then the hotel would have more dead
bodies to deal with, one of which might be mine.

Once I got into my room, I ordered a big room
service breakfast, which Tim agreed to deliver personally so I wouldn't have to worry about who the
waiter was really working for. He's a good man, Tim.

Then I called Lacey and brought her up to date. I
also told her my idea about how to handle a prisoner

from the Church, should we ever get another one. She agreed immediately, and said she'd start looking for a suitable place at once. I told her I'd ask around as well.

After eating, I left the tray out in the hall, took a shower, and went to bed. They say that we all dream, every night. Maybe that's true, but if I had any dreams this time, I was blessed by not remembering any of them.

I'd been at work about ten minutes when the Feebies marched in, intent on talking to McGuire. I received the usual Greer glare, but Thorwald didn't look at me at all. I tried to catch her eye, but it was like I didn't exist for her. Guess she didn't take kindly to being stood up.

I called Victor Castle and told him that the Church of the True Cross seemed to be escalating its efforts to start a "race war" between humans and supes. He said he would do his best to keep the supe community from overreacting to the latest atrocities, but urged me to "bring this matter to a successful conclusion as soon as possible," as if I needed encouragement to do my job. Prick.

Even if it wasn't my job to take down the Church of the True Cross, I'd do it, anyway. Burn somebody alive on my front lawn, I take it personally. I'm funny that way.

On my way to the break room for a cup of what passes for java in the squad, I noticed that some-body had left a copy of the *People's Voice* on an empty desk. The front page headline grabbed my attention – which wasn't hard to do, since the letters were about two inches high.

DEMON MURDER!

it said. Underneath, in somewhat smaller type was,

"Snuff films" show torture of innocent humans

and below that even smaller letters promised,

(Story, page 3)

"Mother*fucker*!" I muttered. Karl must've heard me, because he came up and looked over my shoulder.

"Ah, shit!" he said. "How'd those fuckers get the story?" Before I could offer an answer he said, "Turn the page, will you?"

The headline at the top of page 3 was in smaller print but equally hysterical: *Videos Show Torture, Murder.*

The story was underneath.

Special to The People's Voice by Tod Solin
SCRANTON (Oct. 19) – A series of "underground" videos show the apparent torture and murder of innocent people at the hands of demon-possessed humans, humans who have no control over their macabre actions.

Each video shows two naked prisoners, shackled to chairs facing each other. A voice off-camera can be heard summoning a foul creature from Hell. Then one of the prisoners is "possessed" by the newly arrived demon, who is then freed to commit bloody mayhem on the other screaming, pleading human.

Despite advances in special-effects makeup that allow Hollywood filmmakers to realistically simulate torment and mutilation in the horror sub-genre known as "torture porn," it is highly unlikely that the atrocities shown in these videos are simulated.

The People's Voice has obtained three of these so-called "snuff videos", and this reporter has been reliably informed that others exist as well. The videos have been...

To the left of the story was a shot from the video that Thorwald and Greer had screened for the squad at the beginning of this nightmare. It showed the demon-possessed man at work on the other one, who we now knew as Edward Hudzinski. The image was carefully selected to avoid showing the participants' genitals or any actual explicit torture. But it had a good shot of Hudzinski's face in mid-scream.

Karl stopped reading and stepped back. "Know that that splattering noise is?"

I turned to face him. "What noise? I don't hear anything."

"Sure you do," he said grimly. "It's the sound of all the shit that just hit the fan."

I refolded the paper and took it with me to McGuire's office. The Feebies were still in there with him, but I rapped on the door a couple of times and opened it anyway.

"Boss, I–"

Thorwald gave me the kind of glare that Custer probably grew really tired of in his last moments. "This is a *private* conversation with your *superior*, Sergeant – which you have *not* been invited to take part in!" Hell hath no fury, and so on.

"I know," I said. "And I've been feeling really bad about that, too. But I wondered if any of you folks had seen *this*." I tossed the newspaper onto McGuire's desk.

McGuire reached for it, but Thorwald was faster. She snatched it up, stared at the headline, then ripped the paper open to page 3. She must have been a fast reader, because less than ten seconds went by before she closed the paper, folded it in one angry motion, and flung it back on the desk.

"This is outrageous!" she cried.

"I couldn't agree more," I said calmly. Next to me, Karl said, "Yeah, me neither."

McGuire had acquired the paper by now and was reading the article with a look of horrified fascination.

"This… this…" Thorwald seemed to be having trouble getting a sentence started. "Some cocksucker has *leaked* those fucking snuff videos to the motherfucking *press*. And since *I* didn't do it, and *Greer* didn't do it, do you know what that fucking *means*?"

Normally, listening to an attractive woman talk dirty turns me on a little, but I think even a satyr's lust would have been quelled by Thorwald's fury.

"Um, someone in Washington isn't to be trusted?" I asked innocently. I wasn't going to give Thorwald the fight she was obviously spoiling for. I wondered if she would have been quite this pissed off at me if she'd achieved the two hours of "good hard fucking" that she'd been seeking.

I guess Greer was feeling neglected, because he pointed an index finger at me and said, "I've had just about *enough* out of you, pal."

Before anybody could respond to that, Thorwald turned and headed for McGuire's door, with an expression that said as clear as words, "Don't get in my fucking way!"

Karl and I stepped aside and let her pass. After a couple of seconds, Greer followed. I was glad Thorwald wasn't the last one out. She'd probably have slammed the door hard enough to shatter the glass.

The three of us watched as the two agents made their angry way across the squad room and out the door. A couple of other detectives at their desks turned and looked, too. That much rage is impressive, even when it's not directed at you.

McGuire sighed and tapped the newspaper a couple of times. "Histrionics aside," he said, "this *is* pretty goddamn bad."

Karl and I sat down in the chairs the Feebies had vacated. "Yeah, I know," Karl said. "The public is gonna go nuts over this, which means pressure on the politicos, which means more pressure on us."

"As if we needed it," McGuire said.

"Boss," I said, "have you ever noticed that the stuff that's published in the *People's Voice* always seems like an echo of the bullshit put out by the Church of the True Cross?"

McGuire glanced down at the screaming headlines again. "You figure there's a connection?"

"At this point, I'd be surprised if there wasn't."

"Even if there is, so what? There's no law says a church can't own a newspaper."

"Yeah, but they're hiding it, aren't they? If so, they're doing it for a reason."

"You got any thoughts as to what that reason might be?" McGuire asked.

"No, not at the moment."

"Then bug me about it when you do, not before."

"No matter *who* owns that rag," Karl said, "somebody sent them copies of those fuckin' videos. Since it wasn't us, I gotta wonder–"

Louise appeared at McGuire's door and said, "Excuse the interruption, sir." She looked at me. "Rachel Proctor on the phone. Says it's urgent."

I turned to McGuire. "You mind, boss?"

"No, go on – get out of here, both of you. I've got calls of my own to make. When I tell the chief, I bet he's gonna make Thorwald sound like a Mary Poppins."

I walked quickly to my desk, pushed a blinking button on the phone, and picked up the receiver. "Hello, Rachel?"

"Stan, one of the best ideas you had was when

you suggested I tell the other witches that those murderers were still at large – although I like to think I would've thought of it myself."

"I'm sure you would," I said. "What's up?"

"I just got a call from Carol Ann Cosgrove."

"Yeah, I know Carol Ann."

"Apparently one of those commando assholes made a grab at her, but she had a spell ready to protect herself."

"She froze him, like you did?"

"No, she used a sleep spell," Rachel said. "He's dead to the world, until she wakes him."

"Good for her. I'm glad she was quick enough, and kept her head."

"Me, too," she said. "Thing is, Carol Ann isn't sure who she should call to report it – the regular cops, the Supe Squad, or–"

"Rachel, are you home, or in your office?"

"Office. I could've come up, but wasn't sure if you were there. I was gonna call your personal number if Louise said you were out."

"Great," I said. "We'll be down in a minute."

I put the phone down and looked at Karl. "Come on," I said, and turned toward the door.

As we walked down the hall, Karl asked, "What've we got, Stan?"

"A break. If we play it right, maybe a big one."

"Did Carol Ann say where the perp is now?" I asked Rachel.

"Curled up on the floor of her garage," she said.

"He was hiding there, and apparently made a grab for her when she got out of the car."

"How long will he stay out?" I asked.

"I know the spell she used. It'll remain in place until she lifts it. I mean, she has a moral obligation to wake him before he dies of thirst, or something, but that won't be a danger for several days."

I thought for a couple of moments. "You mind getting her on the phone for me, Rachel?"

"Sure."

Rachel made the call.

"Hi, Carol Ann, it's Rachel again. I've got Stan Markowski from Occult Crimes with me. You know Stan, don't you? Good. He'd like to speak with you, so I'm going to hand him the phone now, OK? All right, just a second."

"Hi, Carol Ann."

"Hello, Stan. Long time."

"Yeah, it is. I hear you've had quite a night."

"To say the least. I don't think my heart rate has returned to normal yet – but it's better than it was."

"You'll be fine, soon," I said. "Tell me, how was the guy dressed, do you recall?"

"He looks like something out of the movies, Stan. Black clothing, even his stocking cap."

"OK, that's what I figured. Uh, Carol Ann, I'm going to ask you to do something kind of… unusual."

Her voice became guarded. "Go ahead and ask."

"Well, instead of sending a squad car over there right now to pick up Sleeping Beauty, I'd like to leave him where he is for a few hours. Think you can stand that?"

After a short pause she said, "Yeah, I suppose so. What's going on, Stan? Are all the cells full tonight?"

"Not exactly. But I want time to arrange for some special accommodations for this fella."

"What kind of accommodations?" Carol Ann asked.

"It's probably better that you don't know that," I said. "But I'll tell you this much – if I can make my idea work, I might be able to find out who's sending these thugs after you and your sister witches."

Actually, I already knew the answer to that question – what I needed was *proof*.

"All right, Stan. I suppose I can go along with that – with one proviso. Are you planning to do harm to him? Because, although part of me would love that, I cannot permit it to happen as a result of my magic."

"Carol Ann, I'm not planning to harm a hair under his little stocking cap. Now, there's just one more thing I need to ask you…"

As Karl and I walked back to the squad room, I reached for my own phone. It only took a few seconds to find Lacey's number and call it.

"Hello?" she said.

"It's Stan."

"Yes… and?"

"We've got one. It's on."

"I'm very glad to hear that."

"How soon can you be ready?"

"Everything's all set up at the cottage," Lacey said. "All I have to do is get there. Say… an hour fifteen, to be on the safe side."

"Fine. We'll see you there."

"Stan?"

"What?"

"Thank you."

When I told McGuire that Karl and I were going to take personal time for the rest of our shift, he looked at me and nodded grudgingly. He doesn't like stuff like that, but union rules say we can, and neither one of us does it a lot.

McGuire looked at me. "Do I want to know how you and Karl are going to be spending the time?"

"No, you don't."

He nodded slowly. "All right. Good luck."

As we walked outside, I asked Karl, "You sure your uncle's not likely to show up in the middle of things?"

"Naw, he's already in Florida. I called him last night, before I gave Lacey the key and directions. He's down there, all right."

In the parking lot, Karl said, "No point taking two cars, is there?"

"None that I can see."

"Which one, then?"

"You've got more trunk space," I said.

"Good point. OK, get in."

In another ten minutes, we were ringing Carol Ann's doorbell. She answered it almost at once.

"Come on in, guys."

She gave me a quick hug. "Good to see you, Stan."

She had a hug for Karl, too. "How've you been, Karl?"

"Not too bad, I guess."

Carol Ann asked him, "I understand you're *nosferatu* nowadays," she said. "How's that working out for you?"

"Ah, it's like anything else, Carol Ann – good points and bad ones."

I asked her, "Did you prepare what we talked about?"

"Yep, got it right here."

She showed me a small statuette. I'd had a bad experience with a Gorgon statue a while ago, but this one looked entirely different. There was nothing evil about it.

"It's a representation of the goddess Hecate," Carol Ann said. "I'd like it back someday. No hurry."

"I'll take good care of it," I said.

"When the time comes, just close your hand around it, like this–" she made a fist "–and say the word *pardac*. It's only charged to work once, so be sure you're ready before you say it."

"It's *pardac*," I said. "Right?"

"Perfect. Here you go." She handed me the statuette, and I carefully put it in my jacket pocket.

"Well, any time you guys want to take out the garbage, he's ready for you," she said.

Five minutes later, we pulled out of Carol Ann's driveway. In the trunk we had an unconscious commando, who was probably in for the worst night of his life.

• • • •

To get to Lake Wallenpaupack, you take Route 84 east from Scranton for about twenty miles, then follow shitty secondary roads that seem to go on forever – or at least they do in the part we were headed for, a stretch of shoreline that mostly consists of smaller houses or cottages. They're empty for about half the year.

Often a bunch of fishermen will chip in and buy one of the cottages, and use it as a base in the summer. Karl's uncle had one all his own, and that's where we were headed, much to the dismay of Karl's shock absorbers. We bounced through the potholes at ten to fifteen miles an hour. Our guest in the trunk should have been glad he was unconscious, although he'd still find himself all bruised and banged up when he awoke. And that was going to be the least of his problems.

Lacey's Dodge Perdition was already there when we pulled into the graveled driveway. Good – that was the plan.

We opened the trunk, and Karl carried the limp form down some sloping ground and around to the back, to the basement entrance. A couple of big doors that belonged on a barn stood slightly open, and a light shone from inside. I pulled one of the doors wide enough for Karl and his burden to get through. He didn't need an invitation – he'd been in here before.

As we came into the big, open room, we found Lacey facing the door, waiting for us. "Good evening," she said. Some people might have said that à la Bela Lugosi, but not Lacey – she was serious tonight. Deadly serious.

I took in the dirt floor, peeling wallpaper, and ramshackle furniture that I figured had constituted all the original furnishings. But Lacey had brought in a few things of her own.

The most impressive of the new additions was a big frame made of black PVC pipe, the stuff they use in industrial plumbing and scaffolding. The freestanding structure was about eight feet square, and the plastic surface of the pipes gleamed in the overhead light. It looked like a big Tinkertoy that had been designed by the Spanish Inquisition.

Next to the PVC structure, but at a right angle to it, was a folding table that I assumed Lacey had also brought with her. Arrayed along it was a collection of implements, which I had described for Lacey from the two snuff films I'd seen.

The macabre smorgasbord included knives of course, and a new-looking blowtorch. Somewhere she had found an old-fashioned corkscrew – the kind that is just a tightly wound spiral of steel with a sharp point at one end and a handle on the other. She had a hammer and the needle-nose pliers, too.

Lacey looked slowly around the room and said, "Nice place your uncle has here, Karl."

"I know it's a wreck," he said, "but fishermen aren't too fussy. All they wanna do is fish, tell lies about what got away, and drink beer."

Lacey shook her head. "No, Karl, I'm sorry – you misunderstood. No sarcasm intended – I *mean* it.

For what we're going to do tonight, this place is *perfect*. I practically fell in love the first time I saw it."

Karl placed his unconscious burden gently on the dirt floor. Lacey looked at the black-clad man for a moment, and something in her face reminded me of stories I'd read about Indians involved in inter-tribal warfare centuries ago, and how their greatest fear was being taken prisoner and turned over to the women.

"Well, you might as well strip him and get him secured to the frame," she said. "Then we'll get started."

Undressing our prisoner was easy enough, although I smiled a little when I discovered the guy wore no underwear – he really *was* going commando. But trying to get a naked, unconscious man tied to a structure like that, arms and legs spread wide, was harder than we'd thought. But finally it was done.

Lacey looked at our work and nodded approval. Then she asked me, "You have something to break the spell?"

"Sure do," I said, and brought the little statue from my pocket. "All set?" I asked her, and she nodded tensely. I closed my hand around the statuette, looked at the naked man, and said, "*Pardac*."

The guy didn't snap awake. It took him ten or fifteen seconds to reach full awareness – and when he did, he was not a happy little camper.

He blinked rapidly, then shook his head, the way a dog will when trying to get rid of water on its fur. Like the other representative of the Church's elite guard that we'd met, this one was in his late twenties and very fit-looking. His black hair was cut short, but his eyebrows were bushy. One of his knees was circled with old surgical scars, as if he'd tried a little too hard when playing high school football.

Our prisoner looked around at us, eyes wide.

"Who are– What did you– How did I get–" Then he seemed to realize the full extent of his plight – he was alone, tied up, spreadeagled naked in front of strangers whose intentions were uncertain. In his place, I'd be scared, too.

"Jesus fucking Christ – let me *down* from here! Let me *go*, goddamnit!!

"Blasphemy. How distressing." Karl sounded disapproving.

"And so early in the proceedings," I said. "Gives us less to look forward to later."

The commando's gaze traveled around the room, and he didn't seem nearly as pleased with what he saw as Lacey had been. "Wh-where am I?"

"Someplace where nobody can hear you scream," I said.

When I spoke this time, he'd stared at me, as if my voice had jarred something in his memory. "I know you!"

I just nodded. Then the guy shifted his gaze to Karl. "And you! I know you, too. You're that vampire cop!" Karl nodded as well.

Finally, he looked at Lacey, who stood there, hands in her pockets, a gentle smile on her face.

"Who – who the hell are *you*?"

She walked slowly over to him until she stood with her face only a few feet from his. "Me?" she said softly. "I am Vengeance."

The commando opened his mouth, but no sound came out. After a few seconds, Lacey walked slowly over to the table and its array of agony. She gently ran the fingertips of one hand along the length of the display, lightly touching each instrument in turn. Then she turned back to our prisoner.

"Do you recognize these?" Her voice was light, almost casual. "They should be familiar. I thought there was a certain… irony involved in taking the implements that have been the source of so much pain for others…" She paused. "And using them on you." Lacey abandoned the teasing tone then, and her voice became hard. "Every one of them."

The naked man was trembling now, as if the temperature in the basement had just dropped twenty degrees. Finally he screamed, "I don't care *what* you do to me – I'll *never* talk! I'll never tell you anything, you *cunt*."

"Ooh, such language." Lacey was playing the tease again. "Do you kiss your mother with that mouth? Or should I say, 'Did you?' Because you never will again."

She was wearing a medium-weight navy-blue jacket, and now she unzipped it to reveal a short-sleeve knit pullover top and jeans underneath. She draped the jacket over the back of a nearby chair, then reached up, crossed her arms, and pulled the top over her head.

At least she hadn't gone the Victoria's Secret route. Underneath the top, she wore a plain black sports bra. I thought it looked pretty damn good on her anyway, but that wasn't the point. The striptease wasn't part of the script we'd agreed on.

Calling a huddle right then might give our prisoner reason to suspect dissension among the ranks of his tormenters, and that would never do. So, trying to sound casual, I said to Lacey, "Um, what're you doing there?"

She was just kicking off her plain black shoes to reveal bare feet. "Doing?" She gave me an innocent look that I didn't believe for a microsecond. "Oh, you mean this?"

As she spoke, she'd been unbuckling her belt and undoing a button on the jeans. Now she yanked the zipper down and pushed the jeans past her slim hips. They fell, pooling around her ankles, and she kicked them free.

"Gosh, Stan, you don't think I want to get a mess all over my clothes, do you? Blood washes off skin *much* more easily than it does fabric."

Lacey bent, picked up the jeans, and placed them on the chair. She had on a pair of those gray women's undershorts that look like the boxers men wear, and are just about as sexy. But, still, on Lacey...

A couple of steps brought her over to the commando, who was staring at her in barely concealed panic, despite his big talk of a few moments ago.

She ran a hand slowly along his inner thigh, just brushing his shrunken penis. "Besides, having a naked woman do all the things that I'll be doing to him adds a touch of piquancy to the whole experience – don't you think?"

Then she reached behind her back for the bra fastener. "If you guys want to stay for the show, it's OK with me. But if you go upstairs, there's beer in the fridge and a working TV in the living room. In fact, you might want to turn it up extra loud."

"Good idea," I said, and turned away just as the fastener came undone and the bra slid down her arms. Karl followed me at once.

We pulled the big door shut behind us, and immediately from inside came the sound of metal sliding on wood. I remembered that there'd been a big bolt next to the knob, and it seemed that Lacey had just shot it, locking the door securely from the inside. I looked at Karl, and he stared back. This part wasn't in the script, either.

Karl and I made our way back around the side of the cottage to the front door and let ourselves in. There was beer in the fridge, all right, but it didn't appeal to either of us – for different reasons. Lacey was right about the TV, too. The old 19-inch portable had extendable rabbit ears that could pull in two of the local channels. We settled on one and watched stupid sitcoms. The reception wasn't all that good, but then I can't say that I paid real close attention. I kept waiting for screams to start issuing from the room underneath us, but all I could hear was the inane dialogue and canned laughter of the

TV show. Finally, I asked Karl if his acute vampire hearing was picking up anything from below.

"No screaming, if that's what you mean," he said. "I can sort of make out Lacey's voice, and sometimes the guy's, but I can't catch what they're saying."

"Let's say we start hearing screams, thirty seconds from now. What do we do about it?"

Karl scratched his chin. "What do you *want* to do about it?"

"You could take that basement door down, couldn't you? Despite the fact that it's bolted shut?"

"Yeah, that wouldn't be much of a problem," he said. "Assuming that's what we decide to do."

"Why *wouldn't* we? The plan was to terrify him into talking, remember? We can't sit here and let her torture the guy, even if he is a fucking scumbag."

"The dude's not under arrest," Karl said. "And Lacey's not acting in her official capacity as a cop, either."

"He's in *our* custody, Karl. We brought him here, which makes him *our* responsibility. And torture, no matter what the motivation, is still a crime. We're supposed to uphold the law – we're the good guys, remember?"

Karl looked at me. "You never bent the law a little, Stan? Here and there, out of necessity?"

"Even if I did, what Lacey's doing down there is more than bending the fucking law – it's *breaking* it."

"Not yet, it's not," he said. "No screaming, remember?"

"What if she gagged him?" I asked.

"He'd still be making sounds through his nose, and I'd hear it."

I sat back and pretended to watch the TV. I was beginning to wish I'd never had the bright idea of trying to scare one of the Church's thugs into giving us information. I should have had Karl try Influence, even if he wasn't real good at it yet, and kept Lacey out of this entirely. Grief and rage had turned her into someone I didn't know anymore, and didn't like very much.

What if Karl heard muffled screams from below and didn't tell me? Or what if I heard them, too? In theory, I was Karl's superior and could order him to tear that basement door down. Except the operation we were on had no official sanction. And what was I going to do if Karl refused – shoot him?

I came up with answers for all those questions – trouble was, I kept changing them every couple of minutes. I was still trying to figure out what to do if it got bad down there when the front door opened and Lacey walked in.

She was fully dressed, I was glad to see, except for the outer jacket she'd been wearing. She was perspiring freely.

I guess she'd familiarized herself with the place during her first visit, because she went without hesitation to a door and opened it to reveal a sparsely stocked linen closet. She found a tattered blue bath towel, looped it around her neck, and began to dry her face and hair.

I was waiting for her to say something. When she

didn't, the best I could come up with was, "Done for the night, Lacey?"

She stopped mopping her face and looked at me, her expression hard to read. "Yes, Stan, I'm all finished."

When she didn't elaborate, I said, quietly, "Did you kill him?"

"No, he's very much alive."

"Has he still got all his parts intact?"

She gave me a half smile. "If he didn't, I'm sure you would have heard the screams. Or if you couldn't, Karl would have." She looked at Karl. "Right?"

He just nodded.

"So what *did* you do to him?" I said.

"I broke his spirit," she said. "Through a combination of terror and sexual excitement, I put so much stress on his psyche that he couldn't stand it, and he broke."

Karl and I looked at each other.

"Sexual excitement?" he said to Lacey.

"Oh, yes," she said. "It can be an important component in an effective interrogation. That's why I was naked. The Gestapo used the technique sometimes, with prisoners they thought wouldn't respond to the more direct approach. Certain prisoners would be questioned by an attractive woman, who would slowly build sexual tension in them, but deny release until she got the information she wanted."

"How come you know all about the Gestapo?" I asked.

"I've been doing a lot of reading, Stan, ever since you told me I might have the chance to question one of these people. God bless the Internet."

"You studied torture, you mean."

"No, I studied methods of interrogation – which sometimes included torture, I admit. Some of the stuff I read grossed me out – or would have, under other circumstances. But I just viewed it as data that might prove useful."

"And was it?" I said. "Useful, I mean?"

"Oh, did I forget to mention that part?" The grin that blossomed on her face reminded me of the old Lacey, someone I hadn't been sure I'd ever see again.

"The next snuff video is scheduled to be filmed two nights from now, in a warehouse at 1634 Stansfield Avenue. Festivities are due to start at midnight, I believe."

"Holy shit," Karl said.

I jumped up, ran over to Lacey and hugged her. "Lacey, that's fantastic! It's all we need to bust these motherfuckers, once and for all."

The grin was still in place when she said, "Well, it's good to know that my little efforts do not go un-appreciated."

"They don't – believe me," I told her.

"Did you get anything else out of him?" Karl asked.

"Just a couple of things," Lacey said. "One is that they've been using Drac's List to identify likely victims."

"Damn, I *knew* there was something wrong about those people," I said, ignoring the look that Karl gave me.

"Once they have a profile that looks promising," Lacey said, "someone pretending to be a vampire member will contact him – or her – and start an on-line conversation. The so-called vampire will find out if he lives alone, has any close friends or relatives, all that stuff. Once they identify somebody who won't be missed for a while, the 'vampire' makes a date – except the poor guy, or woman – gets a lot worse than a vampire bite."

"You mentioned a couple of things," Karl said. "What's the other one?"

"Just that, to the surprise of nobody here in this room, the Church owns the *People's Voice*," Lacey said. "The connection is hidden by a series of hold-ing companies, but the Church is pulling the strings."

"I asked the Feebies to have someone look into the paper and who was behind it. They never got back to me, which isn't exactly surprising." I looked at Lacey. "Congrats, kiddo – you did a hell of a job."

I ran a hand through my hair. "The only other pressing problem is what to do with Rambo down there until we raid the warehouse the night after tomorrow."

"We could just leave him there," Lacey said. The monster was back in her eyes now. "I can come back in a week or so and bury him."

"That's not exactly what I had in mind, Lace," I

said. "There's got to be another way to keep him on ice until–"

"I think I've got an idea," Karl said, and we both turned toward him.

"The county sheriff's an old fishing buddy of my Uncle Ned," he said. "Name's Andy Probert. I used to do a lot of fishing up here myself, and I've known the guy for years. I bet if I ask him, he'll put our commando in a cell for a few days under a John Doe – which is maybe the only name we'll get out of the guy, anyway."

"Hold him on what charge?" I asked.

"Doesn't have to be a charge, does it?" Karl said. "We'll call it 'protective custody'. Sheriff Probert won't ask too many questions."

"That sounds like exactly what we need," I said. "You wanna give the sheriff a call and see if you can set it up?"

"Absolutely," Karl said.

Ten minutes later, the three of us went back to the basement. Our prisoner, who was still tied as before, started when we walked in, but seemed kind of relieved that Lacey wasn't alone this time.

He looked at us dully. His face was streaked with drying tears, and there was a half-absorbed puddle in the dirt underneath him. I assumed that Lacey had so terrified him at some point that he had pissed himself.

"All right," I told him. "In a minute, I'm going to start cutting you free from there. When I finish, I want you to get dressed. Understand?"

"Yeah."

"Once you're loose, you don't want to even *think* about going all Bruce Lee on me. If you do, my vampire partner over there will tear your throat out. He hasn't fed in a couple of nights, and he was telling me earlier that he thinks you look tasty."

Karl smiled, giving the guy a good look at his fangs. "Tasty," he said.

"Yeah, OK, sure," the commando muttered.

When the prisoner was cut down and dressed, Karl handcuffed his hands behind his back and led him out to Lacey's car. She was going to drive them to the Pike County jail, where the sheriff would be waiting to make sure that prisoner John Doe was processed the way we wanted. Guess Karl and I should have taken separate cars, after all – we hadn't thought far enough ahead. I wanted to get back to Scranton as soon as possible, to brief McGuire on what I'd learned tonight.

Lacey started to follow Karl and his prisoner out, but stopped and turned back to me.

"I wanted to thank you," she said, "for leaving before I was completely naked."

"It seemed… I dunno… wrong to stick around."

"I wouldn't have said anything if you and Karl had stayed, but I'm glad you didn't. So – thank you, Stan."

"You're welcome, Lacey." What else was I going to say?

After nearly getting murdered in the police parking lot a couple of times, Karl and I had bugged McGuire to see about getting better lights for the place. He'd impressed upon the chief the importance of what we wanted, and he, in turn, had gone to the mayor. To the surprise of practically everybody, the city council had approved the funds, and our parking lot behind the building was now lit up like a football field during a night game.

The downside of all that illumination is that it makes you a well-lit target for somebody looking at the parking area from outside.

That's why when a deep voice from across the street yelled, "Hey! Markowski!" I scuttled behind my car, dropped into a crouch, and drew my weapon. I heard a car door open, and peered through the chain-link fence that encloses the parking lot.

Ivan the ogre was slowly climbing out from behind the wheel of a big SUV. "Markowski," he called, "I got a goblin!" He made a summoning gesture. "Come on!"

I was torn. I needed to tell McGuire what I'd learned about the next snuff film – but he'd be in his office for another couple of hours. If Ivan had found a goblin willing to talk about who had sent the hit squad of greenies after me, then that was a goblin I badly wanted to meet.

I yelled over to Ivan, "I'll be right there!" Having him bring an unauthorized vehicle into our parking area would require all kinds of time-wasting paperwork. It was quicker for me to go out to him. I stood up and walked rapidly toward the gate.

Ivan was back behind the wheel and as I approached he said, "Get in back, Markowski."

There was a goblin in the front passenger seat. Like all of them, he was short, with matted green fur over black skin. In the close confines of the SUV, I noticed that he smelled like wet dog – a big, old wet dog with bad teeth. The goblin was half turned in his seat, looking back at me nervously.

"This Fred," Ivan rumbled. "Only goblin I could get to come here. Has no English, so I translate."

I looked at Ivan. "Fred?"

He shrugged those enormous shoulders. "Close enough."

"OK," I said. "Ask him if he knows about somebody going out to Goblinville to recruit a bunch of them willing to kill a cop."

Ivan frowned at me. "Goblinville? What's that?"

"I mean whatever they call the place where they live, out near the dump."

Ivan turned to his passenger and spoke in Goblin, which always sounds to me like a mixture of Chinese, Russian, and the sound of a cat fight.

After another nervous look at me, Fred turned to Ivan and answered.

"He say human come, a while ago–" Ivan began.

"Wait," I said. "How long is 'a while ago'?"

"Goblins not good with time," Ivan said. "Could mean a week, a month – who knows?"

"All right," I said. "Go on."

"He say human come, bring meth – but not

much. Give to some goblins, promise more. Want goblins to kill human – cop."

"Did the human say why this cop needed to be killed?"

More Goblin talk followed. Then Ivan turned to me again.

"Human say cop bad for goblins. Say he kill goblin, year ago. No goblin remember year ago, but some want meth. Meth enough reason."

"Ask him what this human–"

Suddenly, Fred stiffened. I noticed he was staring past Ivan, out the driver's side window. He pointed out the window and started jabbering.

I turned and looked where he was pointing. In the police parking lot, Special Agents Thorwald and Greer were getting into what looked like a black Ford Explorer. Ivan had the windows of the SUV closed, so the Feebies couldn't hear the goblin, fortunately.

"What's he so excited about?" I asked Ivan. "What's he saying?"

Ivan said, "He say that the human who come with meth, over there. The bitch."

"Bitch?"

"That what he say," Ivan said. "'That one, that one, the bitch'."

"Ask him if he's positive." I watched the Feebies back out of their parking space and drive away.

Another exchange in Goblin.

"He sure," Ivan said. "Say bitch come to where goblins live, bring meth, want them to kill cop. Some goblins say yes, go off with bitch in big black

car – car like one just drove away. Goblins not
come back."

Damn right they didn't – thanks to me and Sharkey.

Thorwald. The bitch, indeed. She had hired goblins
to kill me. The only reason she'd do that was if she
was working for the Church of the True Cross. Their
own little double agent inside the FBI. Well, well.

I pulled some bills out of my wallet and handed
them to Ivan. "Don't give this to him – he might use
it to buy meth someplace. Buy him a reward – some
food that goblins like, or something. OK?"

Ivan took the money and put it in his shirt
pocket. He looked at me over the back of his seat.
"We square now, Markowski – yeah?"

"Yeah, Ivan," I said. "We square."

When I finished telling him what the commando
had given up to Lacey, McGuire was smiling – but
then the smile faded. He said, "We'll need a warrant
to raid the warehouse, and the judge is going to
want to know on what basis we're asking for it."

"So tell him we received a tip from a confidential
informant," I said. "That's worked before."

"But the confidential informant is Lacey – a *cop*."

"Yeah, but she isn't a cop in this department, or
even in this county. Hell, she isn't even a cop in
Wilkes-Barre right now – she's on extended leave."

McGuire rubbed his jaw. "Yeah, I guess."

"Take it to Judge Olszewski, boss – him or
Rakauskas. Either one of them will sign the warrant
application in a second."

"Hope you're right," he said, and slapped his palms on the desk. "OK, I'll have to alert Dooley, and tell him to have SWAT ready to roll night after tomorrow. And I'm going to assign two detective teams from the squad to go along, for extra manpower. I assume you and Karl want to be one of them."

"Bet your ass we do."

"Where is Karl, anyway?"

"He and Lacey took our prisoner to the Pike County jail. After that, I figure he headed home – the sun'll be up soon. Anyway, we're both on personal time tonight." I grinned at him. "I'm not even supposed to be here."

"OK, then," McGuire said. "We'll send SWAT, plus you and Karl, along with one of the other detective teams. And I'll have to get the Feds in on it, of course."

"No, you won't," I said. "And you shouldn't."

He stared at me. "What the fuck are you talking about?"

I told him about my visit with Ivan and his goblin pal, and what I had learned regarding a certain Federal agent.

"Thorwald," McGuire said, shaking his head. "Jesus fucking Christ. Are you *sure*?"

"All I'm sure about is what the goblin said, boss. And he didn't seem to have any doubts."

"Shit." McGuire closed his eyes for a second, his brow furrowed. "We can't use what the gob told you as the basis for arresting Thorwald, that's for certain. And there's no chance we'd get away with that 'confidential informant' crap twice in the same day."

"Yeah, I know," I said. "We can't bust her – at least, not yet – but that doesn't mean we have to tell her about the raid. If she knows, the Church will know, and then there's no point in having the fucking raid in the first place. All we'd find is an empty warehouse."

"All right, we'll keep the Feds in the dark, and may the ghost of J. Edgar Hoover have mercy on us. We'll have to keep an eye on Thorwald, as well. That'll be tricky – she knows all the detectives in the squad."

"Why not put Lacey on it?" I asked.

"The same Lacey who isn't a cop these days? *That* Lacey?"

"She doesn't have to be a cop just to conduct surveillance," I said. "She can testify under oath about whatever she sees, just like any other private citizen. And she's as good at surveillance as anybody we've got available, that's for sure."

"She's not likely to go all *Death Wish* on Thorwald, is she?" McGuire said with a frown. "The absolute last thing we need is having some Fed burned down by a cop, on leave or not – especially a Fed against whom not a damn thing has been proven yet. Nothing admissible in court, anyway."

"Lacey's got it under control," I said. "If she didn't cross the line with our prisoner, then she's not gonna cross it – period."

"Here's hoping you're right," he said. "OK, put

her on it, if she's willing. Surveillance *only* – be very clear about that."

"I will, boss." I looked at my watch. "Well, I'm not on the clock right now, but if I were, it would be time to go home – or to the Radisson, anyway."

"Yeah, take off," McGuire said. "You've given my ulcer enough to work on for one night."

In the parking lot, I called Lacey – but all I got was her voicemail. Since I wasn't sure when I'd get to talk to her, I laid out as briefly as possible what I wanted her to do. I asked her to get started watching Thorwald as soon as she'd had some rest, and to call me if any problems arose.

As I drove to my palatial accommodations, I was feeling cautiously optimistic about the case. With luck, we were gonna bust a lot of bad guys in less than forty-eight hours, and wouldn't that be sweet?

Yeah, I felt pretty cheerful – that alone should have served as a warning.

I arrived at the Radisson just as the sky was lightening in the east. As soon as the door of my room closed behind me, I knew something was wrong. It took a second or two to realize that it was a smell – an odor both alien and familiar, which hadn't been present in the room when I'd left.

I drew the Beretta and stood, listening. I couldn't hear anything except my pulse pounding in my ears. Then the heater came on automatically, and I almost put three bullets into it.

I took a couple of slow, deliberate breaths, in an

effort to tamp the adrenaline down a little. The rising sun had barely reached the window, and my room was still dimly lit. I reached behind me and clicked on the light. Squinting against the glare, I swept my gun across the room, but found nothing to shoot.

The only thing that seemed out of place was on the bed.

My pal Tim had agreed to instruct housekeeping to stay the hell out of my room for the duration of my stay. But *someone* had been in here, because in the center of the bed, under the blanket, was a lump about the size of a basketball, but irregular in shape.

A bomb? Not too likely. You put a bomb in somebody's bed, the *last* thing you want is to make it conspicuous.

So if it wasn't a bomb, then what? I approached the bed slowly, gun still in my right hand. I flashed on that scene from *The Godfather* when the Hollywood producer wakes up to find a very nasty surprise sharing the bed with him. Good thing I didn't own a horse.

I slowly grasped the edge of the covers with one hand, then threw them back in one swift motion. I had my gun trained on the bed before I could register what I was seeing.

His broad-brimmed hat had been knocked askew by my sudden removal of the bedding, but the sunglasses were still in place. The teeth were bared, so it seemed as if Sharkey's head was grinning at me.

I gaped in shock – which is just what I was expected to do. Behind me, the bathroom door

clicked open, but I registered the sound just a second too late. I tried to turn, but a strong hand
grabbed my gun wrist and an instant later I felt the
sting as a needle went into my neck. I struggled for
a moment longer, but then I was falling, and the
dope worked so fast I never even knew when I hit
the floor.

The first thing I realized was that I was cold – not
freezing-to-death cold, but enough to be uncom-
fortable. The second thing I noticed was that my ass
hurt.

Eventually, I gathered enough of my wits about
me to figure out that I was cold because I was in an
unheated building with my sports coat off, and my
ass hurt because I was sitting on a concrete floor,
and probably had been for a while.

Both of those things had to do with the fact that
my back was against some kind of wooden pillar
with my hands bound behind me. I could feel metal
around my wrists, and realized I was handcuffed –
probably with my own cuffs. Motherfuckers.

My legs were tied together at the ankles with rope.
I squinted for a closer look and saw that the rope was
triple-strand nylon – not rare, but not the kind you
buy at Sears, either. I've learned a lot about rope in
my job.

I thought about the ME's report on the second
witch burning. I don't have a photographic memory, but sometimes stuff sticks in my head, whether
I want it there or not.

The deceased was secured to the tree in two places with ligatures consisting of triple-strand nylon rope.

Funny, the things you remember – and at the oddest times, too.

Having nothing else to do – unless you count panicking, which I figured I'd save until later – I checked out my surroundings.

I could see because of the double fluorescent light in the ceiling, which flickered as if it was on its last legs. The room was about twelve feet square. My view through the single window was blocked by a dirty white Venetian blind, but a little sunlight leaked through, so I knew it was still daytime.

The red brick walls were chipped and pitted, the mortar crumbling here and there. In one corner was a battered gray file cabinet. Ten feet or so in front of me was a severely functional desk, the kind you'd find in high school homerooms back when I was in school. It had seen better days, too, and so had the vinyl-covered desk chair behind it.

Clearly, this was an office of some kind, or had been. It was what you might expect to find in an old auto repair shop – or maybe a warehouse. I shuddered, and it wasn't because of the cold. The word *warehouse* had some pretty bad associations for me these days.

There was a plain wooden door to my left, and I happened to be looking in that direction when it opened. A young guy wearing a black turtleneck stuck his head in, looked at me and said, "Good."

He stepped back out, but left the door ajar, so I

had no trouble hearing him say, "Mister Wilson – he's awake, sir."

Father Duvall had said that the head honcho of the Church of the True Cross, bigger even than Bishop Navarra, was a rich nut named Patton Wilson. I figured I was about to find out just how nutty he was.

I heard footsteps approaching rapidly, and then a man strode into the room and closed the door behind him. He didn't look crazy – but then, they hardly ever do.

Patton Wilson was probably in his sixties, but there was nothing old about the way he moved around. His iron-gray hair was thick, with a moustache to match. He had a tan, but it was the kind you get from a lot of time spent outdoors, not a bottle. His head was large, and his face took up a lot of territory, but the dark eyes were small and mean, like two raisins in a bowl of rice pudding. He had big hands.

"Sergeant Markowski, I presume." His voice fit the rest of him. It was deep and loud – louder than he needed to be in such a small space.

"You ought to know," I said, "unless you're in the habit of having random guys abducted and brought here."

"They said you were over-fond of your own wit," he said. "Pity that they were right."

He dropped his lean frame into the desk chair and rolled it forward until he was sitting behind the desk, hands clasped in front of him.

"Choose your next witticism carefully, Mister Markowski," he said sternly. "It may be your last."

Then he threw his head back and laughed. Looks like I wasn't the only one around here over-fond of his own wit.

When the laughter was done he looked at me and said, "I trust you recognize the reference."

"Sure – it's from *Goldfanger*," I said. "But that stuff's wasted on me. My partner's the real James Bond nut."

"Oh, yes, Detective Renfer. Pity I won't get to meet him as well."

"If you want to wait a few hours, I'll give him a call," I said. "I'm sure he'd love to join us – maybe even bring a few friends."

"No, I'm afraid that won't be possible. Our FBI colleague is attending to him–" he looked at his watch, a gold Rolex "–perhaps even as we speak."

He peered at me. "I note a distinct lack of reaction when I mentioned the FBI. So you know about our mole, do you? Well, aren't you a smart one."

"What kind of 'attending' are we talking about?" If Thorwald was going to try for Karl while he slept, good luck with that – even if there was no more Sharkey around to blow her head off. Karl had made some improvements to the lock on his bedroom door since the last attempt. The codebreakers at NSA would have trouble cracking it now.

"Oh, nothing that extraordinary," Wilson said. "Merely the application of a small amount of plastic explosive to the hinges of a certain door, the removal of said door, followed by the vigorous pounding of a wooden stake into a certain chest. Very simple, really."

I understood my situation very well – there was no way I could get to Patton Wilson right this moment and do what needed to be done – but my hands apparently didn't agree. The short chain joining the cuffs rattled as they followed the impulse to wrap themselves around the bastard's throat, only to be stopped by the cuffs and the pillar behind me.

"Please, Sergeant, no histrionics, especially over what can't be undone." He leaned forward, and a small smile made an appearance. "I am well aware that one of the reasons why that James Bond idiot is able to survive, and thwart his enemies' plans, is that his captors talk too much. Instead of putting a bullet in his head as soon as he is captured, the various villains feel obliged to keep him alive for awhile to explain themselves and perhaps gloat a little. Do you know what I'm talking about?"

"Sure." What else was there to say?

"I never confuse film and life, Sergeant. Nor do I consider myself a villain – indeed, I expect that, in time, the human race will come to regard me as its savior."

Yep – nutty as my Aunt Hazel's fruitcake.

"But putting a bullet in your head at this moment isn't convenient," Wilson said. "We have need of you, alive and in good condition, later tonight. Around midnight, to be exact."

I can't say I was surprised. As soon as I'd realized where I was, the prospect of ending up chained to a chair in front of the cameras was never far from my mind. But that doesn't mean I enjoyed hearing the bastard say it.

"And so," Wilson went on, "since there is time to spare and a search by my associates has satisfied me that you are not concealing a laser in your shoe, I wouldn't mind explaining how you have come to find yourself here – and why. And I confess, I am rather pleased with myself over it all."

Wilson spread his hands, a study in candor. "So, ask me what you like. I'll tell you the truth, since you won't be repeating it to anyone – apart from Saint Peter, or, more likely, Beelzebub. I'm sure there is much that puzzles you about recent events – so ask."

"Anything?" I said.

"Yes, of course."

"OK," I said. "How old were you the first time a troll fucked you up the ass?"

He sat looking at me for a few seconds, his lips a thin tight line.

"Assuming that your adolescent display of bravado is done with," Wilson said, "is there anything you'd really like to know, or shall I just leave you alone until we're ready for you?"

Sitting here by myself until midnight would give me far too much time to think about Karl's fate – and my own. Even talking to Wilson was better than that.

"How did you manage to get Sharkey?" I asked.

"Oh, that was a simple matter," Wilson said. "After what happened to the specialist we imported from Chicago, we knew that Sharkey was watching Detective Renfer's apartment building during the day. We sent a decoy into the building through the front, carrying the same kind of long bag that I understand Mister Duffy had employed. When Sharkey broke cover to follow him, another of our people, stationed on a nearby roof with a rifle, shot him down in the street."

"I guess congratulations are in order," I said. "Sharkey was known as being very hard to kill."

"That was only true because no one with any intelligence had decided to kill him," Wilson said.

"So, how did he get from the street outside Karl's to my hotel room – part of him, anyway?"

"A van with our people in it was parked a block away. Once the shooter reported success, the van sped to where Sharkey was lying and removed the body. Decapitation took place inside the van, and the result we left as a little gift – and a distraction – for you."

"So, you're shooting your next video tonight… not–"

"Tomorrow night – as Jeffrey told you?"

"Who the fuck's Jeffrey?"

"Oh, didn't he give you his name?" Wilson said with a smirk. "He's the young man you captured last night, at that slut witch's house."

"You knew about that," I said.

"Knew about it? We were *expecting* it."

"How could you possibly know that Caro– that the witch would get a spell into action in time?"

Wilson said, "We couldn't be certain, of course. But considering what happened to Charles – the brave young man who took his life while in your custody – we thought it likely. And if perchance the bitch was too slow with her detestable magic, then Jeffrey would have another witch to bring to justice, and we could try again another night. But it worked the first time, I'm glad to say."

I was trying to get my mind around what he was telling me but was having trouble – maybe because I didn't want to believe it.

"Jeffrey was a *plant*?" I said.

"Indeed, yes. He had done some acting off-Broadway a few years ago, before he saw the light and decided to give his life to the Church. I trust his performance was moving. Whatever did you do with him, anyway? We lost track, after you left the witch's house."

I just looked at him.

Wilson gave me an elaborate shrug. "Well, no matter. He has served his purpose – which was to provide what the Russians used to call 'disinformation'. The filming will take place tonight, not tomorrow, and we are nowhere near Stansfield Avenue, by the way."

"So… tomorrow night…"

"There will be no filming at the other warehouse – which is not to say there will be no bloodshed."

I closed my eyes. *Don't try to figure it all out – it'll drive you crazy. Just wait – he'll tell you what he means. He needs to.*

"When your fellow officers raid Stansfield Avenue tomorrow night," Wilson said, "they will find a rather nasty surprise waiting for them. Our resident wizard Malachi, the same fellow who does the summonings, has prepared a spell and put it in place."

"So magic is only 'despicable' when somebody else is using it," I said.

Wilson spread his hands again, like a priest giving benediction. "We all use what we must, in the service of the greater good. Tomorrow night, all Malachi need do is utter a single word, and the spell will cause the deaths of everyone inside the building. Their internal organs will swell and burst. Not a pleasant way to die – although not nearly as unpleasant as yours, of course."

He doesn't know about the prayer team. SWAT deploys with a group of clergy from multiple faiths, and their prayers will disrupt any black magic in the vicinity.

Maybe.

They've never faced a spell that somebody's had a whole day to prepare. But they can stop it.

Probably.

"That conception was my own," Wilson said with a tiny smile, "and it's really quite clever, if I say so myself."

Yeah, you would. Cocksucker.

"Not only do I largely eliminate the police who have been interfering with our campaign, but the deed contributes to the campaign itself. Imagine the headlines, especially in the *People's Voice*: **POLICE MURDERED BY MAGIC**, or perhaps **BRAVE OFFICERS STRUCK DOWN BY EVIL SPELL**."

Then he giggled. He actually *giggled* – like a fucking schoolgirl.

"It should be gloooorious," Wilson said.

"Yeah. Glorious."

I didn't waste any energy on that *You'll never get away with this, you fiend* nonsense you see on TV. It would just make me look like more of an idiot than I already was.

Besides, it looked like there was a good chance he *would* get away with it.

Wilson left me alone soon after that. That's the time when, if I was 007, I'd find a way to stand on my head and open the cuffs with the lockpick I'd concealed in my left nostril. Then I'd use the plastic explosives hidden in my belt to blow the door, karate-chop the nearest guard, and grab his gun. Then I could… aw, fuck it. Thinking about James Bond just reminded me of Karl. Poor Karl – I hoped he had at least died quick. If he had, that would make one of us.

I had plenty of time to think about the horrible death I was going to experience – there was no doubt in my mind who was going to be on the receiving end in tonight's performance – unless I found some way out. After a while, I did come up with an idea of sorts. I guessed I'd find out pretty soon just how good an idea it was.

Nothing much was riding on my little inspiration – just my life, the lives of a lot of other cops, and maybe even the success of stage one of Helter Skelter.

No pressure.

The slivers of daylight coming in through the Venetian blind eventually faded to night. Assuming the ritual was due to start around midnight, that meant I still had several hours to go. My bladder was uncomfortably full, but I was damned if I was going to abandon what little dignity I had left by pissing in my pants. So I held it, and eventually got used to the ache. My throat was also parched, but I figured I'd still be able to scream come midnight, if my idea failed.

Tension and fear are exhausting, and I hadn't been to bed for more than twenty-four hours. Despite being scared out of my mind, I eventually fell asleep, sort of. You can imagine what my dreams were like.

I woke up with a start when the door opened. I realized it was time for the fun to start, and my heartbeat went the equivalent of zero to sixty in about 3.4 seconds.

There were two of them – both young and dressed like members of Wilson's little commando unit. They'd have to unlock the cuffs to move me, and I figured that might give me a chance to try something. I wasn't optimistic about my chances against two Special Forces wannabes twenty years younger than me. But desperation sometimes gives people extra strength and speed, and I was about as desperate as they come. However, the boys had already thought of that – or Wilson had.

One of them went behind me, and I waited for the sound of the key being inserted into the handcuffs. What I heard instead was the guy saying, "We don't want a lot of nonsense while we prepare you, so…" Then I felt another needle in the back of my neck. So much for mixing it up with the guards.

I don't know how long I was out this time, but when I came back to the world it was clear that my situation had gone from bad to worse. I was now naked and shackled to one of the chairs that I'd seen in the videos. The smell like what you'd from get driving by a slaughterhouse in summer, with your windows down – only ten times stronger. I was on the killing floor now.

Since the festivities hadn't started yet, I had time to look around, and I used it. Knowing where everyone was could prove crucial later.

As I knew from the videos, the floor was concrete and the walls red brick. High ceiling, with lights hanging down. Two big windows were built into the wall I was facing, but they were set too high for anyone to see in from outside. Across from me, in the other chair, was a guy I'd never met before. Mid-thirties, red hair, a little overweight. It didn't surprise me that his expression combined confusion with terror.

If the direction I was facing was 12 o'clock, using the Air Force system, then there were video cameras set up on tripods at 12 and 8 o'clock, about twenty feet outside the circle. Guess they had decided to go with a two-camera setup this time. A little more practice, and they'd probably have these atrocities available in 3-D. Behind each camera stood one of the commandos, who I guessed pulled double duty as videographers. I wondered if the things they had seen through the viewfinders ever gave them nightmares.

At the 10 o'clock position and further back stood another one of the commando boys. He was cradling a stocky automatic weapon with a long curved magazine, although who he might be expected to shoot was beyond me. The gun looked like one of those H&K MP5s that the Navy SEALs carry. Once a wannabe, always a wannabe. He seemed to be the only one holding a weapon.

At 3 o'clock and about thirty feet out was the resident lunatic, Patton Wilson himself. He was next to a very tall thin guy in a black suit, whose brown hair was mostly covered by a red skullcap – apparently Bishop Navarra still retained some of the trappings of the Catholic Church he hated so much. The bishop was not looking happy to be here.

Not far from them, at 4 o'clock, a portable podium had been set up. Resting on it was a large, old-looking book, which I assumed contained the incantations. A tall, balding guy, who I assumed to be Wilson's tame wizard, stood behind the podium. One of his hands rested on the book, while the other clutched what looked like a pointed drumstick with symbols engraved on it – his wand. Malachi wore crimson robes and a tense expression. I didn't recognize him, which meant Wilson had imported him from out of town.

And that was it, except for one guest who hadn't arrived yet – but then, he wasn't expected until a little later.

I assumed we were waiting for midnight, the time when the dark powers are at their strongest. Most of those attending waited patiently – after all, they'd done this before. But Bishop Navarra was agitated. In the near-silence I could hear him speaking softly to Wilson.

"I don't see why I should have to be present for this... butchery," he said. "You didn't ask me to be here for any of the others."

"Yes, but tonight's ceremony is the one that will tip the balance," Wilson said, with the utter confidence that all madmen have. "Unlike the others, the policeman's body will be found – and what a stir that will create! Then after tomorrow night, when several more defenders of law and order succumb to the effects of black magic, the outcry will be loud and long, and few among the local community will be able to resist it. And soon thereafter the great, cleansing war will begin."

"All of that will happen whether I am here to watch the bloodletting or not!" Navarra said, although he didn't raise his voice. He probably wouldn't have dared.

"You've been spending all your time in that study

of yours writing sermons, James – or in the church I built you, preaching them," Wilson said. "I thought it was time for you to gain an appreciation of the other side of our crusade – the side where people get their hands bloody."

"Patton, I have *never* failed to appreciate–"

"That will *do*, James." There was steel in Wilson's voice now. He glanced at his watch. "In any case it is nearly midnight, and time for us to commence the ritual."

He looked over at the wizard. "Whenever you're ready, Malachi."

"I'll start now, sir," Malachi said, like a good lackey. And then it began.

The procedure was the same as before. First, they killed all the lights, leaving us in darkness for half a minute or so. It should've been a welcome respite for me, but I couldn't stop thinking of all the wickedness that had been done inside this warehouse, all the suffering and death that had occurred because some lunatic wanted to start a race war. The very walls reeked of evil, and the dark only made it worse.

Then all the lights came on at once, and it was showtime. The conjuration ritual hadn't changed, but this time I paid attention to the name of the demon being summoned: *Acheron*. It wasn't familiar, but that meant nothing – there are lots and lots of demons. But now I had a name. In magic, names are power, and maybe this one would give me the power I needed to survive.

Acheron arrived in the column of smoke – looking almost human, apart from his ears (pointed), his eyes (red) and his jaw (large, misshapen, and revealing several rows of sharp teeth). He snarled defiance at Malachi, and was rewarded with a jolt of agony for his efforts. Demons are no strangers to pain, so Malachi must be administering quite a jolt to impress him like that.

Once Acheron agreed, reluctantly, to obey, Malachi gave him his instructions. The wizard spoke in Demon, and I had to concentrate hard to get the sense of what he was saying.

But I understood when the wizard told Acheron to possess the redhead, not me. Well, that figured. Then he was instructed not to damage my face beyond recognition, and to leave the fingertips of at least one hand intact. That would allow, I knew, for easy identification. If you've never heard somebody refer to your body like it was a cattle carcass about to be carved up – well, I can't say I recommend the experience.

Acheron faded from view, and it wasn't hard to tell when he had taken over the body of the redheaded guy, whose name I didn't even know. When it was clear that Acheron was in charge, Malachi spoke a word and the shackles holding the redhead dropped away. The demon-possessed human moved slowly at first, unused to this new form. He stared at me for a few seconds, and it was the kind of look that a glutton gives a big plate of prime rib. Then he walked over to the table.

I was trying desperately to keep focused, when what I really wanted to do was scream for mercy. *Yeah, and good luck with that.*

When Acheron turned back toward me, he was holding the blowtorch. Panic fought savagely for release inside me, but I kept the lid of that box closed, somehow.

Acheron tested the blowtorch to be sure it worked. You just squeezed a lever, and the mechanism got the gas flowing and generated a spark to light it. Once he was sure he knew how to get a nice hot flame going, he headed my way.

I swallowed hard a couple of times to lubricate my vocal cords. I needed my voice to work at the first attempt, or I'd be too busy screaming to try a second one.

As Acheron bent over me, I croaked, in Demon, "Hail, great Acheron, Lord of the Underworld!" I could have spoken in any language and been understood, but this had gotten his attention, as I'd intended.

He stared, then gave me a vicious open-handed slap on the side of the head, probably just as a warm-up. The redhead's voice snarled, in Demon, *"Who dares speak to me in the tongue of the Fallen?"*

"I am Markowski, a mere human and unworthy to address such as you," I said in his language. At least, I *think* that's what I said. "But this insignificant human can give you what you desire."

He laughed scornfully, and whacked me again. But at least he hadn't started with the blowtorch, yet. *"I desire your blood, Markowski, and your tears, and your screams. And I will have them, whether you give them to me or not."*

I swallowed again, hoping that my throat wouldn't constrict with fear and make speech impossible. "I offer more, great Acheron – I can give you vengeance."

More laughter, and another hard slap to the head. I'd had a bad concussion a few months ago, and blacking out right now would mean the end of me.

"Vengeance against whom? And how?"

OK, he was interested. Now to close the deal.

"Vengeance against those who would dare to summon you from the Netherworld, and would have the impudence to give you orders." I hadn't even realized that I knew the Demon word for "impudence", but the old memory came through when I needed it most.

I took a breath and continued, "I can free you. I can break the circle that you are forbidden to touch."

Another blow, but this one hit the back of the chair – and barely touched me. I didn't think that was accidental.

Acheron bent over me, the blowtorch in hand. *Oh shit, did I fuck up? Is he turning me down?*

Then I noticed that he had released the valve, and allowed the flame to go out. Acheron moved slightly, to block what he was doing from the cameras. He brought the flameless nozzle closer to my chest.

"Scream," he said. *"Scream as if you feel the fire on you."*

So I screamed – but *good*. If Laurence Olivier was watching from the Great Beyond, I bet he applauded a little. I screamed, I struggled against the chains, I pleaded for mercy. It's amazing what talents you discover in yourself when trying to avoid being tortured to death.

Acheron withdrew the blowtorch a little, as if giving me a respite. *"If I try to release you, that fool with the book will smite me,"* he said softly.

Fortunately, I'd had plenty of time to work this out.

"Use the blowtorch to sever the chain holding my right hand," I said. "Pretend you are using it on me. Then strike the chair again, knocking it over. If I am close enough to reach the circle, I can break it."

He gave a loud snarl – for effect, I assume – and brought the blowtorch close. *"Scream again,"* he said. *"And continue to scream until I tip the chair. Do this for me, and you will be spared."*

I resumed my Academy Award performance. Acheron restarted the blowtorch and brought it over to the chain holding my right hand to the chair.

That was when I realized something – iron is an excellent conductor of heat. As the link Acheron was working on turned cherry red, the other links and my shackle also started to glow. Then the heat reached me, and I started to scream for real.

It only lasted a couple of seconds, but seemed a lot longer. Then the link that Acheron was working on began to melt, and my frantic struggles broke the rest of the chain free. At once the demon struck the back of the chair hard, knocking it, and me, over.

Finally the wizard realized that something was wrong. "What are you *doing*, disobedient one?" Malachi shrieked in Demon, then said the word of pain again. Acheron let out a howl of anguish – *and I had fallen short of the circle*.

I had to reach the red circle or I was cooked – maybe literally. Using what traction I could gain with the edge of my shackled right foot and my elbow, I jerked forward, mere inches at a time, like a snail on Adderall.

My progress was slow, so slow. Meanwhile, I could hear Malachi screaming "Obey me!" in Demon, and Acheron's bellows of pain.

Then at last I reached the circle painted on the concrete floor. The paint was already fading a little, and I went to work on it like a madman – maybe that's what I was, by then. I made my right hand a claw and dragged my nails through the paint, bearing down as hard as I could. And *again*. And *again*. My fingertips were starting to bleed now. And *again*. And *again*. Then I heard Acheron say something that chilled my blood. He told Malachi, "*Very well, cease, I will obey you.*"

Acheron walked slowly over to me, intent on righting the chair and starting the torture for real, since he had no choice. Claw the paint *again*. And *again*. And–

I felt something move *over* me and through the circle, where I must have scratched a tiny break in the paint's continuity. That sliver of a gap was all Acheron needed. The red-headed man, whose body the demon had been using, collapsed limply to the floor. A shrill cry of triumph echoed through the warehouse, although I couldn't see its source.

"Cease!" the wizard Malachi screamed. "Return to the circle! You must obey my commands!"

Then the shit really hit the fan. And what a bloody mess it made.

I tried to follow Acheron's progress as best I could, lying on the floor with three of my limbs still shackled to the chair. His first stop was Malachi. Smart move. I could hear the wizard scream "Noooo!" as he felt the demon take over, but Acheron didn't linger – he stayed inside Malachi just long enough to force the wizard to pick up his wand and plunge it into – and through – his left eye. Malachi collapsed, blood spurting from the ruined socket.

There was chaos in the room now. Some of the men were yelling questions, others were trying to issue orders, and a few were running around to no particular purpose. I made a bet with myself about who Acheron's next victim would be – and I won.

The commando wannabe holding the automatic weapon jerked suddenly, as if touched by an electric current. I watched his face change from surprise to malice as the demon took over. Then he started firing.

I'll say this for Acheron – he had good fire discipline. He didn't expend all his ammo in five seconds, like an amateur, but instead fired controlled, three-shot bursts.

His first target was Bishop Navarra, who took three in his lower belly. Acheron really knew how to hurt a guy, but then he would.

The two commando camera operators then decided to rush their demon-possessed buddy. In my personal dictionary, there's a word for unarmed men who run toward an enemy who's holding a loaded automatic weapon – *morons*. Acheron cut them down like wheat at harvest time.

I looked around for Patton Wilson, who I assumed would be the next target, for either bullets or possession. But he was gone. The cagey bastard must've run for the door the instant that Acheron was free. *Damn*.

There were only three humans still alive in the warehouse. Acheron, gun still smoking, ignored Red and me and walked slowly over to Bishop Navarra, who lay moaning in a pool of his own blood. That's what's so bad about being gutshot – you take such a long, painful time to die.

Acheron put the gun down gently on the concrete floor and began going through his commando host's pockets. I saw a terrible smile on the boyish face as he produced a good-sized jackknife. Guess he forgot about all the torture implements on the table, or maybe he just liked to improvise.

I don't think I want to describe what happened next. I stopped watching after a few seconds, anyway – although there was nothing I could do to block out the screams, or the wet sounds that Acheron was making with his knife. After a while, I began to envy Red his unconscious state.

I don't know how long it went on. In real time, it probably lasted ten minutes, but to me it seemed a lot longer – although not nearly as long as it probably seemed to Bishop Navarra.

Finally, the screams and pleadings were silenced. I heard footsteps approaching, and looked up to see the blood-splattered commando heading our way, the dripping knife still in his hand. He crossed the circle without difficulty – now that it had been broken, it was just so much red paint on a floor to him. He stood over the redhead's unconscious body for a moment, then bent over. One hand grabbed the red hair and pulled the guy's head back, while the other sliced his throat.

"Hey!" I cried, "You didn't–"

I'd been about to say, "You didn't have to do that!" But of course, he did. He was a demon, after all.

Once Red was well on his way to bleeding out, Acheron walked over to me. He stopped a few feet away from the chair I was tethered to and said, "Your turn, Markowski." He spoke English now – maybe because Demon had been the language of his tormenter.

"You said you'd spare me," I said, but I didn't say it very loudly. I'd never really thought he would.

He laughed – it wasn't a pleasant sound. "The One whom I serve is known as the Father of Lies," he said. "Did you think I would stint at one of my own, if it served my purpose?"

He weighed the bloody knife in his hand. "I will, however, spare you the kind of death just suffered by His Excellency the Bishop over there, as well as the far worse one you would have had at my hands, had I been forced to remain inside this circle – but do not expect similar mercy, should I encounter you in Hell. Now, lie still."

As he stepped toward me, there came a loud, insistent banging from behind him. He twisted his body to look, which allowed me to see past him.

Two figures were clinging impossibly to the big windows set high in the back wall – well, it would have been impossible for humans. Vampires do that kind of thing very well.

One of the vampires was Christine. The other one – I had to squint, to make sure my eyes weren't combining with wishful thinking to fool me – was *Karl Renfer*.

An instant later, I realized why they were still outside. I snatched in a breath and yelled, as loudly as I could, "*Come on in*!"

At once, the glass in both windows shattered. I saw a pair of blurred images moving in our direction, and then Christine and Karl were crouched between me and the demon-possessed commando, their fangs bared.

"Careful," I said. "He's got a demon inside him."

Acheron looked from Christine to Karl and took a couple of steps back. "You two seem to have some affection for that fool on the floor," he said. "Perhaps I should use one of your bodies to cut his heart out."

"Won't work, asshole," Karl growled.

"Yeah," Christine said. "We're already dead."

Acheron nodded slowly. "That does pose an interesting problem."

"Don't ponder it too long, hellspawn," Karl said. "Cops are on the way. Hear that?"

Now that I was listening for it, I could hear the sound of sirens – a *lot* of sirens.

The commando's face produced half a smile as Acheron looked down at me. "We will continue this discussion another time, Markowski." Then, looking at Karl and Christine, he said, "And perhaps I shall have a few words with each of you, as well."

Then he turned, folded the knife, and walked rapidly toward the nearest exit.

Christine said to me, "Should we stop him?"

"No, let him go," I said. "Otherwise he'd just abandon the commando's body, and God only knows where he'd end up."

The sirens were very close now. "Karl," I said, "maybe you should go out there and show your badge, before SWAT comes in shooting."

He nodded, and started toward the main doors. Christine knelt beside me and began breaking the shackles that still held me to the chair.

"Hey, Karl," I called after him.

He turned. "What?"

"It's good to see you, man. I thought you were dead."

He gave me his sharp-toothed grin. "Yeah, I get that a lot."

• • • •

I had a bad burn on my wrist from when Acheron used the blowtorch to melt the chain. That meant I was due for a long spell in the waiting room of Mercy Hospital's ER. They do triage in that place strictly based on what kind of condition you're in, not how important you think you are. So, if you're not actually bleeding or suffering a heart attack, you can expect a long wait, even if you're a cop.

Before I left for the hospital I had a few words with McGuire, who had arrived with the SWAT team and about six other cops, including two more detectives from the squad.

I gave him the quick version of what had happened to me in the last thirty-six hours or so, with special emphasis on the fact that the warehouse on Stansfield Avenue was not only empty but had a dangerous spell on it.

McGuire had been making notes. He looked up from his pad and said, "I'll get Rachel in on that. Maybe she can also call on a few of the other local witches to help disperse it."

"No hurry — the guy who was supposed to activate the spell won't be showing up," I said. "I'm hoping that right about now he's making the acquaintance of several of Acheron's friends."

I also mentioned that Patton Wilson was still at large, and recommended that an arrest warrant be issued ASAP.

"I'll take care of it," McGuire said, "for all the good it's likely to do. A guy with his money is probably halfway to Australia by now."

"Could be," I said. "Although I have a feeling he won't stay hidden very long. Mister Wilson's determined to start Helter Skelter, and he can't do that while hiding out at a sheep ranch in the outback."

I also made a point of reminding him that Thorwald was a double agent, or whatever you'd call what she was doing.

"Yeah, that one's going to be tricky," he said.

"We can't just let this slide, boss," I said. "The bitch tried to have me killed – and for all we know, she could've hired Duffy the Vampire Slayer to get Karl, too."

"I have no intention of letting it slide," McGuire said. "I'll be having a word with a couple of people at FBI headquarters, as well as her boss at Quantico. And if she ever shows her face in Scranton again, I'll have her brought in for questioning on a material witness warrant. I have a feeling the questions could take quite a long time."

Christine and Karl both insisted on accompanying me to the ER, in case Acheron decided to try again.

"I'll be glad of the company," I said, "especially because there's a lot of stuff I wanna know. But I'm not too worried about Acheron – it isn't anything personal with him. He was just going to kill me because I was here. If anything, he owes me a favor for setting him free."

"Maybe," Christine said, "But I wouldn't hold my breath waiting for him to send flowers."

"And if he does," Karl said, "I'd call the bomb squad, and then run like hell – so to speak."

Once the folks at Mercy established that I wasn't going to die on them anytime soon, they sent me out to the waiting room for what figured to be a long stay. Karl, Christine, and I sat down on a couch, as far away from the other patients as we could get.

"All right, Karl," I said. "This is where you explain to me how you were able to avoid getting a stake pounded into your chest – not that I'm complaining, you understand."

"Not much of a trick," Karl said. "I wasn't home during the day yesterday."

"Why not?"

"It took us longer than I'd planned to get our commando buddy processed into the Pike County jail. By the time we were done, it was almost dawn, so Lacey let me spend the day in the trunk of her car."

"Nice of her," I said.

"More than nice," he said. "When I woke up, I found that she'd pressed my jacket . Even let me take a shower at her place."

"Let you shower, huh?" Christine said with a smile. "Sounds like she's hot for you, Karl."

"Lacey? Nah, not me – she's your dad's girlfriend."

"Give it a rest, Karl," I said. "So, you haven't been home at all?"

"Nope – Lacey drove me right to work. She dropped me off, then said she was going to go keep an eye on Thorwald, like you asked her to."

"Then she got my message. Good."

"If Thorwald blew the hinges off my bedroom door," Karl said, "I'm gonna be fuckin' pissed."

"Just make sure she didn't leave you any little surprises while she was there," I said.

"Booby traps, you mean?" He shrugged. "Not too many of them can harm us bloodsucking undead."

"No?" I said. "How about a thermite bomb under your bed, with the timer set for noon tomorrow?"

"Fire," Christine said, and shuddered.

"You make a good point there, Stan," Karl said. "I'll check the place over before I crash."

"Why would Thorwald bother with Karl now, Daddy?" Christine asked. "I mean, the Church is history, right? Navarra's dead, Wilson's in hiding, and any commandos still alive probably ran back to Kansas, or wherever they came from."

"Maybe," I said. "But if Thorwald's been working for the Church, it's because of idealism, not money. And some fanatics just don't know when to quit."

"Fuckin' A," Karl said.

From time to time, a nurse would come to the door of the waiting area and call somebody's name. I kept hoping to hear mine.

"You two don't know how glad I was to see you banging on the windows of that warehouse," I said. "But how'd you know to go there? The only address we had was for the decoy, over on Stansfield Avenue."

"We have Louise to thank for that," he said. "For some of it, anyway."

"Louise the Tease?" I said. "Our PA?"

"That's her. I guess she doesn't want to keep doing that job the rest of her life – can't blame her for that."

"Louise," I said. "Damn. What'd she do that got you to the right place?"

"I guess you gave her a message for the Feebies a while back," Karl said. "Something about finding out who owns the *People's Voice*?"

"Yeah, but we found out later that it's the Church, just like I figured. Commando boy told Lacey, remember?"

"Louise didn't know that. She tried to give your message to the Feebies when they came through, but she said they went right by her, like she hadn't said anything. The way she put it to me was, 'Guess the bimbo in the tight dress wasn't worth their attention.' So she got mad."

"Guess that makes it unanimous," I said. "Everybody's pissed at the FBI these days. So, what did she do?"

"She checked it out for herself," Karl said, "when things were slow around the squad. Louise is persistent, especially when she has something to prove. She went from one holding company to the next, to the next. All dummy corporations."

"And she found out that the Church owns the paper," I said.

"No, I guess that's not on any public record. She got as far as something called 'Crossman Investments, Inc.' Couldn't find anything else about them."

"So, how does that get you and Christine to the warehouse in time to save my butt?"

"When you didn't show up for work, McGuire told me to find you – which I would've done, anyway. Called the Radisson, called your cell, even called the landline at your house. When that got me nowhere, I even called Christine at work and asked if she'd heard from you."

"Which, since I hadn't, managed to scare me shitless," Christine said. "I made Karl promise to call me back as soon as he learned something."

"It was pretty clear that something nasty had happened," he said. "The Church had either killed you, or grabbed you. I couldn't do anything about the first possibility, so I focused on the second one. Then I started thinking about warehouses. It'd be just like those fuckers to have you slaughtered in front of their cameras."

Another nurse showed up at the door and called a name that wasn't mine.

"Once Louise realized what I was doing, she told me about Crossman Investments, Inc.," Karl said. "After thinking about that for a minute, *I actually made a fucking deduction* – Sherlock Holmes would be proud of me."

"Go on, Great Detective," I said. "Show us how you did it."

Karl said, "We knew that the Church owned the *People's Voice*, right? But what Louise showed me was that in the official records, the paper was owned by Crossman Investments. So I wondered what other properties in town had Crossman Investments as the owner of record."

"Fantastic, Mister Holmes," I said. "I mean it – that was fucking brilliant, Karl."

"Thanks, but it still didn't get us an actual address. And the property records aren't computerized."

"They're all in the courthouse basement, right?"

"Yeah," he said, "and the office was closed for the night."

"Ouch," I said. "Still, the fact that I'm still breathing means you must've figured something out."

"I told McGuire, and he called the mayor direct, instead of going through channels. He said the life of one of his best officers was in danger, and we needed to get at those records, pronto."

"He really said that?" I asked. "One of his best officers?"

"Yeah, he wanted to make the strongest case possible, so he exaggerated a little."

I was going to whack him for that, but Christine beat me to it with a punch on the arm.

"Ow!" Karl said. "OK, so the mayor sent somebody over to open up the room where they keep the property records. You got any idea how many books that stuff takes up?"

"Um – lots?" I said.

"Fuckin' A. And it's organized chronologically, by date of sale – *not* alphabetically."

"Yikes," I said. "So what did you do?"

"Got some help. McGuire assigned Aquilina and

Sefchik to pitch in, and Louise volunteered to take some personal time and help, too."

"Louise seems like a very nice lady," Christine said. "I think *she's* got a thing for you, too." She shook her head. "My old man, the sex object. Jeez!"

"Wait – how'd you get to meet Louise?" I asked her.

"I called Christine, just like she told me to," Karl said. "When I explained where things stood, she said she'd be at the property records office in five minutes."

"I'm pretty sure I made it in four," Christine said. "Don't tell the cops, but I ran a couple of red lights."

"All those people, busting their ass to save mine," I said. "I'm touched." My voice contained no sarcasm, because I intended none.

"It was about ten after midnight when Louise came across a listing that said Crossman Investments had bought a property three years ago, at 647 Montgomery Avenue – a warehouse."

"Is that where it was?" I said. "I didn't pay any attention to the address when I was leaving – had other things on my mind, I guess."

"We knew that the Church liked to do their summonings at midnight," Karl said. "So I asked the others to keep looking, in case Crossman owned more than one warehouse. Christine and I hit the vampire afterburners and got over there. Once I saw you were inside, I called McGuire and told him. You know the rest."

I sat there quietly for a while, thinking about how close I had come to dying in the ugliest way possible. And if it weren't for my friends and my little girl, I would have. Good thing I'm such a tough guy, or I might've even cried a little.

"What's wrong, Daddy?" Christine asked me.

"Ah, it's just my allergies acting up again," I said, blowing my nose.

A few minutes later, a nurse came to the door and said the sweetest thing I've heard a woman say in quite some time.

"*Stanley Markowski!*"

A doctor at Mercy's ER treated my burn – which she described as "second degree" – bandaged it, told me to see my family physician, and gave me some pills for the pain.

I decided I'd only take the pain pills at bedtime, if at all. I know from experience that they make me logy, and in my job, that can be fatal. As it was, I hoped I wouldn't have to try a fast draw until the burn had healed somewhat. Scranton isn't Dodge City, and I don't go around looking for gunfights. But there are times when I need the gun, and if I don't draw it fast, I may not live to draw it at all. And right now, the burn would slow me up, maybe fatally.

Christine and Karl had brought me to the Radisson's front door, then taken off, since dawn was only about twenty minutes away. We'd been at the ER so long, Karl hadn't had the chance to go home early and check his place for any nasty surprises Thorwald might have left him. So, after getting my ok, Christine invited him to spend the day at our place. "I'm pretty sure we've got an extra sleeping bag," she'd said, "and there's enough plasma in the fridge to make breakfast for two." After a nod from me, Karl had accepted, with thanks.

Under other circumstances, having my partner sleeping with my daughter would have bothered me – a lot. As it was, I can't say that it didn't still bother me a little.

I went up to my room and packed. I was relieved to see that someone had removed Sharkey's head and changed the bedding. They hadn't done much about the smell, though. Good thing I wasn't planning to spend the day there.

I wanted to go home, get in my own bed, and sleep for a long time. McGuire said I should charge a couple of days to medical leave, and I hadn't argued with him.

I checked out, thanked Tim for all his help, and carried my suitcase out to where I'd left the car. Dawn was just breaking over the city, and the hotel parking lot was deserted. I was standing at the Lycan's trunk, gingerly digging for my keys, when a man's voice behind me said, "Hello, Markowski."

My right hand was deep in my pants pocket, so I didn't even try for the gun. Instead, I turned slowly.

Standing between two cars in the next aisle was Special Agent Greer of the FBI. His hands were out of sight, so at least he wasn't pointing a gun at me.

I nodded and said, "Agent Greer. Where's that partner of yours? I'd like to have a word with her."

"Linda? Haven't seen her since yesterday sometime.

Word is, there's a material witness warrant out on her, so maybe she's lying low until she gets some legal advice. What's that warrant about, if you don't mind me asking?"

"Among other things, my boss wants to talk to her about a woman who allegedly went out to the goblin camp to recruit assassins, and sent them after me."

Greer smiled, which I thought was strange.

He said, "A woman, huh?"

"That's what the witness says." I didn't mention that the witness was a goblin who didn't even speak English and would never testify in court.

"Sounds pretty bad," he said.

"Yeah, we take conspiracy to commit murder pretty seriously around here," I said. "Agent Greer, do you know anything about the Church of the True Cross?"

A slow nod. "I might've heard something about them."

"They're a dangerous organization, or they were. Your partner is also suspected of working for them, as a kind of double agent."

"Is that right?" The smile reappeared for an instant, then vanished. "Why do you say they *were* dangerous?"

"Guess you're not up to speed on recent developments. Go on over to the squad – McGuire will fill you in. I'm going home."

"Just give me the short version," he said. No smiles now.

"All right. Their head guy, Bishop Navarra, is dead. The power behind the throne, a rich nut named Patton Wilson, is at large and facing a list of indictments longer than *both* of my arms. The members of the Church's praetorian guard – the survivors, I mean – have dispersed and are all wanted for questioning. Get the rest of it from McGuire – I'm tired."

"First explain what you meant by *survivors*," Greer snapped. It sounded like an order, instead of a polite request from one cop to another. But the simplest thing was just to answer him.

I said, "Two of the commando boys died last night, and a third one is currently dealing with a little demonic possession problem."

"I see," Greer said grimly. His face hardened into a mask of hatred. His arms came up, and I saw that he was holding a pistol, and it was pointed right at me. "I told Mister Wilson we should've just put a couple of pounds of Semtex under your house some morning – take care of you and that abomination you call your daughter at the same time."

"Semtex," I said. "That's plastic explosive, isn't it?"

"Bet your ass it is," he said. He thumbed back the hammer of his pistol, which looked like one of those new Sig Sauers. Trust the FBI to have the latest model.

"My only regret right now," Greer said, "is that you're going to die not comprehending the *enormous* damage you've done to your own race's chances for survival against the godless scum of the Earth."

"It was you all the time, wasn't it – not Thorwald." Even without the second-degree burn, my chances of drawing and firing before Greer could put ten bullets into me were nonexistent. I wondered if I should go for it, anyway. There was always the chance his gun would misfire. *Right. Snowballs in hell, Markowski.*

Greer gave a scornful laugh, but the pistol didn't waver. "Linda? You're joking. She's as clueless as they come."

Three cars to Greer's left, a door opened and Thorwald slid out, gun in hand. "Maybe not so much," she said. Bracing her elbows on the car's roof, she took careful aim at Greer. "I've been wanting to say this for a long time, Brian," she said. "You're under arrest."

Greer turned his head maybe two inches in her direction, then I was back in his sights. "Linda," he said. "I wish I could say it's good to see you again."

"I'll say it for both of us," she said. "Now place your weapon on the ground and step away from it. Do it!"

The smile reappeared on Greer's face, although it looked kind of strained this time. "I don't think so, Linda honey. What we've got here is what they call a Mexican standoff. If you pop me, with my last heartbeat I'll drop the hammer on your cop buddy over there. Didn't you tell me once you thought he was kinda cute? He won't be with a bullet through his face."

"Put down your weapon, or I'll shoot!" Thorwald said firmly.

"I really don't believe you will," Greer said. "I know you've never shot anything except targets at Quantico, Linda. You've never killed anybody in your life, especially in cold blood. I don't think you've got it in you."

"*But I do.*"

Lacey Brennan, gun in hand, rose from where she'd apparently been crouching, two rows behind Greer and a little to his right. With people popping up from all over, this whole thing resembled a farce – or it would, if somebody wasn't about to die.

At the sound of Lacey's voice, Greer couldn't stop himself from looking toward her for an instant. And it was in that moment that Lacey fired and blew the top of his head off.

That's the thing about head shots. More often than not, the motor synapses stop working instantly. Greer fell against a car, then slid to the ground without firing a shot. He died with a look of surprise on his face.

I was pretty surprised myself.

I called 911, identified myself, and told them to send some black-and-whites and an ambulance. I asked the dispatcher to be sure to tell the responding officers that the shooter was already in custody.

Lacey heard me. She managed a smile of sorts. "Is that what I am, Stan? In custody?"

"I just said that so the uniforms wouldn't arrive thinking there was an armed suspect lurking around. That makes them nervous, and nervous cops sometimes shoot first and ask questions later."

"Yeah, I think I heard that, someplace," she said.

"Better give me your gun, though."

"Sure. Here." She handed me the compact Walther she'd just used to shoot Greer.

"Nice piece," I said.

"It's mine, not the department's. I had to turn in my duty weapon when I went on leave. But I used to carry that for backup."

"I don't mean this the way it sounds," I said, "but what are you *doing* here?"

She jerked a thumb toward Thorwald, who was leaning against a nearby car, arms folded. "You said to keep an eye on her, so I did."

Thorwald gave me a tired smile. "Were you actually having me followed, Sergeant?"

"Yeah, sorry about that," I said. "Until about three minutes ago, I thought you were one of the bad guys."

I found out later that the goblin words for "bitch" and "faggot" – neither of which is a nice thing to call somebody – sound very similar. Ivan the ogre had mistranslated, so whenever Wilson had referred to "our Bureau colleague", I'd assumed he meant Thorwald

"The Bureau thought the same thing about Greer, and has for a while now," she said. "That's why they assigned me as his partner – to keep an eye on him, and wait for him to slip up – which he finally did, a few minutes ago."

I could hear sirens now.

"I think Greer was suspicious of me, too, after a while," Thorwald said. "I wanted to let you know

that he shouldn't be trusted with sensitive information, but if I had a private conversation with you,
or asked you out to lunch alone, he'd know something was up."

"Why didn't you just call me?" I said.

"I don't trust the phones," she said. "The Church
is believed to have some people at NSA, the National
Security Agency. They can pull any conversation
they want out of the air and listen to it."

"Well," I said, "being paranoid doesn't mean that
they're not really out to get you."

"For sure," she said. "That's why I invited you to
my room that morning. It was the only plausible excuse to be alone with you that Greer would accept."

The sirens were closer. The police cars and ambulance would be here any minute now.

"Wait a second," I said. "That's why you invited
me to your room – to warn me about Greer? Not
for the 'hard fucking' you were talking about?"

"Well," Thorwald said with a toss of her head, "the
two weren't mutually exclusive, I suppose."

"Is that what you really had in mind – both a
warning about Greer *and* sex?"

The smile she gave me would have made Mona
Lisa envious. "I guess we'll never know, will we?"

You know how sometimes you're asleep, and you
dream that you've just woken up? That happens to
me, sometimes.

I opened my eyes and slowly came awake – or
thought I did. The room around me was unfamiliar,

and the pale light coming in through the window had that translucent quality you sometimes find in dreams. Awake or asleep, I felt *good* – I knew that. In fact, I couldn't stop my face from growing a smile so wide I could've been running for public office.

From my left, a woman's voice said, "That's the kind of grin I associate with the Cheshire Cat – the morning after he got his rocks off, well and truly."

Lacey Brennan propped herself up on one elbow and looked down at me, her blonde hair disarrayed in what my partner Karl, who is known to be crude, would call a "freshly fucked look".

"Where am I?" I asked.

"My place. It's your first visit – who knows, maybe it won't be your last."

"If this is a dream, I've had something like it before," I said. "But it never seemed this real."

"Really?" Lacey gave me a wicked grin, all traces of the monster gone from her blue eyes. "You used to dream about fucking me, Stan?"

I nodded. "Oh, yeah. Often. But I never had the nerve to try it in real life."

"Until last night, you mean."

"Is that what I did last night? Put the moves on you – and it worked?"

"Don't you remember? You must've had more champagne than I thought. Although, come to think of it, I had quite a bit myself."

"Maybe that's what accounts for my success. We were drinking champagne, huh? Must've been celebrating something."

"'Course we were," Lacey said. "This nasty bastard of a case is finally over, and we all came out of it more or less intact. So we celebrated – the three of us. With champagne and… other things."

"*Three*? Three of us?"

"Sure – you, me, and Linda – who really isn't such a bad person, once you get to know her."

"*Linda*? Who's Linda?"

"Linda *Thorwald*, dummy. Remember her – Federal agent, eyes bluer than mine, black hair, nice tits?"

I closed my eyes, but when I opened them, Lacey was still there. "You, me, and Thorwald… celebrating? Together?"

Lacey nodded. "I don't normally do things like that, but it *was* a special occasion. And, besides – you know what they say."

"Uh, no, Lace – what do they say?"

"That every straight woman is just two drinks away from bisexuality. And I *know* I had more than two."

"OK, now I'm *positive* I'm dreaming," I said. "But the only complaint I have is, sooner or later, I'm gonna wake up."

Lacey nodded sympathetically. "Probably with a bad hangover, too. Poor baby."

I felt weight shift on the mattress to my right. The sheet moved a bit, and then Linda Thorwald was looking down at me from the other side. Her hair was pretty mussy, too.

More of the freshly fucked look, I thought. My God, this is a *great* dream.

The grin that Thorwald was giving me matched Lacey's for wickedness, and maybe even surpassed it.

"Still think you're dreaming, Stan?" she said. Her voice had a huskiness that I'd never heard in it before. She leaned forward slowly, and Lacey did the same. Their noses touched, and then they were kissing, less than a foot from my face. The kiss went on for a little while.

Then Thorwald took hold of the sheet that was covering us and slowly pulled it down. All the way down.

"In that case," she said, "I think this dream of yours is about to get a whole *lot* better."

Acknowledgments

Jurgen Kleist, Professor of German at Plattsburgh State University, helped me make Victor Castle briefly bilingual.

John Carroll, my oldest friend, continued to provide valuable information about the Wyoming Valley whenever my memory and the Internet failed me.

Jeanne Cavelos, director of the Odyssey Writing Workshop and sole proprietor of Jeanne Cavelos Editorial Services, does plotting better than anyone I know. She was kind enough to share her facility with me, to the book's great benefit.

My agent, Miriam Kriss at the Irene Goodman Agency, negotiated a nice three-book deal for Stan Markowski, of which this volume is the second. Miriam rocks.

Linda Kingston did a great job of morale maintenance, especially during the latter stages of writing this book.

Terry Bear served in his usual roles as confidant and menu planner. He excels at both.

And so are you.

Twitter **@angryrobotbooks**

FILL YOUR BOOTS

Own the complete Angry Robot catalog